Burma Sahib

ALSO BY PAUL THEROUX

FICTION

Waldo

Fong and the Indians

Girls at Play

Murder in Mount Holly

Jungle Lovers

Sinning with Annie

Saint Jack

The Black House

The Family Arsenal

The Consul's File

A Christmas Card

Picture Palace

London Snow

World's End

The Mosquito Coast

The London Embassy

Half Moon Street

O-Zone

My Secret History

Chicago Loop

Millroy the Magician

My Other Life

Kowloon Tong

Hotel Honolulu

The Stranger at the Palazzo d'Oro

Blinding Light

The Elephanta Suite

A Dead Hand

The Lower River

Mr. Bones

Mother Land

Under the Wave at Waimea

The Bad Angel Brothers

NONFICTION

The Great Railway Bazaar

The Old Patagonian Express

The Kingdom by the Sea

Sailing Through China

Sunrise with Seamonsters

The Imperial Way

Riding the Iron Rooster

To the Ends of the Earth

The Happy Isles of Oceania

The Pillars of Hercules

Sir Vidia's Shadow

Fresh-Air Fiend

Dark Star Safari

Ghost Train to the Eastern Star

The Tao of Travel

The Last Train to Zona Verde

Deep South

Figures in a Landscape

On the Plain of Snakes

PAUL THEROUX

Burma Sahib

A NOVEL

MARINER BOOKS
New York   Boston

BURMA SAHIB. Copyright © 2024 by Paul Theroux. All rights reserved. Printed in the United States of America. No part of this book may be used or reproduced in any manner whatsoever without written permission except in the case of brief quotations embodied in critical articles and reviews. For information, address HarperCollins Publishers, 195 Broadway, New York, NY 10007.

HarperCollins books may be purchased for educational, business, or sales promotional use. For information, please email the Special Markets Department at SPsales@harpercollins.com.

FIRST EDITION

Designed by Chloe Foster

Map by Mapping Specialists, Ltd.

Library of Congress Cataloging-in-Publication Data has been applied for.

ISBN 978-0-06-329754-8

24 25 26 27 28 LBC 6 5 4 3 2

There is a short period in everyone's life
when his character is fixed forever.

—George Orwell, *Burmese Days*

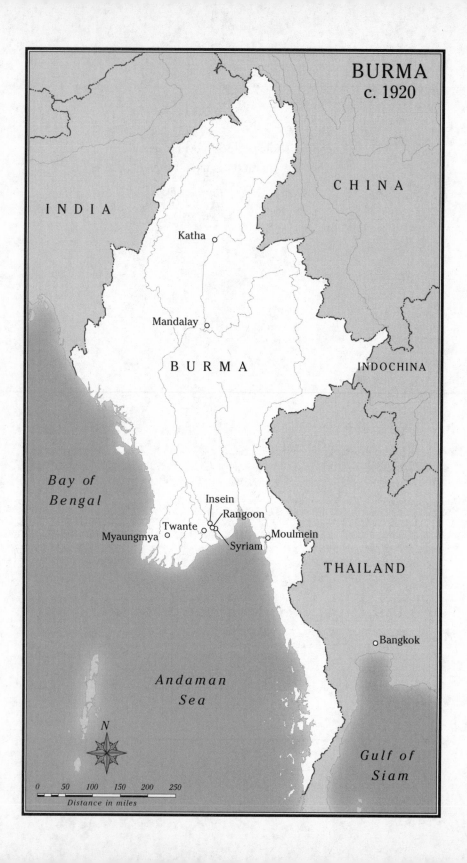

BURMA
c. 1920

CHINA

INDIA

Katha

Mandalay

BURMA

INDOCHINA

Bay of
Bengal

Insein
Rangoon
Twante
Myaungmya
Syriam
Moulmein

THAILAND

Bangkok

Andaman
Sea

N

Gulf of
Siam

0   50   100   150   200   250
Distance in miles

Part I

THE ROAD TO MANDALAY

THE *HEREFORDSHIRE*

East of Suez

T hat braw lanky laddie," the woman in the upper-deck first-class sa- loon said, squinting and hitching herself forward in her chaise longue for a better view.

Her white summer dress tickled her ankles, and today—the sun slanting through the window—she wore a pale, wide-brimmed hat, crowned like a lampshade and with a similar tilt, to cut the glare.

As she raised her binoculars and peered through them toward the bow of the ship, her loose sleeves slipped to her elbows, the whiteness of her dress making her skin seem yellow. She scowled, sour-mouthed, dazzled by the sun, showing her teeth, then pawed at the adjustment wheel on the binoculars to focus on the young man. He was facing the stern, and so facing in her direction.

"He's there again, Alec," the woman said.

He wore a creamy, new-looking linen jacket, baggy gray trousers, and scuffed plimsolls. Watching the shore recede, he leaned into the breeze, his tie lifting sideways and beating against his shoulder. He saw the distant shore slipping beneath the water, a low brown hill where, minutes earlier, men in biblical robes, one leading a plodding camel burdened with bales and others with hoes, had been chopping clods of earth, working in the early November sunshine, under a cloudless sky. The last of Egypt.

"Same spot. In that pairishing heat."

She studied him intently; scowling, he was smoking a cigarette, frown- ing as he contemplated the flattening shore, the afternoon sun on his young earnest face.

"*Ek aur,*" the mustached man next to her said to a hovering waiter. Un- like the alert woman, propped up and fascinated, he reclined on the chaise longue, his feet on the leg rest, toes upraised. Now he tapped his empty glass. "Burra peg."

"Always alone," the woman said. "Quite often he has a buik under his arm."

The man did not reply. Holding his gold wristwatch in his hand, he began winding it, having set it to the new time the captain had announced earlier. He buckled it to his wrist and admired the way the prism of its crystal caught the sunlight. As he was smiling at the blaze on the glass, the waiter returned and bowed, lowering his tray with the drink on it, murmuring, "Sahib."

"He was yip-yapping in French, when we went ashore. In Marseille. And French again to some hawkers in Port Said."

"Bloody Frog, Edith," the man said, lifting his drink and sipping, then lapping droplets from his mustache. "Mystery solved."

"Not at all," the woman said, and smiled with certainty. "He's English."

"With an attack of the parly-voos."

"Don't be wicked, Alec."

Smacking his lips, and with a hint of impatience, the man said, "Can't see why you're taking such a desperate interest."

The woman steadied her binoculars and held her breath, in the manner of someone trying to identify a bird on a branch. "He's refained."

"Pardon?" the man said sharply.

"I'm thinking of Muriel," the woman whispered, as though the young man might hear, though he was forty yards distant, still at the bow rail, watching the shore.

Sighing and lifting his glass, the man drank, and swallowing seemed to swallow whatever he was going to say.

Still whispering the woman said, "He might be just right for her."

"Really." The word was plummy with disbelief. "Probably a planter's bairn, off at Colombo, up to the tea estates."

"He's booked through to Rangoon."

"You talked to the chap?"

"I talked to the purser," the woman said, setting the binoculars onto her lap and staring at the man, with a smile of defiance.

"Half the ship is going to Rangoon."

"He's in first class."

"Along with masses of others."

"He's single."

"I should jolly well hope so, he's hardly twenty-two."

"Nineteen," the woman said.

"Unsuitable."

"But his tie," the woman said and handed him the binoculars. "Have a dekko."

The man muttered "dekko," in a tone of annoyance. He hummed as he looked through the binoculars, then said, "Blue stripes."

"Eton," the woman said, clamping her teeth on the word.

Now the man jammed the binoculars against his eyes and looked closely at the tie, flung over the young man's shoulder, where it still flapped. He returned the binoculars to the woman who had just lit a cigarette. Making a fish mouth in triumph, she blew a plume of smoke at the man.

Waving the smoke aside, the man said, "I'll arrange to have the captain invite him to dinner."

The tall young man—Eric Blair—had been waiting for this moment, the ship released by the local pilot who'd guided the *Herefordshire* through the canal and who'd just reboarded the escort boat that had drawn alongside. The *Herefordshire*'s captain grasped the handles of the ship's wheel—easily seen through the slanted windows of the bridge—and the engines began grinding and groaning, louder as the speed increased, and also thumping under Blair's plimsolls. The smudge of a small coastal town slipped below the horizon.

"'Somewheres east of Suez,'" Blair was murmuring with emotion. He hadn't felt this at Port Suez, among the souvenir sellers and the gully-gully man producing a live chick from a startled child's ear; nor at the crowded bazaar, buying his solar topee; nor seeing some crew members spread small thin carpets on the afterdeck and kneeling to pray. That was prologue. He held the poem's words as pleasure in his mouth—he didn't want to be seen smiling.

That was when he had turned, his tie blowing over his shoulder, as he faced the blue water of the gulf, the sun behind him heating his head, the low brown profile of the shore on both sides receding so quickly he could easily imagine he was in the open ocean—even though he knew from the map in the lounge that the Red Sea lay ahead, and later the Indian Ocean.

Where the best is like the worst—the lines running through his mind. *Where there aren't no Ten Commandments* . . .

Now he could not resist smiling—no one could see him—he was facing forward, gladdened by the accelerating engine, the obvious speed and slosh, after the plod through the canal. The bow wake parted the sea, a greeny-blue spearpoint.

An' a man can raise a thirst.

For the rest of the glowing afternoon he remained on the bow deck, peering ahead, thinking, *I'm on my way,* his decision seeming somehow more serious and strange as the heat of the day burned against his head—this heat reminding him that he was entering a new zone, a new climate, sailing to the far corner of the British Empire where it was likely just as hot, maybe hotter.

What pleased him was that Eton was in the past—he was no longer a schoolboy, and in his mind's eye he saw himself in his school uniform—the top hat, the tailcoat—he shook his head at the memory, with his friends, fat little Connolly, spotty Hollis, round-shouldered Runciman, walking solemnly to chapel or to exams, or garbing for combat in the Wall Game. It was hardly like study at all, but rather a pompous version of youthful folly, odious little snobs innocent of the world. The misery of trudging around Agar's Plough with his parents after tea on a visitors' day. Then, remembering his tutor Gow chalking Greek letters on the blackboard, Blair admitted to himself that without Gow's teaching, his India Office exam results would have been poorer—he might not have passed.

He saw himself bent over Greek prep, he saw himself defying the master of the college, bossy John Crace, he saw himself in the exam hall, he saw himself now, as though he was a spectator standing apart on the deck, a second self, keenly aware that he was playing a role—this nameless alter ego, clear-sighted and quiet and rational, and sometimes appalled by what Blair was doing, or saying—a weird self-conscious detachment, intense now, surrounded by the greasy-looking surface of the Red Sea, sailing to a fate he could not guess at, but in progress, and irreversible. He had committed himself to it for five years, and as the ship plowed on, the vibrating engines numbing his feet, he realized that he could not think for a moment about going back. He sensed the weight of his parents' concentrating on him—their hopes, their seriousness, their need for him to make a success of his job. And that wearied him, his necessity to please them—his father especially, old and sullen and disappointed in himself, Opium Agent Fourth Class (Ret'd), fixing his eyes on him and saying gruffly, "Don't let us down, Eric."

That was a needle. He'd posted a letter at Port Said, describing the ship, the food, the passengers, the weather in the Mediterranean, their first sight of Egypt. He'd write again, he said; Colombo was a week away—he'd mention the camels and Kipling and the canal, and his reading, the H. G. Wells novel, and he added his wishes to his sisters, Avril and Marjorie. Blair had written, too, to Jacintha Buddicom, a short note, with a poem he'd composed after Gibraltar, mentioning the ship's bow "thrusting majestically through the Pillars of Hercules," the memory of its mawkishness embarrassing him now.

His detachment remained, the hovering, watchful self, seeing the young man in the jacket and tie on deck, like a character in a story, knowing what the young man was hesitant to admit: that he was uncertain; that he really didn't have a clue; that he was to be a policeman.

The click of shuffleboard discs woke him from his reverie—two men behind him, poking their cue sticks at the discs and bantering.

"Chance your arm, Basil!"

"I will and all. But I need a wee sharpener. Allow me to fortify myself with a bit of barley-bree. Steward!"

"Sahib!"

It was the hour of deck games and strollers, the sun hanging low, leaving the port side in shadow, the hour that Blair always chose to slip away, back to his cabin, hoping that no one would speak to him. And trying to avoid seeing David Jones, his fellow candidate in the police, also headed to Rangoon, who occupied a nearby cabin.

"You may have to face the ugly fact that you can't do it anymore."

"Not"—and Blair saw the mustached man push with his cue stick— "perhaps with the same penetration. But you might be surprised."

"Perish the thought. Oh, crumbs, a near miss!"

"Deck wants scrubbing."

As the two men jawed, a turbaned waiter approached with a tumbler on a tray.

"Stop right there, my man!" the mustached man shouted.

"Sahib."

"Lussen, when I push I need a guid clean thrust. I can't have you dancing attendance. I want you absolutely rigid."

"Yes, master."

"And bring us each another chotapeg of Jameson's."

"Yes, master."

Wary of slipping past the men and being greeted, Blair had crept to the rail, out of sight of the men but still within earshot.

"Our friend Alec."

"Poodle-Wilmot. Ha!"

"There's talk his missus put the shutters up."

They were whispers, but audible enough.

"Sairten latitude on this vessel for rumpty-tumpty."

Blair feared being seen, he felt complicit, hearing the men talk, the shuffleboard discs clicking. He sensed his face heating and knew he was blushing, hearing the whispers, the insinuations. He slid along the rail toward the lifeboat and the door to the stairwell. On the cabin deck two women walked past, their skirts swishing, not greeting him, hearty with each other.

"Rafe's a bounder—"

"My Frank's no different."

They knew each other well, the men talkative and fraternal, the women like sisters; all the passengers seemed on good terms with one another, even if half the time they were gossiping. It was a seagoing community of Anglo-Indians, clerks and bureaucrats and their memsahibs, brothers and sisters.

The Raj afloat, with intimacies that Blair found astonishing for its clubby candor, or more than clubby, an extended family of smug overlords and philistines—not one of them he'd seen in a deck chair had been reading a book, though many of the women had their nose in a magazine. He'd felt conspicuous with his book, the *Tono-Bungay* he'd wanted to reread. A book told so much about the person reading it. But these were outgoing, social creatures, chatting among themselves, dining together, dancing and changing partners. And many had the peculiar plummy accents of English people who'd lived abroad for years, who'd refined and improved their lower-middle-class accents, making the women sound actressy and the men bluff, honking and huffing, "I say, my dear chap . . ."

Blair cringed to think he was judging them so harshly, that he found the Scots the most tedious and at times uppity, sometimes echoing the porkers he'd known at St. Cyprian's, boasting of hunting or fishing attended by "Our gillies . . ." What appalled him was a fear he could not share in any letter home, that he was facing a future with these people, that they would be his superiors. Painfully conscious of his youth, he longed for June, when he would turn twenty.

And something else niggled him about the other passengers, and it was unbearable at times. Listening to them reminiscing about India, or complaining about babus and servants, they spoke in the Anglo-Indian tones of his father and mother, of the chowkidar and the amah, the chai wallah and the syce. The common language was the language of the Raj, and Blair hated being reminded of it. They knew each other well, but he did not want to know them. *And I don't want them to know me.*

It was easy enough to avoid them. They were occupied with games, with drink, with food, with music in the first-class saloon—he could hear it now, as on every other night, the ship's small dance band, Reg Melly and his Mello-Tones, vibrating in the steel plates of the deck, the walls of his cabin, seeping through the portholes.

I found my love in Avalon
Beside the bay . . .

He hated knowing the words, they lodged in his head, but that one, "Avalon," was better than Reg Melly's snarly, winking version of "Ain't We Got Fun":

Every morning, every evening
Ain't we got fun . . .

By now, past Suez, he'd unwillingly learned Reg Melly's whole reper-
toire, and he despised himself for it, the way the songs worked their way
into his head and jarred his evenings, reading Wells to the lyrics "Though
April showers may come your way."

Those were the tunes tickling through the walls; but it was worse above
decks, much worse in the dining room and the saloon, the smoking room and
the library, the eye-blinding music from seven to eleven, and the drunken
hoots afterward as the roisterers made their way back to their cabins.

How do I avoid knowing them, and their knowing me? It was perhaps
simple: *stay in my cabin.* The bed could have been bigger—his legs were
far too long for this berth—but it was luxury to have such privacy after the
continual intrusions of Eton and his parents sniffing scrutiny at their small
house in Southwold. Blair knew he was a boy, but there were moments on
board the *Herefordshire* when he imagined he might pass for a grown man.

The band was playing "Avalon" again. He'd heard it in Southwold on
the wireless when he was cramming for his exams. Thankfully, tonight Reg
Melly was conducting the Mello-Tones, and not singing the words, and as
the band played he knew from the syncopation that the passengers were
dancing—he'd seen them in the Mediterranean, as he walked the deck,
glancing through the window of the lounge, thinking, *I could never do that,*
glad to be anonymous.

American music, most of it; the English were besotted—they loved Al
Jolson in blackface. Blair wanted to be satirical, yet the songs made him
melancholy and somehow reminded him in a mocking way of his distance
from home. And though the passengers listened to be soothed by the music, they seemed more ridiculous and sad, cheering themselves with the
mawkish sentiments of popular songs and dancing like fools.

When at last the music stopped, he immersed himself in *Tono-Bungay*
and thought of a line for a poem he might write, "The last of England sank
below the sea, and—something-somebody—remembered me." It would be
a frightful poem. Why bother?

In the morning, Ramasamy, the Indian steward, tapped lightly on his
door as usual and brought him a tray, his cup of tea, and on another saucer an envelope with the Bibby Line insignia of a red flag on the flap, and
blue lettering, *EA Blair Esq.*

"What's this?"

"Chit, sahib. From captain, sahib."

Blair waited for the steward to leave, and then tore open the envelope
and read: *Captain Robertson requests the pleasure of your company at the
Captain's Table on November 10, 1922, at 1900 hours.*

2

THE CAPTAIN'S TABLE

Blair's method of pondering the unwelcome invitation was to scrutinize his face in the shaving mirror as though to discern the truth in his expression. He despaired of his pale schoolboy face, the weak evasive eyes, the plump cheeks, most of all the soft mouth, which a mustache might improve. And the angle was lopsided and wrong, because he had to stoop to see himself, he was too tall for the mirror, as he was too long for the berth. He knocked his forehead whenever he entered the lavatory. He knew he would be conspicuous for his height at the captain's table, and for his youth, and for having nothing to say in the way of conversation. The invitation was a challenge, it made him uneasy, he saw helpless anxiety and indecision in the reflected face in the dimpled mirror.

"Going out to be a policeman, sir," he heard himself saying, and thought, *Oh gawd.*

Apart from a few words with Jones, or the steward, Blair had not spoken to anyone on the ship. He had mainly kept to his cabin, with his books; he'd taken his meals alone, vaguely disturbed by the excessive amounts of food. On deck, he'd hidden himself, strolling with his head down, or keeping to the bow rail, forward of the cranes and the citadel of lounges, stacked one on another, his back to the windows and the passengers. As for small talk, he'd always made a dog's dinner of it and hated talking about himself.

But the invitation was an order.

He brooded all the next day, imagining an interrogation, improvising answers and explanations. It was not that he felt intruded upon, but merely that he was losing his anonymity and would need to be resourceful in devising plausible responses. He had no fear that anyone would get to know him—he knew from Eton, the posh boys, the beaks, how to be implacable. His objection to the captain's table was his vague annoyance that he would be dining elbow to elbow in forced intimacy with passengers who knew one another well. That, and the regret that he would be denied the pleasure of reading H. G. Wells over his meal alone in his cabin.

All dinners on board were formal, and he was not used to evening dress, but how was this so different in any way from his schoolboy plumage at Eton? Still, he was tying his tie with reluctance, frowning at his face in the mirror, when his door chime rang. He opened the door to an Indian in a white uniform, red cummerbund, red turban.

"I am Ranjit Singh, sahib," the man said. "I am charged with guiding you to captain's table."

"Lead on, sardarji," Blair said. "I won't be able to find it without you."

But the man had paused to smile and stroke his beard and say with feeling, "You are knowing this word *sardar,* sahib?"

"I got it out of Kipling, who knew Sikhs."

"Thank you, sahib"—bowing and turning sharply on his heel—"Captain's mess, sahib. Adjacent to first-class saloon."

The Indian steward, trimmed beard threaded with white hairs, his turban wrapped tight, had a military bearing, his shoulders squared, his posture erect, and though Blair saw that he was only a few years older than himself, there was something about the man that suggested hardship, the white in his beard, his lined face, his wounded eyes, and he walked with a slight limp, his left leg dragging, scuffing the edge of his blancoed shoe—yet he kept in stride.

"Will many others be there, along with the captain?"

"Always full table, sahib," Ranjit Singh said, without turning.

Blair groaned inwardly and braced himself. *A full table,* he thought, then pondering it—*Maybe it's better that there be many rather than a few: easier to conceal myself among the many.*

Down the passageway and along the bulkhead to the ladder leading to the first-class saloon, making way for couples heading to dinner, Blair felt conspicuous, following the limping Indian. He decided not to ask any more questions for fear of being overheard. As always, among others, he was conscious of his height, instinctively lowering his head, almost bowing, when encountering other passengers, such as the red-faced man in tails at the entrance to the lounge, biting on a cigar and with a grimace of curiosity as he bit, turning to stare at the tall young man with a prowling gait following the bearded foot-dragging Indian.

Through an alcove to a varnished teak door with an oval window, its glass etched with a floral motif and the one word *Private.*

"Come in!" The summoning voice was assured and somewhat gruff, but when Blair entered, the speaker—in a dark uniform trimmed with gold braid—stepped forward with a welcoming smile and blue friendly eyes.

"Who do I have the pleasure of welcoming?"

"Blair, sir."

"What's your poison, Blair?"

"Sherry, sir."

"We have an assortment of venerable whiskeys," the captain said. "But as you wish. Singh, a schooner for our friend Blair." He turned aside. "These fine people"—stepping back to gesture to a group nearby—"will also be dining with us tonight."

As he gave the names, the people smiled and hummed hello, and Blair murmured their names in his mind, to remember them—Alec and Edith Peddy-Wilmot; Hamish and Rebecca Christie—"Jamie and Becca," Hamish clarified; the Reverend MacIntosh; and as the captain was introducing them, Singh began guiding an old woman through the galley door. The woman wore black, a draped dress that fluttered at her ankles, and she seemed spectral, her thin face like parchment, the bones showing through, less a face than a skull.

"Our dear Mrs. Hargreaves," the captain said. "I believe you know these people, but Mr. Blair might be new to you."

"Good evening," the woman said, without interest, keeping the words in her mouth, and she clutched her bag with both hands and raised it as though to defend herself.

Behind Blair a man was saying to Singh, *"Muje pyaar lagi hai,"* as Blair turned to smile, baffled by the words.

It was Hamish Christie. He said, "I'm thirsty."

"Have some wayne, Jamie!" a woman called out.

Blair edged toward the sideboard, and he felt excluded as he had the previous day—and most days—that everyone on the ship seemed on good terms. He continued to smile, sipping his sherry, not knowing how to acquaint himself with the others—their loud good humor seemed clubby and patronizing, elbowing him away. He wished to be in his cabin, in the shadows at the bow of the ship, in a corner of the smoking room—anywhere but here.

"Good evening, my boy. You're Blair."

It was the Reverend MacIntosh, smiling softly, pinching a small glass of sherry near his chin but not drinking.

"Yes, sir," Blair said and, stumped for something to add, said, "Is your church in Rangoon?"

"Goodness, no," Reverend MacIntosh said, disapprovingly. "I'm in blessed Moulmein, the whole of Mon State is my parish."

And Blair stammered, reminding himself that he must not say that he had family there, his mother's people, the French Limouzins, whom he thought of as "the Lemonskins," his grandmother and his uncle and cousins, an old colonial family. *Visit them, Eric,* his mother had urged. But they had done the unthinkable, two of the men marrying local women, producing half-caste children, and the whole lot of them were hanging on and probably despised. The very thought of them in Moulmein, a living embarrassment, deterred him from imagining any sort of visit, except covertly, under the cover of night.

"I should like to see Moulmein one day," Blair said, sipping his sherry, hoping he sounded sincere.

"You'll always be welcome at St. Matthew's."

Someone was insistently tapping his arm. It was the woman Edith Something, grinning, clownish, her gleaming lipstick enlarging her mouth. "I'm seated next to you, young man. Aren't you the lucky beast."

The rest of the diners shuffled around the table, examining the place cards that had been propped behind the plates. Blair found his card and sneaked a look at the woman's—*Mrs. A. Peddy-Wilmot.*

As the captain took his seat at the head of the table, the skeletal Mrs. Hargreaves removed a handkerchief from her sleeve and pressed it to her mouth and coughed into it, her shoulders heaving.

She gagged a little then said, "Where shall we be tomorrow, Captain?"

"Passing Jeddah at first light."

"And Aden?"

"Day and a bit, taking on some passengers and fuel. I'll have Reginald Melly rouse his men and do the usual—play 'The Barren Rocks of Aden.' Then a straight shot to Colombo. I'll arrange to have fine weather for you."

No one spoke—soup was being served by an Indian waiter, ladling it from a tureen—and then the Reverend MacIntosh said, "Bless us, O Father, Thy gifts to our use and us to Thy service. For Christ's sake, Amen."

"Amen," came the murmurs and throat clearings.

"Thank you," Mrs. Hargreaves said. "I'll be so glad to be back in Colombo."

Hamish Christie said to Blair, "Dear Mrs. Hargreaves was in Colombo when the *Worcestershire* was sunk."

"Bibby liner," the captain said. "That was in '17."

"One of your ships," Blair said, and he felt eyes on him as he faltered for anything more to say.

"Mail steamer," the captain said, filling the silence. "Hit a mine set by a Hun ship, the dreaded *Wolf.*"

"Hun battleship?"

"Merchant vessel, filled with guns and torpedo tubes. Battleships were tied up in the Channel."

"News to the lad," Alec Peddy-Wilmot said.

"It was shocking," Mrs. Hargreaves said.

"Why on earth—Ceylon?" Blair said.

"To impress the wogs with German power," Hamish said. "It was delu-brate."

"They talked about nothing else afterward, the natives," Mrs. Hargreaves said. "They could see the whole show from the harbor, the great ship going down, the Germans slipping away. They were cock-a-hoop and knocked my garden about."

Hamish said, "Filthy monks in Burma, too." In a low scarcely audible mutter he added, "A ghastly little bawbag in the bazaar had the cheek to gloat to me about it."

"Jerry got what was coming to him," Edith Peddy-Wilmot said.

"My grandson served in Flanders," Mrs. Hargreaves said. "He was inva-lided out."

"Our Singh can tell you a bit about that part of the war," the captain said.

"Ye sairved, did ye?" Hamish said

"Oh, yes, sir," Singh said, as he limped to the buffet, carrying dinner rolls on a silver bread basket.

"This ship, our dear *Herefordshire,* nearly bought it in a convoy in the Med just a year later—1918," the captain said. "I knew the skipper. Safe pair of hands. He was on the bridge and saw a brace of torpedo tracks coming straight toward him. Ordered the helm hard over and one engine full astern"—the captain raised his soup spoon and spun it slowly. "One torpedo missed his stern by about a foot, the other torpedo hit the *Sardinia,* just behind him."

"And sank it?" Blair said.

"No fear. *Sardinia*'s skipper, Millson by name, was a clever chap. Trans-ferred his passengers to a warship, and seeing that his starboard bow was close to collapse from the hit, he ordered the ship to be sailed backward—I repeat, backward—for sixty miles to the port of Oran in Algeria. Saved his ship."

"Bibby has a heroic impeedial record, laddie," Hamish said.

"We're so prood of them," Edith said. She tapped Blair on the arm and said, "Our captain's too modest to say he was an awardee. Aye, Dougal Rob-ertson, mentioned in dispatches."

The captain shook his head and gave a grim smile. "We all did our bit."

"Puling togaither," Alec put in.

"*Oxfordshire* was converted to a troop ship, carried thousands of men, and dear old *Herefordshire* was also a troop ship, hospital ship, merchant vessel, what not—and now your home for some weeks."

As the captain spoke, the soup bowls were collected, Singh supervising, the waiters scurrying, bending low.

"And what sort of duffrent muschief were you getting up to at that time, laddie?" Alec said to Blair. "Give us a hent."

"School," Blair said and, realizing he was fingering his tie, hid his hands beneath the table.

But it was prep school, not Eton, that came to mind. Hearing the hated burr at the table, the jaw-twisting haws, the pretentious fluting, he remembered the curious cult of Scottishness at St. Cyprian's, the headmaster's sadistic wife, "Flip" Wilkes, pestering the Scottish boys to wear kilts in their ancestral tartan instead of the school uniform, loving the Scots for being grim and dour and "prood," and extolling Scottish chieftains. She claimed Scottish ancestry and regarded Scotland as her private paradise, shared by the moneyed English boys who spent their holidays there and boasted of "our gillies." Blair glanced around the table at the gabbling faces and thought how he was once again stuck in a glottal-stop ghetto of Scots.

"My grandson left school to volunteer," Mrs. Hargreaves said gravely. "He was gassed. Third battle of Wipers."

"Was he badly injured?" Edith asked. "Poor chap."

"Can't bear to talk about it," the old woman said, squeezing her eyes shut.

"What school, laddie?" Alec asked, his face forward, persisting.

"Eton," Blair said, pressing his damp hands together beneath the table.

"I know what he was getting up to," Hamish said, nodding to Alec. "Being debagged at bump suppers."

"I reckon you were a proper little swot," Alec said.

Blair attempted a smile. "Bone idle. Absorbing wisdom unawares, if at all."

"And whit pray tell will you be doing in Burma?" Alec asked.

"Police," Blair said. "Training in Mandalay at the outset."

"Alec's fushing for clues," Hamish said. "Do ya ken what you're getting yourself into, lad?"

"Not entirely sure. I have, I suppose, a few equivocal notions of what the job entails."

"Dinna fash yoursel'!" Alec said. "I'm with the police—superintending Insein Prison—and I can assure you the job entails three things. The first is supairvision. The second is supairvision. The third is supairvision."

"Duly noted," Blair said. "Very helpful, sir. Thank you, sir."

"I've had shattering rows with my deputy at the prison on that score."

"Putched battles, more like," Edith said, sniggering.

Before Blair could reply, Singh was beside him with a platter of vegetables, spooning them onto a corner of his plate. Blair had leaned back to give Singh room to serve, while two other Indian waiters fussed, refilling glasses. Hamish canted his head toward Edith with a stage whisper, cupping his mouth, saying, "Bandar."

"Yes?" Edith said.

"Monkeys," Hamish said, more loudly.

But the attention at the table was on a man in uniform who had entered the dining room and was conferring with the captain on what seemed an urgent matter.

"Our quartermaster," Alec said to Blair. "He's frightfully grand. Our lives are in his hands."

The man was young, blond, fresh-faced and fit, dignified even as he bowed his head to speak confidentially to the captain, while unfolding a sheet of paper—a ruled chart—which the captain studied, tapping his finger on it.

"You have my blessing," the captain said.

As the quartermaster was leaving, he stepped aside to allow a waiter to pass, the waiter with a tray on his shoulder, custard puddings in thick bowls.

"The famous Wall Game," Edith said. "Were you a dab hand?"

"I reckon I was adequate," Blair said.

"Your first time out this way?" Alec asked.

Blair was on his guard, feeling interrogated by the man who said he was a policeman.

"Born in Bengal," he said. "Brought to England when I was just a tot."

"Our Muriel was born in Poona," Edith said. "Such a bonny lass. Was your father in the sairvice like Alec?"

"Opium agent," Blair said, and regretted that he was giving information, but it was unavoidable, these were direct questions. He cautioned himself against revealing that his father had been a lowly subdeputy in obscure Motihari.

"My church is in Moulmein," Reverend MacIntosh was saying to Mrs. Hargreaves. "The local Karen have become quite pious. A lovely lot."

Blair reminded himself again that he must not inform the table that his mother had been born in Moulmein, that his grandmother still lived there. And so he listened, bending over his custard, but merely poking it with his spoon, feeling too full to eat it. When Reverend MacIntosh said he visited a parish across the river—"the *ruvver*"—in Martaban, Blair thought, "*The wildest dreams of Kew, are the facts of Khatmandhu, and the crimes of Clapham chaste in Martaban.*"

"You nae finished your fuid," Edith said.

"I'm full up. Not used to so much custard."

"Aye, it's a right bug bowl," Hamish said.

The captain said, "You good people mustn't mind me. I've been summoned to the bridge, but you're welcome to enjoy your coffee in the lounge if you like. And there's brandy and port, of course, and a selection of cheroots for the gentlemen."

"Our dhobi loves her cheroot," Edith said.

Whacking great cheroot, Blair thought and almost said so. But as soon as the captain left he seemed to take the vitality from the room with him—conversation slowed and stopped. The diners flapped their napkins and tossed them on the table, and they left in pairs, first old Mrs. Hargreaves and the reverend, then Hamish and Rebecca, and, last, the Peddy-Wilmots, Edith saying over her shoulder to Blair, "It would be ever so nice to have you for tea when we arrive in Rangoon—that is myself and my daughter. Insein is quite near, but Alec's terribly busy with his prison."

"Supairvision," Alec said. "Desperate little babus and evil dacoits, and some political monks. My deputy is new and naïve. Don't you be new and naïve, my lad."

"I'll endeavor not to," Blair said.

"Laddie looks nairvus," Edith said with a wicked smile.

"And my assistant superintendent—another new chap, not the crabbit one I refaired to—won't be laughed out of his ludicrous ideas."

Left in the room alone, Blair reflected on his performance and judged it a failure. He had said too much. He had felt mocked for being a schoolboy, he knew nothing of the sinking of the *Worcestershire,* which had meant so much to them, and Wipers was just a name attached to slaughter.

"Sahib, may I fetch anything for you?" It was Ranjit Singh limping toward him.

"I'm fine, but tell me, sardarji. You served in the war?"

"Ninety-Third Burma Infantry—but we were based in Barrackpore. Our unit fought in many places."

"France?"

"And Egypt and Mesopotamia."

"And Wipers?"

"Passchendaele, in '14. Same area as Madam Hargreaves's grandson."

"Beastly luck."

"No, sahib. Good luck. I was invalided out. Many of my comrades were less fortunate. I met Captain Robertson in hospital in Kent, and he hired me as steward. Excellent luck, sahib."

As he limped away—ah, it was a war wound—Blair slipped out to enter the first-class lounge, but seeing the Peddy-Wilmots and the Christies at a table laughing, drinking, he hesitated and stepped back, not wishing to be seen and beckoned ("Laddie!") for fear he'd have to sit and chat and be questioned further. So he returned to the passageway that led to the captain's mess and searched for another exit.

Just then a door was flung open and a man entered and blocked the narrow passageway—the blond quartermaster in his smart uniform, who'd conferred with the captain on what seemed a matter of grave importance. But the man was startled and lifted his hands, which held a bowl with Blair's dabbed and uneaten custard pudding, brimming as he halted and spilling over his fingers. He grunted, as if in objection, and turned his affronted face away and pushed past, still clutching the bowl.

3

ALL AT SEA

Blair concealed himself after that. Until then, he'd been circumspect, but now he hid: he kept away from the first-class lounge, he avoided the smoking room, he attempted to fold himself small and ate quickly in a corner of the dining room at lunch and stayed in his cabin through dinner—too much food, he was never hungry enough to risk seeing those people again. And he hated them for *Proper little swot* and *He looks nairvus* and *We're so prood* and *Puling togaither*. Instead of risking the lounge, when he felt peckish he asked his steward, Ramasamy, to bring him tea and sandwiches. Ramasamy was a dark rail-thin Dravidian, with black close-set eyes and a cringing manner, but when Blair quizzed him about his language, which was Tamil, the man relaxed and laughed and said, "*Nanri aiya*," which he explained was Tamil for "Thank you, sir."

"Teach me Hindi."

"*Acha.* I am know Hindi, sahib."

And Blair learned *Kya haal hai?* How are you? And *Tumara naam ke hai?* What's your name? as well as *Mujhe den*—give me, *jildy karo*—do it soon, and *Bahut dhanyavaad*—thank you very much. And sometimes for tea Ramasamy brought him Tamil rice cakes from the crew's mess.

"What are these?"

"Idli, sahib. Like my mother make. Madras idli."

They were soft and plump and aromatic, like small white pincushions, and always accompanied by a bowl of ocherous lentil stew, for which they were a sop, the stew Ramasamy called *sambar,* but said there was no word for *sambar* in English.

Ramasamy, who'd become an ally, understood Blair's need for privacy and was watchful on Blair's behalf, seeming to twig that Blair had precious secrets he wished to protect—the evidence was the scattered pages of manuscript on his desk, blackened with scribbled notes that seemed priestly and scriptural, sacred texts, which Blair had indicated, saying "*Mat chhuo*"—Don't touch.

"*Main nahin choonga,*" Ramasamy said. "I will not touch, sahib."

Blair felt safe in his nook behind the stanchion at the bow, among the nests of coiled mooring lines, and often at sunset he lingered there, immobilized by suspense. The night air was warm, the ship growling through the Red Sea, delivering him into bafflement. When the ship docked at Aden, Blair heard a rapping on his cabin door, not Ramasamy's knuckle tap but an unwelcome hammering. He was reluctant to answer it, so he stayed in his berth, but when the hammering came again, and louder, he rose and crept to the door.

"Who is it?"

"Jones—just a word."

Blair slid the bolt and opened the door to the glare of day and the face of David Jones—pale, his black hair slicked close to his oval head either with pomade or perspiration. He had a jutting chin, his mouth twisted in concern.

"Blair. You had me worried, you've been so scarce. I've hardly seen you since Gib. I thought you might be poorly."

"I'm fine—just reading and lying doggo."

"Some passengers were asking after you when I mentioned I'm also going for the police."

"What did you tell them?"

"That I'd look you up."

"Inquisitive sorts, were they?"

"Seemed nice enough. They wondered if they'd been a bit short with you. Two couples, actually. Usually in the library."

"Bookish types?"

"Playing cards—bridge or bezique, the four of them. The bearded one rather likes the bottle."

"His wife told me he's governor at the prison in Insein."

"Who knows, we might fetch up there eventually."

That thought silenced Blair, he wanted to shut the door.

But Jones asked, "Where'd you meet them?"

"Captain's table. I somehow earned an invitation. The captain's a rum sort—Dougal Robertson, mentioned in dispatches. But a very queer thing happened afterward—two queer things, actually."

Perhaps anticipating a long story and feeling awkward standing before the open door to Blair's cabin, Jones said, "Might I come in—I'd love to hear about it."

Blair hesitated. On the deck talking he might be observed, and this he wanted to avoid. In the cabin, among his books and papers, the fragments of a poem, a letter in progress scattered on the table, Jones would be admitted to his privacies.

"I'll be brief," Blair said, and stepped out of his cabin to the deck, shutting the door behind him. He walked to the lifeboat station and slid between the suspended boat and the rail, Jones following, perplexed by the detour, snorting a little in his confusion.

"We had custard pudding for afters," Blair said in a low voice, as though divulging a deep secret. He then described how, so full of the big meal, he hadn't been able to tackle the dessert. He did not say that after the meal he'd been trying to avoid the others, or that he'd decided not to enter the first-class saloon. He told how he'd reentered the passageway by the captain's mess and seen the quartermaster ducking out, with the custard pudding he'd snatched, and holding it as he'd scuttled away.

"Sounds comical," Jones said.

"It's grim, more like," Blair said. "He knew that I'd guessed he'd pinched it, or else a waiter had handed it to him on the sly. In any case, here's a man who has our lives in his hands, the quartermaster, and he's scurrying away with our leftovers."

"Why is that queer?" Jones said.

"You don't see how desperately pathetic this is?"

"I expect the chap was jolly hungry," Jones said. "What was the other queer thing?"

"The steward, Sikh chap, he said he'd fought in Passchendaele. Invalided out."

"My father was a sapper in the Royal Welsh. He told me there were Indian divisions all over the Western Front, and natives in uniform everywhere—didn't they teach you that at Eton, you poor booby?"

"I suppose. But I'd never met one."

"Aden tomorrow," Jones said as a farewell. "Care to go ashore? We could tour the town—crater, actually. And the purser told me there's shops at Steamer Point. A church as well."

"I'll keep to the ship. I've got some catching up to do."

Jones shrugged, and when he was gone, Blair thought, *What a frightful tangle of lies one has to tell in order to be left alone.* And the next day, in port, the ship's great engines silenced, he lay and listened to the Reginald Melly orchestra—somehow Melly had found bagpipes and snare drums for "The Barren Rocks of Aden." Blair was appalled by the screech and thump of the martial tune, Scottish shrieks at the ship's rail calling for an encore. He covered his face with his book and groaned. It was as though he was being not floated into the empire, but marched to the sound of bugles and drums.

At sea again, from his cabin during the heat of the day Blair was dazzled by the shimmering ocean and could hear the high spirits of passengers strolling, making plans to go ashore at Colombo, to tour the market, to meet for drinks and games, chaffing each other with lame jokes, the women whispering, the men booming.

He usually rose early and hurried to breakfast before the crowds arrived—they were later and later these days, and many seemed only to show up for elevenses. Back in his cabin, he read through lunch, having Ramasamy bring him high tea—sandwiches and cakes. "And this we call *gulab jamun,* sahib—it is Indian sweet"—small milky dough balls drenched in syrup, but it was another word for his Hindi list.

The music began just before sundown, "Avalon" and "April Showers," bringing the strollers into the lounge, and then it was safe to go on deck. He did so with his head down, yet still feeling conspicuous for his height, averting his gaze when he passed anyone, dreading that he would encounter Alec or Edith Peddy-Wilmot, who'd press him to join them.

His place at the bow was secure, and he remained hidden there, inhaling the night air, reflecting on Jones, his father a veteran of the war, and a miner from the Valleys—and Blair's own personal history an encumbrance if not a complete embarrassment, his father too old to serve, now retired and idle in a poky cottage in Southwold. In a letter posted to his parents at Aden, Blair reported, *Fair weather, ripping teas, Rangoon in a fortnight.*

Through the Indian Ocean, his nook on the boat deck was safe enough to linger in during much of the day if he wished and was shady in the late afternoon. The binoculars he'd brought for birdwatching he used for searching the sea for passing ships, or sea life—dolphins one day, while near Socotra (the captain had announced it on the Tannoy), another great Bibby ship sliding by with a blast on its horn and its decks full of waving passengers, homeward bound, filling Blair with melancholy for going in the opposite direction, wondering whether he'd be better off on the other ship.

The easel with the map propped on it was always at the entrance to breakfast in the first-class dining room, a line of redheaded pins indicating the ship's progress. He was passing it one morning and heard a man behind him say, "Looks like Colombo tomorrow, by teatime. With the tea planters gone we'll have a spot of breathing room."

Blair ate with his back to the other diners and prepared himself to avoid sociable Jones, whom he feared would want to go ashore with him, and what excuse would he invent then—what plausible lie—when all he really wanted was to read in his cabin, or escaping the cabin's stifling heat find some seclusion in the bow and look for birds—gulls, petrels, lazy gliding frigate birds: another list he was keeping.

He hated the childish screeches of passengers who sighted land, and he remained on deck as the ship drew into Colombo, the horns blasting, the great vessel slewing sideways near the dock, its screws grinding, the deck aslant, the lascars tossing lines to skipping men on shore, who were looping them over bollards, the Reginald Melly orchestra playing "Rule Britannia," a waiting crowd of Europeans in white drill suits and silken dresses, some with parasols, waving in welcome.

Blair positioned himself at the rail, just above the gangway, to watch the progress of passengers embarking, the exchange of papers by officers, the crew members guiding the older men and women, keeping near them like nannies, hands raised in anticipation, not touching them, but alert for any mishap. A policeman—European, red-faced, panting—supervising the luggage, caught Blair's eye—because he was a policeman, because he was white, because he happened to be shouting, "*Jildyi karo!*" which Blair now knew meant "Hurry up!"

A bearded man had appeared next to Blair at the rail, causing Blair to cringe and turn aside.

Seeing him stiffen, the man took his pipe out of his mouth and said, "You're Blair, the Eton chap." And before Blair could respond the man went on, "Alec—we had dinner with the captain. My wife noticed you up here. She's frightfully interested, I can't think why."

"Of course," Blair said. "Just watching the embarkation."

"Bloody Fred Karno's army."

What to reply? Blair said, "Bit of a bottleneck."

"Have a dekko at that monkey."

"That man?"

"That coolie."

A skinny brown man, a porter in a white turban and a blue knee-length skirt, was struggling with a long tin uniform case, trying to hoist it to his shoulder, as departing passengers skipped past him, crowding him on the gangway. And then a young English couple let him pass as he stumbled.

"Look sharp!" Alec cried, and again snatched the pipe from his mouth. "Going to bloody smash someone's heid with that case."

The porter was unsteady, the tin case swung to the side as he attempted to find his footing at the end of the gangway, and as he tottered the white policeman dashed from the dock and screamed something in Hindi. Bracing himself on the handrail of the gangway, the policeman leaned like a rugger hearty and kicked the porter in the backside. The porter staggered and fell hard onto the dock, his turban coming loose, the tin case dropping with a clatter.

The passengers on the gangway and at the rail whooped and whistled in approval, as Alec slow clapped, his pipestem clamped in his teeth. Then he turned to Blair and said through his teeth, "Good show, what?"

"New to the job, one imagines. Those cases are the very devil."

"Bloody monkey," Alec said. "And you know why?"

"Haven't a clue, sir."

"They let him pass—those young people." Alec looked furious, as he clutched his pipe and stabbed with it. "Ye dinnae give way tae a native. Ever. Natives are scum."

The proper response to this, Blair considered, was: *The captain's steward, Ranjit Singh, fought valiantly at Passchendaele for king and country. And was wounded.*

But he said mildly, "And if there's no room to pass?"

"Crowd the bastard into the street," Alec said. "Or in this instance into the sea." He chewed his pipestem again. "That policeman deserves a medal for that kicking. You'll be a policeman, Blair—so you said. That's how it's done, lad."

He snarled and stared at Blair, with icy blue eyes, a schoolmaster's severe gaze, demanding an answer.

"Valuable lesson, sir."

"I'm up here for a reason, Blair."

"Sir?"

"My good wife wishes to have you for tea."

"Thank you, very good of you, sir," Blair said. "Topping."

The Peddy-Wilmots had found him, the captain had found him, Jones had found him. But Blair used the hour at tea with the Peddy-Wimots to practice being noncommittal, avoiding a yes or no, never divulging anything personal that could be repeated or used against him—polite laughter and euphemism instead of affront, replying with anodyne questions instead of submitting to interrogation, asking for information, being thankful. "That needs to be said" and "Filling the unforgiving minute" and "Quite right" and "I wish I knew, sir." The fine art, perfected by the English, of saying nothing.

The lesson was that the only safe place on the ship was his cabin, his only protector Ramasamy. He remained there and read, usually H. G. Wells, sometimes Samuel Butler's *Notebooks*, and the Conrad collection that Connolly had pressed on him, *Twixt Land and Sea*. He began poems for Jacintha—bold couplets that dwindled to doggerel. His meals were brought by Ramasamy, whom he pumped for Hindi words and phrases. And one day Ramasamy said excitedly, "Rangoon *nagar*, sahib, *pahunchane*"—more words for his Hindi list, "town" and "arriving."

4

THE CHUMMERY IN RANGOON

Under the twisted branches, dense with twitching leaves, the tangled tree seemed to have multiple trunks—not one thick upright pillar but an intertwined clutch of musclelike strands, a tree from an exotic dream. It was the first thing Blair saw as, chugging through muddy water, the *Herefordshire* swung sideways and churned the water to brown froth as it approached the pier, the half-naked men on shore, howling with raised arms, calling for the mooring lines.

More trees were revealed as the ship neared the pier, some of their branches upflung, an orderly row of them, small boys clinging to their lower boughs, like imps in the same dream. Farther in, the palms seemed vaguely familiar from the glass house at Kew Gardens, but very tall, leaning awkwardly, as though too slender to support their own weight and remain upright. Finally, scrubby bushes, coated with a frizz of yellow blossoms.

To the right, across the harbor, the chimneys, thick black stacks lettered BURMAH OIL, and rising in the distance past the red tile roofs of shop houses, a massive gold stupa, the one sight he'd anticipated, a pagoda looking lazy at the sea, the Shwedagon, like a fabulous bell, upright, at rest.

"Rangoon, sahib," Ramasamy said, coming up behind him at the rail, with a plate, Blair's luggage chits stacked on it. "Godvin Jetty."

"Those trees," Blair said.

"Bodhi tree, sahib. Peepul tree, sahib. Holy tree."

"Why holy?"

"Lord Krishna tree, sahib. Also Buddha tree."

"Under which he was enlightened."

"Exactly so, sahib," Ramasamy said. "And Lord Krishna, sahib. He resided beneath."

A grove, a garden, the sweet smell and dusty smack of pulpous sun-heated foliage. After the derangement of the voyage, this beauty was a soothing welcome, and the December weather was mild, nothing like the heat of Aden or Colombo. For the first time since Liverpool, Blair felt hopeful.

"There's Beadon," Jones said, on the gangway, pink-faced, dragging his fat Gladstone bag. "Roger!" he called out. "I say, Roger!"

Beadon waved his arms to be seen, then thrashed seeming to swim through the crowd, nudging a man with an umbrella—Burmese, Indian, Blair could not tell—but the man staggered, half bowing, stepping aside, losing control of his umbrella as he was jostled further.

"Mind your brolly, you clumsy bugger," a mustached man in a topee snarled, his sharp words causing his mustache to jump under his nose.

The dark man backed away, bent double in apology.

"Sergeant Haggan," Beadon said. "This is the rest of our crew, Jones and Blair."

The mustached man saluted, tapping the brim of his topee. "Sholto Haggan—'Haggis' to many—here to accompany you to your billet, the chummery, and to squire you on your official visits."

Beadon said, "We're expected to pay our respects to officialdom—Sergeant Haggan here knows the drill."

"Let's see your chits, lads. I'll have the boy here sort them out and convey them to your quarters at the chummery."

But Blair didn't hear—he was numbed by the noisy crowd, English mostly, greeting the arriving passengers—deafened by the shouts and the commands; and he was still entranced by the shapes of the trees.

"You there, Lofty," he heard.

It was Haggan, poking his arm.

"Your chits."

Blair glanced at the sergeant's upturned sweating face and twitching mustache.

"Your *bojh*, your clobber, your cases, Lofty."

"Dreadfully sorry," Blair said and handed him the scraps of paper.

"I've got a motor waiting," Haggan said, passing the chits to a porter in a small tightly wrapped headcloth and a loose blue skirt. "Come along. I don't expect you want to trudge around here. I'll take you to quarters and"—he was signaling as he spoke—"bit of advice, have a bite of lunch, a wash and brushup, and consider an early night. I'll fetch you in the morning. Slap-up breakfast. When you finish your tuck-in, we'll make our calls. And this is Corporal Figgis, the driver of our Crossley."

Figgis was a thin, loose-limbed man, dressed like Sholto Haggan in a khaki jacket, and shorts and knee socks. He used one thumb to lift his topee in greeting. He swung himself into the boxy open-topped Crossley, as Sargent Haggan climbed in from the opposite side; Beadon, Blair, and Jones got in the rear seat, elbow to elbow.

"Strand Hotel, pity we can't billet you there," Haggan said, narrating. "Post Office, Sule Pagoda, Anderson's—they do a decent beefsteak . . ."

The smells were strong: the tickle of manure, as the street was thick with horse-drawn carts; the reek of sweat from the soaked backs of hurrying barefoot men pulling rickshaws; the sourness of decaying vegetation; the itch of choking dust; the smoke from cooking fires; and the stink of hot oil and burnt food. Women with baskets on their heads dodged the car— Figgis complaining as he had to slow for them, but he could barely be heard above the creaking of buggies, the clop of hooves, and the cries of hawkers. Nearly all the pedestrians were natives, but here and there Blair spied a white man in a solar topee, seated in a car or a rickshaw, looking like a lord. Seeing the men dragging overloaded carts or rickshaws, the women burdened with bundles, Blair thought: *pack animals*. The Burmese men were dressed alike, most with a head wrapping and loose blouse, and instead of trousers they wore a cloth that was knotted at the waist.

"Those skirts," Blair said.

"That, my lad, is a lungyi," Haggan said. "Very sensible, cooler than our bags or shorts. As good as a kilt. Imagine the updraft!" And chucking his cheroot into the road, he said, "Ah, here we are. The chummery."

It was a two-story wood-frame house with large windows and a roofed veranda over a porte cochere, where Figgis parked, poisonous exhaust fumes swirling over the car as he came to a halt.

At lunch in the shadowy dining room, a punkah swinging slowly overhead, stirring dust motes into the shafts of sunlight, Haggan said, "Tomorrow—up with the lark."

"I was hoping to visit the famous racecourse," Beadon said.

"You'll see it's rather miles."

"Is there a chapel hereabout?" Jones asked.

"No need. You'll be out of here and on your way by Sunday." Haggan was spooning his soup. "Good weather now, but the rains are coming. And the hot months are a caution. The Burmese year has two seasons, a wet and a dry—wet from the end of April to early October, dry the rest of the time. So-called hot months from February till the beginning of the rains." He swallowed some soup and brushed droplets of it from his mustache. "Know what's good for the hot weather, besides whiskey? You want hot tea for a good sweat. What's wrong, Lofty?"

"Not very hungry," Blair said.

He waved away the plate, collops of mutton cut from a joint, and brown gravy and what Haggan said were bottled peas—soft and pale—though he ate part of the plum duff and joined the others for coffee in the lounge.

"I like to see a man with initiative," Haggan said as he rose to go, seeing Blair rolling a cigarette, licking the paper, smoothing the cylinder. "Mind you, your house girl will be good at that—chiefly the licking part."

After Haggan left, Blair said, "I'm going to put my feet up," and wandered away, pausing at the window to look at a bird flicking its beak into a blossom, then he climbed the stairs to his room.

Beadon inclined his head, and when he heard a door slam shut, he said to Jones in a low voice, "Rather a dull dog."

"Lofty aroused some interest on the ship from an older couple," Jones said. "They seemed to be beating the bushes on behalf of an unmarried daughter, so I gathered—looking for someone to take her on. I had tea with them—mind, you can hardly avoid other people on the ship. The memsahib was keen on Blair—kept mentioning Eton. But her forthright husband pulled her up, and said—oh, lord!"

Here, Jones gasped with embarrassment and mirth, unable to finish his sentence.

Eager to hear, Beadon put his face near Jones's and hissed, as though conspiring, "Out with it, David."

Slowly and in a stern Scottish voice, Jones said, "Och, he is no beauty."

"Off we go, Figgis—let's fuck back, *jildy,*" Haggan said, as he slammed the car door and saw that the three men had squeezed into the rear seat. He squirmed to look them in the eye. "We start at the top, the governor. He's new at the job, like you, but he's been here a bit longer. You want to mind your manners—the governor is rather grand."

"Sir Spencer," Jones began, as the car lurched out of the driveway and into the road, among the horse-drawn wagons and rickshaws.

"Harcourt Butler," Haggan said. "And behold Lofty, eyeing the rickshaw wallahs."

Blair straightened in his seat. Watching the rickshaws, the brown sinewy men trotting like nags, bearing a sahib dressed in white, his arms crossed—it was exactly what he'd been doing, but he hated Haggan remarking on it, he disliked being observed. So he denied it, laughing as he said, "Not at all. Just taking the air. Feeling a little green after that voyage."

"My word, that's a tram car," Jones said.

"Only natives ride the trams," Haggan said. Then, "You'll want to be on your toes with the governor. I'll tell you what you're in for. Coffee, biscuits, and a huge jaw on drill."

At Government House, Blair was struck by its massive façade, its elegance, the freshly painted pillars of the colonnade, the vastness of the building, its look of permanence, its solidity as a statement of strength, the Raj as immovable, something imperious and everlasting. Anyone who looked upon it, or entered, would be overwhelmed with a sense of awe, feeling small.

They were shown inside by a clerkly looking white man in a pale suit, but with trousers not shorts, and wearing a black tie, looking harassed as he tugged at his lapels. Blair instinctively held himself back, so as not to tower over him.

"This way," the man said, and glancing at a note card, "Beadon, Blair, Jones—you'll identify yourself to the governor, when the time comes."

Down the hall, through a set of doors; a portly balding man rose from behind a wide desk and greeted them, not words but a friendly growl, as though digesting something substantial. He too wore a pale linen suit, but a bow tie, and a white waistcoat, a mauve handkerchief tucked into his breast pocket. The visitors gave their names, the governor leaned on his desk. "Do sit, chaps."

His shoes were white, with black toe caps and black laces, and looked foppish to Blair, who found himself seizing on details for a letter home.

"Will you take coffee? Yes?" The governor nodded to the man who'd escorted them into the office. "I bid you welcome. Which of you is Beadon?"

Beadon said, "Sir."

"I knew a Beadon at the Delhi Gymkhana Club in '13."

"My uncle, sir."

"Excellent polo player, but he took a fearful toss in a match against Poona." And jerking his head, as though expressing sympathy, he directed his attention to Jones, like a master at morning roll call.

Anticipating the next question, Jones swallowed nervously and said, "Jones, sir."

"I knew many Joneses, one way and another."

"None of my folk, sir. Our people kept pretty close to the valleys. Rhondda, that is."

But the governor had moved on. "By elimination, you must be Blair. I believe your father was in the civil service."

"Opium Department, sir," and thought, as always, *Subdeputy Fourth Class*.

"Not my line, I'm afraid, although their diligence as exporters filled our coffers to the brim, and so your father must be congratulated." He was tapping a paper on his desk. "I see here you were at Eton."

"For my sins, sir."

"I forgive you. I speak as an old Harrovian. And what were you—an oar? Wet bob? Dry bob?"

"Wall Game, sir."

"Make a goal?"

"The last goal in the Wall Game was scored in 1909, sir."

"Oh, yes, of course. What about a shy?"

"Modesty forbids my saying so, sir."

"Modesty will get you nowhere in the Raj, my boy. Sergeant Sholto Haggan will back me up on that. You'll want to keep your head well above the parapet."

The coffee arrived and was served by an Indian in a khaki uniform. When the visitors were sipping coffee, nibbling biscuits, seated upright, at attention, the governor spoke again.

"As you may know, I'm new at this job. I was appointed just the other day. But I should say that I was just your age when I joined the Civil Service—I was twenty, and green. I learned from the best of our people, some old troopers who remembered the Great Mutiny, which I can say was a baptism of fire for me." He stroked the silken handkerchief flopping from his pocket. "And a cure for appallingly progressive ideas. What?"

"Yes, sir," Beadon said, and the others murmured in agreement.

"What is our mission in Burma?" the governor said. "In my view, it is not in aid of the political education of the masses. That is the road to anarchy and upheaval." He released himself from leaning against his desk and stepped forward until he loomed over the three seated recruits. His open mouth went square. "We are here to bring law and order to parts of barbary, and to maintain that order. At times, as you will see, the present situation taxes human intelligence to the limit." He paused with his mouth open. Then, "Democracy? I say, democracy?"

He spoke the word sour-mouthed as though naming an affliction, and Blair became attentive for what might come next, though he could not imagine what it might be, certainly not a refutation of the word.

But it was. "It is a thumping lie!"

"Sir," Beadon said, and Jones and Blair emitted affirmative grunts.

"Above all, let us avoid the pernicious cant of thinking that our mission in Burma is the political education of the masses. Our mission is to conserve, not to destroy, their social organism. With a fertile country, with no pressure of population on subsistence, with few wants, why should the Burman strive or cry out?"

He paused and glanced at Jones, who nodded furiously.

"Here is my point," the governor said. "For the Burman, progress and the strenuous life have no attraction. We are trying to teach him our ideals, to show him how far superior is our civilization. When we shall have succeeded, we shall have spoiled the pleasantest country and the most delightful people in the world."

Blair had begun to smile, and seeing him, the governor seemed provoked, continuing with force.

"Political power is to be deposited in the hands of a natural aristocracy, and not—and never!—to be surrendered to the claims of abstract democratic ideals. And you, gentlemen, must help exercise it with justice and mercy."

With that, he patted the mauve handkerchief at his breast pocket—over his heart—perhaps as an expression of his seriousness, or maybe his palm was damp from the energy of his peroration.

In the silence that followed—the governor seeming to pause to let his words sink in—Jones said, "Thank you, sir."

Blair looked stunned, but when he saw the governor staring at him he spoke up.

"We'll do our best, sir."

Beckoning to the doorway, the governor summoned the clerkly man who'd shown them in.

"Good luck, gentlemen." The governor turned his back on them and seated himself at his desk, sliding a document toward himself on his blotter.

"Gave you a huge jaw, am I right?" Sergeant Haggan asked afterward in the car.

"Natural aristocracy," Blair said. "I fancy he means us."

But he quickly realized, when no one responded, that he'd gone too far and had sounded satirical and spoke again.

"He provided us some decidedly acceptable advice."

In the circumstances, that seemed much more satirical, yet Beadon replied by saying, "The governor is a jolly sensible fellow. He has placed his trust in us. We must make ourselves worthy of it."

Haggan widened his eyes at Beadon's solemnity, and said, "Just one more visit. The inspector general of police."

It was a short drive to Sparks Street and the Secretariat, another gleaming building of the Raj, a fortress of indestructible stonework; but Figgis fretted at the wheel, slowed by the throngs of horse carts and rickshaws, and wincing, distracted by the shouts of pedestrians.

"Hear that? Chap calling us names," Haggan said and yelled back, "*Barn-shoot!*"

"That's a new word to me," Blair said.

"Suster's fanny," Haggan said.

The inspector general's secretary met them at the entrance, saying, "We're rather pushed for time." He held an appointment book with lined pages, like a ledger. "You're being squeezed in. The inspector general is in a meeting—he said he'd absent himself to greet you. He mustn't be detained."

With the snap of a salute, Haggan said, "We're at his service."

The foyer was cool, the ghost of a breeze swelling from the far end of the long corridor that was open to the courtyard, where a barefoot man, on his knees, was sweeping leaves, with a brush that seemed no more than a whisk of limp ineffectual grass.

The secretary tapped at a tall varnished door, and within seconds the door swung open and a man in uniform appeared, looking fussed, smacking his lips, blinking in the light from the street; and yet his uniform was impeccable, his khaki jacket surmounted by gilded epaulets, a row of medals on his breast pocket, his shorts stiff with starch, delicate tassels at the tops of his knee socks, his black shoes gleaming.

"Chaps," he said, a bit breathless. "I'm sorry I can't formally greet you with the requisite durbar, but you're welcome all the same. I'm sure I'll see you in training in Mandalay. That's not far from my usual beat. Sergeant Haggan here will look after you in the meantime."

"Thank you, sir," Beadon said, and now Blair saw that it was done to acknowledge with emphasis anything that was uttered by a superior, and he, too, offered his thanks.

"Two points," the inspector general said, clenching his fists and holding them chest high, as though he was clasping two objects and holding them upright. He extended one fist toward the men who were standing at attention in wide bands of sunlight created by the exterior columns. "The first is, we're in December, fast approaching the crime season, which is January to June, our most testing time."

"Permission to speak, sir," Jones said. "Why those particular months?"

Wagging the same fist, the inspector general said, "Ask the first dacoit you arrest, note the answer, then beat him senseless about his head and shoulders."

"I shall do, sir."

"Second," the inspector general said, weighing his other fist. "Always remember, we are sahib log and they—*they*—are rabble."

"Thank you, sir," Blair said promptly and as the others piped up, the inspector general executed an about-face and pushed past his secretary and slammed the door behind him.

"Bit of luck, him being flat-out," Haggan said in the car. "He's rather a terror. I've seen him bang on for hours."

"We are sahib log," Jones said, in a soft remembering tone.

"And they are dirt," Haggan said, breathing deeply as the car rattled through the city. "Fine weather. It's such a fag, bashing from office to office in the hot months."

"Where to?" Figgis asked.

"The chummery—lunch," Haggan said. "The chaps can sort themselves out. Later on, a tour of the town."

"I should like to see the big pagoda," Blair said. "And maybe try one of the local dishes."

"Och, yes, Lofty. You'll find the local muck better than Beecham's Pills. Worth a guinea a box! You'll be garshly with the squitters for a fortnight."

Over lunch—boiled fowl, mashed potatoes, and a slimy vegetable no one could name—Blair said, "That governor."

"Makes you think," Jones said. And when the steward crept to the table to collect the plates, Jones said, "What is this?" and stirred the bowl of green slime.

"Frog spawn," Haggan said.

"Bhindi, sir," the steward said.

They were served coffee in the lounge, a small boy standing by with a tray of milk and sugar, as the steward poured. Blair considered fetching his book from his room and reading it over his coffee but reconsidered: *I don't want them to know what I'm reading.* It was another Wells. Books revealed so much of a person. And what would they say if they knew he wrote poems?

They dozed where they sat, and Figgis arrived at five in the coughing Crossley; the three recruits squeezed into the rear seat, Blair apologetic, his knees under his chin. Directing Figgis from street to street, Haggan identified the vehicles—"Tonga . . . bullock cart . . . tram . . ." And mingled with the smell of horse dung and heated dust and cooking oil was something else, something syrupy, the aroma of incense. Blair closed his eyes, threw his head back, and inhaled the sweetness.

"Government offices," Haggan said. "That's a Cameron—the Highlanders are in change here, and they don't let you forget it. Merchants—no natives allowed."

"Why is that?" Blair asked.

"Because they're bloody exhausting."

Passing a park with a pavilion, Haggan announced Sule Pagoda, the grass near it scorched and tussocky, and Fytche Square—he spelled it—and Rangoon Lunatic Asylum; he made a joke, but he was smoking a cheroot and his words were incoherent with his coughing.

"Prome Road," Figgis said. "The clubs."

"Gymkhana's good value," Haggan said, and they reversed, driving back to Sule Pagoda Road.

"'Bookshop,'" Blair said, reading a sign.

"Smart and Mookerdum," Haggan said. "You much of a reader, Lofty?"

"Once in a way," Blair said, attempting to be phlegmatic about his greatest passion—the only activity he truly cared about, verging on a sacrament. "Passes the time."

Haggan turned, puffing his cheroot. "There's a chiel among us."

Blair thought, Burns, and was going to say the name, but laughed instead, the too-loud laugh for when he was being insincere. He was going to mention the Shwedagon Pagoda again, but he imagined more of Haggan's derision and so he waited to see the slender spire of the stupa up ahead, and nearer the crowds of worshippers, carrying baskets of fruit and flowers.

"There you are, Lofty. In all its glory."

As Figgis slowed the car a beggar clasping a bowl approached the car.

"*Ma-maik-we,*" Haggan said, and the beggar stepped away. "Useful expression."

"Give us a hint," Beadon said.

"Go hame!"

But he was *home,* Blair thought, and he smiled and attempted a chuckle he knew was a hideous sound.

"Might we stop here?"

"Bloody mob," Haggan said. "Monks, beggars, riffraff. Fucking nuisance. Careful, Figgis—hit a nig-nog and he'll die on purpose, to spite you."

Blair winced, saying, "Is that a fact, Sergeant?"

"Where shall we make for, Sholto?" Figgis said.

"Monkey Point."

Haggan had lit another cheroot, blackish and blunt, that he chewed between puffs, and Blair now understood the man's stained mustache; the sergeant grew heartier as Figgis drove on, east again, past the Secretariat and the bazaar, cheerier than in the morning, muzzy with drink, whiffy with whiskey as he turned and said, "You chaps much good at girls?"

They were now near the river—the mud smell, the decay of the warehouses lining it—but Figgis carried on, turning down a bouldery road, overhung with trees.

"Those trees," Blair said.

"That's a tamarind," Figgis said. "The ones with red blossoms are gold mohur trees. Quite lovely."

Farther on in the shade of trees Blair now recognized as peepul trees, the bumpy road narrowed to a track and, ahead at the end of a path, he saw an elegant two-story house, with porches on two sides, top and bottom, all its windows open, the pale curtains slack, the low sun behind it shining through its rooms, lighting the windows, framing a woman seated with her arm on a sill.

She wore a shawl, and with the sun behind her, her face was in shadow, but still she seemed like a Madonna in a portrait, the shutters of the window flung open. She turned and in profile her lips were reddened, she was smiling; she reached and with the back of her hand she tucked up a loose lock of hair.

Figgis had shut off the engine, and so they sat in silence—not silence, really, there were voices from the river, the whine of a saw cutting wood in the distance, bird squawks, a dog, the gabble of children somewhere near. Blair's attention was fixed on the woman at the window, and now he saw silhouetted in the interior of that same room the movement of draped women, backlit by the low sun, their bodies revealed in their diaphanous gowns.

"That one in the window," Haggan said. "Giving you the glad eye, Lofty."

Blair, breathless, sensed he was blushing, but he was stirred, too, trembling, his hands damp, holding on to his knees.

"Welcome to Monkey Point." Haggan turned to grin at them.

Jones and Beadon squirmed, struggling to see, ducking to peer through the dusty windscreen, then leaning out of the sides of the car for a better look. Now there was movement on the lower veranda, a stout woman in a shawl, scuffing to the rail and beckoning.

"The lady of the house," Haggan said. "She's a chee-chee—half-caste. Quite an armful. Goes by 'Auntie.'"

Blair was too flustered to speak, his mouth was gummy, he was perspiring, his hands sodden.

"One of the pleasures of Rangoon," Haggan said. "I found it quite by chance. The villain I was chasing took refuge there. When I confronted him, he tried to nobble me, offered me one of the ladies. I arrested him on the spot. Charge-sheeted the bugger."

Haggan gurgled with satisfaction, remembering.

"I went back later that night." He tossed the wet stump of his dead cheroot into the dust and watched a rooster dash for it and begin to peck furiously at it. "Found a popsy. A chee-chee. She made herself very agree-able." He sniffed then drew a deep voluptuous breath and exhaled slowly. "Spot of fun."

The young men in the back seat stared in silence at the house; the woman was gone from the window, and the stout woman who'd been on the veranda had slipped inside.

"Lots of knocking shops like this," Haggan said. "Mandalay's heaving with them. Think of it as a standing invitation."

That night in his room, Blair could not sleep for thinking of the pavilion by the river at Monkey Point, the woman smiling at the upper window, the sylphlike figures drifting inside, their bodies glowing through their gowns, the shawled woman on the veranda, rotating her fat finger and showing her teeth—teeth stained bloodred, the rank smell of the riverbank groping through the whiff of incense from the pavilion that promised the prospect of flesh.

5

MANDALAY FORT

Seeing his bumped, ribbed steamer trunk hoisted onto the Night Mail's luggage van by grunting Burmese porters at Rangoon Station, Blair was possessed by a morbid fancy, of the sort he might turn into a poem. The trunk was not a trunk but a coffin, E A BLAIR stenciled in black across the paper label glued to its lid. His corpse inside was being conveyed up-country, he was helpless to prevent his remains ending up in Mandalay—and what then?

A ghastly revenant, condemned to haunt the bazaars and ruins of Upper Burma, his living death as a ghostly policeman, like one of those tormented wraiths in a Kipling tale, a lost soul exiled from his people, doomed to wander as a phantom. He was not going to be traveling with Beadon and Jones in the sleeping car: he was in that trunk that was piled with others in the van, and only his fraudulent self was standing in the vestibule of the carriage, smiling at Beadon, but with nothing to say. The poem would begin, *I saw my corpse conveyed one day, in the luggage van to Mandalay* . . .

A breeze had sprung up, whipping a lacy veil of ashes from the smoke-stack of the locomotive, depositing soot on his arms and face, which smeared and went blacker when he swiped at it with his fingers.

"You're all smuts," Beadon said. "You look like bally chimney sweep."

I look like a corpse, Blair thought, when he slipped inside the carriage and glanced at his face in the mirror of his compartment. The sun was setting behind him as he sat by the window, the ashy smoke still swirling over the platform.

Then a familiar sequence of sounds, the clang and grip of the coupling, the clunk-jerk of the bogie, the long moan of the whistle, and the grinding wheels—steel against steel, with the click of rail ends—as the train began to roll out of the station.

I am making a great mistake, he thought, and at that moment a hawker—Indian, Burmese, he couldn't tell—saw Blair's mournful face at the window, and the man, emboldened because the train was moving away, pursed his lips and leaned and spat a gout of betel juice in his direction, then hooted—an ugly man, laughing at him, wishing him ill.

I hate this, I shouldn't be here, I will never succeed. He saw the soot on his arms, the smear of smut on his cigarette paper from his stained fingers, and felt filthy. He was being drawn into the bowels of this beastly place, among implacable natives, and imperious officials, because he had agreed to his father's demands and his asinine promise: *it will make a man of you.* And Blair had had no reply.

These were disappointed thoughts he could not set down in a letter, nor share them with anyone, not with his father or mother, not with Jacintha, who had flirted with him but stiffened and drew away when he touched her, saying, "Don't be saucy, Eric." Like all his other misgivings, these desperate doubts would have to remain unspoken.

But fifteen minutes into the journey, a matter of miles, his spirits revived. They had left the hot glare of the city and its risen dust, the shop signs and hoardings and the clatter of carts, the sullen faces of natives stalled at level crossings, the noses of their bullocks and horses pressed against the horizontal pipe of the barrier. They had entered the jungle and its green shadows and its leaf-scented air, its sheltering trees, the glimpses of green fields and fences, a geometry of gigantic earthen trays of standing water, with rice shoots poking through, his first sight of paddy fields that he'd known only from an illustration in a schoolbook—and those pictures had not revealed the beauty of them he saw now. And bamboo—fountains of it in tight clumps, and some of it dense in thickets, birds nesting in the green striped canes. He smiled when he saw the tree whose name he knew now, the peepul tree, as well as one he wished to know—thick trunk, wide leaves.

He went to the vestibule for a better look and found Beadon smoking, rocking to the jolt of the train.

"Those trees," Blair said.

"Teak."

And then to his relief, Beadon left him alone, perhaps thinking that Blair had snubbed him earlier.

He was happier in this forest and farmland, the trees dusted gold by the sunset. He felt hopeful—or at least calmer—at dusk, and in the humid darkness he smelled the fragrance of the damp foliage and fresh grass and the lotuses crowding the ponds. When night fell the darkness was complete and it was as though they were tunneling underground, perfumed by night-blooming trees. He relaxed, the tightness in his body gone; he rolled another cigarette and smoked some more. *Maybe I'm not dead.*

The dense forest gave Blair hope. He saw no sign of a village for miles, and when he did he glimpsed dimly lighted faces as they sat near lamps or in open doorways, squatting men, tiny figures in small huts, dwarfs in a dollhouse world, surrounded by the immense darkness, a shadowland of chittering insects and of earthen odors. He found the odors agreeable, suggesting tilled soil and muddy rice terraces, with a reality that the sweetness of blossoms lacked, though at one station he was dazed by the fragrance of jasmine, the smells so much sharper in the dark.

He'd been daunted by the crowded streets in Rangoon, the bustle of scuffing pedestrians, the clatter of tongas, the running men pulling rickshaws, the packed trams, the shiver of unintelligible shouts. He could not see how he belonged among so much strangeness. Yet here, rolling north, he could get to know the trees, and he was consoled by the great empty spaces between stations.

Unable to sleep, craving fresh air, Blair left his compartment and walked along the narrow corridor to the far end of the carriage, where the vestibule was open to the night air, rocking to the rhythm of the train, the clack of wheels rolling over points, the clicks at the gaps in the track, a syncopation that dramatized the passing of time, ticking closer to Mandalay.

He was comfortable for the first time in Burma. In Rangoon they'd boasted of the mild weather, and he'd agreed, but he'd sweated from office to office, suffering the formal welcomes. His bedroom at the chummery had been stifling, and the memory of the women at Monkey Point, their slim bodies outlined by the sun shining through their silks, had unsettled him, keeping him alert. His apprehension, fearing what lay ahead, unprepared, left him wakeful, feverish with anxiety.

But the breeze from the speeding train refreshed him and his mind was eased as he stood in the vestibule, enveloped by night odors and darkness. He clung to the handrail, swaying with the train, as though guiding it forward, bathed in the cool air.

The train slowed to circle a low hill that was dimly visible in the feeble light of a sickle blade of moon, and at this speed he was able to stand without holding to the rail. He rolled a cigarette and struck a match—shielding it with one hand to keep it alight—but before he could apply it to the cigarette in his lips, the carriage door clanged. He shook out the match and palmed the cigarette, as a figure emerged, jarring him in his reverie.

Jones—in his pajamas, looking untidy, his hair wild, his collar askew, shuffled toward him in fat ragged bedroom slippers like a sleepwalker, yawning loudly without covering his mouth, a halitotic growl that Blair found repellent. And the sight of the loosely hanging pajamas, the man's obvious nakedness beneath them, caused Blair to step away.

"Can't sleep, Lofty."

"Don't call me Lofty." Blair became hot again in his anger.

"But you're such a tall chap." And Jones yawned again.

"Did you not hear me!"

The shout startled Jones, who took a sudden step backward, treading on his pajama cuff, and when he stumbled and steadied himself by grasping the rail, Blair confronted him, looking down, Jones's face seemed more frightened and deranged by his wild hair.

"It's not my fucking name." With both hands Blair snatched the collar of Jones's pajama jacket and held tight, tugging the small man upright.

"Eric then?"

"Not Eric to you," Blair said, and he jerked the collar with his damp demanding hands, his knuckles against the stringy sinews of Jones's throbbing neck.

"Leave off," Jones said, in a low whiffling moan.

But Blair held on, furious, shoving him down.

"What then?" The man was choking, nearly breathless. "What name?"

"I'm Blair, you little bastard!"

And saying it, he slammed Jones hard against the iron frame of the carriage door and tightened his grip on Jones's throat. As he did so he was startled by his own anger, the uprush of sudden fury, the man's popping eyes and strangled squawks. And when Blair let go, Jones slumped and gagged and felt for the door handle, then was gone. Blair was flustered, shocked by his response, his hands damp and trembling, his head hot, as though he'd been assaulted.

Back in his compartment he locked the door, fumbling with the bolt, cursing, then lay in his berth, but awkwardly, his legs too long to stretch out, breathless from his rage, nerved from shame. He thrashed, unable to sleep—but he must have slept, because the harsh sunlight of dawn was a surprise.

He tottered along the swaying train, through the corridors of a succession of sleeping cars, until he came to the dining car. He spotted Jones and Beadon having breakfast at a far table. To ignore them was to invite scorn. He could not cut fellow candidates. Joining them suggested companionship, but he had no choice.

Taking a seat next to Jones he faced Beadon, as he sensed Jones stiffen and bristle like a cat.

"Blair," Beadon said.

Beadon's narrow smile indicated he knew everything, so there was no point mentioning it, and it was fruitless to apologize. He regretted having shown his anger, and yet they now seemed respectful, more polite, less chatty than they'd been the day before.

"We ought to be in Mandalay by midmorning," Jones said in an oddly formal manner, as though reciting lines in a stage play. Seeing Blair glance at his plate, he added, "Kedgeree—it's awfully good, Blair."

Afterward, in his compartment, watching at the window he was surprised that, deep into the country, penetrating its heart, there was so little lushness. He'd expected more trees, entangled vines, bigger blossoms, the bamboo again, perhaps tea estates on hillsides. But the train traveled into a flatter dustier landscape, the tracks dead straight, the carriage hardly rocking now, and in this dry plain the trees were smaller, spindlier, the huts meaner, and the only notable landscape feature was the occasional whitewashed temple or six-story pagoda in the distance.

Later, smoking in the vestibule again, taking the air, Blair was cheered by the sight of ducks in village ponds, by chickens nearer the houses, and once a dog with an anguished expression, sitting by the railway line, scratching at fleas, an upraised paw nagging at its neck. Women at creekbanks slapped laundry against great smooth boulders, and the train slowing as it passed a house close to the track revealed a woman on her knees, her head down, her skirt tightened against her boyish buttocks, washing her lustrous hair in a basin.

"Dry zone," Beadon said as a greeting, stepping out of the door.

Blair said nothing, but he looked around to see if Jones had accompanied him, peering past Beadon's shoulder at the carriage door—self-conscious, because that was the very spot where he'd raged at the short-arsed Welshman who'd cheeked him.

Seeming to sense this from Blair's silence, Beadon said, "I gather you were a bit short with our friend Jones."

Blair took a deep breath, inhaling dust, and finally said, "Don't fancy being called Lofty."

"You raised no objection with Sholto Haggan."

"Sergeant Haggan's senior to us. Jones doesn't have a pip yet, or am I mistaken?"

"I can't imagine what inflamed you against him," Beadon said. "Poor chap was shaking like jelly."

Hearing that, Blair's shame became acute, rising in his throat, choking him with self-disgust, and he was on the point of apologizing, searching for words, when Beadon spoke again.

"Shanzu Station," he said, as the train clanked to a halt, its brakes grinding.

At first Blair thought, *I can read the station signs as well, mate.* But he quickly realized that Beadon saying that, changing the subject, meant that the Jones matter was at an end. Jones was an unknown quantity from the Welsh Valleys—he'd mentioned Rhondda, his war veteran father a lowly but worthy collier, earning Blair's respect as a workingman. Beadon was a recognizable sort from school, the confident swot who always had the answer, polite to the masters, hopeless at sports, never caned, arse-creeper. Here he had the confident and cheery air of someone in the know, talkative in these foreign parts, as though he was returning after a long absence, gesturing in a familiar way.

"Arakan Pagoda," Beadon said.

Visible in the distance, like a preposterous chess piece, a seven-tiered capriccio, a pyramid of narrowing stories, thick with gold, topped by a finial like an arrowhead, its flowery and fluted corner pieces and colonnades and gilded pillars glistening in the morning sun.

"Reckoned to be equal to the Shwedagon," Beadon said.

But that glory in the background was misleading, for in the foreground, beyond the station was a jumble of shops, thronged with hawkers and upright bamboo poles on which flags hung as slack as rags in the still air, a nimbus of gray woodsmoke hovering over this bazaar. A blare of brass instruments, too, and screams.

Some departing passengers squeezed passed Blair and Beadon, a British soldier with a rifle and kit bag, an old European woman with a cane, attended by a Burmese girl who opened an umbrella over the old woman's head as soon as she alighted on the platform. And when another passenger appeared—a smiling clergyman, white side-whiskers, dog collar, clapping a solar topee on his bald head—Beadon and Blair descended to the platform to make way.

"What do you reckon?" Beadon said, still seeming at home.

"Flat." Blair glanced around.

"Not all of it." Beadon walked out of the shade of the train to the rear of the platform. "Look."

To the north, in a haze of dust-laden air, a symmetrical hill, bulging out of the plain and the brownish corrugations of low city buildings, a chalk-white structure at its summit,

"Mandalay Hill," Beadon said.

It was lovely, singular, a simple mound rising above the flatness and floating dust and tin roofs. Its beauty lifted Blair's spirits and renewed his hope, as had the majesty of the peepul trees he'd first seen, and the luminous green like fantastic grass in the paddy fields, the white ducks gliding in the muddy ponds beside the tracks—the relief he felt in the scenes without humans.

"You've been here before, Beadon?"

"Mugged it up in Murray's *Guide*."

Climbing the stairs to the carriage, Blair said, "How much farther?"

"A mile or so to the station. And there we'll be met by Detective-Inspector Wynford Beagle, who will see us to the fort and our quarters. And afterward to our principal, Clyne Stewart. I'm assured we'll recognize Captain Stewart by his Old Bill mustache."

Blair envied Beadon his thrust and his eagerness, his willing smile—though he would have been hated at school for these traits. Blair despaired of his own reticence. When they arrived at Mandalay Station and they were met by a man in uniform whom Beadon greeted by name, Blair hung back, feeling awkward and conspicuous. In the car to the fort, seated uneasily next to Jones (Beadon in the front seat), Blair could not think of a question to ask the detective-inspector, though he took some comfort in seeing the lovely hill beyond the fort.

"Wesleyan Chapel," the detective-inspector said, passing a church.

"Good to know," Jones said.

"Here we are, South Gate," the man said. "Welcome to the palace, or I should say, Fort Dufferin."

Past a parade ground, at a row of brick buildings, the car pulled beside the entryway to a two-story, barrackslike structure with a wide steeply pitched roof, its ground floor a succession of arches that seemed to enclose an arcade, but in fact—so the detective-inspector informed them—enclosed the police officers' mess.

And Blair's heart sank, as he experienced the bewildering unanswerable sadness he always felt at an arrival, and the *What now?* as at a dead end. Making it worse for him was the knowing smile of Detective-Inspector Wynford Beagle, because on the walkway he poked Blair's shoulder.

"You can climb it, you know."

The watchful policeman had seen him in the wing mirror, his head out of the car window, wordlessly staring at the hill.

"Thank you, sir. I might do."

The captain, Clyne Stewart, joined them for lunch at the mess. He was, as Beadon had predicted, heavily mustached, with a bluff assertive manner that Blair now saw as the chief characteristic of a colonial policeman—of Sergeant Sholto Haggan, the inspector general, Wynford Beagle, and now his immediate superior, Captain Stewart. Blair thought with regret, *I am not bluff. Am I to be bluff?*

"Classes must be decently attended," Stewart said. "You are probationary. I must emphasize that you are, the three of you, not yet assistant district superintendents of police, but rather candidates on probation."

He was addressing Beadon, who'd become spokesman for the group, Jones too respectful to interrupt, Blair still trying to absorb the fact that he'd finally arrived.

"About the shoe ban," Beadon said.

"Rather an obnoxious stricture," Stewart said. "First it was the monks, then it became general. There have been some serious incidents over it."

"Over removing shoes at pagodas?"

"Our feet are unclean, they say." Stewart stroked his mustache, which twitched as he added, "The pagodas are unclean!" He shook his head. "But there it is, we must live with it."

"The cadets," Beadon said, as a cue.

"A callow lot on the whole, without a spark of gratitude—and easily corrupted, I'm afraid. They're from all over—Burmese, Indian, Gurkha, some hill tribes. You'll be putting them through their paces."

Jones reddened and said, "Looking forward to it, sir."

"The native is a child in every aspect except age," Stewart said. "And should be treated as a child. That is to say kindly, but with the greatest firmness. By firm, I mean don't hesitate to thrash them when necessary. Didn't you find, Blair"—and now he was looking directly at him—"that at your Eton College, being thrashed was a valuable lesson in maintaining discipline?"

"I suppose it also made me efficient when it came my turn to administer what we called a beating," Blair said. "Or a striping."

"Precisely my point."

They were served coffee in the library, and along with the shelves of books, there were mounted antlers on the wall, the skull of a water buffalo, its horns mimicking the contours of Stewart's mustache. Stewart said they'd be free the rest of the day and handed out sketch maps of the fort, drawing their attention to the Upper Burma Club, the Royal Palace, the tomb, the garden, the jail, and the various gates.

"The hill," Blair said. "I'd like to climb it."

"I don't expect you'll want to trudge up there in this heat. It's a biggish climb."

"Might have a go."

"New boy," Stewart said. "Have a lie-down, then think about it again."

The others laughed—hard, eagerly—to gratify the principal, and Blair found himself blushing, hot again and obvious, and hating the lot of them.

But when they'd gone to their rooms, Blair sat and smoked and drank more coffee. He prowled the room, glanced at the dusty taxidermy on the wall, and looked closely at the titles on the spines of the books. He saw a set of Kipling, Sir Herbert Thirkell White's *A Civil Servant in Burma*, Nisbet's *Burma Under British Rule*, *A Handbook of India and British Burmah*, a tattered copy of *The Silken East*, *The Indian Penal Code* in two leatherbound volumes, and an old Anglo-Indian dictionary with the laughable title *Hobson-Jobson*. But he took *Hobson-Jobson* from the shelf and sat, with the fat book on his lap for an hour, turning pages, fascinated.

Around four, self-conscious in the stillness in the library, he set off, using the sketch map to find his way through the fort, to the North Gate, to North Moat Road and the signposts to the hill. The entrance to the footpath was flanked by an enormous pair of toothy stone lions.

And not a path at all, but after thirty yards a stairway cut into the hill. Blair strode to the steps and mounted them, chanting *new boy, new boy, new boy,* for in the secret history of his life, it was the belittling welcome at St. Cyprian's, and at Eton, and at the crammer in Southwold—*new boy*— too green, to silent to succeed. Toadies like Jones, public school pushies like Beadon—they were the ones who made the grade.

And somehow that memory of school reminded him of what Clyne Stewart had said. *Didn't you find, Blair, that at your Eton College, being thrashed was a valuable lesson in maintaining discipline?*

He'd submitted, he'd agreed, and had wished to say more, but what was the point? Eton was an inferno of beatings—from limp-wristed thwacks and spirited cuts called siphonings with a rubber tube, to various canings handed out by martinets in the sixth form who'd risen to be captains. Blair remembered as a senior boy his role as praepostor summoning a terrified victim from his class and leading him to a formal swiping with a cane by the headmaster under the medieval beams of Lower School.

He had never shirked games, an offense that merited the fiercest beatings, but Blair remembered in his first year the boys' disciplinary authority known as the Library whose members tested him on the antiquated lore of the college; when he failed, they were entitled to beat him, which they did with fury. He was bewildered by the brutal injustice of it, but was impressed by a boy named Eliot who was stoical, not to say defiant.

Blair was in his room one evening when two members of the Library walked past. One, named Buchanan, said, "We haven't beaten Eliot much this half—bumptious little sod, needs taking down a peg." And later that evening a squad of sadistic older boys emerged from the Library, walking toward Eliot's room, rattling their canes against the corridor's wooden cladding, and finally they slapped those canes against Eliot's door, demanding he open it.

Eliot was quite unfazed. Some weeks later, Eliot saw Blair leave the Library, with a look of shock on his face, his eyes glazed, after a beating for being late to prayers. Eliot said, "Blotting paper, Blair. Always put it inside your shoes. Draws down the blood from your bum. Makes being beaten less painful."

The next time Blair was beaten—and it was always for a negligible infraction—he used Eliot's trick and it seemed to work, though unaccountably there wasn't the slightest medical evidence to support it.

In time, with his success in the Wall Game, Blair rose to be captain and took particular pleasure in administering a beating to Buchanan's younger brother—Buchanan Minor—bending him over a chair, drawing a chalk line across his striped trousers and thrashing him with the sort of unrestrained brutality that he now felt sure would merit the approval of Clyne Stewart.

The memory winded him, yet the higher he climbed the worn cut-stone steps, the freer he felt, and to take his mind off the miserable images of school beatings, he began humming a tune, one from the ship that had lodged in his head. It was Reginald Melly's crooning as he gripped the stand of the microphone and wagged his baton at his orchestra.

> *I found my love in Avalon*
> *Beside the bay . . .*

Ridiculous, really, but in a clowning crooning fashion of his own it set his mind at rest. To his delight he saw that he was being followed by a bird, a beauty, nipping from branch to branch, and when he kicked up an insect the bird swooped on it—a sort of thrush, black wings, white-rumped, with a wagging tail and warbling like an ascending meadowlark, fearless in its hunger, still following him, his first friend in Mandalay.

A monk in an ochre cloak descended from above him, plodding from step to step in thin sandals, a bag slung at his side and carrying a staff that he clumped onto each step. Blair drew aside and paused to let the monk pass.

What to say?

"Good afternoon."

But the monk grunted and faced Blair and narrowed his eyes, swagging his mouth sideways in an expression that might have been respect, or fear, or a grimace of disdain, and walked on.

I am a new boy and I know nothing. As he climbed he composed in his head another letter to Jacintha, deploring Burma and his fate, and expressing his sorrow at his being so far away and engaged in such futility. *You have no idea,* he'd write.

After about thirty minutes he could see he was nearer the top, the foliage denser and, on some outcrops and cliffs, squat buildings like follies and pillboxes, but more likely shrines. One of them was the haunt of a dozen monkeys, seated upright and eyeing him, scratching their hairy bellies, picking their teeth, like tinkers by a roadside. Past them, the steps opened to views to the west of the immense plain and the wide brown river, the grid of Mandalay city surrounded by emptiness, a smoky residue of dust and haze hanging in an obscuring layer over all of it.

Still climbing the stairs, plodding now, weary from the long day that had begun on the train, Blair resolved not to write Jacintha the letter he had envisaged. He would not contemplate quitting—could not, in fact, since he was contracted to remain for a minimum of three years, or else he'd be forced to repay the cost of his passage. And there was also his having to face the certain wrath of his father if he bolted.

He felt some satisfaction in leaving the fort and climbing the hill alone—he could make it a weekly outing, to enjoy the solitude, make lists of birds and trees, and rehearse his objections to being in Burma, write letters in his head that he would never send, or compose poems that he would show no one except Connolly.

A granite Buddha statue twice life-size bulked near a thick-walled pagoda on the plinth of a fenced platform at the midpoint of the hilltop. Children chasing one another laughing and calling out, and flags and pennants strung from poles, gave the summit the spirited atmosphere of a funfair, unlike anything he'd seen at an English church fete much less a churchyard—and yet this was a holy temple. Under a nearby tree—he wondered what sort—a picnicking family was seated in a circle on a red blanket, parents and three children, each one holding a small bowl to his chin and twitching the food into their mouth with chopsticks.

Burmese in skirts—men and women—formally removing their sandals and bowing, hands raised in prayer, entered the pagoda. He was reminded of Clyne Stewart's mention of "the shoe ban" (*Rather an obnoxious stricture*). Blair wouldn't enter, he'd never found churches or religious sites anything but lugubrious and moth-eaten and false—chapel at Eton had been torture. But he admired the piety of the Burmese, their solemn faces, their air of veneration that made them seem weightless.

He walked to a small terrace and unfolded his diagram of the fort and the nearby streets, and oriented it, to pick out his progress.

"Good afternoon, uncle—may I be of service, uncle?"

Blair turned to see a man—probably Burmese, but with a difference: this one, unlike any others he'd seen, was wearing a tweed jacket over his green blouse and purple skirt, and he pinched and adjusted his wire-framed spectacles as he approached, slowly as though in caution. There was a tremor of fear in his smile, and though Blair knew "uncle" was a term of respect in Burma, he thought of the Fool in *Lear,* saying "Nuncle."

Blair said, "Finding my feet."

A shy figure crept just behind the man, small enough to be his daughter, but seeing Blair's glance, the man said, "My good wife, uncle."

"You speak English."

The man straightened and said with exaggerated dignity, "The sun is setting soon but I have miles to travel before I reach my destination."

Was that a quotation? Blair was amused by the man's pomposity in reciting it, but he hadn't a clue.

"I am Joseph. This my wife, Sarah. We are Christians, uncle."

"I was under the impression the Burmese are mainly Buddhist." But thought, "*O nuncle, court holy-water in a dry house is better than this rainwater out o' door.*"

"That is certainly, true, uncle. This is a Buddhist shrine. But we are Karen, and many Karen are Christian." He stepped to the edge of the platform and pointed downward toward the fort. "That is our church—the American Baptist Church in the near corner, just outside the wall, on the canal. Street number Thirteen."

"Karen—a tribe?"

"Karen—a people. We have our language. We are situated in the southern mountains, but we travel for commerce and work. I am myself employed as a law clerk in the High Court. My posting is a term of three years, and then I await a transfer."

"I'm pleased to meet you on this sacred hill that gives the town its name."

"Not sacred to us, uncle."

With the "Mandalay" entry in *Hobson-Jobson* in mind Blair said, "Representing Mandara, the holy mountain in mythology."

"Hindu belief, uncle." The man pointed again. "We have our Christian church. We have a missionary from America, Pastor Miller. Our previous pastor was Mr. Grover Albee, now at a church in the Delta. But we have few friends outside the church." He stepped away, suddenly self-conscious. "You must forgive me for intruding, uncle."

"Not at all," Blair said. "I've just arrived in Mandalay. You're my first human friend."

"'A man that hath friends must show himself friendly, but there is a friend that sticketh closer than a brother.'"

Sticketh, he thought—nice. "Is that a Karen saying?"

"Proverbs, eighteen, twenty-four," the man said and turned to gaze at the city again. "You know the fort." He pointed. "That is Thibaw's palace, and the moat, and the river. That rising smoke is from the Zegyo Bazaar. In the grid of streets—Chinese merchants there, Indians in that quarter. And there Sagaing Hill, the monastery."

"King Thibaw," Blair said.

"The wicked king whom the British wisely deposed. He is presently languishing in India with his evil queen."

An' 'er name was Supi-yaw-lat—jes' the same as Theebaw's queen.

"Supiyawlat," Blair said.

"You must be a scholar, uncle."

The sun had slipped below the brimming tide of purplish clouds, though a glint of light from a slash in the cloud struck the river, giving it the look of a surging torrent of quicksilver.

"The Royal City," Blair said.

"British City," the man said. "I hope they stay for two hundred years!"

Surprised by the force of the utterance, Blair chuckled and said, "I must be going. Sun's down. It will be dark soon. Work to do."

"The night cometh when no man can work, uncle."

Beadon was seated on the veranda of the mess, smoking, his feet up, when Blair entered.

"What do you reckon? That hill."

"I could see you and Jones from the top."

"Chaps here reckon it pongs."

6

SCHOOL DAYS

He was back in the classroom, it was school, it was swotting, a routine so familiar that Blair was reassured by its oppression. Life was a muddle, but he understood school. Tea in darkness just before six, brought by a servant after a tap on the doorjamb and a whisper, like the soft knock of his fag at Eton, and here Beadon the self-appointed fag master, all of the probationaries like senior boys—Jones aspiring to be a collager—and the newcomer, Angus McPake, surly Glaswegian, always late, as though begging for the cane. The morning break was no different from chambers at Eton, the teachers, except for the Burmese and Hindi language teachers, no different from the Eton beaks he'd known, especially Captain Bailey Balfour, an all-rounder, whose father had marched with General Prendergast in the invasion in '85, to expel the king.

There was a form of messing here, too, and a passion to have a pip on your shoulder, the equivalent in the Police Training School in Mandalay of being an Oppidan scholar at Eton. Blair had been a bugler in the Cadet Corps at his prep school, St. Cyprian's, he'd marched in parades at Eton, he was in the corps again. He knew how to study, he was at home with books, though he had less time for *Tono-Bungay* and the *Notebooks* of Samuel Butler, and would have to wait until the new Lawrence novel, *Women in Love,* arrived at Smart and Mookerdum's bookshop in Rangoon.

School was snobbery, a system of rigidities, the rituals of obedience and punishment. In Mandalay he was a sixth former again, lording it over the native cadets, seventy-odd of them, drilling them after breakfast and licensed to bray orders and, when they lapsed, to bend them over a chair and cane them, another Etonian ritual, the wisdom of the whip.

"Gentlemen," Captain Clyne Stewart said on the second day—the first had been devoted to sorting out books and learning the geography of the school—"we are fortunate to have one of the authorities on Burma's recent history on our staff."

Stewart had entered the classroom followed by the history beak, now in uniform as an officer in formal dress, medals, tassels on his stocking tops, his topee under one arm, a sheathed dirk in his belt. The probationaries shoved their chairs back and stood at attention. The officer stood a bit apart, glowing as Stewart introduced him, by mentioning his father, Sir Duncan Balfour, who'd distinguished himself in Upper Burma, in the years of pacification.

It seemed you were someone in the Raj if your father was someone, and Blair knew his father was no one.

"I give you, Captain Balfour."

"At ease, chaps—be seated," Captain Balfour said, stepping forward, and setting his topee on a nearby table. "I've knocked about Burma for a good many years. I'm here to put you wise to a few home truths and to clear up some misconceptions. First of all, as you aspire to be policemen you must know this. To mention a policeman to any Burman has much the same effect of squirting hot water into his ear. He becomes voluble and abusive on the spot. A Burmese word you will soon learn is *awza*—authority. Everyone wants it, few people have it. The result is that Burma is a benighted province, some of its natives mild enough, others inclined to disorder and dacoity. Let me ask you, what have you heard of our methods? You, sir."

He pointed to Jones, who replied, "Methods, sir, I've heard nothing but praise of them."

"You have not heard anyone speaking rather violently of our rule here?" the captain said. "That we are liberal with the cane and busy with the gallows?"

"Not at all, sir."

"You, there," the captain said, gesturing to Blair.

"Sir," Blair said, "I've heard nothing contradicting the empire's mission to govern fairly, nor anything inconsistent with its ideals."

"A canny answer," the captain said. "Your name?"

"Blair, sir."

"But, Blair, you say you've *heard* nothing—yet that does not mean our methods are universally approved. I am thinking of General Dyer's decisiveness at Jallianwala Bagh, putting down a violent native insurrection led by fanatics. In the official report just last year, the Hunter Commission rebuked the general, stating among much else that the general had overstepped the bounds of his authority by killing a thousand revolting badmashes." He paused to grin. "And members of the government, including I regret to say the secretary of state for war, Mr. Churchill, proved himself something of an old woman with his blather, and many in the government dished up a mass of objections. But what were the precise circumstances—who was General Dyer facing? You, sir."

He indicated Angus McPake, who said, "Natives, sir."

"He was confronting a revolutionary army of many thousands of typically villainous Punjabis," Balfour said in a tone of correction. He then placed his hands on the table and extended his upper body toward the students. "And what was the consequence of the commission's report for our maintaining law and order under duress? We were rubbished. And for General Dyer? He was given the bird!"

Raising his hand, Beadon said, "Permission to speak, sir."

"Yes?"

"The poet Kipling spoke on General Dyer, saying, 'He did his duty as he saw it.'"

"He did indeed," Balfour said. "But the guff about Jallianwala Bagh was not the first of public misunderstandings of our methods, nor will it be the last. When you come to learn the language, you will hear much more, and not all of it will be entirely favorable. Yet in putting down that mob, Reginald Dyer was the savior of the Punjab."

Sensing Balfour nodding at him for a response, Blair said, "Understood, sir."

But he was nagged by an opposing thought: Ranjit Singh, the wounded veteran of Passchendaele, was a Punjabi.

"We have disorder here. We could right the ship in a brace of shakes if we chose. It only needs a pennyworth of pluck. Consider how the natives caved in after Amritsar." He strutted toward Jones. "Dyer knew the stuff to give them."

"Quite right, sir," Jones said, trembling in his chair, perhaps because Balfour had been staring at him, his eyes glistening, one hand hooked on his belt at the handle of his dirk.

"When was this police force established—the one you chaps represent? I'll tell you. Just thirty years ago, after the pacification. And why?"

Conscious of Balfour's sudden silence and his interrogating stare, Blair said, "Supervision, sir. To maintain order, sir."

"Precisely. Jallianwala Bagh was a frolic compared to native events in Burma, little known to the British public," Balfour said. "There have been massacres here. Scores of natives strangled, stabbed, poisoned—by each other. Small children thrown against the wall, or their skulls smashed with clubs." He began to shake his head. "Not our doing, chaps. Not our doing at all. We are sometimes accused of being harsh toward the natives, but the natives know better. They know how Thibaw found his way to the throne, they know the cruelty of their brethren."

He paused and walked in a stately way to the window that faced the parade ground.

"The cemetery there," he said, and the students elevated themselves awkwardly in their chairs to see. "It is filled with the victims of the massacres of the eighties. Thibaw's mother-in-law, the unpronounceable Hsinbyumashin—queen of the central palace, Mistress of the White Elephant, and her evil, conniving daughter Supayalat concocted a plot to dispose of all pretenders to the throne. King Mindon had many wives—there is no law of primogeniture in a polygamous monarchy. He had upward of seventy sons and had not named a successor. It was the Mistress of the White Elephant who named his successor. As the king lay dying she invited Mindon's sons and the princesses to visit, as an example of their piety, and no sooner had they arrived than they were seized and imprisoned and brutally killed—strangled, hacked with dahs, the prison running with blood. And why do you suppose their screams were not heard? You, sir."

It was Blair again. "Can't imagine, sir."

"You can't imagine musical entertainment laid on in the royal pavilion just there, to drown out their hideous screams?" Balfour bared his teeth and in elaborate mimicry pretended to raise a violin to his shoulder and sawed with his right hand upon the invisible instrument as he continued. "The king's musicians played all night. And in the morning the corpses of the princes and their wives and children were set down and trampled by elephants and buried"—he stopped sawing and extended his arm toward the window—"there!"

He let this sink in, he stroked his chin, McPake murmured, "Och."

"Mindon expired, Thibaw ascended the Peacock Throne unopposed, the Mistress of the White Elephant had her wish, her evil daughter now Thibaw's royal queen."

All this time, Blair had meditated on what Balfour was saying. He saw the gunning down of the Indians in Jallianwala Bagh, and General Dyer pilloried but defiant. He pictured the old king on his deathbed, and the plotting mother-in-law—it was Shakespeare in its gore and its lust for power and a crown. He saw the surprised and slaughtered princes, their blood-soaked silks.

"You must understand that what passed for royalty in Burma was a bloody scrum," Balfour said, and somehow a baton or swagger stick had materialized in his hand. He swished it and went on, "There was no law or binding custom determining the descent of the crown within the family. Everyone with royal blood in his veins—however little, a drop will do— was a pretender. When all the princes were dead as mutton, Thibaw ascended the throne, unopposed." He batted with his baton and poked it at McPake. "Ah, did I say all?"

"Aye, sir, you did."

"Silly me," Balfour said and tapped the side of his head as though administering a reprimand. "Not all. Some suspected in advance there might be a bloodbath and never came. Others who were hiding in the palace slipped out—one outfitted as a monk, another as a common coolie. They huddled in their precincts as compact and motionless as monkeys in the rain."

McPake sniggered, and hearing him, Balfour whipped around, flexing his baton in anger.

"Picturing it in my heid, sir," McPake said. "The monkeys."

"They were as stubborn and as stupid as monkeys," Balfour said. "And that is why in '87, another massacre was planned by that awful old creature and her wretched daughter. Four hundred murdered—battered, choked to death, buried alive—and they especially reveled in dashing small children against the wall and committing other outrages. These barbarities, mind you, were done in the presence of Thibaw and Supayalat and the demon mother-in-law, who heartily applauded."

Balfour strode to the window once more and wagged his baton in the direction of the cemetery, as the students turned to see, Beadon managing an expression of disgust and fury, Jones's face ashen, McPake smirking, Blair determined to remain enigmatic.

"Is it any wonder we took up arms?" Balfour said. "We made a vow to fight, as we knew we must. We planned a campaign, with our keenest minds. We amassed an army, as we knew we should." Balfour paused and stared in silence at the students' faces, then resumed. "General Prendergast, and many others, including my late father, led regiments of troops, mainly Indian, and invaded by sailing up the Irrawaddy, according to the battle plan, meeting little or no opposition from native soldiers. A military picnic, the general was to call it, not a jot of damage. What resistance they met was improvisational and rash."

Balfour grinned as though in self-congratulation, reminding himself of something, as he marched back and forth before the young men, smacking his baton against his thigh.

"I want you to remember this when you are at your work, up-country, in the bush, faced with dacoity," he said. "It is the Burmese way of dacoity—desultory, spasmodic, and without definite plan or purpose. But because of those features, dangerous and unpredictable." Seeing no reaction, he grunted, "What?"

"Yes, sir," came like a chorus from the young men.

"General Prendergast accepted the king's surrender and though the king begged for a few more days, the general put him and his ghastly queen in a bullock cart and sent them to the river." Balfour turned to the windows facing the west side of the fort and pointed with his baton. "The steamer *Thooriah* bore them down the Irrawaddy to Rangoon, and thence to India and oblivion." He smiled his crooked unbelieving smile and stared at Jones. "Was the job done?"

"I can't say, sir," Jones said, stiffening.

"And neither could Prendergast!" Balfour roared. His shout startled the young men but had the effect of lightening the mood, the men shifting in their chairs. "It was to be five full years—within living memory—before the last of the large gangs was dispersed, the leaders captured and peace and security established in Upper Burma." Pausing, flexing his baton again, Balfour added, "But that is hyperbole of a sort. There remains an ingenious criminal class in Burma, and still dacoity and brigandage throughout the country. In the past ten years the population has risen about nine percent but the increase in serious crime has risen shockingly, a thirty percent rise in murder and over a hundred percent in dacoity. The jails are full, and so in many cases, whipping is substituted for imprisonment. There's enough to keep you on your toes. And so I say to you"—wagging his baton at them, like a conductor facing an orchestra and bringing a symphony to a close— "carry on, chaps, for king and country!"

Instinctively, as so often after a stirring lecture by a beak, at a desk at Eton, Blair rapped a table near him with his knuckles. Balfour squinted, as though at something unfamiliar and quaint, and Blair blushed, as the others stared.

"Tea," Clyne Stewart called out from the back of the room.

The following day, they met the padre, Father Fitzmaurice, who led them in prayers—"Bit of puja," Clyne Stewart said, and McPake murmured "Holy Willie" and later "Where's Maurice?"

After prayers, they were introduced to the rest of their teachers—all of them English police officers, except the language teachers—the *saya*, Po Thit, who would instruct them in Burmese, and Pundit Shastri, the Hindi specialist, both of them honorary inspectors of police, though never in uniform. Po Thit was genial and talkative, Pundit Shastri severe and exact, a taskmaster, who reminded the young men that the sacred thread he wore indicated he was a Brahmin—"I am not taking meat"—and provided his own brass bowl in the staff mess.

Because Po Thit's spoken English was poor, he lectured using Burmese as well as English words, and this was an advantage, his supplementing his explanations in two languages, one clarifying the other.

"*Mingala khin byar,*" he said the first morning, with a slight bow.

And the young men responded, "Good morning, sir," their first acquaintance with the language.

Pundit Shastri had said, "Good day, gentlemen, I hope you don't mind if I bung these textbooks your way," and handed out a selection of sewn and smudged pamphlets.

"*Kyaung-thar,* to speak a language is like *ka-pwe,*" Po Thit said, and through Po Thit's hand gestures and smiles Blair understood he meant that language learning was a form of play—not intellectual, nothing to do with reason, but a happy activity. And *kyaung-thar* meant students.

Chalking the word *la* on the blackboard, Po Thit said, "This *sar-lone-lay—* little word—can mean 'come' or 'mule' or 'moon,' according to tone," and then he spoke it whinnying in his sinuses, signaling its various meanings.

"The Burmese spelling book is the *Thin-bone-gyi.* The great basket of learning."

Pundit Shastri was a believer in the textbook he himself had self-published on yellowish unbleached paper in Rangoon, containing drills and sample sentences and vocabulary lists. His emphasis was on the protocols of formal and informal Hindustani, how to a child or an inferior one always used the word *tum* for you, as in "*Tum kaise ho?*" But with an adult or a stranger or anyone senior it had to be *aap,* as in "*Aap kaise hain?*"

"Just wondering," McPake asked him, "which one are you?"

"Sir, you will kindly address me as *aap,*" Pundit Shastri said, coldly. "I am Shastri, a man of learning."

"I take it you've met our Shastri?" Captain Digby said, in his first class on the Penal Code. "Indians abound in Burma. You might think of India as a country, but it is much more a continent and has a greater variety of people and more languages than you'll find in Europe. Bags of them in Burma. Pundit Shastri hails from somewhere in the UP—United Provinces. The Bengali babu will be a clerk, the Tamil a coolie, the Gujarati a merchant or a pest like Gandhi. Even here in our Sepoy army in Mandalay we have a great variety—the hardy Punjabi, the wild Pathan, and the still wilder Baluchi. And there's the jolly little Gurkha who stands in good repute as a first-class fighting man. The weedy Madrassi does not rank high for valor, in contrast to the Sikh, who is more than adequately brave and soldierly— though he has a religious scruple against cutting his hair. Yes?"

Beadon had raised his hand. "I've seen many Chinese in Mandalay."

"Then you have been down China Street, Chinese on either side, an important community. John Chinaman is usually a shopkeeper and valued as a useful class of worker. But John is also capable of great mischief, corrupting people wherever he goes—keeping liquor shops, spreading the opium-smoking habit, and pandering to the natural love of the Burmans for gambling."

"And what of the Burman?" Beadon asked.

Captain Digby smiled. "The Burman, ah, lets most employments slip past him."

Blair was cramming again, and the stupor induced by memorization pre-occupied him to the point where he was protected from the world beyond the walls of the fort—a world of stinks and gongs and a gabble of voices. He read lawbooks; he memorized the prohibitions and the consequences of transgressions; he learned the grammar of Burmese and Hindi, and the squiggle of their different scripts, Hindi resembling laundry hanging on a line, a vest here, trousers there, over there two pairs of socks representing *pani,* water. Burmese writing, Po Thit suggested, was a set of doodles and ovals that looked like animals—a rabbit, a cat, a dog, a cow. Immersing himself in these details, all of them new to him, eased Blair's mind. The contradiction in it all was that the study meant to habituate him to the world of Burma beyond the walls isolated him from it. He was grateful for that. His studies absorbed him and gave him peace.

Each of the candidates excelled at something different, Jones at criminal law, Beadon at police procedure, McPake at map reading ("I was in the Boy Scouts, wasn't I? First Glasgow—Waverly!"), and for Blair it was languages, impressing the others by being able easily to switch from Burmese to Hindustani, and he improved his fluency by practicing it on the cadets at morning exercises.

Speaking in Burmese or Hindustani, reading out instructions, asking for names, Blair became someone else, an order giver, an officer, a servant of the king, and that too pleased him, allowed him to relax, like an actor reciting lines, masked in his role, in this case an anxious nineteen-year-old comfortable in his role of impersonating a probationary assistant district superintendent of police, striding along the parade ground, not meaning to lord it over the cadets, but being a foot taller than any of them, the effect was one of superiority and hauteur.

He hid his attempts at writing poetry—he knew he would be mocked. He had known greater privacy and better companionship at Eton. He disliked eating with the others in the mess, he avoided the club, where he found the drinks expensive and McPake's bawdy stories growing stale. Activities were downstairs, the lounge, the billiard room—he was no good at billiards, or small talk, or jokes. He kept to his room.

Of the twelve bedrooms upstairs only four were occupied, and the far bedroom off-limits. Beadon explained, "Haunted."

"I like a good ghost story," Blair said. "We had an English master at school who told them."

He didn't say the school was Eton; he didn't say the man was M. R. James, the provost, an odd duck who enjoyed wrestling with the boys in his rooms after prep, or that he said, "Masturbate all you want, lads, I've no objection. But I draw the line at buggery."

"Seems there was a probationer who went absolutely doolally," Beadon said. "Got a shotgun and stretched himself on his carpet in number twelve and stuck the muzzle in his mouth. Found a way to pull the trigger."

"Grim but decidedly not ghostly," Blair said.

"That's not the story," Beadon said. "The story is that one of the wags in the class a few years ago put an Irishman in the room, without telling him of the suicide. Just a jape. At breakfast, the Irishman said, 'Couldn't sleep a wink. I had a vision of a desperate chap on the floor holding the muzzle of an Enfield in his mouth.'"

"The Irish, they scare easily," Blair said, but he relished the story, and later went to the room and in its stillness imagined the corpse and looked for traces of a bullet hole in the wall.

The worst aspect of the bedrooms was that their adjoining walls did not reach the ceiling: snores and whispers and grunts were audible from other rooms—hardly rooms, more like cubicles. And none had proper doors, but instead at chest level louvered flaps on hinges like the swinging panels you pushed to pass from the public bar into the saloon bar in a country pub.

The cadet subinspectors were on their way to becoming constables, to serve the assistant district subinspectors—the role for which Blair was preparing—the cadets destined to assume most of the investigative duties, dogsbodies compiling reports for charge sheets.

"Think of them as maids of all work," Captain Digby said. Besides his chores as teacher, Digby was also quartermaster. "Drill them accordingly. Yes, sir—no, sir—three bags full, sir."

After a month, the probationers were instructed to take turns as duty officers, supervising the cadets. They drew straws to establish a roster, Blair pinching the short straw, which occasioned a lewd remark from McPake.

"Insist on good order at breakfast, elbows off the table, no chopsticks, no Indian fingers squashing the food," Clyne Stewart said. "Inspect the drills—bayonet exercise, marching, proper formation. Finish with the obstacle course at the perimeter of the parade ground. Take names, if they're warranted. Get used to it—this is your future."

Keen to find an infraction, Blair strode through the kitchen and paused at a steaming tureen of rice, dusty smelling and dark, an obvious example of filthy food, something to report.

"This muck is muddy," he said, swishing a wooden paddle through the thick brownish rice in the tureen. "It's not fit for human consumption. Reminds me of school slop"—he had seen bowls of such sludge at St. Cyprian's. "I'm pulling you up on this."

"What shall we do, sir?"

"Dump it in the pig bin. Replace it with bread today. Use different *pani* to cook the rice tomorrow, not this stagnant stuff from the Irrawaddy."

He called for the logbook and entered his action, with a terse comment, and the date and time. Before heading to the parade ground to supervise the colors and the march past, he handed the book to the kitchen steward, who stared at him, impassive, and then saluted.

"Sahib."

Later that morning, Blair was whistled off the parade ground, where he'd been overseeing the stowing of the flags, and summoned to the office of Captain Digby.

"I'm striving to understand this order, Blair." The kitchen logbook was on Digby's desk, Digby's finger pressed upon the line of Blair's entry.

"Rice too foul to eat, sir. I suspect the cooking water was tainted, sir."

"You do, eh?"

"Yes, sir. Worse than school food back home, sir," Blair said, and when Digby did not respond, Blair added, to fill the silence, "Rice ought to be proper white, sir."

"You've not encountered unpolished rice, Blair?"

"Not to my knowledge, sir."

Clapping the logbook shut, Captain Digby stood, at first craning his neck, looking up, then disconcerted by Blair's height, he stepped back, saying, "That's what you binned, Blair. A tureen of very tasty unpolished rice, the preference of native trainees." He was smirking now, as though from the moral high ground, in the right and gloating. "Perfectly edible and much healthier than the nursery pudding you're obviously accustomed to."

"Unpolished, sir," Blair said and was aware that his face was hot and damp and reddening with shame. "I'm not familiar with it, sir."

"You might think of yourself as unpolished, Blair," Digby said.

He allowed a few moments to pass, Blair at attention, visibly twitching. Digby turned away and tapped at the papers on his desk, head down, in a posture of indifference, his back to Blair.

"Dismissed."

Blair was not surprised that the story of the rice got around; its absurdity lent itself to gossip. But he was unprepared for the exaggeration, the mockery, the ferocity of it, which showed how much they disliked him, using the incident against him, as though resenting his height and taking him down a peg. Or was it the fact, now well known, of Eton?

"Don't mind the blather, Blair," McPake said. "It's just ragging."

It was worse than ragging; it wasn't funny, it was hostile, reminding him of his tormentor at school, the ghastly Verrall. *Care for some more rice, Blair?* became a catchphrase.

His silly mistake was the occasion for more assaults on his privacy and made him conspicuous—as if he wasn't conspicuous enough at six foot two, taller than anyone at school, looming in the back row like a freak in the group photograph with the staff and the other candidates, his uniform ill-fitting, his mustache refusing to grow. He hated being obvious and wrong. He wished to be inscrutable, and his model in this was a cadet called Lockhart, who never spoke, never showed up for games, ate alone, was feared for his silences, and was cultivating a narrow pencil mustache, like a leading man in the cinema. Lockhart was unapproachable.

But the mere desire for privacy in such a place as the police school was regarded as a form of subversion, worse than not playing the game, it was bolshie. You had to be comradely, you had to mess together, you needed to be good at football and play on the team, you needed—this was the most beastly—to be social. He'd thought that nothing could be worse than the arcane formalities of Eton, but at least at Eton he'd been able to hide, he'd had a room of his own, and a door he could lock. Here in his cubicle Blair heard whispers, he saw others drifting past his swinging doors, and the walls didn't reach to the ceiling, so there were ambiguous moans and the jangle of bedsprings at night.

You got whispered about by staying away, he knew, so he forced himself to mess with the others, he exerted himself at billiards, he made a point of buying rounds of drinks in the lounge. But in such close proximity, all that this accomplished was his feeling a greater awkwardness, and the more he knew of his fellow students, the keener his sense that he didn't fit in. Why had his father not warned him?

One morning at breakfast, Beadon and Jones sat side by side across the table. They shoved their plates of eggs aside and began conferring as they passed small white cards back and forth.

"I sprang for engraved," Beadon said, running a fingertip across the lettering.

"Printed does the job, though," Jones said.

"I'll be the judge of that," McPake said. "Hand them over to Angus."

The cards were passed to him, and he held one in each hand, so that Blair could see. They were name cards, Beadon's name enhanced with squirts of gilt, his rank just beneath, and in the lower left, *Upper Burma Club*. Jones's card was plainly lettered in black, though his full name was revealed, David Gruffyd Jones.

"Gruff by name, gruff by nature," McPake said, passing the cards to Blair. "Not so, dai?"

"Engraved may be a shade more elegant," Blair said, "but it verges on pretension. I prefer Jones's understatement. What's the objective?"

"Calling cards, usual thing," Beadon said. "Make visits, drop cards, wait for an invitation."

"Because you want tea."

"Because Digby's daughter is a stunner."

"His wife is a decent piece," McPake said. "But I'd rather find a tart in town here."

"Better value, no airs," Blair said, affecting to be worldly.

"And a cunt like a horse collar."

"And a dose of the pox," Beadon said.

The word *tart* had jolted Blair; he wondered what McPake knew. Perhaps he, too, was affecting to be worldly and intending to shock. But Blair said nothing more. Handing the calling cards back to their owners, he wondered what would come of distributing them. He wasn't social, he didn't aspire to be so. He was most comfortable supervising parade ground drill, and the routine of classes, and the solitude of studying. He hated the holidays, Christmas had been grim, with a banquet and church and the singing of carols about snow ("In the bleak midwinter, frosty wind made moan . . .") as the sun scorched Mandalay. Days off, weekends, all festivities left him feeling at sea, and he was reminded of his conviction that he was destined to fail.

Mind you, what about those tarts? he wanted to ask McPake, but he knew that should he raise the question he would be revealing himself and might be inviting more mockery than over the rice business.

Mandalay Week, meant to be festive, was an ordeal that drove Blair again to his room. The week's events were posted by Captain Stewart on the corkboard in the mess, under the duty roster. They were set out in the form of a campaign schedule, the day, the time, the activity—polo matches, sherry parties, the notice of a shoot, and at the end of the week, the Military Police Ball at the Upper Burma Club.

"This shoot," McPake asked, tapping the schedule. "What are they bagging?"

"Snipe," Beadon said. "There's masses in the woods outside town."

Blair said nothing; holidays were a burden—you needed to join in, to dance, to sing, to risk being a fool. He slipped upstairs to his cubicle, finding refuge in reading, resuming *Tono-Bungay*, which he'd put aside, renewing his acquaintance with the characters who'd become familiar, and friends, smiling over their foibles. George Ponderovo listening to his uncle natter made Blair happy and took his mind off Mandalay Week.

He loved the language, the uncle "a short, fattening, small-legged man with stiff cropped hair, disobedient glasses on a perky little nose, and a round stare behind them." Blair reread the description, marveling at its felicity, seeing the uncle clearly, wishing he could write like that. And he laughed out loud when, in the voice of a "squeaky prophet," the uncle said, "George! List'n! I got an ideer. I got a notion, George!"

I got a notion, George, Blair reflected. He dodged the teas and the parties, and the polo matches. But on the Saturday he heard the music floating across the parade ground from the club—fiddles, reels, the thump of dancing feet—and became curious. He put his book down and listened. He couldn't read with that carry-on anyway. He put on his dress uniform in case he might encounter an instructor or a senior officer and walked out to the Mall.

The club's windows were ablaze, he saw circles of uniformed men kicking and prancing, sweeping across the dance floor in eightsome reels, linking arms, the women flushed in the heat, damp ringlets clinging to their foreheads as they skipped, skirts twisting, bosoms heaving. Civilians, too, obvious in their formal attire. Tailcoats and white ties and gloves, men in kilts and sporrans and black bonnets—all were joining arms and strutting and kicking, red-faced and gasping, the music blaring, the urgent fiddlers. *Bloody fools.*

Seeing them, feeling futile, Blair thought again, *I will fail,* and stumbling in the darkness back to his room he mumbled to himself disgustedly, "*Bhaaltotmha,*" meaning to say "Never," and realized that he'd muttered it in Burmese.

It was a queer mistake, but one he could not correct. And he could not go back, there was nothing to go back to.

7

CAPTAIN ROBINSON

S o ye throttled Dai the Welshman," McPake said to Blair with a wicked grin, his bad teeth bulging against his lips. Then he screwed up one eye in a wink that made his face uglier. "Ye squelched the pure Taffy!"

Blair happening by on his way to the tailor's for a fitting had been whistled over to the viewing platform, where McPake stood in the shade of the awning to mention that unpleasant episode.

Before them, assembling on the parade ground, the cadets jostled like schoolboys, tramping in the dust, awaiting the command from McPake, whose day it was to supervise the morning parade.

Surprised by the gibe, Blair reddened and pulled at the brim of his helmet, hiding his eyes. But McPake persisted, poking him in the ribs with his baton, and laughing, a snort of glee.

"Just a nudge—to get his attention," Blair said. His face was hot, he turned aside, pretending to take an interest in the cadets. "And it was bloody months ago. All forgotten."

"Ya nae remember a wee nudge," McPake said. "Ya nae forget a throttlin'."

Still grinning, McPake seemed to discern in Blair's silence and shame a significant evasion, his concealing a rebellious side that matched McPake's own rash pugnacity and made them brothers in disgrace.

"Must have hurt a fair bit," he said. He tucked his baton into his Sam Browne belt and buffed his buttons on his tunic with the pair of gloves he held in his fist. "Och, Blair, the number of times I longed to throttle a Welshman! Puny little chap, Dai Jones. He's such dim Taffy."

"He's from the Valleys," Blair said, with a note of respect for what he imagined the hard, dirty work at the coal-face, and not this cushy order-giving. "Father's a collier. Fought in the war."

"My father's a vicar. He wanted me to be a padre." McPake snatched the baton from his belt and whipped the air with it. "More larks to be a sinner, I reckon. Though there's a price. Wickedness comes expensive."

"Mining's a real job of work," Blair said to get McPake off his obsessive subject, faith and damnation, and he'd start soon on tarts. "Jones isn't a bad sort. Better rider than I am. I'm hopeless on a horse."

McPake turned his full freckled face on Blair, and he was still grinning. "Aye, you're a canny one, Blair."

"I simply took exception to something he said."

"And what was it, lad?"

"In retrospect, something trivial."

"Always the way, ain't it. Luikin back, ye canna sort out the great frae the sma.'"

"It was small."

"But deserved a bloody great throttlin'!"

McPake shook his head, doubting but still with a smirk of admiration. This talk—and who had whispered it?—of Blair choking Jones in the train last year seemed to signal a bond. He poked Blair in the ribs once more and clapped on his helmet and descended the viewing platform, striding toward the cadets.

"Fall in on parade! March!"

Just then a sudden skirl of pipes, a squad of military policemen, tall Indians, some in turbans, others short-arsed in cloth caps, strutting Burmese in khaki, marched toward the lines, a sturdy Gurkha boy, his terai hat aslant, playing the bagpipes ahead of them.

Blair was glad to be free of McPake. He'd hated looking at his wide gloating face, his mass of freckles, and yet the man had spoken as a conspiratorial brother.

McPake had called Jones dim, but though McPake was fierce on the parade ground, he was slow in the classroom, and Beadon was a plodder. The classes Blair had easily managed at Eton had taught him how to study and prepare. He now excelled at Burmese, he had learned how to give orders in Hindustani, he was acceptable in the Penal Code. His gaffe over the brown rice was forgotten amid all the lapses of the others, some much worse than the rice—McPake in a drunken scuffle with a gharry wallah who claimed he'd been cheated of his fare from town, Beadon fainting in the heat of the parade ground, flopping forward before the cadets, Jones blubbing at breakfast over some upsetting news from home—Blair hoped it wasn't the boy's father. Blair's suffering was not dramatic; it was a dull ache, not a sharp pain, more of an awkwardness, yet persistent, like a stammer, or a gammy leg, or a visible birthmark.

It was the uniform. Often in the classroom—or in the mess, the lounge, or as today on the parade ground—he saw the others in shorts and knee socks, the tabs just so, or in bags and boots and belts, the leather highly polished, the tunic with epaulets, often gloves, always a topee or a helmet, and he thought—the ache searing him with shame—*That's how I look, I'm the same, I'm one of them.*

It was worse on Wednesdays or Saturdays, with boots and spurs for morning parade of the cadet subinspectors in training, and formal dress at dinner once a month, boots and spurs then, too. And what was deemed "casual dress" meant a dinner jacket. He hated his trips to the Indian tailor's cubbyhole in the arcade near the West Gate ("Such an upstanding sahib," he said—he was Deepesh, a Tamil, who then chattered in his own language to his groveling assistant who handled the chalk). Blair felt burdened by the wardrobe that took up half the space of his cubicle and was thick with required clothes and stank of mothballs.

I have been wearing a uniform since I was eight years old, Blair reflected: the green jersey and blue cap and corduroy knee breeches at St. Cyprian's, the black tailcoats and gowns and wing collars at Eton, and now the khaki and boots and helmet of the Burma police. A uniform was a costume, like fancy dress—it hid you, it made you look like everyone else; it was a disguise, but it was also a straitjacket.

"Your bags, Blair—they're in a shocking state," Captain Digby had said to him one morning, frowning at his trousers, wrinkled behind his knees, and loose at his boot tops. "Your boots want polishing. Your salute is slack. Are you doing this on purpose?"

"No, sir." But he thought, *Perhaps I am. Perhaps this is a form of stubborn objection.* Still, he regretted that it was so obvious.

"Set an example, Blair."

He was surprised by Digby's vehemence. Blair intended to conform, yet his instinct to resist seemed to show in his untidy uniform. Hating the thought that on the evidence of this disorder someone might see into his heart, he vowed to be correct—more than correct, a model of police decorum. A swine like McPake could be easily summed up, but when you were pukka you were implacable, and unknowable. Blair didn't want to be noticed or made visible by a lapse in dress or in voicing a strong opinion.

The Upper Burma Club was a challenge. By seldom going to the club, as the others did every evening, Blair was singled out, conspicuous for staying away. It wasn't only the chatter and the idleness he objected to, it was also the expense—signing chits and being faced with a bar bill at the end of the month. But he decided that going to the club was a way of staying invisible, the absurdity being that he was ignored when he showed up, and only ragged when he was absent.

With these thoughts he entered the arcade and was greeted by the tailor. "Burma sahib," Deepesh said, bowing low.

Surrendering his solitude with a sigh, he put his book aside. It was Lawrence—*Women in Love* had been posted to him from Smart and Mookerdum's. It was his refuge these days, Birkin's rants about humanity and "The old ideals as dead as nails," and the romantic longings of Gudrun and Ursula, the ugliness of the miners' huts, which brought Jones to mind, the pretensions of Hermione's Georgian house with Corinthian pillars, and its posturing intellectuals inside, aspects of England he'd never seen before, the novel admitting him to another world, of nobs and moneyed beasts and miners blackened with coal dust. The keenest pleasure in his life at the fort was retreating to his cubicle upstairs after dinner and immersing himself in his book, mentally going home.

For the others, the club was larks; for Blair, it was tedium. But he resolved to put in an appearance twice a week and drink a pint of beer by the billiard table—seated, because standing at the bar he'd be noticed as the tallest man there. He pretended to be absorbed in the progress of the billiard game, lulled by the click of the balls, the bump of a carom, glancing forlornly at the slow hands of the clock.

The conundrum was that he was not visiting the club, but that he was at the club waiting to leave. He was offended by the smell of the place as much as the boisterous men—and the boisterous men contributed to the smell. The peculiar odor of taxidermy, mounted heads of dead antlered creatures, the sour pong of the billiard felt, the stinking air stirred by the mildewed fabric of the swinging punkah.

McPake was a regular, who always brightened when he saw Blair; he seemed the only member who befriended him, and he was watchful. He remarked on Blair's improved appearance, his glossy boots, his neatly pressed tunic, his shined buttons, and his military posture, to preserve the prescribed creases in his clothes.

When he mentioned this, he added, "I've had a right bollocking from the chief. He blew me up. Claimed I look like a stable boy."

McPake did look like a stable boy, that was his virtue, Blair thought, with a degree of envy. McPake was an unapologetic misfit, fleeing his father's vicarage, but seldom troubling to conceal his disdain for good order. McPake's freckles seemed like another sort of untidiness, a constellation of them across his piggy nose, and on his cheeks, and the backs of his hairy hands, darkening by the week in the Mandalay sun.

"Let's not bide lang in this poxy club," McPake said one evening in a surly voice, and then seeing a man enter the billiard room with a drink in his hand, he perked up. "There's Robinson."

The man—middle-aged, clean-shaven, a bit haggard, his hair close cropped—was dressed as a civilian, in a pale linen suit. Yet his tie looked regimental, and he had a military bearing, shoulders back, a slight strut in his step, his head erect, chin up.

"Robinson's got the answer."

"What would that be?"

"He told me the other day," McPake said. "Getting into trouble kept him young."

"What degree of trouble?"

"He were cashiered," McPake whispered. "A woman." He eyed Robinson slow-marching across the room. "Messing about with native cunt."

The leer left McPake's face as Robinson, seeing him, picked up his pace and swaggered toward him. And unused to the informality of the club, Blair instinctively stood, as though out of respect, as he would have done for a senior officer here or a beak at Eton.

He could see that Robinson was older, and the man was weathered, too, a slightly battered look that made him seem superior and sagacious, with one of those strangely waxen faces that Blair had seen in other white men in Mandalay—and women as well, faces like bruised peaches, sun avoiders, keeping to the veranda and the indoors, favoring solar topees and big hats, looking as pale as they might have done in England, but more sallow, their eyes bright and defiant. They were the ones who didn't play games—no polo, no cricket, no shooting, no tennis—and they would have seemed another race entirely except invariably they drank, and when they drank changed color, became pinker.

"And how is our padre tonight?" Robinson said.

Blair could not conceal his smile, McPake the blasphemer called a padre.

"He was billed for something grander than a gadabout in the police, you know," Robinson said, seeing Blair's unbelieving expression. "Game little beast, though. Angus may yet inherit his father's vicarage."

"Chairch people," McPake said. "They hate the bottle, they love sweets, they're bloody thrawn in that regard."

"Thrawn," Blair said and narrowed his eyes.

"Contrary," McPake said. "My father, my mum, the folks in the kirk—Christians generally—they're mad for shortbread, tea cakes, clootie dumplings, buns and biscuits. It's either hymn singing, or flapping your mouth in prayer, or tea parties."

Robinson laughed and said, "Indians, too—the sweet tooth of the non-drinking races. Those godawful Indian sweets—*jalebis*, sticky buns, syrups."

"I had some of those on the ship; my steward introduced me," Blair said. "*Gulab jamun*—I fancied it."

"This is young Blair," McPake said. "He'll try anything once. Even that muck."

"Hello," Robinson said. "My men couldn't get enough of them."

"Where in India?" Blair asked.

"Not India—Mesopotamia." Robinson spoke between sips of his drink. "The war. Ninety-First Punjabis. Light infantry." He dragged a chair toward the two seated men. "They were a wonderful lot of warriors. How I loved their spirit—in the desert, miles and miles of fuck all, and there they were, flashing their sabers and hoisting their bundooks and calling out '*Raja ki jai*.'"

Robinson began to describe a particular skirmish, the regiment of Sikhs, fixing their bayonets and then flattening themselves behind a hillock, watching for a patrol of Ottoman Turks, preparing for an ambush with enfilade fire, and at last when the enemy failed to appear, rejoicing, believing they'd been frightened off by the Ninety-First's reputation for ferocity.

"Where was this?" Blair asked.

"Basra." Robinson sipped again. "The arsehole of the world."

"You'll have another dram of whiskey," McPake said. He summoned a waiter. "Two chotapegs and—what, Blair?—a pint of beer."

"How was your war?" Blair asked.

"Brief—though the desert's a bloody place even when there's no fighting. Toward the end of '17 I had a bad case of dysentery and was evacuated to India—hospital. After that, Rangoon, the regimental depot."

"The local grog rises," McPake said, hiccuping, his shoulders in spasm with each grunt. "Tell Blair about Konglu."

"Konglu!" Robinson said, taking a glass from the tray a bowing waiter extended to him. "Ends of the earth! Imagine, three days on the train north to Myitkyina and you're still nowhere near Konglu. It's a two-hundred-fifty-mile march farther on, with mules and a Gurkha orderly and howling Chinese muleteers. We left on the first of December and stopped along mountain paths, over dripping jungle and white mist filling the valleys." He gasped with another swallow. "Got to Konglu on Christmas Eve. A little hut on a hilltop was my home as district officer for the next year and a half. But I was not alone."

"How many other chaps at your place?" Blair asked, imagining the remoteness—Kiplingesque, the far outpost of empire, a distant Kafiristan.

"No other humans, apart from my Burmese servant. But ducks, hens, pigeons, five monkeys, and a bear—a little Asian brown bear, given to me by some Kachins who killed the mother in one of their paddy fields. He had the run of the house. I fed them all on rice, little buggers. They were constantly in mischief."

Blair said with feeling, "That sounds ripping. What I wouldn't give for a pet of some sort. I'd settle for a dog."

But McPake, waving his arms in impatience, interrupted Blair and in a convulsive hiss at Robinson, "Not that one—the one about the woman."

"The woman," Robinson said with the ghost of a smile, settling back in his chair and glancing around. The billiard players had racked their cues and headed for the bar, leaving the three men in the nook by the table.

"With the handcuffs," McPake said.

"Her name was Ayaw," Robinson said, speaking more loudly. "She was a hill girl, accused of poisoning her husband. The charge was that she'd concocted a fatal potion for him, and he'd drunk it all, not knowing the cup had contained a measure of quicksilver." He raised his hands, to indicate effort, and went on, "Ten days' march to her small village on the North East Frontier—you could spit to China! I fetched her back to Konglu for her trial. I had no choice in the matter. Among my many other duties as the district officer, I was subdivisional magistrate."

"No, no," McPake said, becoming fussed, wiping his mouth with the back of his hand. "The night before the verdict."

"Oh, that," Robinson deadpanned. "Let me see." He tapped his teeth, making a business of remembering. "We'd kept her in handcuffs and leg irons, pretty little thing, maybe a bit more attractive for all those restraints. But she'd tried to escape from the lockup—actually squeezed herself through a gap in the bamboo wall. She was that petite, a child bride. It had taken us days to find her."

"Never mind that," McPake said. "Get to the point, man."

"I'm explaining why she was in irons," Robinson said. "For our friend here."

Blair was not impatient. He saw the young girl, the irons on her skinny limbs, her pretty face, her little hands, and somehow silks and ribbons across her slender body, as she sat in the bamboo enclosure, head up, awaiting her trial.

"I fell." Robinson averted his gaze, or was he smiling?

"Och."

"It was the night before the elders on the panel made their decision," Robinson said. "It was as if everyone in Konglu expected it except me." He sighed. "I asked for her to be brought to my hut, and there she sat, warming herself before the fire. I crept over to her and took her hands in mine, and I helped her to her feet, bemused by the *clink-clink* of her handcuffs, a little tinkle like fine jewelry. I'd hardly heard her speak before then, but at that moment she looked up—stared intently at me with a blush like a glow on her cheeks."

He paused, and Blair clearly saw the pretty girl, the handcuffs like bracelets, the big man beside her, the fire, all this on the remote hilltop.

"'*Duwa*,' she said. Chief, in her language—Kachin. And she allowed me to lead her to my bedroom, slowly of course, because she was still shackled. I didn't remove her restraints—she seemed not to care." Now Robinson took a deep breath. "It was, I can say, a night of love. I lay in the chains of passion, and she in those of iron."

"She fancied it," McPake said.

Robinson considered this. "She was lovely, she was talkative. She confessed to me that her Chinese lover from over the border had given her the quicksilver for the poison and she'd put it in the old man's drink." Robinson waved this thought aside. "We lay in each other's arms until dawn."

"Handcuffs!" McPake said, nudging Blair, who sat, unable to frame a response, his mouth dry, his palms damp, grateful when Robinson spoke again.

"The charge of murder was not proven—the panel disagreed about the potency of the quicksilver. Ayaw was unshackled and when she left the courtroom—free—I saw a slight smile and a flicker of her eye at me on the bench. I thought as I had many times in my life, 'That's the way the wind blows.'"

Blair, rapt, had imagined it all, the handcuffs on the fragile wrists, the slight body, the tryst in the mountain hut, the prisoner and her judge, making love. A feeling of warmth had spread over him, a thickening heat, as though he'd grown a coat of fur and was cooking in that pelt.

Robinson clapped his hands on his knees, and as though inviting a confidence, he whispered, "But what of you chaps? What do you know of Mandalay? Have you seen a Burmese entertainment—a pwe? Have you found a great Chinese eating house? Have you climbed the hill? Have you been cunny-hunting by the river?"

"Plenty of time for that, presently," McPake said.

"Climbed the hill," Blair said. "First day."

"Blair's a reader," McPake said. "He's a right swot but a good lad, are you not, Blair?"

"I was like you once," Robinson said. "Kipling said it best. We've only one virginity to lose. And where we lost it, there our hearts will be."

8

PROWLING

He'd hardly seen or known a native, except as a servant or a cadet. Apart from his impulsive hike up Mandalay Hill that first day, he hadn't left Fort Dufferin, and for him the fort was the city. Robinson seemed to twig this—Blair's lack of knowledge of Mandalay town, his diffidence—not timidity but shyness, the new boy wary of surprises. It was four months since he'd arrived in Burma, the weather growing hot and they were only in March, the officers saying, "You think this is bad? Wait till May—it'll be stinking then!"

Blair felt isolated by the wide moat, lily pads and decaying lotuses floating on its greenish surface, and walled in, peered at by the sentries in the watchtowers of the fort, preoccupied by classes and drill. He'd resisted prowling the town, as McPake had done, yet even Beadon and Jones mentioned that they'd visited the Zegyo Bazaar—Jones had bought a lacquered bowl, Beadon a dagger. Traders and coolies congregated at the West Gate, but only to plead for work inside as menials. Blair didn't speak to them; he seldom spoke to anyone except Po Hit in Burmese and Pundit Shastri in Hindustani, or he shouted orders to the cadets. He stayed within the fort, he studied, he followed orders, he often missed meals, smoking instead; he kept to himself, and he hated the life he'd signed up for.

The people of the town were spectral; he glimpsed them through the gates, small figures framed spectacularly by the massive doors of the fort, dimmed by dust-laden air—they were shrill voices, piercing yells, they were the tinkling bells of the tongas and rickshaws, they were laughter, they were shouts and smells, chiefly of woodsmoke and cooking oil.

Blair had always tried to maintain a shadow existence, of reading, of letter writing, of making lists—trees, flowers, Hindi and Burmese words—or composing poems he knew to be bad. His other life, his teasing and talkative classroom side, agreeable, rubbing along, gave no hint of the anxiety he felt in his solitude that he could not put in his letters home. In a recent letter to Jacintha, he'd written, *You have no idea how ghastly this place is—*

what a grave mistake I've made. But this admission shamed him. He vowed to write to her no more. Describing his misery made him more miserable.

And confounding him, in letters his mother sent, after a few casual mentions of Moulmein, of picnics she'd enjoyed there as a girl, she recalled her widowed mother, and her uncles and nieces, and wondered, in her schoolmistress's copperplate: *Should you find yourself in that pretty town of Moulmein might you pay a call to your grandmama and pass on my fondest wishes?*

Not a chance, he thought.

After class, or morning parade, or meals, Blair disappeared to his room, to read, or add to his lists, avoiding the club when he could, hating the laughter, resenting the expense of the drinks. He was not the swot McPake mocked: he was simply a solitary drudge, and—though he was appalled by the word—homesick.

Then Robinson—the misfit, the man of the world (*He were cashiered*)—had asked, *What do you know of Mandalay?* It was a challenge that silenced Blair. He knew nothing of Mandalay.

"One of the great towns of the Raj," Robinson said. "Palaces, pagodas, eating houses, the bazaar—and this, a little bit of heaven."

They sat, legs outstretched on teak deck chairs on the veranda of Robinson's bungalow on Hodgkinson Road. The veranda faced a canal, where a small boy was catching frogs, drawing them up in a scoop net, dumping them in a basket, and singing in a sweet lilting voice. The sight consoled Blair—the patience of the boy, his vigilance, the way he was lit, gilded by the setting sun that also shimmered on the canal, the boy's song most of all, a melody of contentment.

It was Robinson's suggestion that they meet at his bungalow rather than at the Upper Burma Club—it was near, only three streets south of the fort. Blair was glad of this. The club was a fishbowl, and it was often loud, late in the evening it was drunken, and that was when Blair was teased—"You've been scarce"—and Robinson was chaffed too, singled out for his reputation as having been cashiered from the army as too chummy with natives, especially native women.

"And look who's talking," Robinson said to Blair on his first visit to the bungalow. "The lot of them—poodle-fakers."

But Blair changed the subject. He wanted to talk about the town, and he did so to the accompaniment of tinkling bells, and shouts, the clop of hooves, the rippling of the canal, all of this background noises to Robinson's praises, enumerating the monasteries, the pagoda, the Royal Garden, the singular hill.

"Mandalay—also a great poem," Blair said.

"Bleeder never got here," Robinson said. "He stopped in Rangoon, heard the name, and got it all wrong. 'old Moulmein pagoda'? 'China cross the bay'? China's up north, Putau District, my bailiwick. Kipling knew bugger all about Mandalay."

While they reclined on the veranda drinking tea, a small pretty Burmese woman shuffled to the side table in pink slippers, refreshing the teapot with a black kettle. Her gauzy white blouse was fringed with lace, her reddish lungyi of raw silk shimmered, and her head was wrapped in what Blair now knew was a gaungbaung—green threaded with gold, giving her an air of majesty, a loose hank of the lovely cloth partly hiding her face. After she poured, she set out a plate of rice cakes on a blue plate. She had tiny hands and feet, and when she straightened after seeing to the teapot, she flicked at the hank of cloth to reveal a doll's face—round, smooth, with dark eyes and full lips, a lustrous strand of hair curling from beneath her head wrap.

"My servant, Ma Lat," Robinson said, seeing Blair staring. "You'll get a servant when you're posted. I should push for a billet near here or Rangoon. You'll be swallowed up in the Delta."

The doll-like woman was near them again, whisking flies away from the cakes with a napkin. Robinson muttered to her in Burmese, and she giggled, covering her mouth, and scuffed away into the house, leaving an eddy of perfume as she passed Blair.

"I said, 'You've got an admirer.'" Robinson laughed a little, a satisfied grunt of mirth. "She knows me pretty well. Like the Burmese say, 'The hen sees the snake's feet. The snake sees the hen's tits.'"

In Blair's fluctuating existence—the formalities of classes and drill, his solitary retreat to his room, reading—this was something different and welcome, Robinson's bungalow a refuge, and a preparation for penetrating the town. That, too, resembled his first year at Eton—it was months before he'd wandered any distance from the college and knew anything of Windsor. After more than four months at the fort he'd hardly ventured into Mandalay.

"I arrived here from Calcutta after the war," Robinson said. "I know every corner. There's no end of the things you can do here."

He was staring at Blair as he spoke. He had brown deep-set eyes made more soulful by heavy brows and a thin-lipped mouth, giving little away, his hair cut short, military fashion. There was something pious in his demeanor, something contemplative, and the simple furnishings of the bungalow suggested a kind of monasticism, even if the winsome well-dressed servant—more girl than woman—seemed proof of the opposite.

"I'd like to have a go," Blair said.

"I was like you once," Robinson said. "Green. A bit at sea in the fort. Found my way in the town. And I confess I took to writing poems."

Blair nodded slowly and finally said, "I write poems."

It shocked him to hear himself admit this; he'd never mentioned his poems to anyone here, never shown them to anyone, except the odd one to Jacintha, never told anyone of his wish to be a writer.

"Good for you," Robinson said. "Speaking in verse. It's a civilized way of sorting out your thoughts. Saying one thing and meaning another."

Darkness had fallen. The canal was black, the palm trees in Robinson's garden were silhouetted by the starry sky, and the fronds scraped in the slight breeze, gently buzzing. The night smells were strong—fried fish, wood fires, the perfume of flowers, the sourness of horse shit from the road, the hum of decay from the ripe canal.

"Come back—I'll show you."

Blair left by the veranda, his last glimpse of Robinson's bungalow the lighted side window, the pretty servant, Ma Lat, leaning on the sill, placidly smoking a fat cheroot.

"Would it put you out very much if I went alone to Robinson's tonight?" Blair said a week later to McPake after class.

"I don't care a dead rat one way or the other."

At the bungalow Robinson said, "Where's the padre?"

"Probably at the club. I think he's a bit sick I came alone."

Blair looked for the woman, Ma Lat, as he sat on the veranda chair, glancing aside at the window where he'd last seen her smoking. He'd thought about her in the intervening week and matched her to Robinson, picturing them alone together in the half dark of the house. He imagined them as characters in the sort of Kipling story that would fit in *Plain Tales from the Hills*—the English policeman cashiered for relations with a native woman, living defiantly near the fort with another native beauty pretending to be a servant. That was not the whole story. What next—the consequences—was the actual story, because in Kipling there were always consequences, even if the waywardness was love. Such liaisons always ended badly.

"She's fetching the tea things," Robinson said.

Blair cringed; he knew he was blushing. He was ashamed that Robinson had noticed his glances. He hated being obvious, caught seeking the woman.

Then she entered the veranda and served the tea and set out the cakes and a dish of a thick muddy substance.

"Fish paste—*ngapi*," Robinson said. "Try some."

Blair spooned a gob onto a biscuit, took a bite, and was nauseated as soon as he swallowed.

Robinson laughed. "It's rotten fish! The Burmese adore it, along with that other pungent item, the durian fruit." Then he spoke to Ma Lat, who covered her face again and hurried away giggling.

"I told her you're glad to see her. There's a nice word in Burmese for that. *Pyaw-shwin-sa-yar-par.* 'Ecstatic.'"

Blair repeated the word and had noticed how Robinson's features had altered, becoming animated, and he seemed another man, a better man, speaking Burmese.

"There isn't much ecstasy in the fort," Robinson said. "How old are you, Blair?"

"I turned nineteen last June, sir."

"And already a pukka sahib. All your life ahead of you."

Blair squirmed at the word *pukka*—he was not pukka at all. He was a doubtful sahib, a melancholy sahib, a sad Burma sahib, in his heart not a sahib at all, and embarrassed divulging his age.

"Coming to the end of classes in a few months. A spell in Maymyo, and our first postings."

"Then the fun begins."

Blair searched for a smile on Robinson's face. But all he saw was a grim frown and a dark stare, Robinson faintly nodding in reflection.

"What's the worst of it?" Blair asked.

"The worst of it is you get used to it."

"To what?"

"To wog-bashing," Robinson said. "I'm well out of it." He sat up and grasped Blair's arm and said, "But you're young—you'll see. It's an education. It'll be the making of you."

"I wonder if I'll last."

"You'll last, and it will serve you well. There's a short period in everyone's life when his character is fixed forever."

Just after sunset, Robinson stood and said, "Let's prowl," and led Blair through the garden and west on Hodgkinson Road toward the bazaar. Blair had expected the town to be more subdued after dark but saw that in the cool of the evening the shops were active, the streets busy with carts and rickshaws, the sidewalks crowded with people. And this being the dry season, dust was raised by the vehicles and the tramping feet, and the air was thick, the town existing in what seemed subaqueous light, the pedestrians looking like approximations of themselves, strange shapes in motion blurred by the risen dust.

Blair liked this dreamlike blur, the camouflage of it, and was reminded of walking in an English pea-souper on a winter day, when he seemed masked and anonymous by fog, like another ghost, his feet hardly touching the ground.

"London was once like this," Robinson said. "All great cities, in point of fact. Each street devoted to a particular trade."

They were passing lamplit shops and stalls, fronted by glass cases displaying gold and silver jewelry, glittering in the flames of the lanterns.

"The goldsmiths and silversmiths—masses of Indians. Over there the workers in base metals, the lead beaters, fashioning pewter." And walking on, he said, "Lacquer—baskets—tattoo booths."

Some of the shopkeepers called out to them, beckoning, holding up merchandise, and Robinson replied in Burmese.

"You said, 'We'll come back.'"

"Good lad, you understood."

"I'd like to come back," Blair said with feeling, heartened by the enlargement of his world, the color and bustle of the crowds—the buoyancy, as though they were truly floating—so different from the severity and seclusion inside the Fort. *Prowling*—he savored the word, it suggested anonymity.

At an arcade, brightly lit, stacked with books, Robinson said, "All printers here—more Indians. London had Paternoster Row, near St. Paul's, the booksellers and printers. Here it's Thirtieth Road. You're looking at a medieval town plan—this is a visit to the past. The same employments, the same entertainments. That"—he indicated a group of musicians, men with drums and gongs, not playing but standing and stretching, among men and women in silken robes and turbans—"that's a pwe, shutting down for the night."

"I want to see it."

"Next time."

Blair was impatient for the next time, but the expectation that he'd see Robinson again, and perhaps be granted another glimpse of the servant, Ma Lat, soothed him in classes, allowed him to believe that he could manage here and not feel oppressed by routine—the drills, the exams, the strict order of the day. Digby's classes in police procedure alarmed him for warning of the severe duties that lay ahead.

He'd avoided the town, as he'd once avoided Windsor and Slough, intimidated by the shoppers, the expensive goods, the sheer confidence of
commercial activity—or was it simpler, that he'd had no money? But Robinson's guidance, his friendship, gave Blair hope that he'd be able to accommodate himself to his rash decision to be a policeman and live in Burma.
So, happier having penetrated the town, he was happier as a student, and
happily remote from the others, vanishing once a week to visit Robinson's
bungalow.

"Lovely clothes," Blair said of Ma Lat's dress—after some weeks, he'd ceased
to hide his interest.

"A *htamein*," Robinson said. "A skirt but not properly a skirt—not
a wraparound, a lungyi. Notice the slit on the side. She teases us with a
glimpse of her shapely leg. And the blouse—her *ingyi*. See the flare at the
shoulder and hips. Very clever tailoring."

Ma Lat seemed to understand that she was the subject of Robinson's
talk, and she looked away, but at the same time with a twist of her small
body within the silks, she managed to swish her skirt widening the slit, and
sweep with her lacy sleeve, sweetly swanking. Then she stood straighter,
her head crowned with the elaborate wrapped gaungbaung, green and
gold, that gave her height.

When they left, she drew the curtain aside on the doorway and clasped
her hands below her chin, as though in prayer.

"*Thakin.*"

Blair returned the gesture, and walking away he said, "Master, fancy
that."

"Lord, rather. I much prefer it to sahib."

The pwe was in progress at the gateway to a small temple near the
bazaar, a chattering crowd having gathered, jostling to see, roused by the
clangs of cymbals and gongs, the snatches of singing.

"They had street theater in London, too. Just like this," Robinson said.
"Tumblers. Dancers. Punch and Judy."

The actors in gowns raised their arms for emphasis, and sang, their
sleeves billowing. One actress carried a parasol, facing a man on a throne,
each gesture accompanied by a clash of cymbals or the trilling of a flute.

But what fascinated Blair was the audience, as highly colored as the play,
dressed as well, some carrying lamps, old women in their finery smoking cheroots. The women Blair found beautiful, their faces glowing, their
smoothed unmarked skin like the silk slipping over it. Children ran among
them—lovely children, their laughter lifting Blair's spirits. In the drudgery

of the fort he'd forgotten how to be happy, but here in the street, among the laughter and loud music—and children and dogs and pretty girls—he was content.

"What's the story?"

"Always the same," Robinson said. "There's the spurned lover, poor chap."

It was a man costumed as a prince—turban, gown, glittering rings—dancing away from a princess, taking small regretful steps, a triumphant and gloating lover, much more regal, beckoning the princess forward, in a screeching welcome, to the sound of gongs and drums.

"It's the national amusement—sometimes it's marionettes, *yote-thay- pwe.* Sometimes ballet—*A-nyeint pwe.* Or the *nat pwe*—placating the ghosts and wood demons." Robinson beamed as he beheld the dancers. "This is *zat pwe*—dancers and clowning. It is really too killing in its absurdity."

Blair said, "At last I feel I'm really in Burma."

"I knew this would interest you," Robinson said. "That's why I brought you here. You've read books and been in civilized places. You're not like the rest of us savages here. Don't you think this is worth watching in its queer way? Just look at that princess's movements—look at that strange, bent forward pose like a marionette, and the way her arms twist from the elbow like a cobra rising to strike."

"There's something sinister in it."

"Listen, Blair—there's a touch of the diabolical in all Asians. And yet when you look closely, what art, what centuries of culture you can see behind it! Every movement that girl makes has been studied and handed down through innumerable generations." He turned to Blair and said with feeling, "In some way I can't define, the whole life and spirit of Burma is summed up in the way that girl twists her arms."

The pwe washing over him, Blair caught some of the words—*gold, king, come, love.* Engrossed in the performance he was not in the police; he was enchanted, transported to a pleasant land by music and dance, watching the progress of the pwe through the faces in the crowd, standing apart because he didn't wish to be noticed. For the duration of the pwe he thought: *I could be happy here, I am happy now.*

When it ended and Robinson summoned a rickshaw to take Blair back to the fort, darkness closed in—and the smoke and dust clouding the streets like fog—the cries, the stinks, the thickening heat, and classes tomorrow.

But they met again most weeks, usually on a Saturday night, when the others were at the club, Blair slipping out to his secret life, sometimes dining with Robinson at the Bristol Hotel, more often meeting him at a Chinese restaurant. This was the Woh Sing Bai Eating House, on the upper floor of a row of shop houses, where they sat at a veranda table because of the heat, Robinson sometimes disappearing into an inner room.

"You mentioned your father was in the Opium Department."

"In Bengal—inspected the muck."

"I fancy some of his merchandise ended up here," Robinson said and sniffed. "The fume of poppies."

On one of those evenings at Woh Sing's, sitting before the leavings of their meal—gnawed chicken feet, a residue of threadlike noodles, splintered duck bones, a platter of greasy rice, empty beer bottles, the tablecloth splashed with brown sauce and spilled gravy—Robinson pushed something across the table, a small disc that he steered with one finger.

"What do we have here?"

"Rubber goods."

Blair pinched it and lifted it to see the label. *Three Merry Widows* stamped on the lid. He had no reply.

"For safety's sake," Robinson said. "French letters."

Blair palmed it, like something forbidden, taking a deep breath.

"One of these nights prowling, you're going to find yourself by the river at one of the pavilions. There are many—I recommend Mother Majumdar's. If you go early, before the drunks from the fort turn up, you'll not be seen. Slip in, slip out. Hugger-mugger. London was once like this, too—the stews, the nunneries. Instead of Mistress Quickly you'll find a Bengali matron and lots of her girls."

The tin disk was slippery in Blair's hot hand and now seemed like a coin to gain admission to a secret chamber.

"It's going to happen to you eventually. Might as well be soon. Oh, and by the way, you'll learn some useful Burmese."

A party at the club one Saturday night—Robinson was invited but declined—gave Blair an opportunity. Some of the men would end up at Mother Majumdar's, but not till the party was over. Blair made his way to Robinson's.

"It'll be quiet now," Robinson said. "You'll have the pick of the lot. We'll go early."

Blair sat beside him in the rickshaw, saying nothing until it occurred to him to ask.

"We?"

"I'll tag along to introduce you. I've got a previous engagement at Woh Sing's." He gave the rickshaw puller directions. "Got some rupees?"

Blair patted his pocket. He was dressed in his linen jacket that he'd brought from England, a loose shirt he wore untucked, like a Burmese clerk, and his old drill trousers, the nearest he could find to civilian clothes. But his shoes were police issue—heavy-soled brogues. He'd plucked the insignia from his topee.

Past the pagoda where they'd seen the pwe, past Woh Sing's veranda, past the Zegyo Bazaar, and onward west of the town, past the marshes, where the air was heavy with the sharp smell of the muddy riverbank, and the night-dampened leaves of the overhanging trees, the croaking of frogs that sounded like mockery. Blair had anticipated an awkwardness he associated with failure, yet he was relieved to see that he needed no guidance from Robinson when they arrived.

It was a shadowy house upraised on pillars by the river, its veranda illuminated by paper lanterns, and they were greeted by an Indian woman in curtains of cloth, a green sari edged with red. She peeped from beneath the folds of a green shawl that might have been part of the drapes of the sari.

"Mother Majumdar."

"Sahib, sahib."

They were welcomed as though they'd been expected, as familiar visitors, and his mind racing, Blair thought, *Yes, I am a man, you are a tart, you know me, you know what I want.* They were led upstairs to a balcony that was concealed by a tangle of trees, they were offered bottles of beer—Blair accepted, Robinson declined, "I must be going." There were no introductions, no names, only smiles; Mother Majumdar withdrew, and as Blair drank his pint of beer, Robinson said, "You're on your own now, lad. They'll look after you."

Yes, they knew him here. He was a man, he was British, he was either a soldier or a policeman. He was young, he had rupees. After Robinson left, three girls tiptoed in, wearing shawls, half-hidden in silks and flimsy blouses, looking evasive. They were barefoot, they giggled like schoolgirls, they knelt before him and one poured him more beer, and they murmured among themselves.

He heard "tall," he heard "soldier," he heard "young."

They got to their feet and stretched and seemed to dance before him, to seize his attention. He found himself staring at one in particular, more modestly dressed than the others, her blouse buttoned to her neck, a frilled collar, and she was taller than the others. The girls seemed to recognize his intention in his steady gaze, and two of them slipped away. And now the one he'd seemed to single out with his uneasy smile dropped to her knees and sat at his feet. She placed her folded hands on his leg in a gesture of innocent affection, as a child might.

"*Lar*," she said, a single breath, a slight lisp, a gentle summons. "Come."

He knew what was expected of him—Robinson had warned him. He said, "*Nhit-se*"—twenty.

She lowered her eyes—demure, almost bashful—and held to his knee, her fingers laced, tugging a little.

"*Nhit-se-ngar*." Twenty-five.

In the upper room of incense, her perfumed silks, her fragrant skin, a hint of coconut oil in her hair, the spice in the breath of her sigh as she shook herself out of her blouse—Blair found himself trembling, looking down at her. She unwrapped her lungyi and stood naked, then took his hand and led him to the string bed by the window, the river still light in the afterglow of sunset.

She smiled as he fumbled with the Three Merry Widows tin.

He heard from below on the riverbank or perhaps in a bobbing sampan a cry in Burmese.

"I can feel it." A boy's eager voice.

"Let me," the girl whispered—naked, unashamed, sitting cross-legged on the string bed—and she took the tin from Blair's damp hands.

"Slow"—another boy's voice, and a splash, a whicker of expectation.

She had plucked a rubber and was rolling it between her fingers, and while Blair sat on the edge of the bed she crawled like a cat to the floor and knelt before him, holding the tip of the rubber in her teeth as she sheathed it onto his stiffness, as though slipping on a sock, so expertly he was ashamed and grateful, still distracted by the whispers from the riverbank.

She lay beneath him, small, submitting, and as he thrust, impatient to finish, his head hot, the smack of their sweating bodies like the sounds of struggle, he heard the voices again, one of them triumphant.

"I caught it!"

They were fishing.

Later he remembered how she had lit a taper in a dish, the pinch of incense in his nostrils, as he breathed hard in his frenzy. The boys fishing. A boat passing on the river when, afterward, he lay back on the bed, watching the flash of its running lights sliding across the wall. She nestled beside him, her skin like silk, saying softly, "Come back to me."

"What is your name?"

"Mima."

"Woman."

She squealed, she did not kiss him, the Burmese did not kiss, but she nuzzled him, she inhaled him. It was another sort—a better sort—of consolation, and a kind of completion. She told him the Burmese word for it: *nanthe*. And a week later when he went back to Mother Majumdar's he looked for the same girl, Mima, who said, as a lover might say, "I have been waiting for you."

He saw less and less of Robinson, and was glad of it—the knowledge that he could find his way alone to Mother Majumdar's soothed him in his solitude. In that place, with the girl Mima, always speaking Burmese he was confident, like the nameless shadow self in his secret narrative.

Living two lives, the student, the shadow, he studied harder during the week and ranged more widely, prowling the town, returning to Mima, disturbed one evening when he could not find her, desolated to know she was with another man, and he left, like a lover spurned.

He bought an old Matchless motorbike and rode some days with Beadon, who also had a bike. He resigned himself to finishing the course, to staying on, sustaining himself with a routine—classes, drill, supervision at the fort. Woh Sing Bai's Eating House, the bazaar, Mother Majumdar's, Mima, drilling the cadets—his days absorbing and protecting him, his routine like a refuge.

And then it ended, weakened with a feeling of loss when he was handed his assignment.

"Myaungmya," he told Beadon, though he was not sure where it was.

"I'm not far off—Bassein."

"Yes?"

"The Delta."

Part II

THE DELTA

9

WATER WORLD

He could see nothing in the distance but a green stripe that was the horizon flattened by a hot white sky, and before him the river, brown and opaque from runoff in the rains up-country. But at the banks where it slopped against the black cakey soil of the edges the water was thickened, and soupier, like beef gravy.

Blair was sitting under an awning in the bow of a small river steamer of the Irrawaddy Flotilla Company, chugging through the reaches and bends of the Delta. At the outset of the trip between densely wooded banks, the passage in places was so narrow that branches of trees crashed against the wood walls of the cabin, and by midmorning, on banks laid bare by the tide, crocodiles slept half sunken in the mud. The solitude was perfect, save for a few huts huddled in palm groves, or a casual fisherman in his dugout.

By noon the Delta flattened, and they glided past a featureless shore, the paddy fields indistinguishable from the marshes, except that they were fenced with spindly palm trees, and buffalo pulled plows through the shallow water—lost in the swampland of the tidal creeks. The width of the waterway had changed, the narrow stream when they'd set out that morning from Wakema was now, at noon, like the Thames at Richmond, but without trees or settlements, nothing for the stranger's eye to seize upon or report, a great emptiness, under the staring whiteness in the sky.

After lunch beneath the awning on the foredeck—pigging it, he thought, a tin of bully beef, and coarse bread and a mug of tea the color of the river—Blair saw the first tall palms, but far apart and solitary, like an afterthought, some with their fans of fronds lopped off, but why?

"Toddy," the Indian captain said, pointing to the palms on one hand and making a motion of drinking with the other, cupped to his mouth, wagging his head, smiling insincerely, ingratiating himself, thinking the Englishman would be pleased with this wicked mention of alcohol.

The smaller sticklike palms, each one like a ragged parasol, emphasized the simplicity of the landscape. Once, in the water, he saw what looked like a twisting branch, but pulsing, olive-hued, headed upstream, a novelty.

"Naga," the Indian said. "Esnake."

Blair shrank back but became curious, the diligent snake, whipping, sinuous, just below the surface of the dark water, making for the shore. And when Blair stood to get a better look, he saw past the bank to the land in the distance. *Like the Norfolk Broads,* he was thinking, for his next letter home. *A water world, not of nightmare or fancy, but of indescribable boredom.*

He steadied himself, holding to a stack of crates—tins, beer, biscuits, wine—and looked for more, anything to describe, to report, but he saw a dark darting bird and nothing else. The muddy river was opaque, the green banks unvarying; there was no sun but only a gray glow of hot smothering cloud. He was grateful when the flutter-blast of the engine startled a heron, and the leggy bird struggled to lift itself and flapped away.

Blair yawned, heavy with lunch, hoping for something to remark upon, something to remember, anything, high ground, a hut, another boat, a tree—surely the town, Myaungmya, small as he'd been warned it would be, might sit on a mound of land and be visible from a distance. But he saw nothing ahead except the flat green stripe.

"This river—it has a name?" he asked the Indian.

"Ywe River."

The word *Ywe* had no meaning for him. He sat and smoked a cigarette and half dozed, his head drooping. He was jerked into wakefulness when the Indian skipper called out, not to him but to a man standing on a landing stage, built against the shore. Seeing Blair alarmed by his shout he wagged his head amiably and said in a softer voice, "It is your Myaungmya, sahib."

Beyond the floating wharf of the landing stage Blair saw a wood-framed warehouse and a flat-roofed open-sided structure, rows of tables inside, a market. On this January midafternoon the market was empty, smelling of dead animals, of decayed fish, of fur, of gunny sacks, of rancid fruit, of blood. A street led at right angles to the landing—shops, the police station, bungalows, so the Indian skipper said.

Squawking crewmen began passing loaded crates and bulging sacks from the steamer's deck to porters on the floating dock, as Blair stepped to the ramp and mounted it to a platform beside the stinking market. He lit a cigarette to kill the smell and watched his trunk and bags piled into a wheelbarrow by a porter who saluted him when he caught Blair's eye.

From where he stood he could see to the far end of town, down the street lined with one-story shops, and past the crossroads, at the far end a paddy field or a swamp, an expanse of emerald green. The visible limit of the town, tinier than Southwold, was two streets, one crossing the other at right angles. He felt conspicuous, swaying in confusion, and because no one had come to meet him, he thought, *What now?*

He turned to face the river, the water greenish, almost arsenical, in this light, and saw a boat being rowed, the hull an elegant shape, reminding him of a woman's fancy slipper, a pile of yellow baskets nesting in the heel of its stern.

The small town, the rutted streets, the muddy river, the flooded paddy fields, the shouting men, the stink of squalor—*this is my world now.*

Just then a barking dog, hoarse with ferocity.

The dog lunged at the porters, growling, barking at the man steadying the wheelbarrow and setting off, but it merely sniffed Blair's boots and whined, wagging its tail.

"Fingal!"

The dog backed off at the shout, leaving Blair crouched in the act of petting him. He looked up and saw a white man in khaki approaching him, arms pumping as he marched—shorts, knee socks, a shirt with buttoned epaulets, raising one hand to the brim of his solar topee, half in greeting, half in salute.

"Blair," he said and stopped and stamped the dust from his shoes and snatched at the dog's collar. "I'm Swann—good trip?"

When he grinned, he showed a space between his two front teeth that a half-crown coin could fit into, and somehow that space—that slot—made him seem amiable. His pencil mustache resembled Lockhart's and reminded Blair of his intention to grow one.

"Smashing."

"You arrived with bottles," Swann said, seeing the crates still being stacked, now a low wall of them at the edge of the platform. "That's merciful. We're low on grog, down to our last buckshee ration of gin, confiscated from the evidence locker."

All this time the man was wincing in the glare of white sky, showing the gap in his teeth, looking up at Blair. Swann was in his twenties, so Blair had been told in Mandalay—late twenties perhaps—but he had the severity of someone much older, a kind of weariness in his wounded eyes, creased face, and stern mouth. Apart from the tiny strip of mustache, he was clean-shaven, which made his fatigue more obvious. It was as though he'd suffered a serious illness and had only just recovered, but showed the effects of having been laid low, somehow still damaged. He spoke with effort, his jaw fixed.

He might have been self-conscious because Blair, studying him, said nothing.

Swann spoke up again, saying, "Sutherland—my deputy—has a fat head from last night, the buckshee gin, or he'd be here too. I chained him to his desk. We'll meet later."

He then turned and shouted to the porters in Burmese—Blair understood "baggage" and "hurry"—and snatched at the dog again, which had made for the man with the wheelbarrow. "I'll see you to your bungalow, just up the road in the compound."

The dog trotted ahead, Swann striding behind him talking, Blair loping along, still stiff from the whole day on deck. And now Blair understood that the man was not talking to the dog but rather calling out, indicating a small chapel, the pagoda, the jail, the police station, and behind the station a small green-painted wooden building, upraised on posts, chickens pecking beneath it, a strutting rooster, and, as with the dog, Blair smiled, solaced by the sight of animals.

"This is yours, Blair."

An elderly Burmese man in a white turban and faded green lungyi hurried from the doorway and descended the stairs laughing, to greet Blair with a bow.

"Poh Sim—he was Gilmore's houseboy—Gilmore's posted to Akyab. You can keep him or find another boy, if he comes up short."

"*Thakin,*" the old man said, clasping his hands before his lined face, his hooded eyes.

"Sort out the sahib's boxes, Poh."

The man looked pleadingly at Blair, as though he knew he was being evaluated, and bowed again, a deep bow of respect, what Blair knew as a shiko. And then the man called out in a sharp summoning bark to the porter on the path pushing the wheelbarrow with Blair's trunk and bags.

"You can sack him and find another boy to skivvy for you if you wish," Swann said. "Or girl for that matter, if you're inclined."

"I'm sure he'll do fine," Blair said, but thought of Robinson's Ma Lat, serving tea, looking decorative, perhaps sharing his bed.

Boy seemed an odd word for a man who might have been fifty or sixty, with a deeply lined face, thin arms, yellow nails on his bony fingers, almost skeletal.

"We're in the bungalow just behind the office," Swann said. "Poh will see to your bath. Pop over at seven. We'll have a drink and something to eat and we'll make a plan. We've got a case pending that wants sorting out."

He turned to go, though the dog remained, growling at the porter, snapping at his sandals, making the porter shuffle his feet and laugh in fear.

"Fingal!"

The two men were seated on the upper veranda of the bungalow, in the shadows just at sunset, but spotting Blair, Swann got to his feet and went to the rail and called out to him in greeting.

"Come and meet Deputy District Commissioner Sutherland!"

"Sir," Blair said.

As always on a first meeting, Blair felt the constraint of being too tall, a bit freakish, as though suffering a noticeable handicap, and so he instinctively stepped back, rounded his shoulders and nodded, wishing he were smaller.

But the man was saying, "Welcome," and holding something in his hand, not a drink but a shallow tin, and before Blair could respond to the greeting the man said, "What's this?"—proffering the tin, filled with a puttylike substance, with the look of gummy brown boot polish. "Go on, sniff it."

To oblige him, Blair held the tin to his nose, still suffering the awkwardness of being taller than both men, but—younger and newly arrived—feeling somehow unworthy, a conspicuous boy among grown men.

"Haven't a clue. Smells of treacle gone sweaty."

"Opium," Sutherland said, poking into the tin and licking the dab of black on his finger.

"My father would be ashamed of me. He served in the Opium Department."

"Och, aye—where, lad?"

"Motihari in Bengal. Latterly in Monghyr. Retired now."

"We found this muck on a chap the other day. He's in lockup now. Blighter was selling it in the villages up the river. Probably a *bein-sar* himself."

"Opium eater," Swann explained.

"What will happen to him?

"You tell me, Blair," Swann said. "You've been through the Penal Code."

"Charge-sheet him, try him for possession, fine him appropriately. Jail him."

"No room in the chokey—bend him over," Sutherland said. "Flog him unmercifully until he's sorry."

"Yes, hurt him a little," Swann said. "No need to make a song about it. Leave a few stripes on him, to remind him."

Saying so, Swann made caning motions with his hand, as though he held a birch.

"A proper schoolie," Sutherland shouted. He was a ginger-haired Scotsman, hardly thirty, beefier than Swann but with a pale complexion that flushed pink when he laughed, as he did on the word *schoolie*.

"Quite right," Blair said, tugging at his Sam Browne belt to steady himself.

"You can supervise," Swann said. "You're here to learn. Which reminds me—before we eat there's something I want to show you. This way—"

The three men descended the stairs past a garden, and Swann led them beyond the station to a large windowless shed, where he fitted a key into a heavy padlock. But he did not open the door.

"You'll want to hold your nose, Blair," Swann said, tugging the door. "This here's the morgue. Mind the bluebottles."

The burr of blowflies whined like a whirring fan as the door swung wide, and the smell was so strong it hung in the air like a rotten cloth, something palpable, a mass of filthy rags that stank in Blair's face and dragged across his nose. He reached as though wishing to push the stink aside, as it gagged him—and his other hand was pinching his nose.

"Hark at this for a rancid dumpling, lad," Sutherland said. "Where's me nose rag?"

Swann was slipping a gray-stained sheet from a bulging form on the table—a man, Blair saw, a dead man, strangely bluish and stiff and swollen.

"A white man," Blair said, gagging, and the stink stung his eyes, too.

"No. That's what happens when a native's been in the river for a while. The upper pigmented layer of the skin slips away. They go all white and crepey."

Blair braced himself, choking, though he'd pushed his handkerchief against his nose. Leaning for a better look he saw the man had no face, a great chewed wound that had left his nosehole and teeth exposed, the skull beneath the skin.

"The rats had begun on him when we found him in the ditch," Swann said. "Rats are rather bad in these parts."

"It's the rice," Sutherland said. "Cheeky buggers get into the sacks."

The man's face had been eaten away, the eyes were hollow sockets, the cheekbones were prominent, the yellow teeth protruded—the lips had been gnawed. The face of a ghoul, the flesh of its edges scratched with the teeth marks of the rat.

Blair had already begun to back away toward the half-open door, retching, his throat swelling with disgust, wanting to leave. But Swann had not moved from beside the table, he was holding the stained sheet up by a corner as though to highlight the horror, a streak of late-afternoon light shining on the chewed face.

"Aye, some corpis are more rotten and rank than this," Sutherland said, and *corpis* was his odd word.

"Masses more," Swann said. "Mark the skull, split by a dah. In the normal way we hand them over to be burned. But this one is special. Notice anything besides the cracked skull?"

Blair had not seen the slashed skull, he pressed his handkerchief harder, pinching it against his nose and, holding his breath, turned to look. He saw nothing else, he tried to speak, he gagged and shook his head.

"That hand," Swann said.

It was glovelike, fattened with decay, the blackish fingers chewed to stumps, yet on one finger, the wink of a red stone, probably a ruby, the size of an acorn, set in a gold ring, sunk in puffy flesh.

"Not stolen by the miscreant," Swann said. "This was a man of some standing."

"Any idea who it might be?"

"That's the question, lad. And you're going to find the answer."

Blair wanted to speak but his throat was clogged, his eyes watering, and he could barely breathe. He stepped away, reaching for the door.

"It's fair choking him," Swann said, with a chuckle.

"Dinnae forget the bauble, lad," Sutherland said.

"You'll want the ring as evidence," Swann said, and motioned to the mangled hand, the ring shining weirdly on the puffy finger stump.

Seeing Blair hesitate, Sutherland said, "Hasten, lad—supper's getting cold." He tapped the chewed finger. "It's bangers tonight!"

Just then, as Blair approached the table, he was startled by a dog barking outside the shed—not the yap-yap of a cautioning dog but a maddened and insistent howl.

Swann screamed, "Fingal!" and kicked the door shut, putting the room in darkness, intensifying the smell, the stink now like a cloak flung over them. "He smells the meat."

"Dark as a pocket," Sutherland said, sounding cheerful.

"Can't see a blooming thing," Blair said. He heard a faint squeak, as of a rusty hinge.

"We want a wee vesta," Sutherland said—he'd struck a match and swept the flame above the hand.

But still Blair heard the squeaking, and still the dog barked outside, rattling Blair's nerves, nearly blinding him with the noise. But he knew he was being tested. With the handkerchief against his face, desperate to oblige, he grasped the ring and twisted, yanking hard, and when it was free of the stump he saw that the knuckle softened by decomposition had come away and that dead flesh adhered to the gold prongs that supported the red stone.

"Let's eat," Swann said, opening the door wide, filling the shed with sunlight.

Blair heard the squeak again and saw against the far wall two rats, mottled, weirdly spotty with sparse hair, tumbling over each other as though in play, but in fact trapped in the corner and desperate to escape.

Blair clung to the doorjamb but found he could not stand, and helpless before the barking dog, he sank to his knees and fell forward.

The next thing he heard as he was hoisted to his feet—nauseous, unable to speak, still dazed—was, "Let's shunt Lofty home to lick his wounds."

He was helped to his bungalow, braced by the men, one on either side. Greeted by Poh, he groped to his bedroom. He slept, waking in the night, soaked in sweat, fearful in the dark, the corpse smell still on his shirt. He stripped it off and thrust it outside of the mosquito net, and clutched his face, imagining rats in his bed.

THE DAH

Blair was woken by a rooster screaming, and he smiled at its full-throated boast, the morning sun slatted through the bamboo blinds and gilding the folds of his mosquito net—somehow, he'd been deposited in this gauzy cocoon and felt safe in daylight, reassured by birdsong and the clucking of hens and the rooster again, a chorus, a kind of welcome. Then a hoarse imploring bark. *I want a dog.*

But he remembered, as after a drunken night, the morning-after shame, the chewed corpse, the ring, the rats, his panic, fear, and fall, and was stewing in the awful memory, replaying it in his mind when with a soft knock, Poh appeared, carrying a tray, a cup of tea, and a folded note, *Please join us for breakfast. We're just over the road.*

He dressed carefully, the uniform wrinkled from being in his trunk, but he saw that Poh had polished his belt and boots. On his way to breakfast, he summoned the will to be jaunty, and climbing to the veranda where they were seated at a table, he greeted Swann with, "I feel I rather disgraced myself yesterday."

"No need to make another song about it. No worse than coming down with a fat head."

"Blotted my copybook."

"Don't be downhearted, lad," Swann said, but he was glancing at the creases in Blair's jacket. "Have a banana!"

Sutherland speared a thick sausage on his plate with a fork and held it up, wagging his finger. "Remind you of aught?"

Swann said, "Thanks for this," indicating a bottle of brandy on the table. "Came on the boat with you."

"Have a dram," Sutherland said. "Good for colic—very binding."

"Just tea, thanks very much."

"I recommend this potion from Assam," Swann said, with the pot over Blair's cup. "Flushes out the kidneys."

As Blair was sipping his tea, a serving girl appeared with a plate for him—a mound of fried rice, topped with a poached egg, some slices of ham beside it.

Self-conscious, sitting stiff-backed at attention, Blair poked the egg and stirred the yolk into the rice and began to eat. He was aware that he was being closely observed. He could think of nothing intelligent to say, and though the day was very hot, the air close and humid, the butter melting in its dish, the marmalade gone soupy, he resisted the cliché of commenting on the weather, or the flies buzzing over his eggy rice, the dog flopped in a shady corner of the veranda. In this silence he heard himself chewing ham.

"Aye, they were a bonny pair all right," Sutherland said. "Them rats."

Blair gagged, unable to swallow, and as he pressed his napkin to his mouth, thinking he might vomit, he dropped his fork. When it clattered to the floor the serving girl dashed to pick it up. She bowed and just as quickly replaced it with one from the sideboard.

Through watery eyes, Blair saw she was beautiful, and there was sympathy in her smile.

"*Thakin,*" she whispered.

"I'll tell you something you don't know," Swann said, and he sounded a bit tight—perhaps the brandy. "Men find more comradeship through a trivial episode like that rat-bitten corpse than the most noble of obligations."

"You want to take a pull on yourself, Blair," Sutherland said.

Blair, not *lad*—he felt reprimanded this second day in Myaungmya. And he saw that in fumbling with his fork he had splashed a gob of yolk onto the cuff of his jacket; he thought better of wiping it, though, fearing to make it conspicuous.

"Fuckin' rats," Swann exclaimed, a bit breathless, as though he'd spent these last moments bursting to speak. "I've seen rats in the hundreds, twice that size in the trenches, shoals of them and always fucking about in the camp—fat as piglets from feeding on corpses. They'd be climbing all over us when we were asleep. Reached into my pocket once to fish out a smoke and put my hand on a rat, idling there."

"Christ," Blair said, nudging his plate away. "What did you do?"

"Sloshed him one in the clock and tossed him to buggery."

Sutherland put his hand on Blair's sleeve and winked at him. "Our Duncan can be a fluent liar on occasion," and sipped his brandy.

"You know sweet fuck all about it, Fraser, ya daft Jock," Swann said. "Where were you? On parade in Rae Bareli in that cushy barracks. And we were up to our necks in shit, crawling toward a show in Mametz."

"My sappers would have been an asset—gone through the Huns like a dose of salts. But we weren't summoned to march."

"Good thing you didn't, a bloody cunt like you's sufficient to demoralize the whole fuckin' battalion." In his fury, his teeth clenched, Swann turned to Blair. "Second Battalion, the Gordons. We captured Mametz from Jerry in '16. Trenches were fuckin' heaving with rats."

He paused, wheezing like a rheumatic, and to calm himself Blair lit a cigarette. As he shook the match out a brass ashtray was slid under his hand—the serving girl bowing, a deep shiko, then stepping away. He tried to thank her but she bowed again in deference. Her delicacy, her beauty, made him feel clumsy and ugly, and there was that stain on his cuff.

"I've been around rats so long I've made a study of the buggers—there in the Somme, and here in this fucking swamp. They're randy great breeders, masses of babies. You see a few and before you can say 'knife' there's fifty. They can leap three feet from a standing position. If you're sitting, like you are now, they'll jump to your lap and end up on your head. Toss one thirty feet off a ledge onto stone and it won't be injured. They can climb anything, up a wall, up slippery bamboo. Squeeze through a crack the width of a farthing—they could squeeze through this"—and he grinned and showed the gap in his front teeth. "I've seen them gnaw through lead pipe, chew through a brick. They can swim like fish. Those two in the shed, they weren't afraid. They were larking about. Listen, I've heard rats laugh—it's a queer kind of purring." He grinned at Blair and sucked air through his tooth gap. "But the rat has its uses. He consumes the corpses on no-man's-land, a task the rat alone is willing to undertake." He sighed with satisfaction. "Pass the poxy marmalade!"

Blair handed Swann the shallow dish and said nothing, though he wanted to. He felt unwell again, dizzy, his face hot, his hands damp, the paper on his cigarette stained with sweat from his fingers.

"Rather be rat-arsed than a rodent," Sutherland said.

Blair steadying himself with a deep breath, like a drunk pretending to be sober. He said, "From Latin, I reckon. *Rodere*. To gnaw."

And immediately heard himself as pompous.

Sutherland snorted. "Sassenach."

"Enough," Swann said. "We've got a crime that wants solving."

"You've come at the right time, lad," Sutherland said. "Crime season."

Blair did not betray his irritation. He'd heard this repeated so often it sounded more like a boast than a warning, a singular interlude, rich in the drama of mayhem and arrests.

But he said, "I'm here to help—and still on probation."

"You're green," Swann said. "It's perfectly understandable. Your rank's sitting a little stiffly on you—oh, yes . . ." He dug in his pocket. "You'll need this," and he handed him the ruby ring. "Mah May scrubbed the mince off it." He nodded to the serving girl who was crouching at the doorway. "She fancied it was tagged with a morsel of chicken meat, and a good thing too—the Burmese are fearfully superstitious."

"Shall we introduce him to the men?" Sutherland asked.

"Finish your breakfast first."

"I'm done," Blair said, feeling queasy and hoping it didn't show.

As they walked to the parade ground behind the station, passing Blair's bungalow, Swann said, "You've got some shit on your cuff. Nip inside and put on a decent tunic."

They saw everything, it was exhausting, it was shaming; but Blair reminded himself that his being on probation was his excuse. He changed—Poh had ironed his other jacket—and he met the men at the margin of the parade ground, a dusty field, the subinspectors forming in ranks, thirty or more of them, in the morning sun.

"Here are your men," Swann said, and lowering his voice, "More than half are Indians. Your Burmese are much too casual for the police. But even these men will be skulkers if you're not firm."

Blair stood straight, head up, shoulders back, and for once he felt he was at an advantage, that the men would respect him for his height.

"Ten shun!" Sutherland commanded, and the ranks became symmetrical, the men stamping in place.

"Assistant Superintendent Blair," Swann said, speaking to the men, but referencing him, like an actor in a play addressing an audience. "You've come at the right time, sir. Crime season. What is it you'd like to learn about? Simple murder, we have masses of that. House breaking, burglary, thievery, assault. You've come to the right place. Rape? It's a common occurrence—rape of women in the paddy fields, rape of schoolgirls, heinous rape of children—it never stops. Added to which"—Swann paused, he grimaced, he beat the air with his baton—"the incineration of some of the victims, doused with paraffin and set alight like fiery torches. Not to mention the plague of dacoity—"

He continued in this vein, elaborating crimes and denouncing them, and finally said, "These are your men. You will expect the best from them. There's work to do—you have your orders. Now carry on."

In the inspection that followed, Swann remained standing, observing Sutherland and Blair walking the length of the ranks, each subinspector presenting arms and calling out his name as Blair saluted. They were young, they seemed like schoolboys, he like the head prefect.

When they were done, and the men standing at ease, Swann summoned Blair to confer.

"They're all yours," Swann said. "I suggest you make a plan. I'll give you a map of our district and you can start on patrol tomorrow. In the meantime, choose your men. Take five or six. You need them for beating the bushes."

Blair said, "I'll take Kohli, Chandu, Vasant, Ba Sim, U Min, and Maung Mint—the sturdier chaps. It's a murderer we're after, he might resist when we find him."

But Swann had begun to stare and for once he was silent, seemingly puzzled. In the ten minutes of the inspection, Blair had remembered the soldiers' names and guessed at their abilities, based on their size. They were big men, with a glint of ferocity in their eyes.

In the still air just after dawn, the shafts of light made the paddy fields seem like puddles of molten gold and gave the clouds of early morning mosquitoes a glow like gold dust, as they sifted through the air then formed and made for an early riser poling his sampan downstream to the west. But no ripple of current was visible. The tide was slowly ebbing past the paddy fields into the Bay of Bengal.

The men were squatting on the deck of the steam launch, Blair and the six subinspectors studying the sketch map of the river system that Swann had given him.

"The body was found here, in a ditch, between these two villages," Blair said and tapped the villages that had been circled.

"Moke Soe Kwin," Maung Mint said. "Big place. Pagoda. Market. Got pigs."

"I know Taung Dee—not so big, sahib," Kohli said.

"We'll look at the smaller village first," Blair said. He took a twist of paper from his pocket and unwrapped the ring. "This is the key to the dead man's identity. We'll find out who he is, then we'll look for the chap who killed him. Evidently no one's reported him missing."

"Mogok ruby—best kind," U Min said.

"We are having rubies," Vasant said. "So many in Western Ghats, Mysore State. This big, sahib"—and he made a fist.

"Maybe they no report missing because they not know he missing," Ba Sim said.

Blair signaled to the skipper—it was the Indian, Chandu—and they cast off, heading downstream, passing the sampan and the man poling it, and rounding a bend into the flat featureless emptiness of paddy fields and swamps, gliding along the brown river under a sky smoldering with glare, though there were creamy clouds in the distance. The men had taken up positions on the shady side of the wheelhouse. Blair stood in the sunlight, uncomfortably, feeling that it was expected of the sahib, that it would diminish his authority to be huddled with the men in the patch of shade.

The Indians and the Burmese kept themselves separate, as he'd seen in Mandalay; the Indians having little respect for the Burmese. The Burmese resented the Indians' presence in Burma and sometimes screamed "Kalar!" at them, their word for Indians. It was why Blair had chosen three of each and was not surprised—he had smiled—when the qualities of national rubies were compared, Mysore gems against Mogok gems.

Lulled by the rhythm of the engine, some lines of a possible poem came to him.

The hurrying rat in my room
Goes lewdly round my legs
And shames me with a gloom
That something, something begs.

Rubbish. Never mind. He was briefly self-pitying, yet the thought of a rat anywhere near him made him weak and fearful, and the dead man's gnawed face appalled him. But seeing farmers knee-deep in paddy fields, bent double, grubbing in the water, among the shoots, he thought how much worse their lives were, how hard, how hopeless. It was as though he'd plunged into a Wells scientific romance, floating across a planet composed entirely of standing water—he the visiting earthling in his boat, watching the inhabitants splashing through their water meadows.

Vasant brought him a cup of milky tea. "Chai, sahib."

Blair said, "You're from Mysore?"

"State of Mysore, sahib, but coast side, Canara side," Vasant said, seemingly pleased to be asked, proud to respond, arms to his side, his fingers drumming on the seam of his shorts. "I am of Bunt community."

"Speaking Hindi?"

"Not at all, sahib. Speaking Tulu language. I am Vasant Rai. We are warrior caste, sahib."

Vasant saluted and with a lordly strut in his step rejoined the other Indians.

Drinking his tea, standing at the rail apart from the men, Blair thought, *I am in charge,* and smiled, and thought again, *I am in charge,* and frowned.

• • •

Toward noon they came to Taung Dee—a grove of palm trees, a scattering of bamboo huts thatched with fronds and bundles of withered grass. A boy on the bank called out in fright, seeing Blair treading the narrow plank of the gangway that the men had fastened to the boat rail and the embankment. The boy ran shrieking in the direction of the huts.

"He is fearing, sahib."

"Find the headman," Blair said, then remembered, "Fetch me the *thugyi-min*."

All the men except Chandu had come ashore and stood side by side at the margin of the village, looking formidable in their uniforms, glowering from beneath their helmets, batons in hand, as though about to lay siege— and the more menacing for their silence. Blair walked slowly in front of them, holding his fist at the level of his chest, and it seemed like a threat, but his fist enclosed the ruby ring.

An old man appeared and tottered toward them from the direction of the huts, one hand on the shoulder of a youth, a stick in the other hand. The stick top was a brass handle, and when they were closer and the old man relaxed his grip, Blair saw the handle was fashioned in the shape of strange creature, shiny from use, with a fat serpent's head and gaping mouth, unexpected elegance in this poor place, giving the old man a measure of dignity.

"He is *thugyi-min*, sahib."

The old man winced when Blair opened his fist, and he seemed startled to see the ring. As he gazed upon it, seeming to marvel, a group of villagers who'd followed him pressed forward, whispering, until Vasant stepped in front of them, holding his baton horizontal, pushing it, and shouting for them to back away.

The old man was shaking his head, murmuring to U Min.

U Min said to Blair, "This ring not from here."

"He's sure?"

"They poor people, sahib. They no have such things."

"Back to the boat, chaps," Blair said.

Pulling away from the shore, the boat slowed, the engine coughing, and with a rattle ending in a clatter like a dropped biscuit tin, it seemed to seize and went silent. Now they could hear the tweeting of birds. The boat turned slowly in the mild current. As it drifted, the skipper, Chandu, began tinkering, unbolting some fittings, blowing on a fuel line. Blair directed the tiffin pots to be distributed, and the men sat cross-legged on the mats eating from tin pannikins of rice, of vegetables, Indians with yellowish dhal, Burmese with fish.

The engine had died, there was no breeze, the river was flat, the boat drifted as though floating in air, not a sound to be heard except the chirping of birds in the reeds. Heat and light and silence, not bliss but a kind of serenity, life suspended. Blair thought, *I don't want to arrive.*

He was dozing, seated on a crate, when he was awakened by the engine chugging to life. Within half an hour they were at Moke Soe Kwin, tying up at a floating dock, a raft of lashed-together logs. The dagger-blade finial of a pagoda was visible in the distance and when Blair climbed from the raft to the top of the embankment he saw a stockaded village, a great sprawl of huts, clusters of them on twisting footpaths, more huts than he could count.

A small spotted dog loped toward Blair—lame in one of its rear legs, unsteady as it barked. When Blair extended his hand, the dog licked it and sniffed his boots. Blair scratched the dog's neck but conscious of the men he didn't hug the dog as he wished to.

"Burmese people eat dog animals," Kohli said.

Overhearing him, U Min screeched, "No! That not true!"

Kohli merely smiled. "And cat, sahib. They are eating."

"Lies," U Min said.

Kohli persisted, "They call them *kyar nge*—little tiger. It is so, sahib."

"Find the headman," Blair said to Kohli to end the dispute. "Get on with it."

"We no eat cat," U Min said. And he stepped in front of Kohli saying, "Not *thugyi-min* for this investigation. This big man ring. Better we talk to *sayadaw*."

"A monk?"

"Big monk," U Min said.

"What's the logic of that?"

"Big monk always know big man. Big man give money to pagoda."

The ring might have belonged to a donor, he was saying, which made sense. They set out for the whitewashed pagoda that stood at the center of the mass of huts, near well-built houses that had not been visible from the landing. Clusters of meaner huts lay farther on, and beyond them low hovels, all the dwellings baking in the sun this midafternoon.

As they made their way along the footpaths, Blair at the lead saw that all activity in the village had ceased: the intruders in uniform were objects of interest. Women who had been bearing fruit and flowers in baskets to the pagoda knelt and watched them pass, men in the shadows of the poles of upraised huts stared but did not speak, children followed them, skipping, gesturing, laughing.

But someone—a child perhaps—must have run ahead and raised the alarm, because a stout yellow-robed monk stood at the gateway to the pagoda. He was shaven headed, with a soft lined face, putty colored, like a withered apple. He was flanked by younger monks, one of whom held an umbrella over the old monk's head. The umbrella was large, of faded elegance, green threadbare silk, with fringes of braided gilt.

"This Sayadaw Wimalar."

Saying so, U Min clasped his hands before him and bowed, as did the two other Burmese subinspectors. The Indians folded their arms and looked severe.

Blair greeted the monk in Burmese, then said to U Min, "Show him the ring."

The monk's solemn face became animated when U Min held the ring before him in his palm, but then he just as quickly looked perplexed and muttered to the monks beside him.

"He want to know where we find ring," U Min said. "Did we take from the man finger?"

"Who is the man?"

U Min conferred with the monk, nodding, asking questions, then said, "It is grandfather, Hpo Thin. Hpo Thin go Bassein two week ago, on boat."

"Tell him Hpo Thin is dead. We found his body and this ring on his finger."

The monks cried out when they heard this, the words repeated, and the clamor passed among the crowd that had grown around Blair and his men.

Amid the urgent whispers, a man broke through the jostling spectators and announced himself as the headman of Moke Soe Kwin village and that he'd heard the terrible news. Seeing the ring in U Min's hand, he demanded that it be handed over and given to the wife of Hpo Thin, who he said did not yet know she was a widow.

"We need to discuss this," Blair said and walked with the headman to the doorway of a hut that lay in the shade of a tamarind tree, the crowd following them. Blair hesitated at the door, seeing he was at the center of a hundred or more villagers, talking excitedly, none of them grieving, and what Blair found odd was that a number of the men were laughing softly among themselves.

The headman began arguing with Maung Mint, U Min chipping in, the Indians sighing in exasperation, some men at the back of the crowd shouting, their cries growing louder.

"It is not safe, sahib," Vasant said. "I have seen such situations become perilous."

"*Thugyi-min* wishes to have ring," Maung Mint said.

"Tell him it's evidence. What can he tell us of Hpo Thin?"

"He is landlord, Sahib."

Seeing that Blair and his men were distracted in the discussion, the crowd pressed forward. The Indians reacted by pushing against the men in front with their batons, as the three Burmese inspectors called to the crowd to be calm.

"Sort yourselves out!" Blair shouted, and when a man stepped in front of him, bumping him, Blair whacked his shoulder with his baton. The man howled, lost his footing and tumbled, and was stepped upon until, protesting, he got to his feet, screaming at Blair.

"We must return to boat," Vasant said, his face gleaming with sweat. "It is becoming mealy, sahib."

Blair said, "Warrior caste, Bunty?"

He turned and as he strode away, roughly shoving several men aside, the crowd drew back—shouting men, shrieking women, gleeful children—making way for the tall English policeman striding toward the riverbank and the boat. But just as he left the last of the crowd, a woman rushed up to him and spat a gout of betel juice on the sleeve of his jacket. He wiped at it, smearing it, making it worse.

"It appears you made a right cock-up of it, Blair," Swann said, when they returned after dark to Myaungmya and the station, Swann brooding by lamplight. Seeing the stained jacket, he sighed. "One doesn't hold a palaver in the middle of a village, attracting the rabble. Breaks down order."

"The headman insisted."

"One does not allow a native to insist."

"Sir."

"See what became of it?"

"Sir?"

"You put yourself within spitting distance, my man."

He turned his back on Blair and left him to lock up. Blair walked to his bungalow, where he was greeted by Poh, but Blair was too dispirited to say anything. He sat in the darkness of the veranda, nursing a whiskey, watching the fireflies winking, until the mosquitoes were too much. He took another drink to his bedroom and lay beneath the mosquito net, sipping it in the dark, thinking, *I cannot put any of this in a letter.* He was weary from the long day, his mind a blank, stifled by the cloud of failure that had settled over it.

• • •

"Duncan's taken the launch to Bassein to confer with the magistrate," Sutherland said the next day. "He'll want to see your report when he's back later in the week. But he left instructions—a wee bambooing for you to see to."

"Bambooing, sir?"

"Caning, lad. As a public school boy—Eton, was it?—you'll be familiar with a thrashing, not so?"

Blair hesitated, annoyed by *public school boy,* and the notion of the brutality of a caning on this hot humid morning oppressed him.

"Beating, not caning at my school," Blair said, to defy him. "Six strokes at the discretion of the beater, usually the captain of the house. But yes, the cane was bamboo."

"Your debut caning—och, sorry, beating!" Sutherland said. "Our opium smuggler. It's scheduled for noon in the wagon shed."

"Understood, sir."

It was not yet eight. Blair sat at his desk and tried to make sense of his visits to the villages, logging the times of the interactions and the results—the pathetic results. He copied and recopied, attempting to create a narrative that yielded some insight into the murder. But all he had was the name of the victim, Hpo Thin, and the fact of his being a landlord; the rest was trivial, the details of the search, the empty day on the river, the singing birds, and onshore being screamed at and spat upon.

"See to the bambooing," Sutherland said, stopping by Bair's office just before noon. "It's twenty of the best. A right schoolie."

The prisoner was spread-eagled, being fastened to the frame of a lashed bamboo gantry as Blair entered the shed, the gantry propped against a large wagon wheel. The man's face was contorted, his eyes widened, his hair wild, and he was naked except for a dirty loincloth. His arms were raised, his wrists having been tied to the extended poles of the gantry. Now, his legs spread, his ankles were bound, and though he could not move his body, he was able to twist his head. He turned his mournful face upon Blair, his eyes bright with anxiety, his lips trembling as though to speak.

"Opium man," a fattish subinspector said, nodding at the prisoner. Blair recognized him from the parade—a Bengali—but could not recall his name, yet he had noticed his paunch pressing against his belt. Today the man was holding a length of bamboo the thickness of a finger.

In his fear the prisoner was looking away from the Bengali, avoiding any sight of the cane in the man's gloved hand. *Like a man with a toothache in a dentist's chair,* Blair thought, *not wishing to see the drill.*

Glancing at his pocket watch in his palm, Blair said to the Bengali, "You may begin."

As the man lifted his cane, allowing it to tremble as he flexed it, Blair gazed at the prisoner's back. He was slender, unmarked, his skin like fine cloth drawn over the bumps of his spine, the nape of his neck blackened by the sun. And in that moment, watching, Blair heard a sharp sound, a smack, like a slapped face, the cane scarcely visible, but in seconds a narrow stripe of blood raised across the prisoner's shoulders, as the man cried out, an animal yell, a sudden bark.

"One," Blair said.

He had seen boys beaten at St. Cyprian's, and at Eton, and he'd been beaten himself, for being late to chapel, for smoking, going out of bounds—to Slough, to Windsor—yet nothing he'd seen at school had prepared him for this, the sadistic slowness of it, the patience of the flogger, the vicious cut like a saber slash, the agony of the man fixed to the gantry, the writhing of his body, his tortured expression, his breathlessness, as though suffocated by the cut. After six stripes, the Bengali grunting with each one, the prisoner was in too much pain to utter anything but a sorrowful gasp.

The man had slumped by the time the last cut broke the skin where the cane had landed, the bamboo cane itself dripping.

"See to his wounds," Blair said. "Unbind him. Discharge him when he's able to walk."

He went to his office and recopied his report for the fourth time and left it in Swann's in tray.

What disturbed him after that was not Swann's severity but his silence—though Blair understood that the man's avoiding him was a form of severity. In the ensuing fortnight, Blair led his men in exercises of the sort he'd learned in Mandalay, and he went on patrol upriver and in the canals and creeks of the tributaries, but he always returned in the evening to his empty bungalow, to eat alone, no sign of Sutherland or Swann, disconcerted by being ignored—or was he being tested?

He'd finished with H. G. Wells, he was reading Jack London now, *Martin Eden*, marveling at the travels, the writing ambition, the fluency. Blair was too demoralized to write a poem, or to finish the one he'd begun on the boat, *The hurrying rat in my room*.

He was relieved at last to be summoned to Swann's office—even a reprimand from the chief was preferable to silence. Blair's report lay before Swann on his blotter, some of the words underlined.

"You may sit," Swann said, and as he tapped the report, Blair folded himself as small as he could in the chair facing him.

"Sir."

"Blair"—still Swann was tapping the report—"you've got as much intuition as an egg."

"Not sure what you mean, sir."

"Landlord," Swann said, putting his finger on an underlined word. "You need to know the type. An angel to the monks and *poongies,* because he gives money to the pagoda, to earn his ticket to heaven. But he's ratty to everyone else. I know the type, you need to study him. An artful bugger, full of shout and swank."

"If I'd had the time, I would have looked deeper. I had a list of history sheeters."

"No, no, Blair! All wrong. A history sheeter would have scarpered with his ring. Study the victim to identify the murderer. What does the victim tell you? That he had position, that he had an enemy. This was not robbery, this was revenge. One of his tenants, at a guess, aggrieved because his rent was increased, or someone evicted for nonpayment. I surmised when we found the body that the murderer was a first timer, all those unnecessary slashes with the dah. A real killer would have scuppered him with one swipe."

"I'll go back, sir."

"Indeed you'll go back. You'll look for the aggrieved party, one of his tenants—there can't be that many. You'll make discreet inquiries, you'll keep your eyes skinned, you'll instruct your men accordingly."

"Yes, sir."

"You're not searching out a dacoit. You're looking for a simple soul, taking his revenge on a landlord with his dah. And I daresay you'll find the weapon, the dah."

"I hope so, sir. Material evidence."

"Upon my word you will. He will still have it. He will be too poor to get rid of it. He'll need it for his work. A dah is only now and then a weapon. The rest of the time it is an essential tool."

Blair returned with his Burmese subinspectors to Moke Soe Kwin, and the villagers hid in their huts seeing them striding to the house of the headman. And as he conferred, with U Min translating the subtler questions, the two other subinspectors roamed the village, making inquiries. The headman was fearful, alone in his house as Blair had insisted, in the presence of the

Englishman, and he agreed that the landlord Hpo Thin had been hard on his tenants. There was one family facing eviction, but the news of Hpo Thin's death had caused them distress—they had mourned him.

"What family?"

"That of Moung Kway U. A poor man."

Moung Kway U was summoned, and while U Min kept him handcuffed in the headman's house his hut was searched, and the dah found, traces of blood still adhering to the cracks in its wooden handle. Moung Kway U was arrested and taken to Myaungmya, shackled, weeping, and confessed his crime.

"I think I've made my point, Blair," Swann said.

And they resumed meeting in the evening, always to drink, often to eat together, sometimes to play the dice game Crown and Anchor. Sutherland chaffed Swann, and Swann told war stories, slipping into furious obscenities when describing its hideous details.

But even engrossed in a war story—"And there we were, shelled to shit by the big Boche guns, the ones we called Farting Fanny"—Swann was alert to Blair's attention, or his wandering gaze. He saw that Blair invariably stared when Mah May refilled his glass or brought him a plate of rice cakes.

One of those evenings, Swann said, "You know, Blair, you can sack that geezer Poh and hire a bint instead—a 'keep,' as we say." The gap in his teeth was dark and strange and mocking as he added, "She'll ply your shoulders with a sponge in your bath."

Blair began to protest and was certain he was blushing.

"Maybe not so canny as a skivvy or a cook," Sutherland said, "but very convenient for a bit of how's-your-father."

UNSENT LETTERS

Another murder was reported, this one at nearby Shan Su Village, another stockade on the river, the rape of a girl of twelve, who was abducted, assaulted, and then strangled, but not before she'd scratched the face of her rapist, a known history sheeter, whom Swann had pursued for two years. Blair and his men spent a week tracking him in the paddy fields and marshes and found him at last at a toddy shop, disguised as a woman, in a pink gaungbaung and soiled *ingyi* blouse, but there was no way he could alter his clawed face. Blair took him, still in his woman's clothes, to Swann, who said, "Good show."

So the killing of the landlord Hpo Thin was forgotten, and his murderer, Moung Kway U, was in the port town of Bassein, awaiting trial, his dah as evidence, his fingerprints on the handle, Hpo Thin's blood on the haft. But Moung Kway U had signed a confession. "Spilled his guts. And we were nae troubled to squeeze it out of him," Sutherland quipped. He'd be hanged, Swann said, leaving a homeless widow and five children. Blair thought, *Like a desperate peasant you might find in Tolstoy, or more likely Gorky.*

Each murder drove out the last, and rape and robbery and toddy-fueled assaults were on the rise, as the Delta days grew hotter.

"Don't brood, laddie," Sutherland called out, and he did not say—but seemed to suspect—that Blair's mood could have been improved if he'd taken Swann's advice and sacked Poh Sim and hired a young woman he could use as a "keep." After all, Blair had seemed to fancy Mah May.

Blair resisted, though he was tempted. Such carnality would seem so obvious and might jeopardize his probation. Besides, Poh Sim—father of six—needed the job. Yet Blair couldn't help but brood, nor could he hide his perplexed face. He regarded the criminals in the Delta as a kind of infection, the contagion of the place taking hold of him. It was not the sad and swampy flatness of Myaungmya that oppressed him—it was something else, something worse, the mournful feeling that he was belowground, underwater, dealing with crimes that occurred as a form of stagnation. The waterways allowed dacoits to slither like snakes from creek to creek and along the canals—the rapist of the small girl had been found miles from his village, at a riverside toddy shop. In this submerged world, civilized life did not exist—it was out of reach, far above the tainted and flooded Delta, where even the air was aqueous.

Seated before Swann in his office, Blair was back at school again, watching the man underlining the reports he'd brought him, swiping at the words he'd written, correcting him—"Say 'slashed,' not 'lacerated.' And 'drunk' has more force than 'inebriated'"—he was like a student seated uneasily before his tutor.

"You're still probationary, Blair," Swann said, sending him out on difficult cases, testing him, smiling grimly but offering little when Blair reported failures or delay. "I'm not interested in excuses," he said. "I'm only interested in a crime solved."

"Very good, sir."

"I need you to know something of crime here, Blair," Swann said. "You hear of a terrible outrage, a village pillaged at night by dacoits, a serious robbery of property, one or two villagers killed, and an old woman tortured for her treasure. And you picture the perpetrators as brutal criminals, lost to all sense of humanity, tigers in human shape—what?" He smiled and showed the gap in his teeth. "And when you come to arrest them—if by good police work you succeed—you find yourself quite mistaken. One or two of the ringleaders might be brutes, but the others are far different. They will be boys or young men led away by the idea of a frolic, allured by the romance of being a freelance for the night, but very sorry now and ready to do all in their power to atone for their misdeeds. Granted it was more common long ago, but nothing has been more striking to me in my years here than the willingness of a criminal to confess."

"In all cases, sir?"

"Not all, no. But I've known many such," Swann said. He became reflective and in his thoughtful silence seemed compassionate. "It is the poor who rob the poor."

Yet what Blair had seen was that rapists fled to distant villages, dacoits vanished downriver, arsonists disappeared in the haze of their own smoke—leaving bleeding women, plundered huts, ashes.

I am not cut out for this, Blair wrote in the letters he decided not to send to his parents, and his life in Myaungmya was a chronicle of unsent letters. And there were letters from home he wished he'd never received—from Jacintha, who dwelled on outings they'd shared, when she was walking together on one of their springtime rambles in the Thames Valley, extolling the bluebells, when all he wanted was to kiss her soft cheek, though he knew it would appall her. Or the unwelcome letters from his mother, more frequent now that he was in a proper post, urging him to visit Moulmein, reminding him of her family there—*Grandmama will be so proud to see you in uniform, and I believe Uncle Frank is still in timber. His daughter, Kathleen, is near to your age.*

It was pressure, and in his unsent replies he said he was too busy for this scattered family in Lower Burma, some of whom had defied custom, married local women and produced half-castes, a breed he now knew were not welcome anywhere and were often mocked.

In the banal and unforthcoming letters he did send he described the bird life, drawing on the lengthening lists he kept from sightings he made on patrol. He remarked on the weather, his meals, his reading, the new uniform he wished to acquire. And without saying why, he vowed to try harder, "to make you proud." But his failures and his muddle showed him just how poor a policeman he was, tall and unmistakable and hopeless.

For Swann, he wrote reports of days spent on the river with his men, on the creeks that fed the river system, on the canals to villages, staying in dak bungalows, interviewing witnesses or victims. They were always reluctant to talk—perhaps intimidated, perhaps hostile, but in any case stubborn— and the result, pages of futile description, the history of another failure, none of it suited for a letter home.

"You claim you couldn't find the weapon, Blair."

"No, sir."

"It was likely sitting there, big as life and twice as ugly. No boy of ten, playing at sleuthing, would have missed it."

"Sir?"

"These are farmers, Blair. A farm implement is a weapon. A spade is a weapon. A common hayfork is a weapon."

Sutherland called from the next room, "Aye, that's the truth. I have known men murdered with a chopstick driven through their lughole—a wee wooden chopstick!"

"I see, sir."

"You see, but you do not observe, Blair. The distinction is clear," Swann said, and Blair hated him for quoting Sherlock Holmes without attribution. "That means—what? That you not only have not identified the blighter, but that he is free to roam and commit more crimes."

"I understand, sir."

"Crimes for which you bear a heavy responsibility." And dismissing him Swann added, "The inspector general will not be pleased."

• • •

Blair was seldom invited as a dinner guest these evenings—evenings plunged into darkness just after six o'clock, hardly relieved by lantern light, and anyway the lamps were magnets for moths and flying ants. After one disastrous night, inattentive at playing Crown and Anchor, he was not included in any more games. He knew he was disliked and probably mocked. All his attempts to ingratiate himself sounded insincere. If they truly knew what was in his heart, they would have disliked him even more, but they were shrewd detectives, who could read the weakness in faces, and the guilt in a man's eyes, and so they probably did know.

To put any of this in a letter home—telling the truth of his situation—was too shaming. Forcing himself to write reminded him of his concealment in writing home from St. Cyprian's and Eton, saying nothing of the beatings or the filthy food or the reprimands—and never mentioning the snobberies, the rich boys describing their father's new motorcar, boasting of holidays, or Flip's Scottish pretensions. And Blair did not reveal to anyone his secret desires—for a woman, for a dog, for a transfer.

When night closed in, the air was still, the surface of the river unruffled—the foliage and the grass along the banks unmoved, as wild ducks streamed to their nests, and crows returned to their haunts, uttering hoarse caws, while flying foxes disengaged themselves from the upper branches of trees and flapped into the darkness in search of fruit. He was struck by the companionship of the wildlife, the flocks of ducks, the sky full of fruit bats.

Blair had no friends. Bhikku the Bengali grocer, with his "Good day to you, sahib," and his presents of Indian sweets, didn't count. Nor did the fishermen on the river with whom he practiced his Burmese. But he was not surprised. Some of the subinspectors sucked up to him, but he'd been warned by Clyne Stewart in Mandalay in training: *As you advance in the police, remember this—you don't become better looking, nor do your jokes become funnier—so beware.* He couldn't in any case be friends with his subordinates; it was bad for discipline, and anyway infra dig. As for fraternizing with his superiors, it simply wasn't done. Swann and Sutherland were cooler to Blair now than when he'd arrived two months ago.

Of course—they knew him better now. Get to know someone well and they end up disliking you, or envying you for your brain, or despising you for your accent or class. That was the pattern in most socializing, discovering people's weaknesses or strengths, and mocking them for it. The absurd snobberies of the Raj made it worse. A common little Scotsman like Sutherland, who'd once let slip that his father was a crofter, made a point of sneering at Blair when he mentioned that he'd known Captain Robinson in Mandalay. Robinson, he said, was well known as a degenerate.

"The bugger was cashiered for poodle-faking," Sutherland said. "Don't want to know him."

"The most disreputable Englishman in Burma," Swann said.

Sutherland, whose wife was far away in the Indian hill station of Naini Tal, who routinely romanced local women, as Swann did his housekeeper; and in his way Swann was also a snob, who longed for an invitation to the governor's mansion, and once let drop as a boast that he'd been part of the security detail at a garden party for the Prince of Wales in Rangoon the previous year.

Blair's secret life, and his release, was reading—Jack London these days, rationing himself to *Martin Eden,* usually five pages a night, ten at most, to prolong the pleasure—and books were scarce. There was no one to share his reading with, but, anyway, he thought, a reader is unsocial, a reader is wounded in some obscure way, a reader hides by burying himself in a book and living through the drama and excitement of the fictional characters, whom he gets to know with more intimacy than any living person. Blair longed for the workday to end, so that he could shut himself up in his bungalow, and smoke, and read. And it sometimes occurred to him that there were readers of books, and the book might be *The Silken East,* and its sensual descriptions of the Burmese people and the landscape, and pages of pretty pictures, that made the readers yearn to be where he was now—the credulous fools.

In the daytime, he welcomed being sent by Swann up and down the muddy river and its stagnant canals, to visit villages, to inquire after the history sheeters, who were usually to be found at local cockfights, the *kyet-tak pwe* that often ended in vicious brawls. The men cheeked him, they defied him, they never cooperated, but at least these inspections kept him away from Swann's scoldings and the dreariness of Myaungmya.

On one of these assignments, at Magwe Village, tucked in a bend in the river, Blair picked up a thief in manacles and delivered him to Bassein for trial, a full day's trip in the launch: down the Ywe River, up the main channel of the Bassein River to the town. En route, the skipper cried out, waking him from his nap, and what he said was at first unintelligible, but later he explained he'd seen a porpoise surfacing in the Irrawaddy.

The thief was chained to a stanchion under an awning, though the sub-inspectors had wanted to leave him to roast in the sun. At Bassein, Blair saw the dock was wide enough, the river deep enough, to accommodate good-size ships, and the town itself was much bigger than he'd imagined, with direct access to the sea. Ships looming over his small motor launch were being loaded with sacks of rice and fat planks of rough-sawn teak logs.

Two of his subinspectors escorted the thief to the police headquarters, while he strode before them. He'd known that Beadon had been assigned to Bassein, but he wasn't sure whether Beadon would meet him—the pedantic and pushy young man hadn't seemed to like him much in training in Mandalay. Yet Beadon was at the station, waiting at the front desk to receive the thief, and he greeted Blair warmly. He was fatter and sunburnt and bluff.

"Well-met," he said, as he'd chucked Blair's elbow. "When this cutpurse is in chokey, let's have a drink."

"This cutpurse," Blair said, mocking the word, "is also charged with grievous bodily harm, with intent, so do prosecute him accordingly."

"As you say, Blair—I well remember your keen grasp of the Penal Code."

Beadon was confident, he had an air of authority, his uniform was in perfect nick, he had the beginnings of the sort of pencil mustache Blair himself wished to cultivate. He seemed years older than the student Blair had known in Mandalay, and it had only been—what?—less than five months since they'd been given their posts. Was it the result of being in Bassein, rather than—as with Blair—stuck in a muddy backwater?

"To the club," Beadon said, after he'd signed in the prisoner, while Blair had watched and smoked. "You can leave your chaps here to cool their heels."

A real club, teak wood paneling and thick beams, a billiard room, a lounge, a punkah wallah squatting in the dining room, yanking his cord, and on the veranda turbaned waiters in white uniforms, with red sashes and cummerbunds, serving cold drinks.

"Ice," Blair said. "I haven't seen ice since Mandalay."

"We get this from Madras. I think it's shipped from America, but greatly diminished en route."

Beadon was greeted by some other policemen, and men in lounge suits he whispered afterward were merchants. He introduced Blair as "one of my fellow sufferers at the fort." Blair, rumpled from the eight-hour boat trip, was abashed by their scrutiny.

Over drinks, Beadon said, "You're looking awfully well, Blair."

But this was insincere—Beadon's bonhomie. Blair knew he looked travel-weary and unkempt, and he felt certain now—the grunted bonhomie seemed proof—that Beadon didn't like him much. And seeing Beadon, his fellow probationary, hearty with his colleagues at the club, he realized how badly he had failed. He'd known that he was struggling in Myaungmya, but he hadn't seen how obvious it was to someone like Beadon. He was cursed by being conspicuous and imagined what the club members were saying about him—"Lofty," perhaps, "scarecrow," scruffy, rag-tailed. He wished he hadn't agreed to the club.

"What I find," Beadon said, "is that one absolutely has to play the game. If one doesn't fit in, one is likely to let the side down."

Beadon saw through him: he knew that Blair was still the misfit he'd been in training. But Blair said, "Quite right," and smoothed his wrinkled lapel. "By the way, got any books?"

A pocket edition of *As You Like It*, some old copies of *Blackwood's*, a stack of the *London Illustrated News,* and after a night in the chummery in Bassein—and no goodbye from Beadon—these Blair took back to Myaungmya. He read the Shakespeare on the way, looking up from time to time for a glimpse of another porpoise, hiding the book (Sutherland would jeer) when they arrived at Myaungmya, this desert inaccessible, under the shade of melancholy boughs.

The heat increased, he was blinded by the glare, the days were worse, more humid and intolerable than ones he'd known in Mandalay; and the nights were stifling inside his airless mosquito net, when he lay awake wondering: *Had I been posted to Bassein, instead of this hole, would I have ended up clubbable and hearty like Beadon?*

It was now late April, which made Blair dread May when he knew it would be hotter, the villagers more idle before planting began, more prone to violence and vicious quarrels, inflamed by drink in places where there were toddy shops but no pagodas.

He sat at his desk at the station, his pen poised over a sheet of paper, intending a letter home. But his head was so filled with thoughts of failure and complaint he did not dare to begin, and got no further than *Dear Mother and Father . . .*

His pen was slippery from his sweaty fingers, a drop of ink at its nib plopping to the empty page, blotting it with a veiny smear.

"Bloody, bloody hole."

On one recce on the river with his men, gasping in the heat of early May, they encountered three men in a sampan, startled by the shouts of Kohli, and who paddled hard to get away. The sampan was intercepted—three dacoits with a sack of loot: silver, Chinese crockery, loose gemstones in a pouch, an elephant's small tusk. The men were seized and manacled and jailed. But the following morning they were gone.

"Absconded," Swann said.

"I specifically instructed my men—"

But Swann interrupted. "Their lapse is your lapse, Blair. I'm writing you up. You can expect to be disciplined."

Night duty was part of his punishment. He didn't mind, though he'd copied a thought from Samuel Butler in his own notebook: "It is seldom very hard to do one's duty when one knows what it is, but it is often exceedingly difficult to find this out." He read copies of *Blackwood's,* always a cracking good story in each issue.

As further punishment, he was ordered to be transferred. It must have been obvious to Swann that Blair wanted to be elsewhere. Now he had his wish.

"You're being assigned to Twante," Swann said—always grinning to display that wide gap in his front teeth when he was especially mocking. "I'm sending you to Oliphant. He's a rum cove. He'll know what to do with you."

Swann and Sutherland saw Blair off; they were smiling, glad to be rid of him, he knew, after four months. But he was happy to go, and liked being on the move, up the river and down the creeks to Wakane, a motorcar to Maubin, and then the river again, narrowing toward the canal at Twante, visible above the embankment a pagoda and a church steeple, and he dared to feel hopeful.

12

OLIPHANT

I say, Oliphant?" Blair called out to the white man onshore, as the crew tossed lines from the deck of the boat to the snatching hands of scrambling dockers.

The white man was nodding absentmindedly as though in vague greeting, his hands shoved into the pockets of his pale drill jacket, his topee tipped back. He was plump and pink, though his face was lined, textured like a biscuit. He stood, feet apart, leaning back in an odd casual posture, as though evaluating Blair. Then he seemed to translate into English what Blair had said, and he laughed.

"Goodness, no," he said, tittering—a wheezy *hee-hee-hee*. "You'll find Neville at the station, or I bet"—he pulled a gold watch from a fob pocket of his waistcoat and studied it in his palm—"as he's mighty punctual, at his house. Gorgeous house."

The voice was American, and its weird twang—mimicking bog Irish—caused Blair to smile, as if he was hearing a sour note from a small instrument, a penny whistle or an untuned flute. And as Blair stepped to the dock he saw the stains on the man's jacket, the unbuttoned waistcoat, the baggy trousers, the dusty shoes. The man's lined face seemed another feature of his untidiness, and yet he was uncommonly friendly.

"Give you some help with that stuff?"

"My chaps will see to the clobber."

"Grover Albee," the man said, putting out his hand.

Blair was flustered for a moment by that insistently reaching hand—Americans shook hands. Blair fumbled for a moment, grasping air, then tentatively raised his hand and the man snatched it and squeezed and pulled with hot damp fingers in a grip that startled him.

"Do you live here, Mr.—"

"Reverend Albee—yes, at the Baptist church. I'm the missionary. Happened to be lollygagging here, waiting for the mailboat from Rangoon. Darn thing's always late."

"Not much happens on time in Burma."

"Oliphant happens on time," he said, and he emitted another wheezy laugh.

"He's the man I'd hoped—"

"You the new Drummond?"

Was that another American trait—interruption?

"I'm so sorry, I don't follow."

"Sergeant Drummond—he's the fellow that just left on transfer. Lovely man, very efficient, quite a crime buster. Assigned to Maymyo, lucky dog—nice cool place. Hot as the dickens here, especially now."

"Apparently I'm the new Drummond," Blair said. He smiled again at the man, grateful for his talk, his greeting that was boyish and unaffected, a welcome that seemed genuine, though the damp handshake still lingered on Blair's fingers, fluttering to dry.

"That there's the pagoda," Albee said, seeing Blair staring past him to the town beyond what was perhaps a maidan. "Supposed to be real old. And kind of a humdinger—pilgrims come from all over to see it."

"The Shwesandaw."

"You read up on it?"

"It's mentioned in Murray's *Guide*. It's said that a hair of Buddha—"

"Oh, sure, but you won't be welcome there. I'll tell you where you will be welcome." Now the man drew near to Blair and poked the lapels of his tunic, expelling sour breath in Blair's face with each word. "Baptist church. We'll throw the doors open for you. And like I tell people here, you won't have to take off your darn shoes!"

"Fancy that," Blair said, and now he backed away, wishing to accompany the men who'd loaded the luggage, squatting in the shade of the cart.

In the space of a few minutes, the man was a stranger, then a friend, then a bore, perhaps the definition of an American, and speaking with him Blair felt more English, prissily so, hearing himself and his plummy accent, in a way he hated.

"Many heathens here have declared themselves for Christ."

"I daresay—"

"What have you got to gain?" the man said, following Blair to the luggage cart. "Nothing less than a wonderful thing called eternal life. You will be saved, my friend."

"I really must go."

The man put his hand out again to initiate another handshake, but Blair's palm was sticky from the last one, and he shrank, though he returned the man's smile.

Following the coolie who pulled the cart, and the two uniformed Indians on either side as escorts, Blair was reminded of his arrival in Myaungmya, the trundling, the dog, the stony road, Sutherland and Swann, to adjust to new circumstances, and that too was like going from school to school. It annoyed him to have to stay behind the slow-moving cart, kicking along. He would have preferred to stride ahead, except he had no idea where he was going.

The gold pagoda, symmetrical and stately, dominated the town, with the usual elegant spearpoint finial, and the town itself was much larger than Myaungmya, rows of shops, lamps burning inside several of them, and some activity even on this late afternoon, native women strolling—their elegant clothes, their beautiful posture—and framed in the archway of an arcade a man toiling at a sewing machine.

"Station, sahib," one of the escorts said, pointing to a squat cream-colored building on a mound in the distance—the only high ground Blair could see. The roof was tiled, the walls plastered, and its solidity gave it the look of a tomb structure that might house the vaults for a wealthy family. In contrast, the church a little distance away was made of weathered wood, with a tin roof blackened by scabby lichens, and its undersize steeple surmounted by a rusted cross: a sign in front was lettered First Baptist Church Twante—Reverend Albee's church.

The land was as dead flat as Myaungmya but less swampy, seemingly less pestilential, and though Blair had passed paddy fields on either side of the canal on his way here, none were visible from the town. He saw banana groves, and stands of palms, and some small trees he could not name, but the most pervasive feature was the muddy smell of the canal that seemed palpable, like a brown cloud, and penetrated the town and dirtied the air.

Before they reached the station, the men stopped in front of a house upraised on poles, much like the one he'd left in Myaungmya. He was heartened to see chickens and ducks fussing beneath it, and a cat yawning at the foot of the stairs, a kind of welcome.

"Your quarters, sahib."

"Where is the superintendent?"

"That side, sahib, big house."

"He's not at the station now?"

"Past five o'clock—now home."

Blair was vaguely put out that he hadn't been properly met—he'd expected some sort of formal greeting, and the offhand banter of the disheveled American made it somehow worse and more offensive.

"I expect I'll meet the superintendent later."

"Tomorrow, morning time—seven o'clock," the man said. "Staff inspection. Seven thirty, parade. Then assignment to cases. Eight o'clock, welcome and briefing, with tea."

"You know this?"

"I have all particulars, sahib."

It seemed oddly formal and remote, suggesting the superintendent a stickler for punctuality and good order, rather ominous to Blair. And there was the uncertainty of the night ahead in his bungalow—what food, what drink, how to fill the hours between now and bedtime—and where was the bed?—a new boy again.

"Those chickens."

"They were Drummond sahib's."

"And the ducks and the cat?"

"Sahib could not convey them to Maymyo."

Now Blair saw at the top of the stairs a woman standing erect, her hands clasped before her pale fox face in the prayerful Burmese greeting, then she placed both her hands on her stomach and bowed. She wore a green lungyi that brushed her ankles, a white blouse, a yellow headscarf, and she was staring with fearful eyes, as though awaiting a command, a slight twitch in the folds of her lungyi, perhaps her trembling knees.

"That is Mah Poo, sahib. She was also Drummond sahib's."

"*Kyun?*" Blair said, wishing to be clear. Servant?

"*Aain-hpa,* sahib."

"Housemaid," Blair said.

"Exactly, sahib."

Blair sighed and mounted the stairs toward her, suppressing a grateful smile, as Mah Poo shikoed low as though wishing to conceal her face.

Exhausted from the long day of travel through the Delta, Blair reclined on a deck chair on the veranda and stretched his legs, smoking a cigarette, preparing himself to look further into this agreeable house. It was surrounded by what he knew to be peepul trees, and frangipanis in bloom, the path lined with coconut palms, and he watched with delight the chickens flying to the boughs of the trees, fussing and flapping, to roost for the night.

Seeing the cat's implacable face as it mounted the stairs to the top step he made a kissing sound, and it approached, first sidling against the chair and purring softly. He lifted it and stroked it and was consoled by its purr bubbling in its throat, as it settled on his lap, warming his thighs. The last of the light was slipping from the sky, the gleam of a sliver sword blade of sunset sinking beneath the canal. He felt contented, but could not say why, just a vagrant mood, like a sense of good health and pleasant fatigue, a kind of languor that promised good sleep.

Then a whisper, just a breath. "Food for the sahib."

He did not see the whisperer, she was gone as soon as he got up and turned to look, the cat startled, leaping to the floor. A lamp burned inside at the center of the table, a bowl of chicken and rice on a place mat, a bottle of beer standing on a small white saucer next to an empty tumbler, a round tray near the lamp, a jar of mustard, bottles of Worcester sauce and Branston pickle, a pot of marmalade, a pepper mill, a small dish of salt, a cup of toothpicks—Drummond's condiments.

The cat remained under his chair mewling until Blair dropped a small piece of chicken.

"Now are you happy, muggins?"

In the morning, Blair woke to find a cup of tea on his nightstand, the tin tub in the bathroom half filled with warm water, his uniform pressed and hung up in the wardrobe. After he bathed and dressed, a plate of eggs and bacon on the dining table, a rack of toast, a dish of butter.

More of Drummond: Drummond's house, Drummond's cat, Drummond's chair and bed, and Drummond's housemaid—though she remained hidden; and after Blair left the house for the station, and was walking past the row of palms, he glanced back, but he was not sure whether that small pale presence at the window was the woman or the cat.

There followed a sequence of delays—delays for Blair, duties for Oliphant. "Superintendent sahib is reading his post," was the first, relayed by an Indian in uniform, who showed Blair his office, a map of Burma on one wall, a chart of Twante District on the opposite wall, a portrait of the king behind his desk, and a faded print of British soldiers attacking naked Burmese inside a fort, dated 1824. Blair sat and opened the desk drawer—pencils, headed notepaper, a candle, matches. He heard down the hall the subinspectors being briefed in Oliphant's office, but as he had not been introduced and was only guessing at the voice—which was plummy—he remained in his office, fretting over a blank sheet of government notepaper.

"Superintendent is at tiffin." The same Indian, two hours later.

"Your name?"

"Inspector Mirza Khan, sahib."

"Does the superintendent know I have arrived?"

"He is knowing, sahib."

Invisible housemaid, invisible superintendent.

"Please bring me the pending cases. And tea."

Within minutes, the inspector placed a fat yellow file on Blair's desk, the file bound with faded green ribbon.

"Some in process, some unsolved," he said, pouring Blair a cup of tea.

"And empty this ashtray."

"I will have chokra do so, sahib."

Ah, yes, an inspector might pour tea but was too grand to empty ashtrays.

Blair opened the file and sorted the documents into stacks—criminal cases, civil cases, and the sizable number marked *Unsolved*.

"Superintendent taking tea," the inspector said, sometime later.

Blair looked up from the papers scattered on his desk but said nothing.

And at the end of the afternoon—in the stillness and shadow, the heat in his office unbroken by any breeze from the open window—Blair returned the cases to the file folder and retied it. He was pondering the list he'd made on a sheet of foolscap, under headings, *Rape, Murder, Arson, Dacoity, Theft, Assault,* when there was a soft tap at his door. He sighed, expecting Mirza Khan again, but it was a small slender Englishman, smiling at Blair, then at the desk.

"Oh, excellent," he said. "Initiative. That's a promising start."

Blair had risen at the man's entrance and stepped from behind the desk, peering down at the man's head, his smooth slicked-down hair, neatly parted.

"Blair," the man said and stepped aside, shifting his gaze to the paper on the desk, saying, "A healthy little docket, to keep you on your toes."

"I'd hoped we might discuss them."

Instead of replying at once, the man shot out his arm and tapped his wristwatch.

"It's gone five. I'm off duty. We'll confer in the morning."

Superintendent Neville Oliphant's black slicked-down hair made his pale face paler, almost ivory, and his lips seemed redder in that pallor, though his eyes were deep blue, and he gave the impression of someone acting in a play, the precisely enunciated lines, the business with his thrust-out arm and his finger tap on the face of his gold wristwatch, and even his smart about-face as he left, as though on cue, "Exit, Stage Left."

Another night in the humidity of the hot house, moths fluttering at the lamp, Samuel Butler's *Notebooks* lying open next to Blair's plate, the cat purring beneath his chair, and after that, in bed under the mosquito net, in the dark, wondering about the invisible housemaid, the evasive superintendent, and thought, as he often did, *What am I doing here?* And much else he could not put into a letter.

• • •

"I gather you met our American," Oliphant said the next morning, greeting him as Blair strode toward him on the rising path to the station—the plaster bungalow newly painted, the Union Jack limp on the flagpole.

The man stood at attention, as he had the previous afternoon in Blair's office, as though reviewing his progress up the path, causing Blair to shorten his stride and straighten his shoulders.

He felt awkward, because he felt that Oliphant was finely made, his uniform faultless and close-fitting, his belt and boots gleaming, his buttons polished, the brass like gold. His pale face was pinched, his hair combed flat against his head, slicked sideways, a white strip of his scalp showing in his parting, and now Blair saw what he had missed before, his pencil mustache, thinner than Beadon's, just a shadow on his upper lip, and freshly shaven he seemed almost boyish. His spruce appearance caused Blair to despair of his own.

"The American Albee, I believe?"

"Reverend Albee, our missionary," Oliphant said. "He's been here some little time. He'd previously saved souls in Mandalay, but of course Twante is quite another pair of shoes. He won't last. Americans never do. He's a desperate bore, and did you mark his tessellated face?"

Blair smiled, grateful for the satire, but Oliphant was still talking.

"I love Americans. What a blessing it is that they never talk English. Albee was all right when he arrived, but he's become desperately whiffy."

With that, Oliphant turned to the entrance—the inspector Mirza Khan snatching the door open for him—and he led the way to Blair's office, where the list of unsolved crimes lay on the blotter where Blair had left it.

"Please do seat yourself," Oliphant said, standing. "Notice Drummond's attempt to prettify this room, as evidenced by that fractured vase, that mildewed print of Rangoon." He went closer, reading the caption, "'Storming of one of the principal stockades'—our glorious warriors, handsomely kitted out in scarlet tunics and stylish shakos, firing flintlocks at natives in loincloths flourishing fearsome sticks and dahs. That was a century ago, Blair, the First Burma War—we've come a long way. The Burmese are better dressed for one thing. Oh, yes, the maps are government issue, as is the portrait of His Majesty."

Blair sat hunched forward, anxious. From the name, he'd expected Oliphant to be a big blimpish copper, heavily mustached like Sholto Haggan, brandishing a swagger stick, bullying in manner, laying down the law. As on the day before, he was surprised to find a smallish, somewhat delicate officer, almost exquisite, bordering on an aesthete, with a hint of hauteur in his speech, oddly pale for someone in a sunny tropical backwater.

The neat uniform and belts caused Blair to glance at his own, seeing his ill-fitting jacket too tight in the shoulders, his trousers too loose at the knees, his boots dusty from his morning walk across the unkempt maidan to the station. If Oliphant noticed he didn't say anything, but Blair knew, he'd known from his arrival in the country, the chief characteristic of the police: they were watchful, nothing was overlooked.

"That chart with all the waterways," Oliphant said. "That's our district—two hundred lakhs of natives to supervise, and a crore of headaches. Many are dacoits, the rest are paddy farmers or monks. I daresay you had monks in Myaungmya?"

"A fair amount, sir."

"You will have been schooled by the estimable Swann—frightfully good value. He had an excellent war. Sutherland—another matter altogether, a bit of a lout."

Oliphant pointed at the chart again, revolving his finger, a slender well-manicured finger.

"You see our district greatly resembles a tea cozy in repose on a tea tray, given its shape by these two tributaries of the Irrawaddy. That singular stripe is the canal, the bobble on top is the confluence of the rivers. Heaving with dacoits." He rapped a knuckle against one corner. "We are here, on the finely knitted brim." Another rap. "The pagoda located here."

"Said to be very holy, sir."

"Wholly"—Oliphant shaped his lips like a chorister—"wholly infested with miscreants. The abbot, the soi-disant *sayadaw* one of the worst." He turned to face Blair, squinting as though with a slight pain. "Gives me the pip."

"What I find queer," Blair said, "is I was always led to believe that Buddhist monks were the souls of piety."

"Many are, others are naughty, with their hands in plackets, and some are bolshie, and quite a few are wicked—that abbot an example, with his well-known sedition."

"Would I have heard of him?"

"Sayadaw Ashin Wirathu, a noted rabble-rouser and scamp."

"Pamphlets? Broadsides?"

"Even given the lightly furnished state of his mind, Wirathu is too clever to commit himself to print, and anyway the rabble can't read. It's his strenuous preaching. He denounces our dear king. He's superb in his effrontery."

Oliphant indicated the paper on Blair's desk. "I want him on your docket—right at the top."

"Yes, sir."

"And his odious troop of monks, tricked out with oaths and chants and robes, uttering menaces."

"Understood, sir." He poised his pencil and then began, speaking as he wrote. "Ashin Wirathu."

"In the past, you'd be able to quiet him with a couple in the ribs with your truncheon," Oliphant said. "But the law is a more efficient truncheon. You're aware of that section of the Penal Code, Blair?"

"One twenty-four A," Blair said. "Offenses against the state. Whoever by words, either spoken or written, or by signs, or by visible representation, or otherwise brings or attempts to bring into hatred or contempt to excite disaffection toward His Majesty, shall be punished, et cetera."

"Punishment?"

"Shall be punished by imprisonment for life."

"Full marks, Blair! That was said to be drafted by Thomas Babington Macauley. I think we can use it against this talkative abbot Wirathu. If we don't and he continues, we're likely to have an uprising on our hands, one of these"—and he tapped the old framed print of the redcoats firing upon the naked, gray natives in the wooden stockade.

"Seems a wicked one."

Oliphant raised his arms. "Who shall deliver me from this turbulent priest?"

Another stagey line, but Blair said, "I'll see to it, sir."

"Drummond was making some headway, but for his sins he was posted to Maymyo."

More Drummond, Blair thought.

"Your subinspector, Mirza Khan, will fill you in. As for housekeeping, all receipts and official communications are to be answered the same day, and all documents filed before the end of the day. This"—he tapped the docket list of crimes—"is not to be left on your desk overnight. No loose ends. I'll leave you to get on with it."

He nodded, just a tip of his head, and left Blair's office.

No loose ends, Blair thought. *All I know are loose ends.*

The rest of the day, and the whole of the following day, Blair spent discussing tactics with Mirza Khan, and he made and memorized a list of all the other subinspectors' names—most of them Indian, about a third Burmese. He found Drummond's dossier on the seditious abbot, Ashin

Wirathu, and to show Oliphant he was at work, he resolved to make some arrests.

On his third night at his bungalow Blair found his housemaid bent over his tin tub, filling it with a bucket of water. She was so startled by his greeting at the bathroom door, she stumbled as she stood erect and jogged the bucket, slopping water on her blouse. The water dripped darkening her lungyi, but her blouse was made transparent, as she stood hugging the bucket, watching Blair, her eyes bright with fear, her soaked clothes clinging to her body.

"*Thakin,*" she said. And then, "Master."

But, flustered, blushing, Blair quickly stepped away.

13

THE TURBULENT PRIEST

I t was a test, another test; he'd have to prove himself again, in the way being a prefect at Eton—in Pop—was a test of responsibility, not simply giving orders but making sure they were obeyed. Power didn't necessarily corrupt you and turn you into a tyrant; power was a challenge, a test of character, and if you didn't achieve the desired result, not to be feared but to be respected, you were a failure. What Blair had come to despair of in Burma were natives backing away from him, with a look of hatred or fear in their eyes—it made him hate himself. And he was only a half-made policeman, still on probation after sixteen months in the country, in suspense, needing to prove he measured up in this beastly job, this dreary town by the stinking canal, answerable to the popinjay Oliphant.

In the days following Oliphant's injunction to investigate and record the seditious utterances of Sayadaw Wirathu at Shwesandaw Pagoda, Blair met with his inspectors, much as he'd once met at Eton with his fellow prefects, to locate a troublemaker. It occurred to him that at Eton the most effective way of dealing with a pest was to recruit an informer: a willing snitch in a lower form.

"Tattletale," Mirza Khan said. "We must gain access to preaching. We will take note of his treacheries."

The other inspectors, Krishna Kumar Mitra and Roop Singh, agreed. Krishna Kumar said, "We will form team. We will gain by stealth."

"Too obvious—Indians at a Buddhist palaver. Even I know you're not welcome. The word is that he preaches in the courtyard behind the pagoda, adjacent to the monastery. Have any of you actually been there?"

"In point of actual fact, sahib," Mirza Khan said, and then with throat clearings and tugging his beard he began to waffle vehemently, repeating the word *footwear*.

"I need a straight answer," Blair said, "and your answer appears to be no. That you know fuck all about the goings-on at the pagoda and any possible offenses regarding public order or exciting disaffection toward His Majesty."

"Put one of our Burmese chaps on the case, sahib," Roop Singh said.

Blair hesitated to as whether a Burmese inspector's heart would be in such a scheme to betray an abbot, with a large following, who was both beloved and feared.

"Employ bribe," Krishna Kumar said. "Novice monks are penurious and desirous of baksheesh."

The others chimed in, advocating baksheesh, as Blair reflected: Who would be the likeliest candidate to gather incriminating statements of the seditious abbot—someone reliable and passionate, motivated by moral outrage and an inner drive to bring the man to be charge-sheeted? As the subinspectors muttered among themselves, Blair imagined the ideal spy, concealed in a crowd of the abbot's followers, someone intelligent and Burmese, but loyal to the Raj, deeply offended by such dangerous heresies.

"A Christian," Blair said, bringing his teeth down on the word.

The word hung in the air and silenced the room, which seemed hotter in silence, the subinspectors smiling at the faint echo—now a familiar smile to Blair. He'd seen it in Mandalay among some Indian cadets, and really it was not a smile at all, but a sneer of contempt for credulous and superstitious believers in the Bible, the tainted mob, despised by Hindus for their subversion.

"Ample of such in Twante, sahib," Krishna Kumar said. "Christian people."

That same afternoon, feeling purposeful, wishing to have something to report to Oliphant, Blair walked to the Baptist church, a weathered wood structure, a bungalow converted to a chapel by the addition of a slatted wood steeple, with a rusted cross on top, severe in its simplicity, facing the maidan. Just behind it was Albee's house, boxlike, flat on the ground, which might once have been a paddock. The front door was ajar.

Blair knocked, then called out, and hearing no response, he poked the door open wider and saw Albee asleep on a sofa. The floor was littered with newspapers, some rags that might have been discarded clothes, an overturned bowl, a soiled spoon. Albee lay in his shirtsleeves, his shirtfront unbuttoned and open to his undervest, his trousers rucked up to his plump calves, fish-belly white, though he was still wearing his shoes.

Albee smacked his lips in sleep, as though dreaming of food, while Blair beheld him, marveling at the squalor, the scattered objects, the clutter of paper, the hot wheezing man, glowing with perspiration.

"Sorry!" Blair said, then coughed, to announce himself.

Now a fretful servant appeared with a cup and saucer in a tray, and he too grunted a greeting, yet even so Albee slept on. The servant became agitated, backing away at the sight of the uniformed sahib, a policeman standing over Albee, and he bobbled the tray. When the cup and saucer smashed among the litter Albee awoke, still somehow chewing, focusing on Blair.

"Resting my eyes," Albee said, yawning.

"I don't mean to intrude."

The servant was on his knees, picking broken fragments of china from the litter and placing them on the tin tray. But Albee merely smiled, as though this was nothing unusual, like a man watching his small child at play on the floor.

"I have a request to make."

"Take a chair," Albee said, and yawned. "I'm all ears. Is it something your boss wants?"

"Why do you ask?"

"He's snooty."

Blair remembered: *He's whiffy.*

"I'm looking for a good Christian," Blair said, and as he explained his need for someone to report on the seditious speeches of the *sayadaw,* he was overcome by the smell of stale food, of dust, of unwashed laundry, and the human smell, which was the most offensive, the pong of a malodorous man, that clotted the air.

"What's a *sayadaw*?"

"An abbot."

Albee yawned again and wiped his mouth with the back of his hand, and Blair imagined that the man's expelled breath fouled the air further.

"My sexton," Albee said.

"I'd like to meet him."

"Why, that's him right there on the floor." Albee leaned over and tapped the kneeling servant on his shoulder. The man winced at the touch. He had just about finished gathering the remaining shards of china. He got to his feet and bowed, holding the tray of broken china like an offering.

"*Min-ga-la-ba khin-bah,*" Blair said in greeting.

"Wow," Albee said.

"Good day to you," the servant said, slowly, nodding with each word. "I am quite well, *thakin*. Thanks be to God."

He was Burmese—a Karen, he was pious, he was reliable, Albee said, emphasizing that like many in his congregation, probably all, he was very pro-British. The sexton was small, but wiry, and though an older man—

gray hairs showing at the sides of his head wrapping—he stood straight and kept his gaze on Blair, as though awaiting an order.

"I am Simon Sin Kwa, *thakin*."

"Picked him because he speaks good English," Albee said.

"I am reading and writing as well, sahib," Sin Kwa said.

"Writes up the hymn numbers and names on the chalkboard in the chapel," Albee said. "Saves me tons of time."

Blair questioned the man. His replies were forceful. Yes, he knew the *sayadaw*; yes, he was aware that the monk made speeches against the British.

"Wirathu is the devil," Sin Kwa said.

Albee shouted his approval at this and got to his feet, hitching up his trousers, and beaming—a teacher's pride for a prize student. Only when Albee chucked the man on his shoulder did Sin Kwa recoil, the Burmese hatred of being touched that Blair now understood. But Blair stepped back, forcing himself to glower, so that he wouldn't explode in laughter at the contrast between the two men—the small skinny Burmese standing at attention in his neat white shirt, his elegantly wrapped gaungbaung and purple lungyi, his hands folded before him. And beside him, the big pink American in his sweat-stained shirt and rucked-up trousers, unshaven, his hair wild, sighing in fatigue.

"I'll send along a copybook," Blair said. "Go to the meetings, listen well, write down everything you hear from Sayadaw Wirathu."

"Yes, sahib."

As Blair turned to go, Albee grasped his sleeve—what was it about this man, tapping him, squeezing his fingers in a sweaty handshake, and now snatching at his arm? Were all Americans like this, poking and prodding?

"Listen, I want you to promise me you'll come to a service," Albee said. "How about this Sunday?"

"Of course—I'd be delighted to," Blair said, stepping away, disengaging his arm from Albee's tugging hand.

Oliphant discouraged interruptions, he welcomed memoranda. Blair wrote a proposal, stating his intention to form an antisedition unit, seconding one Burmese informant from the community, who would report on the *sayadaw*'s speeches and outlining his approach, listing the members of his team, naming his subinspectors, Indians rather than Burmese. He passed this in a sealed envelope to the station secretary, Chunder Dass, who delivered it to Oliphant. At the end of the day, Blair received an envelope, his memo acknowledged with Oliphant's initials, in black ink, thick-nibbed, as elaborate and as imperious as a monogram.

Invisible Oliphant, invisible Mah Poo, and the conspicuous Albee. Restless, feeling untethered, needing a tangible success, Blair ordered Mirza Khan to organize a series of tours of the district, beginning with the canal-side villages but touching each corner of the triangular tea-cozy map. They set off, traveling by boat from dak bungalow to dak bungalow, stopping en route at small villages—paddy farmers, fishermen—noting grievances and recent crimes, conferring with headmen. Theft was common, so was rape and assault—Blair listened, while his subinspectors took notes, and each night Blair logged his interviews and enlarged his report.

What made the canal survey pleasant was his reliable staff, the conscientious subinspectors, the cook, and the way the bearers converted each dak bungalow into a comfortable billet. And because of the diligence of his men, Blair was able to make arrests, bringing dacoits and rapists back to Twante, handcuffed and in leg irons, as trophies, to earn Oliphant's approval.

Weeks of this, past his twenty-first birthday in June that he celebrated alone, and into July, the heat lessening but the air dense with humidity and always the mud-stink of the canal. But he was away from his dreary desk and his stifling office, and at last pleased to think that he was older now, and doing his job and making arrests. In this mood of satisfaction, Blair attended one of Albee's church services. It was more than putting in an appearance—he wished to talk to the sexton, Sin Kwa, to find out whether the man had kept his word to attend the meetings of the *sayadaw* Wirathu and make a record of his seditious utterances.

Arriving early at the church, Blair saw no sign of Albee, but Sin Kwa was busy setting out hymnals on the pews.

"Uncle," Sin Kwa said, pausing and standing to attention, a stack of hymnals in his hands.

Blair went close to him and inclined his head. "Are you making progress?"

"Yes, uncle. I can fetch my work."

The sexton called to some small boys to finish setting out the hymnals and hurried to find the copybook Blair had given him.

"I am needing new copybook, uncle."

The copybook was fattened by closely printed pages of Sin Kwa's orderly handwriting, in looped and rounded Burmese script, and on facing pages verbatim accounts in English of the *sayadaw*'s speeches, each entry meticulously annotated with dates and times.

Blair leafed through the copybook during a service in a back pew of the church, while a Burmese priest in Baptist robes, the *hpongyi*, sermonized and led the congregation in hymns. Albee, in a black gown, clutching a bible, sat in a thronelike chair at the side of the altar, smiling, and when he saw Blair at the back he waved in welcome.

"I'll take this," Blair said to Sin Kwa after the service, as he held the copybook. "I'll arrange to have another sent over to you."

"The man is a devil," Sin Kwa said.

Just then, at the church door, seeing members of the congregation bowing to Albee in a ritual of thanking the preacher, Blair saw a lovely young woman making a deep bow. She looked familiar. It was Mah Poo.

He watched her, as he spoke with the sexton, a little distance from the church as she accepted Albee's blessing, and then starting away, she saw Blair with the sexton and smiled. And that evening he used that smile at the church as an excuse to speak to her. He'd been in Twante now almost six weeks, and apart from a few clumsy encounters—the most memorable one, the soaked blouse—Mah Poo had been invisible, or simply a shadow, a face at the window, serving him Drummond's meals, Drummond's drinks, drawing Drummond's bath.

But discovering each other at the church seemed to soften the mood of their relationship. She did not withdraw when he approached her. She seemed to be reassured by his appearance at the Sunday service. His had been the only white face in the congregation, a full head taller than anyone else.

"Mah Poo," he said.

"My name Margaret."

She smiled when Blair asked how old she was. She didn't know, she finally said. He guessed she was about his own age. Her village was Kway Lay Gyi, half a day downstream. She said she had worked for Drummond Sahib for almost a year. After more questions she simply demurred—she smiled, then lowered her gaze, and didn't answer. She was reluctant, not in an anxious way, more in a manner that reminded Blair of a coquette, not shy but oblique, keeping whatever secrets she had to herself. Or was it something simpler, the reticence of an employee—a servant—faced with the master's scrutiny, using the only power she had, her silence? He was sure of one thing—she was not afraid of him, she was perhaps testing him.

Some weeks later, a memo on Blair's desk one morning—*What progress with our friend?* and the initials, that monogram NO—caused Blair to fret. He had not heard from Sin Kwa since the church service; he had failed to keep tabs on the man. For all Blair knew, he had done nothing with the new copybook, but in any case, Blair had no answer to Oliphant's test question.

The sexton Sin Kwa was sweeping the floor of the chapel when Blair visited. Sin Kwa dropped his broom and welcomed Blair with clasped hands as Blair opened the chapel door.

At first Blair resisted the man's fumbling hands, but then greeted him in Burmese.

"Very well, uncle," Sin Kwa said. "Thank you for visiting our sanctuary. Shall I fetch the missionary?"

"I want to see you," Blair said, was impressed by the neatness and simplicity of the chapel, in great contrast to the squalor of Albee's bungalow.

"I am at your service, uncle."

"What progress with our friend?"

"He is not our friend, uncle."

"Have you anything to report?"

"I have been to the pagoda four times. Please wait here one moment. I will fetch the second copybook."

Sin Kwa propped the broom against a pew and hurried away. Blair stepped outside to smoke a cigarette, but the man was back before he'd taken three puffs.

"It is cooler in here," Sin Kwa said.

Blair ground the cigarette under his boot and joined Sin Kwa in a back pew, gladdened to see thickened pages of the second copybook, fuller than the first one, the neat handwriting on the right-hand page, Burmese script on the left. Sin Kwa began turning pages slowly.

Blair asked, "What's that word 'deer'?"

"The *sayadaw* compares Buddha to the British," Sin Kwa said. "Buddha gave his sermon at Sarnath, in the deer park, where the deer are unmolested. The deer represent happiness and harmony. The *sayadaw* spoke about the deer in Burma."

"I've seen some. What's his point?"

"We have four deer—the golden one, Shwe Thamin. The Sat—sambar deer. The che—muntjac deer. The hog deer—da-yae."

"What exactly did Wirathu say about them?"

"I have written it here. 'The British do not respect the deer. They molest them. They kill them. They eat them. They treat Burmese people like animals.' He says we are made to work for them, we are despised like animals, we are killed with impunity. And"—Sin Kwa turned the page—"the British people came to our paradise of fine weather and flowers and kind people and became owners. They are masters, we are slaves."

"Good, good," Blair said. "This is very helpful."

"It is not good, sahib. Sayadaw Wirathu is preaching against the British people. There is much more in these pages."

"It is good evidence," Blair said. "You're doing fine work."

"Thank you, uncle."

"How often does the *sayadaw* speak at the pagoda?"

"Saturdays, just at nightfall. But Saturday is a busy day for Reverend, Uncle Albee. He writes his sermon on that day, and I must assist with the Burmese language. That is why I have only managed to visit the pagoda four times."

"So there will be a show this Saturday at the pagoda?"

"It is so, uncle."

"I should like to hear him speak."

Sin Kwa closed the copybook and became silent, looking down, and in the pew could have been mistaken for a man absorbed in prayer, possessed by piety.

In a soft voice, he said, "The people are unruly, uncle. They go hither and thither. They make mischief."

"I'm a policeman!" Blair said, angered by the suggestion that he should avoid the pagoda because of its disorder and mischief. He wanted to say that his role was to correct such conditions.

Sin Kwa clutched at his notebook, as Blair stood up, casting a shadow over the small man cowering beneath him.

"I will be there this Saturday."

"Yes, uncle."

"You can keep that copybook for now. I'll pick it up some other time."

"Yes, uncle."

The next morning, Wednesday, Blair arrived at the station as Oliphant walked briskly ahead of him, and at the station entrance, with Mirza Khan opening the front door, Blair said, "I have the *sayadaw* in hand, sir. I'm paying a visit to the pagoda this Saturday."

"Jolly good," Oliphant said. "You'll want to keep your head well down. No need to make an arrest or"—he raised an eyebrow—"to lapse into discourtesy."

In the following days Blair debated bringing the Indian subinspectors, but he rejected the idea for their being too conspicuous; the Burmese he feared would be unreliable. He would therefore go alone, as a witness to Sin Kwa, to lend credence to the sedition outlined in the copybook.

On Saturday, Blair set off just at sunset, walking across the scrub the locals called the maidan—but it was stony and useless for games—and approaching the pagoda he sensed eyes on him, heard whispers, a vibration of curiosity from people in the road. At the entrance to the pagoda itself worshippers stepped aside as he made his way to the rear courtyard, where he heard a loud voice declaiming in Burmese, snarls of indignation.

The place was illuminated by Chinese lanterns strung on wires, small candles burning within them, the paper globes giving the effect of a festival, with their color and light. The crowd was mostly men, all of them standing, a knot of women in one corner of the courtyard, the saffron-robed *sayadaw* seated on a platform above them, cross-legged, flanked by two small pinch-faced boys, each one holding a large circular fan of rattan and rosy silk, attached to a pole that they swept back and forth. Before him a row of monks, their heads bowed, were also seated, but on broad steps at a lower level.

In an attempt to be inconspicuous, Blair kept to the rear of the crowd, yet he was keenly aware of being noticed as he entered the courtyard—for being a white man, for his uniform, for his height. Nearby men in lungyis and some in robes edged away from him, muttering, isolating him, and Blair felt all his old awkwardness of being the tallest man in the room. The head monk looked across the heads wrapped in cloth, to Blair in his policeman's cap.

"The British have made Burma a prison," Wirathu shouted in Burmese— his voice had risen as Blair's presence had become obvious, the tall pale Englishman, the only white face in the crowd, his head cocked, keenly listening. "We once had our own king, Thibaw, who has been banished to India. His throne has been stolen and another king sits on it—not one of us, but the white monkey King of England—"

Blair could not understand every word, but he understood enough. "White monkey King" was actionable—*seditious,* Blair was thinking—and glancing around he saw by a pillar, half in shadow, smaller than anyone around him, the sexton Sin Kwa, a scrap of paper in the palm of his left hand, the stub of a pencil in his right, dabbing at the paper, note-taking. Blair was relieved, because in the *sayadaw*'s fury, growling the words, some of it Blair found hard to translate. Sin Kaw could fill in the blanks, and it seemed that enough was being uttered by the monk this very evening for him to be arrested. Perhaps the sight of Blair standing, facing him, provoked him to rant at greater length.

Wirathu had a fat face, folds of flesh at his neck, a bulge beneath his chin, and his shaven head gleamed in the lantern light. As he spoke, he gestured, reaching from his robes, wagging his stubby fingers, enumerating his objections.

With a shriek he gave an order that Blair had trouble understanding. He looked to Sin Kwa who seemed to crouch, hunching over, hiding his note-taking, and then to Blair's surprise everyone shuffled where they stood and adjusted their lungyis and lowered themselves to the flagstones of the courtyard. Blair struggled with the words in the order the *sayadaw* had given, and it sounded as though he'd told them to sit—but they didn't sit, they hunkered down, squatting on their heels.

This command to the crowd had the effect of exposing Blair to their gaze, the only man standing—conspicuous among the squatting men— and the next shout from the *sayadaw* was, "The Englishman has come here to interfere with us—he wants to punish me!"

Kneeling, bent over, Sin Kwa became smaller and compact, and though his body was lowered he lifted his head, his face tight with fear, his eyes squeezed, and though he seemed to be smiling, Blair knew that Burmese facial expression—it was a rictus of terror.

Blair considered calling out—perhaps, *Don't worry*—but he instead backed away, and as he did, stepping into the darkness of the gateway he tripped, snatching at the gatepost. He fell heavily against flat, unyielding flagstones. He was stunned, jarred by pain that was agony in the dazzle of lantern light, and trying to get to his feet he was impeded by sweaty arms attempting to lift him, and another duller sensation, his being kicked—but by bare feet, toes hammering at his body—small men hovering over him. He had a brief thought, imagining himself as Gulliver beset by furious Lilliputians, but his anger overcame the absurd vision and he wished to stop them and was willing to kill them.

There were so many, grunting and kicking and pulling at his uniform. He batted them away and rolled over and got to his feet—and when he was standing they fell back, briefly awed by his screaming into their faces, "Sort yourselves out!" In that pause, he stumbled away from the light, into the shadows at the side of the pagoda, past barking dogs, into the darkness of the road, and dragged himself across the maidan toward his house.

He had not seen the damage to his uniform, though he could feel pain in his shoulder and knees from his fall, the bruise on the side of his head, and touching his face a sticky substance that had to be blood.

Mah Poo cried out when he mounted the stairs, hoisting himself by the handrail, and now on the lighted veranda he saw his torn trousers, the blood leaking through at the knees, his gashed hand, the blood on his shirt that had dripped from his forehead.

He tottered past Mah Poo, clutching his head, and—faltering—found his way to the bathroom. The shaving mirror reflected his foolish, ruined face, splashed with bloody finger marks. It was too much. He sat on the stool by the tin tub, and as he did, groaning, Mah Poo appeared at the door with a kettle and a basin.

"Master."

She helped him out of his jacket, then plucked at his collar, unbuttoning his shirt and pulling it away from his body. After she filled the basin, she sponged his head wound and patted it dry. Blair had meanwhile kicked off his boots and was rolling up his trousers so that she could attend to his bloody knee.

"No," Mah Poo said, just a whisper, her fingers tugged at his belt buckle.

Blair hesitated and reached, but she brushed his hand aside and unbuckled his belt with a deftness that aroused him, loosening his trousers. He stood and let them slide to his ankles, and then sat again on the stool in his underpants, as she dabbed at his wounds with the warm wet cloth.

She'd moved the paraffin lamp to the floor so that she could see better, and the lamp flung shadows upward. The shadows wagged on the walls as he sat, consoled by her sympathy, her expert hands tending to his wounds, mothering him.

The fall had shocked him, as though he'd been clubbed to the ground, and in the helplessness of his collapse on the stones he'd been set upon by small scurrying men, snatching at him, kicking him with their bare toes— not painful kicks but beastly and insulting. In that moment, lying there beneath them, Blair had wished for a dah, to swipe at their skinny arms and slash their faces. He had never felt so murderous.

And that was why he was so grateful now, having found his way home alone, to Mah Poo's kindness. Because she was not daunted by his nakedness, he was not ashamed—he felt strengthened, she had hardly spoken, she was sighing with concern.

After she'd cleaned his wounds and bathed his shoulders, she dried him and wrapped him in a towel, swaddling him, and helped him to his feet, guiding him to his bedroom door, where she released him. He groped to his bed and there he lay, strangely aroused by her ministering to him, her motherly murmurs as she'd washed him, her nearness, the delicious odor of spice on her skin, her fragrant breath, the freshness of her hair—the ringlets that swung beneath the edges of her headcloth, how they'd tickled his bare shoulder. All this came back to him as he lay in bed, and it seemed like an act of purification, a ritual of intimacy.

He wanted more, he wished to be near her again. He called from the darkness of his room—not "Mah Poo" but "Margaret."

Hearing nothing but the echo of his own imploring voice in the room, and the yap like an answer from a pye dog outside, he felt foolish. But he remembered the touch of her fingers on him, that pressure on his flesh, and he ached to have her near him again. He called out once more, softly this time. He heard nothing; he decided to remain silent, to wait, maybe to sleep.

But in that silence—he had settled into his bed, he had straightened the mosquito net, lying quietly, still hot from his wounds—he heard the lisp of fabric, the chafing of a cotton sleeve, the slight skid of a small foot sole on the rush matting on the floor, a sound like chewing.

She was a shadow at his door, backlit by the lamp glow from a distant room.

"Come," he said.

"Master."

Like a child in a game she held her hands against her face, peeking through her fingers, as he reached to lift the net. She bowed and as she slipped beneath it, the gauzy net draped her head and shoulders like a bridal veil.

14

DEPARTURES

You are cursed for being conspicuous, Blair," Oliphant said. "Must I conclude that it was all a shambles?" Then he frowned as he always did when attempting to be witty. "But that plaster on your bonce makes me proud—the red badge of courage."

Somehow Oliphant had heard of the melee at the pagoda before Blair had time to tell him, intending to do so in the sort of written report the superintendent preferred.

"I believe it was a success, sir. I was a material witness. And I have documentary proof of his sedition."

"I shall be heartened when I'm privileged to see it," Oliphant said.

It meant another visit to Albee's house, to collect the second copybook from Sin Kwa. Again the door was ajar, and in the weeks that had passed since his last visit, the parlor had become more squalid, the litter pushed aside rather than collected, yet much of the disorder looked familiar—the overturned bowl, for example, though it had worked its way across the room. And Albee too looked untidier—was he simply unshaven or perhaps was he starting a beard? He seemed fatter, or was that the effect of his rumpled clothes? He had the sluttish demeanor of a down-and-out, sleepless and deranged.

But he was nodding in welcome, unaware of Blair's scrutiny, his undisguised dismay.

"I was a whole lot happier in Mandalay," Albee said. "But I was a little younger then, and my gout wasn't playing up. And the climate here—and that smelly canal."

"Quite," Blair said.

"Driving me crazy." Albee pulled at his face, scratching his whiskers. "And your boss is a snob. Judge not, lest ye be judged, though, the Lord tells us."

His lined face was spotty with heat rash, his cheeks aflame, and he stood in his socks, his thumbs hooked into his braces, his shirt tightened over his protruding belly. And although Blair was viewing him from a little distance, he had a distinct intimation of the man's odor, a feety stink, the unmade bed visible in the next room.

"Heard about that fuss at the pagoda," he said.

"Bit of a balls-up," Blair said.

"I'd hate to have your job," Albee said, shaking his head in what seemed like pity.

So that's the sort of job I have, that I am pitied by this midwestern cock virgin out here trying to save souls, who hasn't got the pluck to make his own bed? Blair stepped away—annoyed by what Albee had just said—and to call attention to the clutter in the room, he pretended to trip over the litter of papers. That they looked like religious tracts gave him pleasure in kicking them.

"Surely your sexton," Blair began, gesturing to the paper on the floor.

"Sexton looks after the church," Albee said with a hint of anger and nudged the pile with his stockinged foot. "Oh, I know what you're thinking, but I've made a lot of friends here. They'll pitch in with housekeeping." He stroked his whiskers. "Now what can I do for you?"

"The sexton," Blair said. "His copybook."

Albee shouted, "Simon!," and shortly the man appeared. Seeing Blair he rushed to fetch his copybook.

"You'll be compensated for your trouble," Blair said, taking the book.

"If the devil Wirathu is arrested, that will be my compensation, uncle."

In his office the next day, Blair read the neatly written pages—lovely handwriting listing the vicious speeches, the threats, the calls for resistance, the mockery of the king. Blair made a fair copy on government foolscap to be typed by the station's secretary, Chunder Dass, adding Sin Kwa's detail, the dates and times of the speeches, the number of people listening, noting that while many were monks, the ones who predominated at the pagoda were farmers, onlookers, and worshippers. *Peasants,* Sin Kwa had written, summing them up, estimating their number. As Blair had seen on the evening of his visit, Sin Kwa made notes on scraps of paper, which he amplified later on the pages of his copybook, in his clear mission school handwriting, scratching it in Burmese script on the facing page. It would make a wonderful exhibit as evidence at the *sayadaw's* trial.

In the week it took Chunder Dass, sitting at his clacking Remington, to make a typewritten copy of Sayadaw Wirathu's speeches and remarks, Blair was careful to collect each day's pages, to keep them confidential. He read them in the evenings at his house, usually after dinner, still sitting at the table, as Mah Poo cleared the dishes and pottered in the kitchen—seeming more at ease in the house now that they were lovers.

The British have made our paradise into a prison, Blair read. *We have rubies, we have petroleum, we have rice—rice to feed ourselves and to sell to the world. The British have stolen our wealth. They say they are protecting us, but they have imprisoned us.*

In successive speeches, the monk spoke of how the British treated the Burmese like animals, repeating his comparison with Buddha and the peaceful deer—the British killed the deer and ate them.

We are despised like animals. We are paid less than white men, we are punished with taxes, Wirathu said, speaking of how the British had introduced money and greed into the happy land. *We Burmese are poorer now than we were with King Thibaw.*

In another rant, he spoke of how all the profits went to Britain—and he listed timber, and gems, and rice—none of it kept in Burma for the benefit of the people. Blair was fascinated by the vehemence and the detail, the metaphors of control, so clear—so inflammatory—using the simple but dramatic imagery of farm animals. The words *master* and *slave* were repeated and seemed at time to be chanted.

The British have made Burma into a business—a good business for them, a bad business for us, Blair read. *A few thousand white men and Indians dominating fourteen million Burmese people. Is that right? And the British monarch is the boss of it all—the main dacoit.*

Against the line, *The British king must be removed and our own dear king returned,* Blair wrote SEDITIOUS.

On some of the evenings, after reading the speeches of the *sayadaw*, Blair put the typed pages back into the file, tied it with ribbon, then in his bedroom called out softly, "Margaret," never failing to hear the whispered response, "Master."

In this week of the transcribing and typing of the speeches, Blair felt at last that he was doing his job; that Oliphant would approve; that he might take him off probation—not something Blair cared much about for himself, but it would be good news to pass on to his parents, who seldom heard good news from him.

When the typewritten document was complete in a first draft, Blair read it for errors and misspellings, and a final version was typed—another week—and the file submitted to Oliphant.

"Good show," Oliphant said, passing Blair's office that day.

Have I at last done something right? Blair thought. *Have I passed the test?* Oliphant didn't say, but never mind, Blair was content. Leaving work after Oliphant he went eagerly to his house, to a drink and a smoke on his veranda, to his meal, to his lover—never kissing her, but always when they were lying in the dark, sniffing her face, in the Burmese way.

Heading home one evening some days after passing on the report, Oliphant stopped Blair on the footpath and greeted him in his inquisitive thin-faced way, patted his slicked-down hair, and said, "Rangoon is jolly pleased with the *sayadaw* file."

"Delighted to hear it, sir."

"His very words." Squinting at the setting sun, he scowled, his front teeth protruding. "And the thread on which those pearls are strung is pure sedition."

"When do we move on him?"

"Rangoon will take it from here. The arrest. The charge sheet. Your chap might be compelled to testify."

"We could carry out the arrest."

"Better to keep our hands clean."

"Quite right, sir."

"One other thing, Blair. Are you free for dinner?"

"Yes, sir. Awfully good of you, sir." But he thought: *another test.*

"We dress for dinner," Oliphant said.

"My master," Margaret said, helping him with his dress uniform, brushing his jacket, straightening his tie, admiring him in a way that both pleased and saddened him. And when she knelt to buff his boots, he said, "No," and touched her shoulder. Startled, she stood, and he put his face against her cheek and inhaled, as she covered her eyes, abashed but smiling.

He had so far—for almost two months—only seen the outside of Oliphant's house, a large gabled bungalow, upraised on thick pillars, surrounded by palm trees and a low fence of wrought iron, with a gate. A well-raked garden path led to the stairs, greenery lining the path, the Burmese equivalent of a herbaceous border.

An Indian servant in a white uniform and plimsolls rushed toward Blair as he clicked the latch on the gate and led Blair to the upper veranda. Oliphant stood in uniform, his hands behind his back, reviewing Blair's progress toward him. Seeing Oliphant in full fig made Blair grateful for Margaret's close attention, her ironing his jacket, pressing his trousers— but perhaps he should have allowed her to buff his boots.

"My khidmatgar will take your helmet," Oliphant said.

"Yes, sir."

"Sherry?" Oliphant snapped his fingers and a waiter brought a tray of half-filled schooners of sherry. "What's your pleasure? This is fino, this chap is oloroso."

"Thank you, sir," Blair said, selecting the fino, glad that the choice had been simple.

"We shall drink to our quest for justice," Oliphant said. "Mind you, I have nothing against the Buddhists." He sipped then ran his tongue over his narrow mustache. "I am merely pursuing enemies of the Crown."

"Quite right, sir."

"This turbulent monk must be stopped. It is greater than an offense against the state. What he is demanding is the equivalent of attempting regicide."

"That needs to be said, sir."

Seeing Oliphant seating himself on a sofa, Blair sat in an armchair next to a table on which copies of the *Illustrated London News* and *The Westminster Gazette* were stacked, each stack neatly squared, several inches high. What caught Blair's attention was their smoothness—they lay unwrinkled, a slight shine on their surface, as though fresh from a newsagent.

"Smashing," Blair said, running his hand over the top copy of the *Illustrated London News,* which was smooth and cool to the touch.

"My khidmatgar irons them. They're ever such a jumble when they arrive."

"Swann had copies," Blair said. "He sometimes passed them on to me—out of date, but there it is."

"I'm fonder of the *Gazette.* Or *The Strand.* I don't suppose Swann took much interest." He sipped his sherry. "Good soldier, Swann." He sipped again and became thoughtful. "I was too young for the Boers, too old for the Boche."

"Swann fought at the Somme."

"As did my literary hero. He insisted on volunteering. Poor chap bought it at the Somme."

Blair remembered Oliphant's line, *I love Americans—what a blessing it is they never talk English,* on his first meeting—opening lines stayed in the memory, especially quotations. He said, "Would that be—Saki—Munro?"

"Clever boy," Oliphant said. "Yes, and born right here, in Akyab. He was someone quite apart. I often think—Shall we go in to dinner?" he said, rising. "I often think, why should this peerless soul have been induced to fight and be mercilessly killed, for all those slackers at home?"

"I wish I knew, sir."

"Cut is the branch that might have grown full straight," Oliphant said. "Lions led by donkeys."

"Quite."

"Munro was a policeman here in '94, you know, but couldn't stick it. He was my age when he joined up. To my shame. He posted some dispatches to the *Gazette*—marvelous stuff."

"I've been meaning to read *Bassington*."

"I have a copy somewhere. But I was going to say, one has not perhaps at forty the same zest one had at twenty. Do much in the way of reading, Blair?"

"In Myaungmya I read *Women in Love*. Lawrence, sir."

"Rather common and carnal, Lawrence," Oliphant said, but the bearer was at his elbow and he didn't complete his thought.

The bearer served them—slices of beef, roast potatoes, Yorkshire pudding, and thin discs of a reddish vegetable Blair found unrecognizable.

"Pickled beetroot," Oliphant said. "We've finished the bottled peas and pickled walnuts. As for that . . ." He indicated the dish of butter, which had been shaped to resemble a small animal—a monkey?—a moment ago but was now a melted yellow lump. "I try to discourage my khidmatgar from making the butter a medium for a display of his prowess in the plastic arts, but I'm rarely successful."

A white towel draped over his arm, the khidmatgar, perhaps pretending not to hear, poured wine—"A decent claret," Oliphant said, as he repeated his earlier toast about his quest for justice. The man was pompous and mannered, but Blair was soothed by the wine, the good food, the setting of the dining table, and this order was a distraction from the evening heat that seemed folded to an oppressive heaviness in the room.

"I appreciate your going to all this trouble," Blair said. "I haven't eaten this well in ages."

Oliphant faced him and said in a schoolmasterly tone, "I do this every night."

"Dress for dinner?"

"Anything less is squalor."

The word had occurred to Blair at Albee's and seemed to sum up the man, standing in the clutter of his bungalow. It reminded him of the part Sin Kwa had played in the file of Sayadaw Wirathu.

"Albee's sexton proved incredibly useful."

"Ghastly little man, Albee. So he's good for something?"

"His sexton's a treasure."

"I shouldn't rubbish Albee," Oliphant said. "Though he comes from somewhere quite frightful. Wears a frock coat at service. Looks like Vesta Tilley playing principal boy." He was slicing his beef and using his knife blade to dab horseradish on it. He held the forkful at the level of his mouth but didn't eat. "American men. They cry. They keep their helmets on indoors. They are forever pawing one with their prehensile fingers." He poked the meat into his mouth and chewed. "Extraordinary."

Forever pawing one with their prehensile fingers made Blair smile, and he was won over.

"Cook does a decent treacle pudding," Oliphant said, when the plates were cleared and dessert was served. "What are your plans, Blair?"

"I wish to succeed in the police, sir. I want to make my parents proud. I mean to get off probation. I feel time is passing."

"You'll do fine, Blair."

"I hope you're right, sir. I don't want to lose my way."

"No star is ever lost we once have seen," Oliphant said, seeming to recite. "We always may be what we once have been."

After coffee and brandy, and a smoke on the veranda, Oliphant bade him good night. Blair headed home and laughed at having said, *I don't want to lose my way,* when he saw Margaret at the window, waiting for him. He quickened his step and mounted the steps two at a time.

"Rangoon are making their move tomorrow evening," Oliphant said at the station a week later.

"Are we needed, sir?"

"I think the prudent course would be to give them a wide berth. And, by the way, I hear our friend Albee is rather browned off."

"I haven't seen him since I paid off his sexton."

"It's none of our affair."

"His church is popular enough."

"Low church, befitting yet another footling American," Oliphant said. "And natives, especially the Christians, are so tiresome."

"They'll miss him."

"He's a lesson for you. No bottom, no sense of order. Thick with the natives. Don't you be thick with the natives."

"I try to be firm but fair," Blair said and suspected he was quoting someone. "I take it our men aren't involved in the arrest of the *sayadaw*."

Oliphant tapped the side of his nose and gave Blair a look of complicity. "We're keeping it dark. We'll make ourselves scarce. Come to dinner."

The dinner was memorable for two reasons. That it was the night of the arrest of the *sayadaw* was incidental. Blair remembered it for Oliphant selecting a copy of the *Westminster Gazette* and reading a review of *Women in Love,* the novel he'd mentioned at the previous dinner.

"'Not only do all the heroes and all the heroines of this crowded tale cast off clothing whenever there is any excuse, such as seeing a good pond on a hot day, but they do it unexpectedly at garden parties, after dinner, over cigarettes, while talking round the fire on a winter morning.'" He put down the *Gazette* and tapped it. "What?"

"Yes, sir. But this has never happened in other novels I've read. In one bit the talk is of following the impulse, taking that which lies in front, responding to the primal desire. It's something new, and I suggest daring."

"Oscar Wilde was new and daring, and after a spell in chokey he died penniless in Paris."

"Lawrence publishes his poems in the *Gazette*."

"They're tosh. They're like prose."

Surrendering, Blair said, "What do you recommend besides Saki?"

"Try Kipling. At his best, no one can touch him. Look at the first sentences of the story 'Love-o'-Women' in *Many Inventions*. See if you can better that."

And the other memory was of an occurrence at the end of the meal (veal chop, mash, brown gravy, bottled peas). The boat that had brought the arresting officers had also brought provisions: crates of wine, potted meat, packets of water biscuits, tins of salmon, and a chest of cheeses.

Wearing gloves, the khidmatgar placed a cheese board on the dining table next to Oliphant. Grasping a cheese knife, Oliphant tapped it on a large wedge of Stilton, lowering his head so that his slicked-down hair gleamed in the lamplight, scrutinizing the Stilton. All the cheeses on the board were sweating slightly, a moist double Gloucester, a damp cheddar, a softening brie.

"Mousetrap," Oliphant said, dismissing the cheddar, giving it a slap with his knife blade.

"Before you commit yourself to a cheese, you need to study it," he went on, beholding the Stilton, with his knife raised. "Do you follow, Blair?"

Shouts from a distance—from across the maidan, the direction of the pagoda—caused him to scowl, as at an awkward interruption.

"Yes, sir."

"You see"—but he said nothing for some moments, as he prodded and poked the Stilton, dabbing at it, prizing large crumbs away, worrying the wedge with his knife blade, smearing it, before moving on to another corner. "Consistency at its core of Filboid Studge—not a bad thing."

There were more shouts, a yelping from one person, a woman's shrieks, and Oliphant paused.

"Not committed yet."

And that was the moment Blair heard the ruckus—yells from the pre-cincts of the pagoda, the frantic jangling of bells, hoarse shouted orders from the arresting officers. Oliphant did not look up but instead studied the cheese.

Then, "Ah," he breathed and brought his knife down on it.

In the morning, Sayadaw Wirathu sat, his shaven head held high—superb, majestic, indignant—chained to the deck of the boat to Rangoon. Albee, too, sitting on his trunk, going home, his head in his hands.

15

NITS WILL BE LICE

O ver time, Blair understood that Oliphant was unwilling to talk to him unless he—Blair—were seated. It was his height, so much taller than Oliphant, and the ungainly way Blair leaned when he was standing, one shoulder higher than the other, hovering. Nor did Oliphant address police business outside the office, but instead responded to any question Blair might ask by pressing a slender finger to his lips, indicating *shush*, like Matron at St. Cyprian's. And Oliphant had Matron's way of cocking his head sideways, querying silently anything he regarded as unwelcome—a word, a smell, the sound of the gong at the pagoda, a barking dog.

Punctual as usual this morning, passing Blair on the station veranda, brisk, unfazed by the heat, in crisp khakis, Oliphant pursed his lips and gestured to his office, indicating that Blair was to follow him. This was three days after the monk's arrest.

"Victory," Oliphant said, shutting the office door and going to his desk. "Our *sayadaw* is on the mat. Rangoon is overjoyed, and you're mentioned in dispatches, Blair. Good show."

"Thank you, sir."

"For the love of god, sit down, Blair."

"Yes, sir."

"One is so daunted by the steep angle of your sloping shoulders."

In his confusion at being summoned so quickly, Blair had forgotten the rule. He bowed, half in panic, half in apology, and lowered himself into the armchair. Sitting there, facing Oliphant's wide teak desk, was a privilege accorded to very few—none of the subinspectors, none of the merchants in town, never a woman; only a superior, visiting from Rangoon, or a superintendent from another district—Swann had once dropped in—or a delegate from Bassein in the Opium Department. Oliphant regarded his office as his sanctuary, off-limits to Burmese. It was in his view a remote corner of Britain, not to be violated by the intrusion of a native. A Union Jack was pinned to the wall, and on the wall opposite a map of Burma, next to the tea-cozy-shaped chart of Twante District. On a shelf, a commemorative mug—*Prince of Wales investiture, 1911*—and a framed photograph of an elderly woman in black bombazine and a gray bonnet—white-haired, a face in meditation, hands clutching the ends of a shawl that was draped over her shoulders—Oliphant's widowed mother? One didn't ask. And a noble portrait of the king, bearded, clear-eyed, in ermine—trimmed coronation robes.

"The formal charge of sedition, with a bouquet of other offenses," Oliphant said. "He is being reminded that he was sadly in error."

The *sayadaw* would be tried at the High Court, and he would certainly be convicted, based on the violent content of his speeches and the treasonous references to His Majesty—and Blair glanced again at the portrait.

"Chokey—in the Insein part of the world. A good long sentence, I should imagine. Give the blighter some time to think."

"He had a certain presence."

"You look smitten, lad."

Blair thought hard and finally said, "We're bound to become fascinated by the thing we punish."

Oliphant pursed his lips, expelling a doubting puff of air, then leaned forward across his desk and peered at Blair. "Let me see your battle scar."

Blair inclined his head and traced his fingertips lightly on the bandaged wound at his temple.

"Just about healed. But I didn't want it to go septic."

"A neatly contrived plaster."

"My housemaid saw to it."

"Dab hand with a plaster, your housemaid—splendid work," Oliphant said, squinting slightly as though conjuring a vision of the young woman, a cloudy image coming into focus. In a comfortable voice, sitting back, Oliphant said, "That would be Drummond's Margaret, the comely Karen lass."

"Indeed, sir."

"I've seen her." He squinted again, seeing her. "A bit vixenish, what?"

Blair had recoiled at *Drummond's Margaret,* and *vixenish* jarred him again. He was sure he'd begun to blush, his face heating, his palms damp, from Oliphant's tone, with its tone of with confidence, *I know everything.*

And he seemed to perceive Blair's discomfiture, because the superintendent then said, "The estimable Mrs. Drummond preferred to fox-trot at tea dances in Rangoon rather than be rusticated here. Even so, she paid conjugal visits and kept her spaniel eyes on Drummond to keep him from straying."

Blair could not think of a reply. He nodded, hot faced, trying to smile.

"Hardly a fit subject for discussion," Oliphant said, sniffing slightly and sliding his flattened hand to stroke some loose papers on his desk.

Did this mean Oliphant was reassuring him, that Drummond had not had relations with Margaret; that he was giving him a little history, clarifying, but also in his oblique way inquiring without wishing to be obvious? But he must have known the truth from Blair's squirming, from his pink cheeks. *He knows that I'm fucking my housemaid.* That Oliphant had the tact to change the subject was proof of it.

"The pagoda's in disarray with the big man gone," Oliphant said, rocking in his chair. "It's an important place, if rather showy—one of the trophies in its reliquary is a whisker from the Buddha himself—so they passionately believe. Monks there have a great deal of influence. I reckon they'll be rabbiting on about the *sayadaw*'s punishment, working themselves into a frightful froth."

"My chaps are on the alert," Blair said, his voice hoarse from shame. "We've opened a file."

"A single arrest is not enough. We must build upon it. The other monks will want dealing with. The banded krait is called the pongyi—why?"

"Pongyi—the yellow robe. The monk, you mean?"

"The snake, Blair. Troublemakers. Riffraff. We'll have to pull them up."

"Masses of monks, sir."

"I'm well aware." Oliphant had a peculiar way of sniffing, which meant, *I've been here for years, my boy.* He sniffed impatiently now, his nostrils narrowing.

"Some of them"—Blair began to smile, thinking of them—"little lads, sir."

They were puppet faced and small, chirping among themselves; like skinny schoolboys at play, they excited Blair's affection. He saw himself in their whispering and frisking, their harmless mischief. Take away their robes and give them a blue blazer and shorts and a cricket cap and buttoned boots and they could be third formers at St. Cyprian's.

But Oliphant merely stared with cold eyes at *little lads,* his nose becoming gristle, his nostrils small in a silent superior sniff.

"It set me thinking," he said.

"Little bald barefoot chaps in yellow robes, sir," Blair said, chuckling softly, clutching his helmet on his lap, his palms still damp. "They always look to me as though they're haring off to a fancy dress party."

"Jackanapes."

"Sir?"

"Winkle them out," Oliphant said sharply. "Put a bit of stick about. No great mischief if they fall."

"Yes, sir."

The sudden order, unexpected, left Blair at a loss, obedient and anxious.

Oliphant's face darkened, he took a deep breath, then clamped his teeth together, doglike, as he often did when he was about to deliver an utterance he wanted to be remembered and obeyed.

"Nits will be lice, Blair," he said through his teeth.

"Yes, sir."

"Know the source?"

"Cromwell, sir. Irish rebellion. Sixteen-fifty, roundabout. Slaughtered the children. Drogheda and elsewhere."

"Full marks, Blair. I like a recruit with an education." Now Oliphant was smiling, but there was no mirth in his smile—he seemed to be fathoming a contradiction. "I say, jolly queer as an Etonian you didn't carry on to Oxford or Cambridge."

"Many of my schoolmates did, sir."

He thought of Connolly and Runciman and Hollis and had a glimpse of them in gowns, laughing, walking together through a cloisterlike archway of sculpted gray stone, still untested, frivolous, privileged—yet spared a withering interrogation of this sort.

"But not your good self."

"No, sir."

"The ball is at your feet, as an Oxford graduate."

"This is my Oxford, sir. The police."

Now Oliphant did smile, a real smile, surprised by the reply, but he just as quickly looked away and seemed to become distracted, perhaps bored. He disliked lengthy interviews for their lapsing into what he called chuntering.

He drew some papers from a stack in his in tray and said, "Set your chaps on the monks, great and small. I do not propose for one moment that we slaughter the monks, or put the whippy little tots to the sword. But they must be restrained. Sort them out before they kick up a racket."

"Very good, sir."

"You're dismissed."

"Thank you, sir."

Blair sat at his desk after that, smoking cigarettes, his mind blank, stunned by the talk with Oliphant, the condemnation of Sayadaw Wirathu who was facing years of punishment in Insein Prison. And the mention of Margaret ("vixenish") and "Nits will be lice" through clenched teeth had rattled him. He needed time to recover, he called for tea, he sat before a sheet of government paper on which he'd written *Monks*, and nothing

more. And he thought of his prompt reply, *This is my Oxford,* and wondered whether he believed it, even half believed it, and shook his head,
no—nor was Oliphant taken in.

Instead of lunch, Blair smoked some more, and when he heard the subinspectors on the veranda rattling their empty tiffin tins, stowing them in
the staff hamper, he called six of the Indians and two Burmese into his
office. They stood before him, stinking of the curry they'd just eaten, the
Indians' jaws bulging with wads of *paan,* the Burmese standing apart.

"Duty roster—new plan," Blair said. "Our objective is the pagoda and
adjacent monastery."

The men became attentive, because it was local, not bush bashing on
foot, or coursing up the canal and the creeks in the launch, and they seemed
relieved, knowing they could sleep each night in their own bed.

"Discreet patrols," Blair said, and he explained how they were to engage
in close supervision in the precincts of the pagoda and find ways to penetrate the monastery.

The Indians nodded. Mirza Khan spoke for them, saying, "We will do
our level best, sahib," but the two Burmese subinspectors, Zaw Tun and
Myo Kin, frowned. Zaw Tun said there had been a rise in crime on the
canal—boats from Rangoon plundered for goods, boats themselves stolen,
reports of assault, rumors of drownings.

"Piracy," Zaw Tun said. "We must crush this."

"Chap is flatly refusing to patrol pagoda," Krishna Kumar said.

"Sayadaw Ashin Wirathu is gone," Zaw Tun said, gasping a little, as
though awestruck uttering the name. "There is no big *hypongyi* now."

"I'll handle this," Blair said sternly to Krishna Kumar. He knew that Zaw
Tun's reluctance as a Buddhist would make him useless in pursuing the
monks. He faced the two Burmese. "I'll authorize a patrol. Write me a report on canal security. Make some arrests." And to Mirza Khan, who was
the most senior of the Indian subinspectors, he said, "I'm assigning you to
the pagoda. The superintendent wishes us to pay special heed to the novice
monks."

Krishna Kumar snorted, shifting the wad of *paan* in his mouth and
seeming to masticate it. In a juicy voice, his lips gleaming red, he said,
"Mere children, sahib."

"That is so," Zaw Tun said, blinking at his sudden audacity.

"Not at all goondas," Mirza Khan clarified.

The Indian who had not spoken, who had stood listening, was the
Dravidian subinspector Veeraswami. He said quietly, "Little blighters. Very
playful. I sometimes see them kicking a ball in precincts of holy pagoda."

The others murmured among themselves, chuckling in acknowledgment, just as—Blair realized, abashed—he had done in Oliphant's office.

"Nits will become lice."

In a palpable air of bafflement, one of the Indians grunted, as though asking for clarification, and the men exchanged glances. Zaw Tun whispered, "Nat is spirit, sahib."

Blair said, "You know the Hindi word *joon*?"

"A disagreeable insect, sahib," Krishna Kumar said.

"*Nitya joon ban jaegee*," Blair said.

"That is matter of fact, sahib. But what is application?"

Blair could sense the men's discomfort turning to resistance. In Oliphant's office the proposal had seemed odd, but at last, under Oliphant's gaze and his impatient sniffing, straightforward and acceptable—"sort them out" was the order.

"The novice monks can be disagreeable," Blair said, hoping they'd see his point.

But explaining the order compelled him not only to examine the expression in detail, and elaborate on it, but to justify it. The shocked faces of the men, who were used to dealing with hard cases, surprised and embarrassed him. They clearly objected to forcibly rounding up and interrogating the young monks. Zaw Tun's face verged on the unreadable, but the other Burmese subinspector, Myo Khin, looked fierce and insulted and unwilling, as though he was being ordered to detain his own children.

"Myo Khin, do you wish to speak?"

Myo Khin hesitated, losing his ferocity, looking anguished, and finally said, "I was a *shin*, sahib. A *maung shin* when I was a boy. I performed the *shinpyuu* ceremony—novice ordination. I knelt to the *hypongyi* and requested he admit me. He is the *kodaw*, the master. Like Sayadaw Wirathu. I stayed for two *wa*, but my family so poor. I stop and join police." Blair had begun to speak, but Myo Khin raised his hand in a silencing gesture. "I still pray, sahib."

"If I may, sahib," Mirza Khan said.

"Yes?"

"Pagoda at present moment is without big man. Is in shambles. Police action to intrude likely will make matters worse. Simply my opinion, sahib—watch and wait."

"Watch and wait is what I'm ordering you to do."

"With respect, sahib, you have said *nitya joon ban jaegee*."

"It's a manner of speaking."

"*Joon* is so disagreeable, sahib."

"I know what a louse is," Blair said.

"We pinch them from hair," Krishna Kumar said. "Pinch is *sanjivani,* so to say, restoring life to hair. You are ordering us to pinch them?"

Blair sighed, and said, "Keep an eye on the young monks. Report to me if you see anything that wants correction."

Mirza Khan glanced at the others and then seeming to speak for them— though they still frowned—said, "Very good, sahib."

"Those are your orders, now get cracking."

Sleepless that night, tormented by the whine of a mosquito that had slipped under the net when Margaret lifted it to leave, he saw the shocked faces of the Indians, the insulted Burmese, and felt himself squirming at the memory. He'd begun with his order to squeeze the young monks, and then sensing the men's reluctance he'd backed away, surprised by the murmurs of the men ordered to take action against—perhaps arrest—the boys. He'd wanted to say, *I am following the superintendent's orders.* But that was craven, they'd see it as weak.

None of his men—even the Burmese—had any love for the older monks, superior and insolent and some of them noted to be dissolute. But the small boys, their skinny necks and pigeon-egg heads, their bony ankles showing beneath their robes—laughing, playing—these delicate creatures charmed them, inspired benevolence; they were indulged. Children weren't nits, they were helpless, they were harmless, and like Myo Khin they would probably drift away from the monastery and spend the rest of their lives knee-deep in a paddy field, planting, harvesting, under the pitiless sun. *No great mischief if they fall* was beastly.

It had all seemed so simple in Oliphant's office. Blair had paused, but it was an order. You didn't question an order. It was the room itself, the map, the chart of the district, the portrait of the king. It was in the nature of such an office of the British Raj for authority to build and hover like a thunderhead—a strangely suffocating cloud, the vapor of power filling the room, stifling doubt, making you submit. Blair was no more capable of refusing an order than one of his prisoners was of disobeying him, and in that respect he saw how he was also imprisoned.

But that was the system. *This is my Oxford, sir.* He had no choice but to submit. Yet the men's hesitation—and they were tough men, handy with their fists, deft with their truncheons—their objections, their imploring eyes—shamed him. He didn't bend, he couldn't bend, yet he'd lost their respect. It was another defeat.

16

A KIPLING RASCAL

I n that same week, before Oliphant could inquire about his progress in investigating the young monks, Blair heard the clop of hooves in the road, the iron horseshoes ringing on stones and mashing the gravel at the entrance to the station; then snorts and snufflings, a horse blowing at its lips, finally the shouts of what could only have been an exasperated Englishman, breathless from hacking.

"I want him brushed and fed and ready for me to ride after tea. I'll have none of you monkeys loitering."

The front door opened and banged shut and Oliphant was heard to call out in an affectionate squeal, "Bunny!"

Blair went to the window and saw the horse being led away by three bearded Indians in uniform, red turbans, high boots, probably Rajputs. And when he stepped into the corridor outside his office he saw Oliphant chatting to a stocky gasping man in riding boots and jodhpurs, fiercely mustached, his helmet in one hand, a riding crop in the other.

"This is our probationary assistant, Blair," Oliphant said. And to Blair, "Major Bratby."

The man growled at Blair as a greeting and slashed with his riding crop, then said to Oliphant, "As I forewarned, I've only time for a cup of tea. I'm expected at Maubin dak bungalow for the gymkhana tomorrow."

"Perhaps Blair might wish to join us," Oliphant said. "He'll be out on mounted patrol next week."

They sat on the station veranda, facing the maidan, Oliphant summoning Chunder Dass to order the chai wallah to serve them. And Bratby sat, knees apart and breathing hard. He had a beet-red face and was sweating heavily, his eyes gleaming with fatigue, and though he'd put his helmet down, he still held his riding crop against his leg, beating the side of his boot.

"Do much hacking?" he said to Blair, blinking sweat from his eyes.

"I rode in Mandalay, but I was posted to Myaungmya—all water there."

"Boats are sheer buggery," the major said. "Natives respect a horse. You handy in a point-to-point? A hunter?"

"In point of fact—"

"Foxhunter?"

Blair said, "Purely a spectator."

"You want a proper pony," the major said. "Think of a mounted patrol as a hunt. The dacoit is your quarry—he's the fox. Sometimes a brace of them. Your subinspectors—your hounds. They must be biddable. They must carry a good head—they must run tight. They have to be canny— low scenting of the quarry—and feather when they find the scent. Do you follow?"

Blair said, "Yes, sir."

Oliphant said, "This is valuable, Blair."

But Major Bratby was still talking: "Then it's full cry and tallyho, the quarry's at bay and before it can run to earth your hounds have at him. Tear him to pieces. If you're a first timer, you want blood on your cheeks— dacoit blood."

The major was nodding at Oliphant for approval, ignoring Blair, who sat uncomfortably, disliking the man for his bluster and his laughter, now holding his cup of tea to his mustache and drinking noisily.

"Must run," he said, kicking to his feet and striding to the veranda rail. "Where are my monkeys?"

After he'd gone, Oliphant said, "Major Bratby. Frightfully good value."

Blair was not fooled. He'd known this obliqueness at Eton. It was a sixth form ploy, and obvious from Oliphant's silence, which was a form of en- couragement, his feigned surprise at seeing the major's arrival, his close attention as the major had lectured in a superior sort of way, his pompous foxhunting analogy.

But the major had said, *As I forewarned,* and Oliphant had to have known that Blair's score in horsemanship was the lowest in his class, that he could hardly stay on a horse and been mocked for it at Mandalay. He was not an able rider, he was the son of a lowly clerk in the Opium Department, he was Wall Game not Equestrian, there were no ponies in Southwold; he was not a foxhunter, it was mockery.

A friend invites someone to meet you. After the brief introduction, the stranger takes over, lecturing you in a jeering tone—he has been briefed, he says what the friend thinks but daren't say, who merely watches with disguised pleasure while the other talks in his hostile way. Oliphant was the friend, Major Bratby the other, and now Blair knew: *Oliphant rather despises me.*

At dinner a few days later, another test: Oliphant asked Blair how his men had reacted to the order to squeeze the novice monks.

"They were attentive to the notion."

"'Notion' meaning the order."

"Yes, sir. My order."

"Please remind me, Blair. How old are you?"

"I was twenty-one in June, sir."

This was theater: Oliphant had his record, he knew his test results, his poor riding, his age. But Oliphant was clawing the air.

"You must remember to sit, Blair. I find your inconvenient height quite disconcerting."

Blair crouched in submission, seeking a chair, duckwalking to the nearest armchair. But even seated he looked down upon Oliphant. He compensated by leaning forward, his forearms on his thighs.

"You have your whole life ahead of you. It will be a rewarding life if you remember to follow a few rules—unbreakable rules."

"I understand, sir."

"Consider yourself very lucky to have observed the behavior of our American friend, Mr. Albee."

"His sexton was invaluable, sir, in helping us charge-sheet the *sayadaw*."

"I don't mean that. I mean quite the opposite. For reasons known only to himself, Albee wished his presence and his low church upon Twante. I've heard that he was in bad odor in Mandalay, and that might explain his fleeing to us. He chose to live in a rather poky bungalow in squalor, with his desperate secrets, and made a sizable pile in donations from his converts. I may say, I didn't entirely believe in his piety, though I was convinced of his transparent longing to leave."

"His living arrangements were—as I saw myself—rather improvised," Blair said. "Pigging it much of the time."

"A rather feral creature—precisely my point—his nerves were in pieces." Oliphant straightened a brass bell on the side table with his fingertips, and Blair smiled to see that in his deftness Oliphant did not coax a sound from it. A freshly ironed copy of the *Westminster Gazette* lay next to it, shimmering under the lamp. Oliphant took up his schooner of sherry and held it, the lamplight striking through it making the liquid seem a live thing. "Albee arrived from Mandalay in rude health. You saw him leave, looking rather washed-out. As soon as the Rangoon boat pulled away he heeled over, looking ghastly."

"Nerves, I reckon. As you say."

Oliphant smiled and touched the schooner to his mouth, his sipping like assertion. He swallowed and spoke again.

"The man has no self-control. He was an example of condescending righteousness. He believed, as some Christ-bitten people do, that his faith was his justification—and his salvation. Of course, in the long run that may well be the case. But faith is not enough in Burma. You want order in your life, you want bottom."

"He was free with the natives, certainly."

"And as mean as cat's meat," Oliphant said. "But that is not half the problem. Tell me, Blair, how far are we from Rangoon?"

"A dozen miles, sir, by the canal. Bit longer by road."

"And yet you may have noticed I seldom go to town, unless there is some pressing business—and why? Because it demoralizes one to be in polite society and then to return up-country to one's village existence, and this disorder."

He reached for the bell on the side table and gave it a shake, then lifted his gaze to the doorway, where his khidmatgar appeared, white gloved, with a sash and turban.

"We are ready to dine."

The khidmatgar bowed, and Oliphant led Blair to the dining room, where two places had been set, as before, at opposite ends of the long table.

"We are living in a lawless place," Oliphant said as the waiter served the soup course, which was clear consommé. Between spoonfuls, Oliphant said, "We do our best, but there will always be dacoity and murder and rape, and turbulent monks as well. A hundred years from now there will be disorder in Burma, and alarm and despondency. What is the answer? Suppress it, while creating a world for yourself. Keep order, exclude natives from it, unless they are trusted servants. Your home"—he gestured to the room and the door leading to the parlor, where the brass bell and the *Westminster Gazette* shone beneath the lamp—"is not to be violated."

What flashed through Blair's mind was his own bungalow. He lived alone but was grateful for Margaret, for her body and her food; for the cat that hissed and drove away the rats. He'd not been social, he slept, he read. In Myaungmya he'd lived a monastic existence, though he'd wished for a friend. Here in his bare rooms in Twante it was much the same, except that Margaret relieved his loneliness. He could say to Oliphant that even without knowing the rule he had, within limits, kept to himself, observing the order he'd learned at Eton.

"Why was Albee a failure?" Oliphant was saying through Bair's reverie. "He had no place to return to. His house was Liberty Hall."

"Indeed, I saw it myself, sir."

"One cannot thrive in the Burmese world. One cannot go native. The notorious Captain Robinson is the prime example of this—a disgrace, known to all. It is not merely insufficient, it is disloyal. Consider the tedium of native life, the emptiness of the native mind."

Pretending to agree, Blair saw Margaret next to him in bed, her luminous face, her smile of satisfaction, the way in her nakedness she hugged herself then nestled against him, murmuring, her sweetness. And how once when he'd risen from the bed and tripped over the hem of the mosquito net Margaret had cried out, "Sorry!"

"Read your Nisbet," Oliphant was saying. "The Burmese are the Irish of the East. No mechanical ability, no inventive talent, lacking in initiative, impulsive and illogical." He was chewing now, as the waiter had served a yellow stew. "Their virtue? None of the groveling obsequiousness of the Indian. And they know how to laugh."

Oliphant continued in this vein, which—although Blair did not agree—Blair found unexpectedly relaxing, for Oliphant's certainty, his fluency, doing all the talking, and all Blair had to do was murmur agreement—"Quite right," "That needs to be said," "Indeed," "Point taken." But he never ceased to think of Margaret's small fragrant body beside him, her smoothness against his skin.

And Blair was seeing her clearly as Oliphant said, "You must always stand apart from the native or you will lose your ability to observe. As for language—with which I see you have some facility—you can only dabble. To my mind, it is something of a handicap to speak the language. The Burmese, the Indian, will regard you as an ally and will take advantage."

Blair listened (and Margaret smiled), the words washing over him as he ate—the yellow stew was curry, not spicy but a dish resembling one his mother often served, chopped chicken pieces with vegetables in a soupy yellow sauce.

"Albee is your lesson, Blair," Oliphant said. "I doubt a newspaper was ever ironed under his roof. And one last thing. Promise me you won't be a Kipling rascal. You've read *Plain Tales* and the others. You see what befalls these misguided chaps when they leave the fold. 'Beyond the Pale,' 'Without Benefit of Clergy.' Need I say more?"

"Point taken, sir."

Now in his mind Blair was smiling back at Margaret, as Oliphant huffed, putting down his knife and fork, saying, "I do wish cook would learn to make proper curry, or have the sense to leave it alone."

Blair could think of no reply—to that, or to the Kipling allusions. He'd spent the evening saying very little, sipping wine—his glass refilled by the khidmatgar who had the stately manner of a sommelier. He realized he was slightly tipsy and grateful that he was not being called upon to do anything except agree. That was his role, to agree, to take orders. As for *You must always stand apart from the native*—all that accomplished was to remind him of Margaret, and in his wine-infused mood he longed to be with her.

"Now to a more serious matter," Oliphant said, after dessert (syllabub, with mango, and cream from the khidmatgar's cow). Presiding over the cheese board, he said, "You're aware of my rule concerning one's commitment to examining a cheese."

Oliphant went on speaking, poking at the mound of Stilton, and now Blair understood, through Oliphant's example, another feature of survival in Burma: the man spent his life here repeating himself, and what at first had seemed original and comic became, after a time, tedious parody.

That night, crossing the maidan to his bungalow, tripping on tussocks, squinting to see if Margaret was at the window, Blair thought, *No, I am flawed and wayward and uncertain, I am possibly a Kipling rascal.*

She was not at the window, but the lurid orange flame of the paraffin lamp burned in the servant's hut. He lurched toward it, unsteady, telling himself he was tight, and on impulse rapped at the flimsy door of lashed-together bamboo.

"Margaret."

"*Thakin,*" came a sleepy voice.

Some minutes passed. She had to be dressing. And when she opened the door she stifled a yawn, like a child awakened in the dark. And something in her easy acquiescence—her readiness—roused his jealousy.

"*Thakin.*"

Slurring his words, Blair held her by the shoulders and said, "Did you ever kiss Drummond?"

"No, *thakin*. On my honor, sir. I would not do such a wicked thing."

It was late, he felt stupid; he released her and staggered past the prowling cat to his bungalow and pulled himself up the stairs.

The next night she was in his arms.

She refused to kiss, in any case; she sniffed instead, the sniffing called *nanthe,* caressed him with her nostrils, and said she was a *musoem,* a widow. "I can choose who I want for *nanthe.* I could not choose before now. But he is dead. I can choose anyone, even a *bo*—a white man—like you."

And brushed her fragrant silken cheeks against his rough ones, inhaling him.

On horseback, riding from village to village, stopping at dak bungalows, Blair missed Margaret but felt liberated from the tedium of the station, and he was glad neither Oliphant nor Major Bratby saw how badly he rode. He was awkward in the saddle, anxious when the horse became skittish or came to a stop and paused to crop grass. Apart from Mirza Khan, who rode beside him, his men walked, often trailing far behind, though Blair tried to slow the horse to a walk and stay abreast of them.

The thought of Bratby's foxhunting analogy made him sigh. Being probationary meant that a torrent of advice was directed at him, the cautions, the elaboration of rules, the disparagement of Albee, the snide insinuations of Margaret ("vixenish")—they had the effect of thrusting Blair away from Twante, so that he could think straight.

In some respects he was glad for the advice, at his age, inexperienced, at sea in the police, fearful of failing or doing the wrong thing. He was receptive to rules for living, for knowing the world better—never do this, always do that, beware of the other. He hated being lectured to but he was content to be guided and warned—it was so easy to go wrong, and being wrong was fatal to discipline.

Guff about "the emptiness of the native mind" he knew to be rubbish. He imagined putting such words into the mouth of an absurd fictional character—Raj policeman, timber merchant—in a story he might write sometime in the future. He'd been around his cadets and his subinspectors long enough to know how shrewd they could be. They needed to be watchful to survive in such a place. As for Albee—he was much worse than an untidy interloper, and it alarmed Blair to think what this American represented—incoherent, clumsy, subverting the Burmese with the Bible, sententious and so easily shocked. *I'd hate to have your job,* said the fat man who, in his stained robes in the pulpit, browbeat his flock with notions of sin, and Blair wished he had said, *I wouldn't want your job either.*

This is my Oxford, sir, had come suddenly to him, provoked by Oliphant's mention of his failure to go to university. And though it had seemed glib at the time, these days on horseback along the paths through the marshes, it seemed inspired and true. Connolly and Runciman and Hollis and all the rest of the Old Etonians were meeting their tutors, discussing dusty poets and ancient history. But history was alive in Burma: the troublesome priest was flesh and blood, his young monks were possibly a threat, and not long ago in Mandalay a weak king and his evil queen had been overthrown and banished to exile in India. Blair was following orders to catch murderous villains and bring them to justice—wickedness was real here, kingship was Shakespearean.

Not tea with the master and moldy books and sour afternoons at the Bodleian and the frivolity of bump suppers and binges, but actual risk, justice, and order. And passion. He remembered his agonized hours with Jacintha, inwardly pleading for a single kiss from her, unable to ask outright, congested with shyness, finally sending her a poem. And then Blair had a vision of himself above the small skinny body of Margaret, glowing in the lamplight, her frantic eager face going pink, and thrusting madly as she moaned, and finally flinging her arms around his neck, pulling him close, pressing her face to his neck, panting *"Ngar luu, ngar luu"*—My man, my man.

What was Oxford, and tittering undergrads, and the dreamy snobs in boaters and gowns, and cock-teasing coquettes compared to that?

And it was possible that in sending him on patrol—"Gather your hounds, you'll be the foxhunter"—Oliphant was separating him from Twante town and testing him in the countryside, pushing him into the greater disorder and the little known. Perhaps he saw that Blair was becoming too complacent in his bungalow and needed to be separated from his housemaid lover, too.

Blair did not let on that he considered himself to be traveling in style, not hunting with hounds—that ridiculous conceit—but exalted, with a train of servants, his able horseman, Mirza Khan, and a cook and an orderly, who doubled as porters, and four of his best men on foot, deep in the murky interior, penetrating the bobble on the tea cozy map of Twante District, where some villages were cursed by dacoits, others by arsonists and rapists and thieves. Often at a village the women fell on their knees, begging for protection, seeing a *bo*, a *luuhpyauu*—a white man on horseback—while the village men at a little distance eyed him suspiciously, and sometimes sheepishly, reminded of their weakness.

The bamboo hut, the naked children, the flooded paddy fields, the cooking fires clouding the village with acrid smoke, the carved images of golden nats, the prevalence of superstition, the mud and the magic—it was nothing like Twante town here. Oliphant seemed to make a point of sending him in the opposite direction from Rangoon, away to the west and north, in the labyrinth of creeks, into disorder, the flooded fields, the strange smells, the precincts of criminals and their victims.

"I'd like you to draw up an extensive *tour d'horizon* of our dacoity in the benighted hinterland."

Soon the days of summer heat drained Blair of energy, he slumped in his saddle, he hated his horse, he grew tired of talking to his men, and glancing past Mirza Khan as they straggled behind him on the path he was disgusted by the sight of them. Veeraswami—whom Oliphant called Very Slimy—was bandy-legged; Krishna Kumar, the short-arsed Bengali, was potbellied, with a gleaming banana of flesh at the back of his neck, and spat gouts of betel juice into the tall grass; Zaw Tun kept abreast of the plodding cook and the bearer. And they all stank of sweat.

But at each dak bungalow Blair could sit apart, or lounge inside, while his men found shelter elsewhere in tents. His cook made curry, the bearer heated a basin of water for the overhead bucket shower. Blair sat and smoked and saw that his life as a policeman was complete.

It was a relief for him to be able to delegate. He had the power to give orders, he had capable men who obeyed him.

"Find the man," "Take a description," "Make a list of possible suspects."

He might linger in the dak bungalow all day, avoiding his horse, amused by the geckos and lizards, and receiving petitioning villagers who brought him fruit and cigars and gourds of toddy.

And one of them—an Indian shopkeeper—whispered to him of a crime that had taken place in a nearby village; the suspect she said was also an Indian. *Dahej hatya* was the Hindustani whisper. Blair did not understand the meaning of the odd joined words, but Mirza Khan became solemn when he heard them, and said, "Dowry murder."

17

DOWRY MURDER

Blair had complained to Oliphant that the violence of some village crimes repelled him to the extent that he could hardly bear to investigate. The evidence was appalling—the hacked corpse, the battered and bruised body of a girl who'd been raped by a band of dacoits, the small boy accused of witchcraft pushed into a well and left to drown, a family of nine (Muslim, from Arakan) incinerated in their flimsy hut of combustible bamboo by Buddhist villagers, with torches, chanting, "*Mwatsalain!*"— Muslim.

"One becomes habituated to this unpleasantness," Oliphant said. "It is in the nature of police work, just as a doctor is habituated to examining the most outrageous maladies, or probing the crevices of the grotesque bodies of his patients, reclining in his surgery in the utter noddy."

The worst in Blair's experience were bride burnings, always the blackened and unrecognizable corpse of a young woman, always an Indian, the close relatives always the prime suspect—the mother-in-law or the husband, but "They are presently in India, sahib, and not obtainable."

"*Dahej hatya,*" Mirza Khan had said, after the shopkeeper had whispered the words to Blair on one of their patrols. "Dowry murder."

Blair had never encountered that expression. But he asked Mirza Khan to help him look into the crime at once. They rode off and found that it had happened that morning in a small village, a cluster of huts and two shops, sitting like an islet in a green sea of paddy fields, the villagers startled to see two policemen on horseback trotting along the levee that was a raised path between their paddy fields, now dismounting before a crowd pressing toward an Indian shop, its merchandise visible through the window over the wooden counter—rice and soap and cooking oil and bolts of cloth.

But the onlookers backed away as the policeman shouted for them to disperse. On the bare ground at the back of the shop, in what looked like the kitchen area—a firepit, a woodburning stove, a shelf of tin pots and clay vessels and some brassware—a black thing lay like an enormous cinder.

It was charred and brittle, twisted but stilled in a death agony, its skeleton showing through the blistered skin and scorched flesh. The crowd that had gathered at the shop had followed Blair and Khan, the Burmese gaping with fascination, a scattering of Indians looking horror-struck.

"This is Mullapoodi," Khan said, indicating a tearful man, his skinny face contorted in anguish. In his gauzy untucked dhoti and a dirty vest he seemed a wraith in rags, skinny, barefoot, his eyes reddened and wet.

Blair addressed him in Hindi, but the man didn't understand, and so they conversed in Burmese but the man's accent and his mustache made it hard for Blair to find a meaning in his mumbles, and so Khan conducted the interview, the man muttering answers to Khan's questions.

"It was a terrible accident," Khan said. "His wife was cooking on the *chulha*"—he indicated the woodburning stove—"and her clothes caught fire, sari in flames. Woman succumbed."

The withered cinder had once been a woman, Blair reminded himself with sadness, burned to a blackened lump. He turned to Mullapoodi, the man's mouth obscured by his thick mustache, but his liquid eyes looking soulful, his arms limp, his fingers plucking at his dhoti.

"Were there any witnesses?"

"None, sahib," Khan said, after translating the question.

"His mother?" Blair knew from other cases that the mother-in-law was often at the center of Indian family mayhem.

"Seems to be not present, sahib."

Blair put his handkerchief over his mouth and knelt near the corpse and at once was stung—not by the stink of burned flesh but by the odor of paraffin adhering to the body and clinging to the charred cloth, pungent and oily and unmistakable.

"She's been doused with paraffin. This was not an accident," Blair said. He walked over to the man Mullapoodi and sniffed and said, "*Dulhan?*"

The man had cringed when Blair came close, but he shrugged now, not seeming to understand the Hindustani word for bride.

"Language is Telegu, sahib."

"Do you speak it?"

"Veeraswami is knowing. It is similar to his Tamil."

"Chap doesn't smell of paraffin—has he changed his clothes?"

"No, sahib. He was restrained as soon as the villagers saw body," Khan said. "We must find mother. Man's mother must be culpable."

Blair summoned Subinspector Veeraswami from Twante, and in the afternoon, the man Mullapoodi was seated handcuffed on the floor inside the shop, the shutters closed, and the interrogation began, Blair giving the questions to Veeraswami, who translated the answers. But after the first questions, Mullapoodi refused to cooperate. He said he was grieving for his wife, and he repeated that his wife's sari had caught fire as she was cooking dhal, and he specified the dish to Veeraswami, who added, "With pachadi and perugu. Pickle and curd. Telegu eatables, sahib."

"Go look for a jerry tin," Blair said. "I'll hold him here. There has to be a jerry tin."

Khan was back in minutes, with an empty jerry tin that stank of paraffin. Mullapoodi swore to Veeraswami that it was not his, that he had never seen it before, and he denied that his mother had killed his wife.

"She has fled out of grief," Veeraswami translated, as the man began to weep.

Then Khan howled at Mullapoodi, gripping him by the throat, as the man helplessly raised his manacled hands, his eyes bugging out, sucking air through his betel-reddened teeth. Blair stood up and was about to order Khan to release him—the man was gasping in distress—when Khan finally let go, as the man uttered some choked words to Veeraswami.

"What's he on about?" Blair said.

Veeraswami straightened, standing at attention, his arms at his sides. "Suspect states, 'I have done this wicked thing. Mother is innocent.'"

"What do you think?"

"Mother is not innocent," Khan said. "In such cases, mother is never innocent."

Yet Mullapoodi had confessed—under severe pressure, Khan's thumbs in his throat; but it was a confession. And although Blair was certain the man was lying to protect his mother, his admission of guilt was recorded, he was chained and led away. Blair's men were sent to the village to gather evidence, and Mullapoodi was charge-sheeted in Twante for the crime of murder. After a week in lockup he was sent under guard to Rangoon where he was conveyed to Insein Prison.

He was innocent, Blair was convinced of that; but he rationalized the arrest by telling himself that Mullapoodi, on the premises, had allowed it to happen. It was a common enough crime, Mirza Khan said: the bride's family agrees to a dowry, and pays the first installment—money, or jewelry, or a cow or clothes—and fails to pay the remainder. "And when nothing more is forthcoming, bride is killed. Dowry murder."

Blair returned to the village weeks later out of curiosity, visiting the shop where he saw the mother-in-law serving behind the counter. She eyed him as he poked at the shelves, Subinspector Veeraswami just behind him.

The woman shrugged when he spoke to her in Hindi and shook her head when he switched to Burmese. She had plump pitted cheeks, and though her teeth were stained with betel, her manner was gentle, and the way her shawl was draped gave her the look of a dark Madonna. Blair could easily imagine her knees, cradling her skinny son in a sorrowful pieta.

Wagging her head, she handed a small brick of jaggery to a Burmese woman who pushed some coins across the counter.

"Shall we charge-sheet this woman?" Veeraswami said, and *vhooman* made her sound wicked.

"The case is closed," Blair said. "But tell her this. 'You smell of paraffin.'"

Veeraswami spoke the words in Telegu, the woman blinked her long lashes but was otherwise unfazed. She faced them, defiant, then turned aside to serve another customer.

Oliphant had belittled the Kipling rascal, but in the parallel narrative of Blair's life in Burma he rejoiced in the color and drama of the jungle and the swamp, even as he shrank from the violence and injustice. He was usually soothed by contemplating the landscape, the water world of the Delta, the singular trees, the simple geometry of the paddy fields, and the way the newly planted ponds—the sheets of water pricked by shoots—mirrored the sky, the floating clouds, what in a poem he would have called the empyrean, and mocked himself for the florid word. But the vastness of the landscape daunted him and he was reminded how small and remote he was, how strange the trees, how sour many of the blossoms, how lugubrious the mud, the catch in his throat at nightfall when he sensed a shadow overhead and saw a flock of flying foxes—fruit bats setting out to feed.

"Your Mullapoodi will hang," Oliphant said.

"Someone else's lookout," Blair replied, and he winced at the thought.

On patrol Blair was free and, until he returned to Twante and Oliphant, he was fully in charge, with able men to assist him, obedient servants and subinspectors. He smiled to think of Connolly and the others swotting for their finals, while he was thriving in police work, deep in the Burmese hinterland, on patrol.

But that hinterland: he was always glad for nightfall, the sudden darkness, because he was able to rid himself of the romance, and that for all its color there could be sadness in the landscape, too—low-lying and flooded and green, the slimy paths, the head-high grass and spindly palms and dead trees—their roots drowned, their black, bare, high-up boughs giving them the look of gallows, the whole of it otherworldly, marshy, and without definition except for the paddy fields, where he often saw herons and egrets or heard the lapwings cry "Did he do it?" and thought of Mullapoodi. He'd seen jackals and wild dogs in Myaungmya, but here only squirrels and monkeys. He was wordless at the sight of floating snakes—the hama-dryad, and the viper they called *mwe-bwe* with its fatal bite. And rats—looking pink and scalded—swimming through the stagnation in the green froth of the creeks.

To mitigate the strangeness of the tidal creeks Blair made lists of birds, of shrubs, of trees, and pressed some flowers—mimosa, delphinium, magnolia, jasmine—between the pages of Samuel Butler. Snipe, teal whistling duck, the graylag geese flying low over the marshes, six kinds of pheasant bursting from tall grass when they were flushed by his patrol (though he looked in vain for a crimson nan), the francolin calling "Have a drink, papa."

Even in this apparent emptiness there were groves and bowers of trees. The ficus with tangled roots, the brittle *sit* tree—albizzia, the jujube, the cotton tree, the mulberry they used to make paper, the *thanat* whose leaves were the wrapping for cheroots. Jackfruit, wild plum, Chinese dates, tamarind. Zaw Tun taught him the uses of trees—the *pyinkado* used for the railway sleepers, the *than* they used for making charcoal, the juniper prized by Chinese coffin makers, the nipa for thatching the roofs of huts, the *thin-baung* and bamboo for beams and frames. These names seemed to confer some order and took the curse off the landscape of the Delta, which in places—unexpectedly eerie in harsh daylight—seemed haunted.

"Haunted" was not fanciful—not in the spongy remoteness of the Delta where so many crimes were violent and beastly, the men the inspectors arrested so wicked, with ghoulish sneering faces—villains who looked like villains; and some women, too, though they might purr like madonnas, who were poisoners or cheats, claiming after being caught with a lover, naked in a nighttime tryst, that the lover was a rapist. That way, they'd preserve the pretense of their virtue, not a matter for the police but for the village toughs who'd deal with the lover by dragging him away to be lashed.

Blair knew he was living a story that Kipling could have written—the same colors, the same heat, the same odors, the same secrets and contradictions and loyalties. The same distress, too, and like the wayward Kipling hero he had a native mistress to return to, her spiced breath, her murmured endearments, her nakedness swimming with perfume.

The rains of July and August that had hampered their patrols began to diminish, and in the dryer days of September and October the arrests fewer. In this cooler weather, the crime season—which extended into

June—had come to a close. The reports from the Shwesandaw Pagoda were favorable, no arrests of the boy monks, and only the jeering of the older monks, adherents of Sayadaw Wirathu, continued.

In the week before Christmas, Oliphant summoned Blair to his office. Blair assumed it was to be an invitation to Christmas dinner at Oliphant's house, something festive—the subinspectors whispered that it was always a great occasion, though they were never invited.

"I was just getting used to your perverse charm, Blair," Oliphant said by way of greeting, handing him a sheet of government notepaper with the subject line typewritten at the top: REF: TRANSFER—E A BLAIR.

"Syriam," Blair said in a querying voice, reading the order.

"You've been bounced to Rangoon."

Margaret remained impassive when Blair told her that night, though he sensed her body stiffen against him.

"I'll come back."

She had never before showed anger, or even dismay; she put her face near his, with a deep intake of breath, not a sniff but a sigh.

"You lie," she said evenly, her whisper worse than a shout. Then she hissed: "You are a white man—a *luuhpyauu*. The *luuhpyauu* tell lies. God will punish you."

Part III

ABOUT RANGOON

18

PUKKA SAHIB

cross the wide river the city lights winked and glittered suggesting a distant funfair at night, glowing in the wisps of rising smoke, reflected like puddles of gold in the eddies of the turning tide midstream. But a howl of voices and motorcars also reached Blair from that far shore, and the clang of trams, the scrape and screech of interrupted music; the whole noisy city was alive and menacing, like a humped and spiky creature half concealed in patches of darkness. He thought "the witchery of the moon," as rags of cloud twisted past it, the City of Dreadful Night. After the evening hush and the solitude of Twante—its simplicity, its mutters— Blair was anxious, thinking, *What now?*

He'd found a cask to sit on, at a wharf on the Pegu River, remembering his first view of Rangoon, near here, the black chimneys of the Burmah Oil refinery, the peepul trees, the palms, the wharves, the godowns, the clatter of cranes, the trudging bum-boats, the nimble sampans—his confusion at arriving at the city, the apprehension of a new boy who did not belong. And here he was, returned, still probationary exactly two years later. Wasted years. *I have been obedient but what have I accomplished?*

Behind him, the foul-smelling smokestacks; before him on the far side the flickering lights of Monkey Point and the sprawl of the vibrant capital, the beckoning hoot of its ferries—daring him to cross. He sat in darkness smoking a cigarette, pondering the distant clamor, the dazzle on the water. He was unused to such loudness and light, he'd been numbed for months in the waterways and creeks, the small towns and the villages in the Delta. He'd overcome the remoteness, he'd begun to be consoled by the birdsong and solitude, to people vanishing at nightfall, retiring to their huts. Margaret had helped him through it, so the memory of her tugged at his heart. He'd forgotten the chaos of a city, its chugging engines, its crowds, its suggestion of struggle, its stinks.

Blair did not want to think he was intimidated, but he knew he was uncertain—he felt it in his throat, gagging him—as he'd felt it in London on field days from Eton, pretending to be brash for his friends but swallowed by the city and fighting for air. Among the chickens and ducks at Twante—with his cat and his willing woman—he'd found a way to live that suited him. The sudden order to leave had taken him by surprise and torn him from Margaret. Had Oliphant despaired of him? "They want you elsewhere," he'd said. "They" meant authority—a big man ordering him away. As always Blair lived with a sense of uncertainty, of incompleteness, of imposture, wearing a uniform that was always somehow ill-fitting, his boots never adequately shined, his bony wrists showing at his cuffs, a scarecrow to be mocked behind his back.

A ship approached from the Rangoon River, having left a jetty on the south bank of the city, passing the timber mills and the dockyards, moving slowly toward the mouth of Pazundaung Creek—a Bibby liner, the *Shropshire*. As he watched it gliding past, Blair picked out a lighted porthole on an upper deck and wished he were in that cabin, reading a book, heading home. He fantasized portions of the voyage—Colombo, Aden, the Canal again, meals alone, and at the end of his reverie his arrival: he envisioned his mother's gaunt disappointed face and heard his father, *Eric— what on earth will you do now!* Not a question but a shout of complaint and despair, the man slamming his fist on the table, *And who's the muggins who'll pay for it?*

Just then near his cask the darting of a silent sniffing rat—Blair had been so still the rat had not noticed him. He stamped his boot to drive it off, then chucked his cigarette into the river and walked back to the house, to unpack his trunk.

"No billet for you at the moment, Blair," the sergeant had said, as he'd disembarked from the Twante boat at the Syriam wharf. "You'll be putting up at Meldrum's."

An impromptu chummery facing the confluence of the three rivers, but nearest to the Pegu, Meldrum's was a two-story house with a sloping triple-pitched roof overhanging a wide veranda. Meldrum himself was tetchy, with a disapproving turned-down mouth, youngish but balding, clapping his hand to his head in impatience, annoyed at having to accommodate men he hadn't planned for.

"At first it was one bloke," Meldrum said, as he entered Blair's name in the visitors' book, adding as a gibe, "*Eric, or Little by Little.*"

"Beastly book," Blair said, from his chair by Meldrum's desk.

But Meldrum kept talking, "Then it was two more, and a straggler from Moulmein, and a rascal from Mandalay, and now you. The commissioner thinks I'm running a bloody hotel."

He poked his pen into the inkwell and blotted then blew on the page. Snatching up a brass bell and shaking it, he summoned an Indian in a khaki uniform, shirt and shorts and a ragged puggaree—but barefoot, who scampered from the veranda at the first clang of Meldrum's bell.

"The coolie will see you to your room," Meldrum said, and he then seemed to remember, as he nodded and held Blair with his gaze, his mouth still turned down. "So you're our Etonian."

"For my sins, sir."

"Do the buggers still dress like toffs?"

Blair didn't answer. He smiled and stood up, looming over Meldrum, who backed away, chewing his lips.

The rascal from Mandalay was Angus McPake. Even before he set eyes on him, Blair recognized his choking voice, his Glasgow gutturals, his snarling. He was blowing up someone in a back corridor, obviously a native from the recklessness of the abuse.

"Ya scabby badmash," McPake screamed. "Dinna come back til ya find it. That Pist-o-Liter's worth more than your black arse!"

Blair stepped into the corridor and saw that he was berating an Indian who was crouching at his feet, McPake kicking him with each insult, the man pleading, "Sahib, sahib!"

"Ya feckin puggly," McPake said, as the man covered his head with his skinny arms. "Ya pinched it!"

"No, sahib, not at all."

"*Chor*—you bring it here! *Idharr aao.* You fetch it back *jildy.*"

"Sahib!" the man whined in a pleading voice.

"*Barnshoot!*" And on the word, McPake kicked him.

"Sahib!"

"Stop your bleedin' *bat* or I'll fetch you another kick."

Then, noticing Blair, McPake straightened and smiled, and in a mild amiable tone he said, "Blair, ye daft bastard, so good to see you."

"Angus."

As the Indian scuttled away, doglike, on all fours, McPake poked Blair in the chest, saying, "Meldrum said ye were coming ashore but he's a fecking waghorn, so how was I to believe him?"

Blair smiled and sized him up. In the year since they'd seen each other, McPake had become fatter, louder, more whiskery, and he seemed to have mastered a range of Hindi insults. His uniform was spruce, as though he'd just come from an inspection. Spruce and abusive—he'd become a pukka sahib.

"Where've you been, lad?"

"Flaming Myaungmya," Blair said. "Beastly Twante."

Over dinner that evening, McPake leaned and whispered, "The work's nae bad, just bashin' sentry duty and keeping the wogs off the fence, guardin' the gates and that. Syriam's full of Yanks—that's how I got the Pist-o-Liter, from a Yank. But the rest of it is foul, the other thing."

"What thing?"

"The reek," McPake said. "It's howlin', Blair. The chimbleys. And it poisons the grass."

Blair had seen it on his arrival, the thick smoke from the Burmah Oil chimneys, the stink of the refineries. He assumed the wind would blow it away, but there was no wind, and hardly a breeze.

Down the table, Meldrum, who had heard him, said, "Pity you don't appreciate the smell."

"What are you on about?" McPake said.

"It smells like money."

Blair had wished for a friend, and he smiled to think the friend was Angus McPake, because a rough Scot was the last man he would have chosen. But he was grateful that McPake was blunt and candid, often voicing complaints that Blair harbored but kept to himself. Imperious with his men, McPake was forgiving, even at times affectionate to his fellow officers. Though he could revert, his mood never far from that of a lout from a Glasgow tenement. McPake's father was the parson who as a missionary had risen through the clergy and used his influence with the archdeacon of Rangoon to find a place for Angus at the fort, hoping the discipline would mold him and tame his rebellious nature—so McPake told Blair with a supercilious grin, scratching his whiskers.

It had worked. McPake had proven himself a strict supervisor, an able horseman, a martinet on the parade ground.

"We had some cadets with a lot of jabber and cheek," he said. "But I had this"—he pushed his sleeve up his arm and showed him his fist.

"What I've heard called a schoolie," Blair said, remembering Sutherland.

"Aye, lad. That's the tairm."

McPake was no longer probationary at Syriam; he'd achieved the rank of assistant district superintendent, while Blair was still on probation. Clearly his superior officers valued McPake for his ability to lay down the law. They were the order givers, McPake the one who saw the orders carried out; he was their weapon, he was their shouting mouth and hard fist. In the year since Mandalay, McPake had greatly altered, adjusting to the police code, mastering the language of command—half of it orders, the rest abuse.

This thick-fingered brute, his punctilio in faultless khaki, his buttons burnished, had become a pukka sahib. The young man who'd boasted of his pranks in "Glesgie" and cheating at cards carried himself differently now, his shoulders squared, his posture tipped back, chin up, helmet tugged down to shield his eyes, a gilt-trimmed baton in his hand that doubled as a truncheon. His sneer was masked by his mustache, but his fierce underlip was visible. He moved in a slow strut as though preparing to march through a solid wall, which was the same gait as striding through a mob of Burmese monks at a pagoda screaming for him to take his boots off. He told Blair how he relished marching into the great Shwedagon in his riding boots and daring anyone to stop him, crying, "*Barnshoot!*—Ya suster's cunt."

"Aye, let the bloody poongees try!"

He knew the talk, he was keenly aware of his privilege, but McPake met his responsibilities. He was the muscle that all senior officers relied upon, the man sent into battle, leading from the front, earning respect.

His superiors might mock him for his broad accent and his bluster as a grinning idiot, but as long as his kit was crisp, his uniform spotless, his boots and belts polished, and his men obedient, he was valued. Privately McPake disparaged some officers—"Nancys," "bum boys"—for avoiding conflict, because he welcomed conflict and never failed to prove himself. He had some close friends among the Scots Command, and the Cameron Highlanders who patrolled Rangoon, but Blair saw that like many Scotsmen—and unlike the English—McPake had a soft spot for Americans.

The welders and oil men at the refinery, he said, many of them Americans, were reckless and loud, free with their money, boastful, loving a spree, dogging the local women, and all had a Burmese "keep."

"One says to me, 'The governor's wife ordered us to leave the local women alone. We sent her a message, No cunt, no oil. That fixed it.'"

Blair smiled at the knifelike rebuke, saying, "That takes the biscuit."

McPake admired the Americans' defiance, taking on the governor's lady, and felt a kinship with them for their jeering at the English.

"Gahd damned Limeys," McPake said, affecting an American accent.

"That would be me," Blair said.

"Nae, Blair, you're one of us, right enough," McPake said, and he seemed to see Blair as he saw himself, a secret rebel, chafing behind the obedient exterior. Blair wondered if this were so. Did McPake see something Blair did not see himself? He thought, *When have I ever resisted?*

And more than once McPake reminded Blair that it was known in the police that he had tried to strangle Jones in the Rangoon up train for cheeking him. He knew of Blair's involvement in Sayadaw Wirathu's arrest, and he had no patience with monks.

Blair said, "You have problems with *hypongyi*?"

"The poongees—aye—they're the worst."

It was a relief to Blair that it was McPake and not the choleric Superintendent Comstock who showed him the drill in the first weeks of his arrival.

"No snatching of dacoits," McPake said. "It's all supairvision, and as for the men, it's 'Yes sir, no sir, three bags full, sir.'"

No charge-sheeting, no caning, no sleuthing, no blood. Nominally they were guarding the docks, patrolling the depot, securing the wharves when ships tied up to receive the oil that was piped into the tanks in their bulkheads. The tedium of standing guard was assigned to native policemen, Indian and Burmese and a handful of Gurkhas, who manned the sentry boxes at the gates and bashed back and forth at the high fence, sometimes taunted by small boys, but nothing worse than that.

"Lovely weather now," McPake said—it was now December, they were strolling on the wharf—"but it was perishing hot in May and June. My men didn't mind. Burmese never broke a sweat. And it were hotter in Mandalay."

"You went up there?"

"To see Robinson. That's a tale. He tried to cure himself from being an opium addict by becoming a monk. Imagine Captain Robinson a pongee!"

"Did it work?"

"Nae. He's back smoking the muck."

"Has anyone breached the fence?"

"Nae, but I'd be tickled to see some plucky badmash try. I'd gie him a right schoolie—guts for garters, skin him alive."

McPake welcomed a fight—no wonder he was popular with Comstock; he'd proven to be a sahib, he spared the higher-ups the indignity of facing down the natives, and Blair saw that his men feared him.

Now they were standing at the edge of the wharf, looking across the river to the city. McPake said, "Remember Sholto Haggan?"

"The sergeant."

"Remember the knocking shop—Monkey Point—'There's a standing invitation'?"

"I seem to recall," Blair said, but the words and the sight of the pavilion at Monkey Point had never left his mind.

McPake raised his arm and pointed across the river. "It's just there, on the waste ground north of the ferry landing—can you make it out—the lights? Monkey Point."

It was now dusk, the best hour of the day, pale light instead of glare, a silkiness in the mild air, the crickets beginning to tune up.

"I've accepted the invitation."

Blair was about to speak, but instead put his cigarette to his lips and puffed, and inhaled, not knowing what to say, wishing for more. McPake's mustache was twitching, his underlip curled beneath it, savoring a thought.

"Satisfactory?" Blair finally said.

"As a place to eat it were a wee nosebag. As a knocking shop it were heaven."

Stroking his chin, Blair mimicked a cockney accent, saying, "Did you, um, take down their particulars, Constable?"

"Hah!" McPake howled, but just as quickly stiffened, seeing Meldrum approach them, striding along the wharf, jerking a small dog after him on a leash.

"Dinner," Meldrum said, walking past them. "Spotted dick with custard for afters."

"Speaking of tarts," McPake said with a wink, as they started across the wharf for Meldrum's. "There's all sorts there, even a chinky-chonk or two from up-country. But the prime ones are the chee-chees, the mongrels."

Blair bristled at the words, but said, "What, half-castes?"

"Aye, one they call Chutney Mary. Fancies herself a flapper, bare legs, bobbed hair, silk frillies and all. I've had 'er more than once."

Blair's head was hot, his face burned, he wondered if he was blushing; he was glad the sun had gone down, and now they were mounting the steps to the veranda, which was in shadow. He longed for a woman, and it would be so simple at Monkey Point. But he craved to go alone, not on a spree with McPake, who'd chaff him afterward.

"They're a funny lot, the half-castes—barely know who they are. The Europeans won't touch 'em with a stick."

Blair said, "Our attitude toward them is rather beastly, I suppose."

"You reckon?" McPake said, seeming surprised at Blair's sympathy.

Blair said, "The Burmese call them *ka-pyar*—half blood."

"Yellowbellies," McPake said. "The blokes work on the railway, some are box wallahs. But the half-caste women don't really belong, so they're natural tarts. There's a Yank here wants to marry one, God's truth."

As McPake spoke—and he mentioned women with an odd hunger in his voice—Blair thought of Margaret, and he wished for a woman, not a half-caste. *I want the perfumed body of a Burmese, the sweet spice of her silken skin.*

After parade at seven in the forecourt of the refinery, and tea and porridge that McPake now called chota hazri at Meldrum's, they were on duty, observing the sentries, from nine until just before sundown. Then the lamps came on, lighting the perimeter fence and attracting moths and beetles, and the night watch took over, and it was back to Meldrum's for dinner, McPake to the billiard room, Blair to the lounge to read. The lamp in his room was dim, his hard chair uncomfortable—the armchair and the standard lamp in the lounge were better for reading.

Oliphant had loaned him his copy of *The Unbearable Bassington*, which at first made him smile, seeming from another time and place that he cared little about, and of a class he faintly despised. Then he read how Comus Bassington had a reputation as "an effective and artistic caner" and some pages later, "'Bend a little more forward,' Comus said to the victim, 'and much tighter. Don't trouble to look pleasant, because I can't see your face anyway. It may sound unorthodox to say so, but this is going to hurt you much more than it will hurt me,'" and Blair was back at Eton in the Library, remembering the sadism of Buchanan, and the mockery of captains for minor infractions. He posted *Bassington* back to Oliphant. He was happier in the company of Wells and Jack London—and Lawrence, who seemed to him a new man, writing in a clear voice of people who'd been ignored until now, and of passions that had rarely been spoken about in a novel.

Meldrum had jeered at him for having been a toff at Eton, but it was Meldrum who, seeing him reading in the lounge, asked him if he'd known Huxley there.

"I read *Crome Yellow* last year," Meldrum said. "Smashing book. A chap here told me that Huxley was a master at Eton."

"Huxley was my French master."

"Do tell."

"Decent chap, but the boys ragged him. He couldn't keep order."

"Rotten little beasts."

"I suppose so. It was just in fun. But you know when a schoolboy sees an advantage he exploits it."

"They want a caning."

"The awkward thing was that Huxley was nearly blind."

"Shocking," Meldrum said. "I know what I'd do with the little bastards." But he was impressed that Blair had known Huxley, and he added that he'd just bought a copy of *Antic Hay* at Smart and Mookerdum's. "It's the book of the moment."

"Haven't read it," Blair said. "*Crome,* though—the house—reminded me of Breadalby in the Lawrence novel, *Women in Love.* All those talkative and mocking intellectuals and their precious opinions in the grand house."

"Bloomsbury," Meldrum said. "Ottoline Morrell." He turned to gaze at the light on the river and lifted his head to see beyond it, into the darkness. "And here we are, on a far distant shore." He sighed. "Among natives."

When Meldrum had gone, Blair put his book aside and regretted what he'd said, regretted the whole conversation, despaired of this kind of talk. Reading was an intimate act, your reading showed who you were. *And my reading shows I'm not a true policeman.*

19

MOULMEIN CHRISTMAS

I'm in need of a Scottish warming pan," McPake said, badgering Blair to go on a spree—"on the razzle," as he put it; first visit the Gymkhana Club—he was a member, he offered to propose Blair for membership— and later to Monkey Point to find a tart.

But Christmas was a week away, and dreading that and the period from then to after New Year's, his hatred of holidays as a suspension of the routines that sustained him—the invitations to parties and dances and polite company, testing him—Blair decided to go to Moulmein, to his mother's family. His mother had been asking him for the past year when he planned to make a visit: *It will be ever so good for you. It will take you out of yourself.* Now, so near, with a direct train to Martaban, he relented and sent a wire.

Keen to visit. I'm posted to Rangoon. I could take the train down anytime— perhaps for the holidays.

It was timely, a way of avoiding McPake's nudges for a spree, and for pleasing his parents. He'd seldom had good news for them, and though he'd written home as often as he could, it was dreary stuff—complaints about the weather, descriptions of birds and flowers, a line or two about his duties, nothing of consequence.

But a visit to the Limouzin family was news they'd welcome. His mother had told him how her father had emigrated from France and started as a teak merchant and shipwright, and prospered in the colony, and raised eight children, how two of his uncles had inherited the business and gone into rice but had got into difficulties. Some of them had scattered, Aunt Nellie in Paris, his mother in Southwold, but Grandma Limouzin was still in Moulmein, and Uncle Frank, too, and with euphemisms his mother suggested that Frank had married a Burmese woman, but that was a whisper ("apparently married a local lass"), and though Great-Uncle William was now dead, he was said to have married an Indian—"Perhaps just talk," his mother said. She had left India long ago, soon after Eric had been born, and before any of these questionable matches, and she had never returned. But Blair knew he had cousins in Moulmein, and there was his grandmother, Therese Limouzin, who was elderly, and ailing, his mother said. *You must call on her, Eric.*

All this was hushed: no one in the police knew of his relatives in Moulmein—but why would they? The Limouzins were French, and that perhaps two of them had married out of their race was not something Blair wished to share—it was in fact disgraceful if it happened to be true, grounds for being high-hatted at any club, as Robinson had been with his Burmese lover in Mandalay. This family history Blair kept to himself, as though concealing something shameful, a guilty secret that would be held against him. He knew the consequences, he'd heard the gibes. He'd once thought, early on, that he'd joined the police and asked to be posted to Burma to see these people, close relatives who were no more than a name to him, Limouzins, whom he thought of as "the Lemonskins" or "the Automobiles." But when he pondered it, especially now, he was not sure why he had come to Burma. He was well aware that it was a mistake, but he tried not to brood: it was a mistake he'd have to live with.

The reply from Uncle Frank was swift. *Come at once. Your grandmother is poorly and would be glad of a visit. Do plan to spend the holidays with us.*

Blair applied for Christmas leave—he hadn't taken a holiday for months— and sent word that he'd be on the overnight train to Martaban, the terminus that lay across the river from Moulmein. He sat upright on the hard seat, dozing over Meldrum's copy of *Antic Hay,* arriving at dawn, the carriage at once filling with sea air and the rank odors of low tide and decaying seaweed, coolies rapping on the windows, pleading to carry luggage.

A stout middle-aged man in a white drill suit, wearing a topee, a tightly rolled umbrella hooked on his arm, approached him on the platform, smiling.

"Didn't know you'd be in mufti, lad, but I was sure it was you the minute I clapped eyes on you—your great height, and your mother's chin. I'm Frank."

No handshake, Uncle Frank chucked Blair on his arm, Blair saying, "Awfully decent of you to meet me, Uncle."

"Don't know why I bothered to bring my gamp—hardly rains in December, but we had a shower yesterday."

Blair saw his mother's face in the man and was moved, missing his mother acutely for the first time, feeling remiss that he hadn't written more often—but this would offer an occasion for a proper letter, and family news.

"The ferry's waiting," Frank said. "As soon as we all crowd on it'll take us across."

And when the ferry finally left the pier, Frank indicated the sights, the Salween River, the hills in the town, the sawmills on the riverbank, and

Battery Point, where a gharry was waiting, the horse stamping and blinking away flies, the driver rushing to take Blair's bag.

"The scenic route," Frank said, as they set off along the ridge, looking down at the districts Frank named—Maunggan and Mopun—some of the family's timber sheds, and the low green island in the river fronting the town.

"Beyond that is Belu Kyun," Frank said.

"Fearful place, one imagines," Blair said.

"What an extraordinary thing to say. It's jolly fertile. Timber price is down but there's masses of paddy in Belu Kyun."

"*Belu* is ogre," Blair said. "*Kyun* is island."

"Fancy your knowing that," Frank said, sniffing and without interest, then drew Blair's attention to a palatial building, which he said was the new courthouse. "But old Colonel Bogle built it for himself originally. Not for the likes of us working folk in trade, old boy!"

The gharry turned into a side road, rocking in the furrows of the ruts.

"This is Montgomery—I had a bungalow here once," Frank said, then, "Upper Main Road."

"That lovely steeple."

"Saint Matthew's—we'll attend services on Christmas—ah, here we are."

The gharry slowed as it drew into a circular driveway, stopping beneath the portico of a house upraised on stucco pillars, a woman servant dashing to assist Frank, taking his umbrella, as the driver hoisted Blair's bag.

"Your gran is over the road, but I imagine you'll want a wash and brushup. The train is shocking, what?"

Frank led him through the house, describing the holiday plans, but Blair was so fixed upon the details of the rooms he only half listened. The house was a wilderness of heavy teak furniture, the creamy odor of polish hanging in the air, the sofa stacked with plump silk Indian-embroidered cushions, and Blair saw the same Benares brassware, pots and bells, Burmese lacquer bowls he'd seen in Oliphant's parlor. There was a commercial calendar on the wall (a picture of an elephant under *Akoojee Timber Products*), where he'd expected a painting, and on a formidable sideboard, which had the dimensions of an altar, a framed photograph of a small Burmese girl with bobbed hair next to a crystal bowl filled with dead frangipani petals.

Passing through the dining room he recognized the iconic Raj centerpiece on the blackish mahogany table, the china plate of glass half-filled cruets, vinegar and the sauce bottles, a pot of mustard, a cup of toothpicks, a dish of salt. It was the dim sour-smelling interior of a colonial house, more acceptable than some he'd seen but with the same whiff of curry and cooking oil and butcher's wax. There were rooms in Burma so shabby and faded and cluttered they could not be adequately dusted, and this was one of them, though the obvious surfaces had been wiped clean.

His room was at the back, facing a low terrace of servants' hovels, a chicken coop and a rough planked shelter, which might have served as a paddock. He stripped naked and doused himself with a bucket from the enormous water jar in his bathroom, then shaved and dressed and felt better.

Blair was on the veranda, smoking, when a young woman appeared at the door.

"Will you take tea?"

It was a servant's question but her manner was forward and impish, she was smiling broadly, holding a tin tray with a cup and a pot on it. She was sallow and black haired and small, her hair curled in the European style, and her dress was English, with a loose collar and long sleeves, her hem reaching to her ankles, black patent leather shoes, the toes narrowing to a point—not a servant's footwear.

He hesitated before he said, "Kathleen?"

"Yes, and you're Eric. Daddy said you'd arrived."

It astonished him to think that this young woman was his cousin, a *ka-pyar*, and he could not rid himself of the memory of McPake saying "chee-chee" and "mongrel" and "They're natural tarts."

"How was your journey?" she asked, and he became aware that he'd been staring at her, saying nothing; that she was speaking to fill a silence. She set the tray on a side table and poured a cup for him, then offered him the milk jug.

"Bit of a fag, thanks—no, I take it black."

"And how is my dear aunt Ida?"

Again he was thrown, the young half blood calling his mother Aunt Ida. But he sipped his tea to hide his surprise and said, "Worried sick about me, I fear."

"You're in capable hands here—you don't mind my calling you Eric?"

"Not at all," he said, and swallowed, "cousin."

"You'll be with us over Christmas," she said. "It's so lucky for you, our English weather in December. Very sweltering is the weather in April and May. We suffer from prickly heat, not like the natives. Pounded tamarind applied to the prickly heat is infallible. I suffer torments each night. Very prevalent ailment among we Europeans. For us, sunstroke ever menaces."

Blair hoped his dismay did not show on his face as she spoke, and she said the word Europeans in the chee-chee way, with the stress on the second syllable; but she was still smiling beautifully, twitching the sharp toes of her stylish shoes.

"And for a New Year's jolly there's always a party at the club."

"I mightn't be able to stay that long," he said, improvising at the mention of "party." "My superintendent most likely will order me back."

"We will appeal to your superintendent," Kathleen said, and now he saw that she was teasing, too, forthright and confident in a way he associated with Jacintha but no one in Burma.

But she sat and became serious, explaining that Granny was ill, that the Christmas Eve dinner would be smaller than usual, just them, her father and mother, and possibly Aimee.

Aimee? Was that Great-Uncle William's daughter from his wife, Sooma—a proper chee-chee, half Indian? But he was too shy to inquire. He said, "I shall greatly look forward to it."

But he must see the sights of the town, Kathleen went on, the festively decorated church, Reverend MacIntosh's Christmas tea, the party at the Moulmein Club, Christmas cricket on the maidan—and there was more, as she became animated. But he sat stupefied, not only at the prospect of all the socializing, but at the intimacy and force of Kathleen's talk. He had not been spoken to in this way by a native for two years—no, not a native, his flesh and blood, his cousin.

But he said, "Sounds ripping."

Uncle Frank returned from his office for lunch, bland Anglo-Indian curry and custard. Afterward, over coffee on the veranda Blair fell asleep in the middle of a conversation, waking himself with the dull flutter of his own snoring, opening his eyes to Kathleen's shrieking laughter and Frank's grunting guffaws.

"I've disgraced myself."

"Not at all, Eric lad," Frank said. "It shows you feel at home."

Yet he was baffled, he couldn't think of anything to say, he felt he was among strangers, and Kathleen's shrieks had sounded like teasing.

"Might go for a stroll," he said, stretching.

Frank seemed startled; he jerked forward in his chair as he said, "It isn't done, lad." And stammered for more to say, finally hissing, "There's riffraff, the monks and such. They're a caution here, always out and about, hooting at Europeans."

"I'm a policeman, uncle. I'm acquainted with *hypongyi.*"

Kathleen seemed bewildered by the word. She had watched him with apprehension, her eyes dancing at the thought of her reckless cousin sauntering down the road alone on a hot afternoon, squinted at by natives.

She said, "Is there anything particular you'd like to see?"

Instead of replying to her, he spoke to Frank. "You mentioned your timber yard."

"Oh, yes, we could jog down later. And there's your gran. We'll stop in tomorrow for Christmas Eve high tea. That's a tradition." He frowned then said, "I'll take you on a tour presently."

Kathleen saw them off, flapping a handkerchief—there was something actressy about her; was it confidence or nervousness? And in the gharry Blair realized the family didn't own a motorcar but made do with this pony and trap, their gharry wallah tapping his whip on the nag's flanks.

"Salween Park," Frank said.

Beyond a thorn hedge and a grove of flowering trees Blair now recognized as the gold blossoms in clusters of the padauk, the geranium-colored petals of the *Amherstia,* a driveway lined with stately palms led to a large house trimmed with green, and above a wide veranda a number of balconies, each one attached to a separate apartment, like drawers in a dresser. Each balcony had its own green-tiled dunce cap roof, a rusted finial on top. As they watched, a mali lazily clawing at the driveway with a mamoty became aware of the snorting horse and looked at them from the far side of the hedge.

"That's Franconia," Frank said.

"Smashing."

"Used to be ours—the larks we had there!" Frank became reflective. "My father built it. My father lost it."

Blair marveled again as the gharry pulled away, but the sorrow in Frank's voice kept him from asking more.

"Holy Roman church," Frank said, farther along the road, and indicating a building with heavy barred windows next to it, "The jail."

The shops on what he said was Lower Main Road were thronged with Burmese and Europeans—Christmas shoppers, Frank explained, as they descended to the river and the warehouses and the timber yards, where beyond stacks of teak logs two elephants were being chained by Indians.

"Those are yours, Uncle?"

"The mahouts?"

"The elephants."

"At one time, yes, the whole blooming show." He sighed. "No longer, my boy. We've got rather a modest operation now."

But they lingered, Frank overcome by what seemed an inertia of sadness. Blair watched the elephants feeding, placidly twisting their trunks around leafy green boughs and cramming them into their mouths. How peaceful, how contented, how kindly they looked, and now nearing dusk, Blair could hear them threshing the mass of twigs and leaves with their molars, an audible almost human chewing of food.

On the way back to Frank's house, the gharry taking a roundabout route, circling the town and its busy streets, the shops now lit, there came a racket overhead, and a sudden sweeping and flapping, like a cloak being drawn across the sky. Blair looked up and saw a thousand black birds, cawing—screeching—as though in warning.

"Rooks," Frank said. "Off to the island."

But the sound and the sight of them made Moulmein seem haunted. For a moment Blair regretted he'd come. Then he remembered his grandmother and mentioned her.

"Tomorrow," Frank said. "Christmas Eve. It's a family tradition."

What they called tea was curry puffs and sticky buns and rice cakes, served by Frank's Burmese wife, Mah Hlim, silent except for inquiring in a whisper to Blair whether he wanted more. He asked for a lightly boiled egg and went to bed early, still fatigued by his train journey, sleepless in his second-class carriage, and the bewildering day with Frank and Kathleen, feeling more like a stranger than a relative. The house was airless and so sealed with screens against mosquitoes the ticklish odor of mildew kept him awake. Worse, he couldn't read, but never mind, he told himself, the Huxley novel reminded him of Meldrum's question about Eton, and Blair telling him of the rowdy schoolboys, who made poor half-blind Huxley's life a hell in class.

He was more dismayed by Moulmein, which did not summon Kipling to mind, or evoke his lusty poem, but was terraced by its roads, each road representing a different class or occupation. The poem was false and misleading, there was no Burma girl awaiting him, and China was not across the bay. As for the house and Frank's evasions, and the anxious teasing of Kathleen, Blair felt like an intruder. He'd come for his mother's sake and now he was sorry, because he knew he'd have to concoct a story to get back to Rangoon early.

Something funereal in the house frightened him, an atmosphere of dust and shadow and failure in the much-too-big colonial edifice—frightened him most of all because the people in it were his family. This was his house, as well, but his relatives were spectral, not whole, oblique, mannered, somewhat in awe of him yet not seeming to share a common language, especially Kathleen with her queer way of talking. *I suffer torments each night. Very prevalent ailment among we Europeans. For us, sunstroke ever menaces.*

How was one to reply to that? Blair could think of nothing to say to his relatives, and he was wary of asking questions because of the awkward answers he feared they'd elicit. They were down on their luck in a seedy netherworld, neither English nor Burmese, in a twilight of playacting that seemed hopeless yet everlasting.

At breakfast the next morning he attempted to speak Burmese to Mah Hlim but she pretended not to understand—was it his accent, or was she shamming?—and she replied to him in English. It was only after she'd left the room, scuffing into the kitchen, that he realized she was wishing him a Happy Christmas—that today was Christmas Eve.

"Christmas Eve high tea, Limouzin tradition," Frank said in the afternoon.

Blair was on the veranda, where he'd battled the tedium of the day by reading Huxley and wishing he'd brought his unfinished collection of Jack London stories.

"Your gran is so keen to meet you, Eric."

At five, they walked across the road and were met at the door of the house by an Indian woman of certain age, with dark deep-set eyes made deeper having been ringed by kohl, her thin face dusted with powder that made her cheeks bluish. She wore a long shapeless dress, it might have been a sari, that dragged on the floor; her hair was gray and somehow frizzed and contained in a net that reminded Blair of what a snood might be. Her lips were reddened, more from betel stains than lipstick. Nor did she smile.

"I am Aimee." And she swung the door open.

My cousin, this aged native, his dead great-uncle William's daughter, a crone peeping from a blue shawl behind her in the parlor cluttered with rattan baskets and porcelain vases—empty baskets, empty vases—the crone's hands before her face, clasped in greeting.

My great-aunt, draped in a shawl, clad in a sari, and—Blair lowered his eyes—barefoot, rings on her naked toes.

As they led him deeper into the house that was stifling with the heat of the day, Frank and Kathleen behind him, Blair saw it all, perversely, with McPake's mocking eyes, then Oliphant's superior glance, then Superintendent Comstock's assessing gaze, and he despaired of anyone in the police ever knowing anything of it. How they would bray with contempt if they saw him here. He became self-conscious with the thought and felt ashamed thinking it, and he again wished he hadn't come.

But he told himself it was his duty, obeying his mother's wishes. He needed to be here to understand who she was, who he might be, and all this while he was thinking of ways to improve upon the experience when he finally got round to describing it in a letter home.

"Just pass through here," Aimee said. "Mind your head."

It was a palm in a pot, its slack fronds brushing his ears, placed at the doorway to an inner room, smelling of cigar smoke. An old woman in the room lay on a couch, a native charpoy piled with blankets. She could have been Burmese—she was emaciated in a way that makes old people look Asiatic; she wore a Burmese lungyi, her head wrapped in a gaung-baung, bangles on her wrists. She was an elderly Englishwoman but her Asian look was not his imagination—she had hooded eyes and thin lips and a look of suspicion. She disentangled her arm from a mass of cloth that might have been a shawl that had slipped to her shoulders and extended a bony hand like an empress, her fingers limp hanging down, the bright blue stone on her ring catching his eye.

"Eric."

"Grandmama."

"Come closer so I can see you."

He crouched before her and took her hand—the hand was cool, as though bloodless, and not only the ring of an empress on one finger but long nails, varnished crimson, more oriental than English. And that was how she seemed to him, queenly—queenly in the way she held out her hand, regal as she reclined on her couch, which had the contours of a throne, and now he saw she had a Chinese bowl in her lap, a dragon motif on its side.

"Frank, Kathleen—do sit down. I hate it when people stand and mill about." She coughed into a ball of cloth that she held with her other hand and she called to a servant who'd put her head in at the door, "Bring drinks for my guests."

"I won't have anything at the moment," Blair said.

The servant looked confused, mouthing the word, *M'am?*

Blair said, "*Ma-sar-tot-buu, kye-zuu-tin-bar-tal.*"

"What is that yip-yap, Eric?"

"I said I won't have anything."

"You speak this language?"

"I'm a policeman, Grandma."

The old woman looked amused, as she raised herself on her elbow, coughing as she did so, and turned to Frank. "Did you hear?"

"Indeed, yes. Jolly impressive."

"It's all a blur to me. I've lived here my whole life and haven't felt the need to learn it."

Aimee said, "Besides, anyone worth knowing here speaks English."

The old woman was grinning at Blair, a smile made more hideous by her discolored teeth. She shrieked, "You monkey!"

Mah Hlim said softly, "Cook has laid tea in the parlor."

"Go, all of you," the old woman said, in her fruity voice, still vaguely gagging. "I'll stop here. I have no appetite. This will do me. Off you go."

To Blair's astonishment she picked up a half-smoked cheroot from the

Chinese bowl and tapped off the cylinder of ash. As the old woman placed it between her quivering lips, Aimee stepped forward and struck a match and held it against the tip of the cheroot, the old woman puffing, blinking and batting at the smoke. Then she lay back, emitting a shallow cough and blowing smoke, chesty and convalescent.

After what Frank called the preliminaries—"Tasters," he said—curry puffs and fingers of toast wiped with fish paste—he announced, "I can't do the honors until the vicar arrives." So they picked at bowls of cashews and sipped their tea, talking of the old woman in low voices—"It's her heart, you know"—while Mah Hlim fanned herself impatiently.

At last, a rattle at the front door.

"The vicar," Frank said. "Part of the tradition."

The man who entered the parlor—white haired, in a dog collar and black frock coat—looked familiar to Blair, though he said nothing. Instead of eating, he lit a cigarette, easing his mind with a smoke.

Kathleen said, "Reverend MacIntosh, I sent our Danpa over to polish the brasses yesterday."

"And an excellent job she did, too—many thanks." Seeing Blair staring, he said, "Hello. Happy Christmas."

"Happy Christmas to you, sir. Remember me?"

"The *Herefordshire*," the vicar said. "I never forget a face, or someone so tall. You're the Etonian. I trust you'll be joining us at the service tomorrow."

"First things first," Frank said, pouring brandy over a Christmas pudding that Aimee had placed on the tea table, and when he lit it and it was blurred in ribbons of blue flames, he shouted, "Happy Christmas!"

The vicar, the pudding, the merriment, the old woman gasping and smoking a cheroot in the next room, Kathleen's attempt at a carol—"God rest ye merry gentlemen . . ."—and the prospect of going to church the next day depressed Blair to the point of inventing an urgency in Rangoon. He said it would mean he'd have to leave after breakfast on an early train. The vicar tried to prevail on him, with stubbornness masked in Christian piety and a menacing suggestion ("I could have a word with your superiors"). But Blair resisted, saying he had urgent business, not in Syriam but in Rangoon. He left the parlor to visit his grandmother in the inner room again, but she was asleep on her couch, a dead cheroot in her hand.

Blair fled on an early train and arrived in Rangoon just before midnight.

As Blair flung his bag into the gharry waiting at the station, the driver sitting up top said, "Sahib?"

"Monkey Point."

20

SEELEY'S FOLLY

As in Mandalay in the upper room of the pavilion by the river, and in Twante those nights with Margaret, Blair felt rewarded and fulfilled, cured of loneliness, relishing his solitude, clinging to a woman, sick with delight. Sex at Monkey Point was magic, mind-expanding, enacted in energetic postures that he recalled later, because remembering, savoring, eased the tension in his brain—seeing himself kneeling, standing, knotted, the woman on all fours, one of them objecting to his reckless eagerness, laughing, "Me no dog!" yet allowing it. Sex was knowledge, too, not blind lust—though wild monkey lust was part of it—helping to illuminate the act, which for him was a secret miracle and a source of serenity.

Blair relished every detail of it, from his first stirrings—contemplating a visit—to the intimation of agreement, the woman's warm glance, his quiver of anticipation, sensing his scalp tighten at the prospect, his face heating, his fingers flexing, the throb of blood beginning to pound behind his eyes, his breath coming in slow sips, his chest tightening, his mouth dry, as though he were treading on a slippery path, spongy with mud through a thickness of livid foliage, following a bird dancing on the path before him, a firebird with brilliant plumage and a flicking feathery tail.

To caress a woman who wished to be caressed was for him the height of pleasure—"Touch me," one had actually whispered to him and he had nearly swooned; to sniff her and be sniffed by her with the same desire, to feel the panicky excitement of being touched by her, the pressure in every fingertip a wordless promise. He changed by degrees from a reflective soul of yearning, sifting through his dreams, to a man gripped by frenzy, his whole body burning. However casual the act may have seemed—he had a tendency to dismiss it as a spree or a boyish lapse in judgment if anyone mentioned it—it was passionate and serious.

It was the slap of bodies, the bump of bone on bone, and it left him breathless. He might groan but that was to signal the pleasure, because he could not convey in words the profound raking of his nerves, the wrenching of his muscles, as he was wrung dry. In the descent into the deepest recesses of his body, he felt an inarticulate animal fury, like a male drone in pursuit of the queen bee in flight, frantic to mate. The ritual and the fury of the act of sex exhausted him and helped him to understand the single-mindedness, the urgent monomania of desire. He was glad to pay the woman, because that made it certain and equal. It was something to anticipate, too, and afterward something to savor, thinking, *I've a neater sweeter maiden, in a cleaner greener land.*

In a perverse attempt at fidelity Blair tried to return to the same woman, Kyaw Thin, who called herself Cha-Cha, a Burmese beauty with an elfin face, the bottom of her *ingyi* curving outward above her hips like the petals on a downward pointing flower, a pink datura on a green branch. But one night she was nowhere to be seen—probably in an upstairs room with someone else—and Blair became upset and realized he was inexpressibly jealous, feeling like a jilted lover. He went with another woman that night but was awkward and unsure, and she said afterward, "Why you sad, sahib?"

Days later he asked Cha-Cha where she had been. But she laughed. She said, "I want you every day."

"I'm here now, Cha-Cha."

"Yes, give me rupees, handsome boy."

In that hollow week from Boxing Day to just after New Year's, he visited Monkey Point three times, always in a fever of anticipation, always alone, slipping onto the ferry, avoiding the cadets and the other officers. McPake that week was either at the Gymkhana Club, or at a party. And when finally he met McPake one morning at breakfast, McPake said, "You missed a right knees-up last night," and laughed. "Don't get the breeze up."

Blair said, "I had my hands full," and smiled, because he'd been at Monkey Point with Cha-Cha.

On weekends, McPake often returned to Meldrum's drunk and boisterous and on the boil, eager to sit and drink some more, and bellow a bawdy song.

"Get over here, Blair, do the chorus," he said one Saturday night, and began to sing "Sipping Cider Through a Straw."

"The prettiest girl," he called out.

"The prettiest girl," Blair sang.

"I ever did see."

"I ever did see," Blair echoed.

"Was sippin ci—"

"Was sippin ci—"

"Der through a straw—"

They kept on, yelling tunelessly.

"And as we sipped the straw did slip—"

"And I sipped cider from her lips—"

This was on the veranda, facing the Pegu River and the lights of Rangoon, and the ferry tracking through the glittering water across to the pier. Some other officers joined in—braying the words.

Afterward, McPake said, "Blair's got a ditty for us! 'Southern Railways'!"

"Let's hear it, Blair."

It was a song Blair had written in his idleness, and recited to amuse McPake, one evening on the ferry to Rangoon. And tonight he was just drunk enough to oblige them. He stood up and swayed holding a tankard of beer, as he sang to the lilting tune, played at Eton by the King's Scholar Delves-Broughton on his violin to his astonished classmates—*Humoresque.*

Southern Railways do disparage
Consummation of a marriage
While the train is still at Waterloo.

Then he paused and sipped from his tankard, and belched, and continued in the plummy crooning he associated with Reginald Melly.

Gentlemen reserve that function
While the train's at Clapham Junction
When in fact there's fuck all else to doooo!

Amid the loud laughter, Meldrum appeared, enraged, banging a tin pot with a spoon, struggling to make himself heard. "Stop that racket! I'll be on the blower to Comstock if you don't pipe down."

And so they laughed and gasped, jeering at Meldrum's furious face. But when Blair turned to go to his room, Meldrum tugged his sleeve and detained him—the man stood appalled, a spoon in one hand, a blackened pot in the other.

"I'm ashamed of you, Blair." His cold tone was a more severe reproof than his shouting had been. "You let yourself down, lad."

Blair was at a loss; he was sheepish now, as the others had gone to their rooms, and standing alone, rumpled, his shirtfront beer-stained, the echo of his song ringing in his head, he felt foolish.

"I thought better of you, an Eton chap. The others are nothing but brutes and ruffians, and that Angus McPake is a pissant. But I thought someone with your background would have standards."

"I have standards," Blair said, still hoarse from singing. "Sadly, I don't always live up to them."

"You assaulted the dhobi—he was limping. He said to me, 'Blair sahib kicked me.'"

"He made a dog's dinner of my laundry. When I complained he cheeked me, insolent little beast—and besides, I've seen you kick him."

"I kick him because he is my dhobi. I pay his wages. You've no right, Blair. As for the other thing—those louts and their filthy songs, you should choose your friends more carefully."

Blair was stung by that and also for being told off by Meldrum for kicking the dhobi, another insolent bandy-legged Madrassi who stank of sweat, who'd provoked him.

"At the present moment," Blair said, facing the river, the light on the far shore, the growl of a passing boat, "one is not exactly spoiled for choices."

"Perhaps another old Etonian," Meldrum offered in a reasonable voice.

"I daresay." Blair smiled at the thought. "If such a creature could be found in this—" But he stopped himself from uttering a disparaging word.

"My insurance chap at H. V. Lowe," Meldrum said. "Decent fellow. His father's the archdeacon."

"Rather," Blair said—wasn't it an archdeacon who'd been implored by McPake's clergyman father to find Angus a billet in Mandalay? It was McPake's boast that he hadn't had to sit all the exams because of this leg up.

"Name of Seeley," Meldrum said.

"Not Eric Seeley."

"The very same."

Seeley, another King's Scholar, in the fourth form when Blair had been in the third: Seeley the choirboy, whose trousers were rubbed and shiny like Blair's, betraying the anxious economics of a humble home; Seeley, who'd debated with Hollis and Runciman, while he and Connolly had swanked and affected to be above it all, with the satirical poems, claiming to be anarchists and atheists—that Seeley.

"In Rangoon?"

"He's got an office in Strand Road, across from the courts. He's a better bet than those louts."

Blair knew the location; he knew most of the streets in the central part of the city, and he knew all the gardens and many of the markets. Strolling through Rangoon had become one of his pleasures, taking the ferry across from Syriam and stopping first at Smart and Mookerdum's bookshop in Sule Pagoda Street, where there was always something new from England.

Recently two new books by Wells, *Men Like Gods* and *The Dream,* and a new Conrad, *The Rover,* and the clerk said, "*Passage to India.* Very popular."

"No greasy babus, thank you," Blair said and bought the new Maugham, *On a Chinese Screen.*

After the bookshop, he'd walk east along Dalhousie to Dufferin Garden to sit and smoke, then west through the bazaar, past the lovely wooden buildings, admiring the latticework and the shutters, the gingerbread on the balusters, the piecrust eaves, and onward to the Horticultural Gardens at the canal. He liked loosening his legs with the exercise, going at his own loping speed, cherishing his anonymity. He was happiest out of uniform, merely another *bo,* an English pedestrian, often smiling at the thought that in mufti he harbored subversive thoughts, of the wrongness of these ill-bred English clerks and Scottish soldiers and callow policemen lording it over an entire country that hated them. Pissants, indeed.

In his white suit and solar topee and walking stick he entertained the idea that the empire was nothing but a racket, his father's years of shipping Indian opium to China a wickedness—yet the old man feeling virtuous and patriotic doing it: the awfulness, the shame. He loved the freedom of being inconspicuous, chatting in Hindustani or Burmese with hawkers at the bazaar or in shops. Alone, dressed that way, as he wished, he was himself. In his khakis and belts and helmet, swinging his truncheon he was someone else, a policeman, an official to be feared, keeping the peace, for king and country. But always, however he was dressed, inhabiting the role of a Burma sahib, and because it was so antiquated a role, he saw himself in the old spelling, Burmah Sahib.

He chuckled to himself to think it wasn't really a question of belief, or a contradiction. It was merely a choice of parts in this playacting—a change of costume.

Blair easily found the building on Strand Road, *H. V. Lowe & Co* lettered in gilt on the plate glass of the front door. He wondered if he should leave a note, but when—pondering this—he entered the foyer to do so, the Indian clerk at the desk jumped to his feet and became solicitous. He wore a skullcap and a cummerbund, and he shikoed—a deep bow—as Blair approached.

"Good afternoon, sir. Allow me to assist you."

Blair had not decided whether he wanted to meet Seeley that afternoon, but he was so surprised by being confronted by the Indian, all he could think of to say was, "Mr. Seeley, is he about?"

"Right this way, sir," the Indian said, opening the gate to the stairwell as he spoke, stepping aside, gesturing for Blair to ascend.

But before Blair mounted to the first landing, there came a shout from another voice, almost a shriek, "Motilal!"

The Indian froze, and when Blair turned, he saw the small man twisting his hands together, grinning in fear, and in a choked voice, smothering a gulp, "Sahib."

"All visitors are required to give written notice!"

That posh English voice from upstairs was tremulous with apprehension, like an exquisite cry for help.

Blair said, "I'll nip back another time."

"As the sahib wishes. But required application form is just here, in tray. After name and signature I am able to issue chit."

Following the Indian back to the desk, Blair looked at the form, which listed: *Name, Title or Rank, Address, Affiliation, Club, Purpose of Visit.*

Blair filled out the form. Under *Affiliation* he wrote *Old Etonian,* and after *Club* he wrote *Burma Police.* This he handed back to the Indian, who folded it in thirds and smoothing the jacket of his uniform, mounted the stairs, bobbing as he climbed.

In seconds, before Blair had time to seat himself to wait for a response, he heard from above the stairwell a hearty voice, "Blair!"

Seeley appeared on the stairs in shirtsleeves and braces, a stouter, pinker version of the schoolboy Blair remembered, panting from the effort of hurrying to greet him.

"Do forgive me for the severity of that form," he said. "It's just—" And he dismissed the thought. "Come up. Motilal, bring us tea."

The blinds were drawn in the office, bright sun piercing the cracks. Seeley dragged a chair from against the wall and offered it.

"I do believe you're a foot taller, Eric. What in god's name are you doing here? 'Police'?—is that a wheeze?"

"No. I'm with the police. Been here for two years—not Rangoon, but out and about, Mandalay, the dear old Delta, now Syriam."

"Two years—you didn't go on to university?"

Blair began to pluck a cigarette from his case and used the delay of tapping and lighting it and puffing it to think of a reason, avoiding any mention of a scholarship. Finally, exhaling smoke, he said, "Thought I'd see a bit of the world."

"Fancy calling the Delta the world—sorry!"

"No, it's beastly, but there are satisfactions. Give me a minute and I might think of a better excuse."

"That's the droll Blair I know," Seeley said. "Sorry for the protocol."

"Filling up forms—that's my life."

"No, it's just"—Seeley looked pained—"I've been subjected to a lot of nonsense lately—unwelcome attention."

The clerk, Motilal, knocked and brought in a tea tray and a plate of biscuits, muttering, "Chai, chai," and set it down then bowed, touching his skullcap, and backed out of the room, bumping one elbow on the doorjamb and staggering.

"As a policeman," Blair said, "I should be jolly pleased to make an arrest on your behalf."

"You might find yourself with more miscreants than you can handle."

Seeing Seeley's face tighten, and the tense way he stirred his tea, rotating his spoon with a kind of fury, Blair said, "What is it, man?"

"I can't go into it just now—some other time." He sipped his tea and went on in a brighter voice. "I can't tell you how good it is to see you, Eric. You're looking fit—even in that suit I'd know you for a copper from your military bearing."

"I get pulled up for slouching though."

"What do you hear from our old mates? What of your chum, the poet Connolly?"

They relaxed and reminisced, and for the next twenty minutes they were back at Eton, reliving classes and outings and the Wall Game and, since Seeley had been a wet bob, rowing. Blair told how he'd been asked about Huxley, and mentioned Huxley's novels, which Seeley knew nothing about—"I scarcely have time to open a proper book." Seeley spoke of his father, the archdeacon, and his own work as an insurance agent and stockbroker—"paper chewing"—and it was only after all that talk that Blair asked, "Might I inquire if there is a Mrs. Seeley?"

Hesitating, seeming to swell and straighten, as though about to deliver a formal declaration, fortifying himself with a deep breath, Seeley said, "Not yet, but soon."

"Excellent news."

"That's, um, the cause of the nonsense."

Seeley looked so flustered, Blair said, "I don't mean to pry."

"Not at all. I love her dearly. It's a delightful prospect. We'll be married in a month's time—not in a church but at her father's house. You'll like her, Eric—she's ever so clever, she's quite lovely, from a very good family. Her father's a high court judge."

In spite of this praise, Seeley still looked strained, as though he had not quite finished and was pausing before he said more. To relieve him in his awkwardness, Blair said, "Where's the rub?"

Seeley cleared his throat, he dabbed at a biscuit crumb on his sleeve. He said, "She is in point of fact a native."

"You're a lucky man to be in love."

"Lucky to be loved," Seeley said. "But her being a native"—he hesitated again—"poses certain problems. There have been strenuous objections to my choice. You must meet her. Come to dinner."

They settled on the following Sunday evening, and then Blair left, continuing his stroll in the city, murmuring, replaying the conversation, reliving the tension, smiling at the necessity for a written introduction— undoubtedly caused by the strenuous objections. Finally, walking back to the jetty, where waiting for the ferry, he faced the river and spoke one word, "Folly."

Her name was Leila Das. Her, father Judge Jyoti Ranjan Das, accompanied her to the dinner as chaperone. Blair's gharry wallah had difficulty finding the right house; there was no house number, though the house name— *Lake View*—was painted on a small board fastened to the gatepost. This bungalow on Cheape Road near the lake at Cantonment Gardens was set inside a high wall, an Indian watchman, a Sikh chowkidar, armed with a lathi standing guard, just inside the gate, looking fierce, and then calling, while at the same time seizing a bell pull to signal the gharry's arrival—the bell a distant *ping* beyond the trees.

Seeley greeted him—the small judge and his small daughter just behind him—as Blair apologized for his lateness.

"We're a bit off the map," Seeley said. "And a jolly convenient thing too."

Leila clasped her hands before her in a namaste and bowed her head. She was petite and pretty and very dark, in a purple sari, with a crimson caste mark on her forehead. She did not speak, but her father stepped forward, a smiling man in a light linen suit and striped tie. He shook Blair's hand, saying, "So you're Eric's schoolmate."

"I'm the lesser Eric," Blair said. "He was senior to me, though I can't say he actually had the pleasure of giving me a beating." He chucked Seeley on the shoulder and said, "A great oar, and an able cricketer, Your Honor. A safe pair of hands."

That seemed to please the judge, and Leila, too, looked affectionately upon Seeley at the words of praise. Blair was moved by the tenderness in her eyes, envying Seeley for this veneration, but still thought, *a native*.

They lingered on the veranda, drinking a concoction of mango juice, though he had craved a glass of beer. Perhaps in deference to the Hindu judge and his daughter, no alcohol was served, and the meal was Bengali, soupy lentil dhal and deep-fried cakes, and a proper fish curry—"Catfish," Seeley said, "though you'd never know it under all those spices"—a platter of mounded rice and vegetables, and dessert of custard that tasted of condensed milk.

Leila named the dishes, she asked Blair about his time in the Delta, she praised Seeley—"A clever stockbroker, but more important than that, a decent man"—and her father beamed, while Blair felt the same ambiguity as before—lovely praise, but a native's praise. He was surprised by her being so talkative; he was used to submissive and silent if not cringing Indian women, and boisterous Bengali men, not this serene well-spoken man in his finely tailored suit.

"And where to next, Mr. Blair?" the judge asked in a soft voice.

"Heaven knows where. I'm still probationary."

"I know your Superintendent Comstock," the judge said. "He's rather a taskmaster. Do you have a club?"

"Not yet, sir. I'm still finding my feet, as it were."

Seeley said, "Ask the judge what his clubs are."

Blair said, "Sir?"

"I was blackballed at the Gymkhana, for the usual reasons—this brown face, for one." The judge tapped the table, as though to announce that he was to make a point. "But I had a solution."

"Do tell—I'm all ears, sir."

"Started my own club. The Orient. Eric might put you up for membership."

"Gladly," Seeley said.

Abstracted as they talked, and as the servants padded back and forth, clearing the table, serving coffee, Blair recalled Moulmein and the Limouzin Christmas Eve high tea, with Uncle Frank, and elderly Aimee, and bubbly Kathleen, and solemn Mah Hlim, ancient Grandma reclining on a couch in the next room, puffing a whacking great cheroot, as they sat around the tea table awaiting the padre. And at this dinner here was Seeley, the owl of the Upper Fourth, and the black high court judge, pinching the deep-fried cakes in his fingers and exclaiming, "Toothsome," referring to the curry as a "collation," while his black daughter toyed with her rice mixture, flashing her eyes at Seeley . . . And Blair thought as he had in Moulmein, *What am I doing here with such people?*

• • •

The wedding was held, not at any of the stately Rangoon churches, but at the Das family bungalow in distant Kokine Road, tucked into the valley. The ceremony was simple, an exchange of vows and rings, Leila resplendent in silks and finery, an array of jewels, necklaces, heavy dangling earrings, and a veil. She looked like a princess. Seeley in a white suit beside her in a chair twisted with flowers and ostrich feathers, a garland of marigolds around his neck. The banquet filled five tables, Indian dishes on several, a baron of beef at a third, desserts and drinks on others, an ice sculpture, butter pats shaped into blossoms. Most of the guests were Indian—Leila's mother was veiled and looked severe and didn't speak; a scattering of nervous Burmese, two or three English couples, a Scotsman in a kilt. Some were obvious half-castes—a sweet-faced woman who smiled at Blair across the wedding cake Leila cut with a dah—and he smiled back at the half-caste but he thought, *I couldn't possibly.*

An Indian servant in a gold-trimmed uniform and turban stood by a gramophone, playing records, winding the machine with a crank when it ran down. Some of the tunes were familiar—Al Jolson, and "Avalon," and "It had to be you—wonderful you," and a new one.

What'll I do
When you
Are far away
And I am blue
What'll I do?

Blair was dizzy with confusion, but fancied the word *blue*—"I am blue"—and was glad to be witnessing social life beyond the pale, as he had in Moulmein with his half-caste relations and his dotty grandma. And here at the edge of Rangoon, the blackballed judge, the veiled Bengali mother-in-law, no sign of Seeley's father or mother, but a jolly if motley crowd of wedding guests and well-wishers.

"Duty calls," Blair said, excusing himself for leaving early, reminding himself of his similar whopper in Moulmein.

And in the gharry, rattling through the city to the ferry he thought again: *Folly.*

21

DESPERATE MEASURES

There was another more boisterous drunken songfest on the veranda, McPake and the others singing "Oh, they say there's a troop ship, just leaving Bombay . . ." and bawling the chorus,

You'll get no promotion this side of the ocean
So cheer up my lads, fuck 'em all!
Fuck 'em all
Fuck 'em all!
The long and the short and the tall!

Meldrum complained to Superintendent Comstock, and staff bungalows were found in the Cantonment in Syriam for McPake and Blair. Though Blair had not been among the rowdies that evening, Meldrum heard that he'd taught them the saucy song, "Riding Down from Bangor," and he was blamed for their shouting that as well.

Meldrum said, "This disgraceful fracas is your fault. Now you can hire your own dhobi and kick him all you like."

Blair had spent that noisy evening in his room trying to finish *Antic Hay,* a book he'd come to dislike for its tedious philosophizing, its cast of moneyed beasts and aimless toffs looking for meaning, none of them with enough bottom to hold a proper job. What they sorely needed to take the strut out of them was something like a spell in Burma, to discover what the real world was like, the sight of a rat-chewed corpse, the unashamed practicality of sex for money, vermin in the larder, and being hated by large numbers of natives. The cheesed-off schoolmaster in the first chapter was real enough, Gumbril recognizable as Huxley, guying himself and giving up. The rest of the book was tedious talk, no landscape, no weather, nothing of the natural world. What it needed was trees, and meadows, and flowers, perhaps a storm or two—or, better, palms and orchids, mangroves and snakes. Tossing it aside without finishing it, Blair thought, *I could do better,* and he took up the Maugham he'd bought some weeks ago, Maugham's *On a Chinese Screen.*

The secret yearning of Blair's hidden self to become a writer was heightened when he read books he hated. The women in *Antic Hay* were coquettes and cockteases, nothing like the fearless but sensual women in Burma who frankly fucked for money, often with a smile demanding five rupees more, but gave value for it with delicious tricks he'd never dreamed of—and deserved to be in books. Margaret deserved to be in a book, so did Oliphant dressing for dinner, the joyous clamor of the drummers and dancers in the pwe, and the haunted landscapes of paddy fields and jungle that gave meaning to the remoteness and the otherworldliness of Burma.

Blair regarded Seeley's marriage to Leila Das as a desperate measure, and Judge Das's being blackballed at the Gymkhana Club as a predictable colonial melodrama—the oaf McPake was a member! And the young recruits in the mess at Syriam depot a pack of blimps—yet who had written of such things? He was reading Maugham. Maugham had passed through Mandalay in '22 but if he had seen any of this he hadn't written about it. Kipling dealt in hyperbole and allusiveness, Maugham knew nothing of women, the recent Forster novel about India sounded like touristic tosh. So much of life, especially the realities of colonial life—not the prettifying and the patriotic—was unwritten about, yet this was the stuff of fiction.

My poems are overwrought and tentative and precious, they hold too much back, he thought. *Not my policeman self, but my other self, my real self, the doubter, the mocker, the brothel creeper, could be a book, if I dared.*

This notion swelled in his mind and possessed his imagination when McPake one morning at parade took Blair aside and said he had news of Captain Robinson. Blair was struck by McPake's whispered urgency and seriousness, more alarming than his drunken shouts for attention.

"Tried to blow his brains out," McPake said, shortening his neck and breathing the haust of his morning dram of whisky into Blair's face.

"Why would he want to top himself?"

"Dinnae ken, Blair. He's just been admitted to Rangoon General Hospital. He's fucking blinded hissself."

Somehow this rash act of Captain Robinson—utter madness—was in accord with Seeley's marriage to a Bengali woman living in Victoria Park, shunned. Seeley had earned the contempt of English society in Rangoon when he was wooing the Indian, but married to her he was now an outcast; in colonial terms he was committing suicide.

It was a dilemma for Blair. He too wanted to shun Seeley, or at least avoid him, but out of old boy sentiment and fearful of showing the disapproval he felt, Blair agreed to dinners at Seeley's bungalow, Leila presiding over the table—she had opinions!—and Seeley beamed as Blair studied his countenance, thinking, *He doesn't have a clue that he's destroyed his career.*

At one of these dinners, Seeley said, "Remember Hollis?"

"Christopher, yes. He was two Elections ahead of me. We weren't at all close." But resisted adding, *And he was a prig.*

"He's headed to Rangoon."

"What's Hollis doing in this part of the world?"

"In Batavia at present with the debating team. He's due in Rangoon in a fortnight. He found my name in the directory."

"My school chums from Calcutta are forever pitching up here," Leila said. "We have marvelous larks, though they hardly recognize me, married to Eric. 'Chalk and cheese,' they call us!"

"Fancy that," Blair said, and Leila laughed, but Blair was speaking of Hollis.

Hollis the swot at Eton, presumably a drudge at Oxford, horrid Hollis, would find Eric Seeley married to a chuntering Indian, and Blair Sahib a Raj policeman cracking natives' skulls with his truncheon, not to mention kicking his dhobi, and he'd be properly shocked at the turnup.

"Converted to Roman Catholicism, so he says."

"I once saw a crucifix—odd little souvenir. You tugged the top and out came a knife. I thought, what a perfect image of Roman Catholics."

"I heartily disagree, Mr. Blair. *Cruci dum spiro fido* was our school motto," Leila said, tapping the table with her ring finger for emphasis on each Latin word. "And I found the nuns very kind."

"Leila was educated at a convent school in Calcutta—Loreto House on Middleton Row, very posh."

"I'm sure I'm mistaken," Blair said, realizing he'd gone too far. "No harm intended."

This was the inevitable awkwardness of being among people with whom you had nothing in common. Eton was a flimsy excuse, really. It had only been a millstone for him in Burma, and as for Hollis the Catholic and Leila the convent girl—it was dire, the religion of criminal popes and poisoners, of vicious hypocrisy and fake piety, services conducted by snooty secretive priests in robes in a fug of incense.

Bloody Catholics, worse than Jews, he wanted to say, but only smiled and made his usual excuses, saying he'd have to have an early night, "Big day on the parade ground tomorrow."

Later in the saloon bar at the Staff Club in Syriam, another Burmese veranda screened like a meat safe against insects, sighing over the duty roster, while across the room McPake leafed through *The Pink 'Un*, Blair had felt—what? Superfluous, he finally decided, his life shapeless and futile in circumstances he found more and more incomprehensible. Captain Robinson had blinded himself, McPake was a pukka sahib, and Seeley with an Indian wife. But Blair thought how even a shapeless existence had consequences. He hated his life here at times with such force he did not dare allow himself to give it voice. But maybe there was salvation in being a writer. There was hope and shape in a book, even the dream of one yet to be written. Consequences were also helpful—consequences formed the essence of a plot.

"Dae ye ken what opium does tae ye?" McPake asked Blair on the ferry to Rangoon, the day they arranged to see Captain Robinson.

"I have a decent understanding," Blair said, but he did not say that his father had spent his working life supervising the growing and harvesting and the packing of tons of it in chests to be sent to China and beyond.

"It's filthy muck."

"Revenue for the Raj," Blair said, looking away.

They found Robinson in the general ward, a crowded place smelling like a doss-house. On Robinson's right behind a screen, an old man lay groaning through his yellowish beard, his leg in plaster, a tattooed squaddie behind a screen on Robinson's left, his foot upraised on a stained bolster, the naked foot swollen and tight and greenish—"Snakebite," he said, when he saw Robinson's visitors staring. "Hamadryad."

"Who's there?" Robinson asked in a small voice, his lips barely parted.

His eyes were heavily bandaged, and the dressings around his head covered his nose as well, so only his mouth and chin were visible, as though clumsily mummified. He lay in sweat-soaked pajamas under a counterpane he clutched with rigid fingers as though to steady himself.

"Harold, it's us," McPake said. "Your mates from Mandalay."

Blair had started to speak, but taking a breath to begin he was choked by the foul smell of the ward, the sour human odors, the competing stinks of urine and carbolic soap.

"Speak up, this dressing's half over my ears," Robinson said, and releasing the counterpane, he beckoned with both hands. "Come closer."

McPake said, "Me and Blair."

"The padre," Robinson said. "The poet."

"I seen you in Mandalay not two months' back," McPake said. "You was braw enough then."

"I was fully medicated at the House of the Deer, five pipes a day and lots of sleep," Robinson said in his small weary voice. "There's been a chapter since then, a chapter of accidents." He clasped his hands to his face and spoke into them in a tone that seemed sorrowful because it was so muffled, like someone grieving into a cloth. "Blair," he said. "When did we last meet?"

"That Chinese eating house near the bazaar—Woh Sing's," Blair said, his mouth filling with hospital odors. "Two years ago in Mandalay."

"My downfall," Robinson said, still through his hands, still sorrowful. "Months of opium after that. I made an excuse. I told myself I was seeking to solve the timeless riddle of the universe."

"What do ye reckon?" McPake asked.

"It came to me," Robinson said, and he intoned in a low voice, "The banana is great but the skin is greater."

"Blimy."

"Wisdom of the banana," Robinson said.

McPake chewed his mustache and turned to goggle at Blair, who was shaking his head, murmuring again the unexpected words.

"But I still had need for smoke. It got so bad I began to think of remedies. I listened to the *hpongy-kyaung*. I talked to the other *hypongyi*."

"Bloody poongees," McPake said. "Sod the lot of them."

"No," Robinson said. "They were wise. I thought, *Buddham saranam gissani*."

"And so say all of us," McPake whispered, his hand against his mouth.

"I take refuge in Buddha," Robinson persisted. "I would find refuge from the terror that had begun to haunt me. I would put on the Yellow Robe." He stopped and then resumed with effort. "I studied. I learned the formulae for meditation in Pali, all the rules, all my responsibilities. I took one last pipe before my ordination, and my head was shaved. Then I was invested in my robes, and given a name, U Nipuna, the Gentle Monk."

As Robinson continued to talk, relating his stories of begging with his bowl, walking in rural villages, going from house to house, Blair became abstracted, detached from Robinson's drama, as though suspended over the screened-in cubicle, where Robinson lay, now holding his head in the manner of the forbidding cloth-draped gods Blair had seen in Hindu temples, seated statues wrapped in stained muslin, the more ghostly and frightening for having no discernible faces.

Blair saw McPake, he saw himself, he saw the bandaged head of Robinson, the dry lips relating his history, and it seemed to him that his other self was witness to the unfolding of this shocking story—weirder by far than

"The Opium Den," one he'd recently read in the new Maugham book—Robinson's story unknown to anyone, a tale yet to be written in his secret history of the Raj, that included scruffy sahibs and willing whores and shunned natives. He felt strangely exalted, privileged to be there, especially so, as neither of the other men present knew what was in the heart of this second self, the desire to use this story somehow, later, when he might be a writer.

"I was in distress," Robinson was saying. "I went back to the kyaung and found U Nyana, the monk who had taught me the Pali texts. He took one look at me and saw that I had failed, that I was a *bein-sar*, one of the most opprobrious epithets that can be applied to anyone in Burma—opium eater. And when I left by the great wooden gate I heard the bell, and a dog began to bark. I thought of the saying, 'A dog that howls at the sound of the temple bell will be reborn a man.'"

McPake turned to Blair again and made a disgusted face, raising his hairy hands in a gesture of futility.

"There was more—disgraceful—debt. I owed thousands of rupees for all the chits I'd signed at the House of the Deer. But I had an answer. I locked myself in my room. I loaded my pistol and prayed. I'd never been so frightened—and I suppose it was that, my fear, that made my pistol unsteady. I tried to blow my brains out, but no—the bullet blinded me in both eyes."

To fill the terrible silence that followed, Blair said, "They'll help you here," and even as he spoke the words, he knew they were meaningless.

"A failure all my life," Robinson said. "I couldn't even make a decent job of killing myself."

Blair thought, *That's how the empire will end, one-sided and rash, in a botched suicide, leaving India wrecked, Burma blinded.*

"You've been a good friend," McPake said, helplessly.

"My woman ran off, back to her village. They'll ship me to England, where I belong, where we all belong." He had raised his voice to such a pitch there were murmurs from the bedridden men behind the screens.

"We belong here, mate. We've got a job of work to do," McPake said.

For the first time, Robinson laughed, a ghastly gagging laugh, not of mirth but of sneering contempt, and that it came from a blinded weakened man made it worse.

"You're outnumbered," he said. "Millions of natives, a handful of sahibs. The empire is a colossal bluff. I can see this now in my blindness. If they chose to rise up, we'd be done for." He laughed again, lips and teeth working beneath the thick bandages. "It's all a bluff—give me your hands."

They reached, each taking one of Robinson's dry withered hands.

"This one is certain," he said of McPake's, and of Blair's, "This one is clammy and uncertain."

On the ferry back to Syriam, McPake said, "Did ye ever hear anything so daft? 'The empire—a racket, a bluff.' The man's doolally."

Blair considered this and thought again of his father, a subdeputy opium agent, and saw him standing at a railway godown in Bengal, among skinny coolies loading wooden chests of opium into the goods wagon of a waiting train, looking pleased with himself, imperious as always, another pukka sahib raising revenue for the Crown. The more he knew of the empire first-hand, the more Blair hated his father. That was his secret history. Robinson, another casualty of the empire, at least he admitted it, but all of this was heresy.

"You look a bit off-color," McPake said.

Woken from his reverie, Blair said quickly, "The poor chap's blind."

"Aye—he's in the dark. What does he know?"

Blair was summoned to Superintendent Comstock's office the following week, just a line on a chit, delivered by a bearer, assigning him a day and time. At once he wondered what he'd done wrong. Was it another complaint about his uniform not fitting, or an objection raised by one of the guards he'd punched in the chest the previous morning for leaning like a scrubber against the sentry box instead of standing at attention—and the punch had toppled the weedy man to the ground? Was it his absence in the mess, or another misunderstanding about singing? Or maybe someone had seen him at Monkey Point and reported him for gross lewdness. Or his mewling and puking cat, just acquired, or the ducks he kept under his bungalow that swam in the green canal that ran through Syriam—the birds returning punctually each evening, quacking as they waddled across the oil-stained parade ground—someone must have noticed how they fouled the footpath.

Blair steeled himself for a bollocking.

"In here, Blair," Comstock called out, seeing him fretting in the outer office. And when Blair entered, "Don't sit down. I haven't much time. I just want to inform you that your probation has been lifted. Good show—shut the door on your way out, if you please."

22

SCHOOLBOYS

*I*t *is just conceivable I am the proof that it is all a colossal bluff,* Blair thought. *Two years of disgraceful concealment and unpreparedness, habituated to failure, shrinking like a girl at the sight of a mere rat in the corner of a dak bungalow, disgusted by my sweaty men when they march, hiding in my room whenever someone mentions a party or a dance at the club, taking refuge in books, appalled when I see myself in the mirror in uniform, slope-shouldered, my tabs askew, my puttees slipping down my shins, blaming my houseboy yet knowing the fault is mine, unashamed at lashing out at my bearer, the old man Myat who bobbled and broke my lacquer bowl—all that, and the hugger-mugger of visits to Monkey Point, pressing money into the tiny hand of a sweet-faced tart, so that I, a well-fed sahib, can have my wicked way with her, a hungry native. Yes, I'm the proof.*

For this I am rewarded, my probationary status lifted, promoted to full assistant district superintendent with a raise of seventy-five rupees a month, for lording it over thirty Indian and Burmese guards at the refinery—in league with the brute McPake—and, oh yes, the underpaid, beleaguered and browbeaten native guards do all the donkeywork.

"See me tomorrow, I'm hideously busy just now," Blair learned to say to a sentry who was groveling, seeking attention, needing a day off ("Family matter, sahib"), and then he hurried to the ferry, to go across to Rangoon, to the bookshop, to the brothel, or—latterly—to the Gymkhana Club, McPake having successfully (seconded by Sergeant Sholto Haggan) gained him membership. Being in the club with the other sahibs was a form of surrender, another kind of failure.

Dear Parents, he wrote after his promotion, his raise in pay, and his club membership, *Excellent news . . .*

The Gymkhana Club was horses and billiards and booze, but Blair rationalized his membership by telling himself that he was there to use the library, that it was less snobbish than the Pegu Club, a convenient bolt-hole across the river. He didn't mention the Gymkhana to Seeley, whose father-in-law, Judge Jyoti Das, he'd disappointed by failing to join the Orient Club with its rabble of Indian pleaders and box wallahs, and Burmese merchants and schoolmasters, as well as half-castes from the railways—that he'd have to explain to Comstock why he was mingling with natives socially. It wasn't done, though he still covertly saw Seeley from time to time.

And, troubled by the empire as bluff, he recalled the disturbing incident at Pagoda Road Station.

It was midafternoon on a Friday, he'd just come from the bookshop, stopping at the Indian chemist on the corner of Fraser Street to buy a tin of Three Merry Widows rubber johnnies. Mounting the stairs to the station platform he'd thought of having a drink at the club, hunkering down with a pink gin until sunset, then going to Monkey Point before the lounge became crowded—he resented the sight of other men there, he hated to be seen by them.

The prospect of a drink and then a woman filled him with nervous anticipation, the promise of pleasure and release, his reward after a week of celibacy at Syriam. That prospect was a distraction, too, making him clumsier than usual. But on this afternoon, no sooner had he stepped on the platform, stabbing the ferrule of his cane onto the teak planks, when he was bumped from behind. Staggering sideways he was bumped again by a group of Burmese schoolboys in uniform.

"What are you monkeys laughing at?" he called out.

"Not your business!" one boy screeched.

In an effort to regain his balance, Blair had stabbed the cane again, and in the same motion—steadied, his feet well planted—he swung the cane at that cheeky boy just ahead of him, who'd turned away, landing the length of the cane across the boy's neck and shoulders with a smack that that sent the boy flying forward, at last stumbling, his schoolboy satchel breaking his fall but not until he'd rolled onto his back, where he lay, whimpering miserably.

The boy was too stunned to react, but one of the other boys said, "You struck my friend!"

"Bloody right I did," Blair said. "Mind where you're going."

Hearing this exchange the other boys ran back to help their fallen friend, who had begun to sob, and—red-faced, breathless with rage—Blair pushed past them to the edge of the platform to await his train. He saw that the knee of his trousers was torn, that he must have bumped his leg on the pillar at the top of the stairway, and not only was his knee sore but there was a stain of oil and dirt on the tear.

He was rubbing his knee and brushing at the smudge when he saw the schoolboys had surrounded him. He was Gulliver once more, surrounded by furious Lilliputians.

"You have done an injury to our good friend," a bespectacled Burmese boy said in a fluting voice. His face was pinched with indignation, as he held the tearful boy by his hand.

"You boys don't belong here—bugger off, or I'll thrash you again."

"We will report you to the policeman on station duty," another boy said.

"Clever stick—I'm a policeman!"

"You very dangerous man."

Blair was disconcerted by their cheeking him in English. He bent low to shout in their faces in Burmese, "*Thwa, thwa!*"

"We will not go away. This is our country!"

"This our home," another chimed in.

"You are an English!"

Blair saw that a monk on the platform was eyeing him with obvious pleasure, the Englishman badgered by screeching schoolboys.

"*Thwa!*" Blair shouted again, and to his relief he saw the train drawing into the station. But stepping into the carriage he was jostled by the boys, all of them shrieking, and climbing aboard, and when he walked to the far end of the carriage they followed noisily, chanting, "Say solly, say solly!"

"Look what you have done to Bo Zin!" one said, picking at the collar of the injured boy and showing the welt left by the cane on the nape of his neck.

Blair said, "If you don't step aside, I'm going to fetch you another cut," and raised his stick and flexed it, preparing to whip it.

The threatening gesture sent the boys backward, and the lurch of the train drawing into Tank Road Station had them reaching for the seat backs to steady themselves. But as Blair descended to the platform they howled at him from the open windows with such insistence he was too rattled to respond, and he knew he was blushing and helpless, suffering the indignities wrought by the pestiferous Lilliputians. He was mortified to see that he was the object of attention of others on the platform—a pair of English ladies with umbrellas, and a disapproving gent in plus fours, chewing a cigar.

Instead of descending to the road and the club, Blair walked to the tea stall at the far end of the platform, taking a seat in the shade of its awning. His knee ached where he'd struck it, his trousers were badly stained—the stains would be noticed at the club as an example of negligence, and he feared, too, that helpless fury still obviously reddened his face. He massaged his knee and cursed the students for provoking him. *Say solly! Say solly!*

As he sat and fumed, he heard the whistle of a train approaching on the opposite side of the platform, the down train to Central and beyond, stopping at Monkey Point Road. He limped, using his stick, and boarded, glad to be in civilian clothes, riding it to the wharf, and walked the rest of the way.

Midafternoon at Monkey Point, full sunshine, the quietest time of day for any Burmese brothel, the parlor empty except for two sleepy-looking girls, chatting in a corner like schoolgirls on break. To his relief he saw that one of them was Cha-Cha.

"Here is my friend," she called out when he entered. He cringed, feeling a peculiar annoyance hearing her speak English, knowing she'd learned it from men she'd slept with. She rushed to him and clasped her hands before her face, uttering a familiar salutation in Burmese and then, "You are welcome, *thakin.*"

It was disconcerting, the hot afternoon, the sun striking through the blinds, the heat seeming to carry the mingled odors of flowers from the parlor and the briny whiff of the river, with a murmur of mud. Voices, too, and the blare of boat horns, the cries of coolies on the wharf, the clang of trams. The whole of Rangoon was still at work, as he lay next to the slender Cha-Cha in her gauzy shift, still recovering—his sore knee was a reminder—from his encounter at Pagoda Road Station, seeing himself, not the reader, the reluctant sahib, the inner man, but the other one, the furious pukka sahib, landing a blow with his cane on the schoolboy's shoulders and raising a welt on his neck.

"You not smiling, *thakin.*"

"I'm thinking, Cha-Cha."

She pouted a little, because he was lying on his back, naked in broad daylight a kind of novelty for him, staring at the dusty blades of the slowly turning fan above him that was croaking yes-no, yes-no with each revolution. Sniffing him amorously, Cha-Cha said, "But what you name?"

Now he smiled. The sun flashed on the river and the gold reflected greenish on the blinds and on the bedclothes—green dusk for dreams, moss for a pillow, he thought, delicious.

He sniffed her cheek, loving her smile when he put his face against her sweetness. In a soft sincere voice, he said, "Call me George."

"King Jaw, King Jaw," she chanted and raised her flimsy shift, her body so pale and small in daylight.

• • •

"Behold the Burma sahib," Christopher Hollis said, in the foyer of Anderson's Restaurant on Strand Road a week later. He seemed to be intoning it for the amusement of Seeley, though Seeley didn't smile. As Blair waved away the bearer who was reaching for his helmet, Hollis stepped back, striking a pose, and said again, "Behold, the Burma sahib."

In this exaggerated way he was remarking on Blair in uniform, his buttons shined, his belt and boots gleaming, a pip on his collar indicating his probation had ended, his stick in his left hand, his helmet in his right—he was determined to hold on to his helmet, for the gold insignia on its crown.

"Just finished with inspection. If I'd stopped to change my kit I reckoned I'd be late—I've come from across the harbor." He tucked his helmet under his arm, the insignia facing Hollis. "Christopher, lad, you've had a touch of sun."

Hollis was hot faced and rumpled, smaller and fatter than Blair remembered, his horn-rimmed spectacles slipping down his nose—he poked them into place with his thumb as he stared. His hands were pale, his hair was parted in the middle but spiky and damp from perspiration, his shoes scuffed. His heavy jaw and his mouth like the letter slot in a pillar box were somewhat familiar, though the spectacles seemed an affectation, and Hollis something of a stranger.

"I wasn't issued a solar topee in Java, more's the pity."

"The belief is that one's brain is seriously damaged without such protection."

"My father often said that," Seeley said. "Shall we go through? The table's waiting."

"All the comforts," Hollis said, when they were seated, and looking up from the menu he said, "I can't believe it's really you, young Blair from the Election of '16."

"But remember I'm a year older than you, Christopher."

"Did you fag for me, I can't recall," Hollis said.

"I did not," Blair said, raising his menu.

Seeley was giving his order to the hovering Indian waiter, saying, "Clear consommé to start, and then the fillet steak with roast potatoes."

"I'll have the same," Hollis said. "You chaps know what's best."

Blair said, "Beefsteaks and butter that have traveled eight thousand miles on ice."

"I don't get much in the way of beef at home," Seeley said.

Blair said, "The consommé for me as well, and I think game pie today."

"Very good, sir." The waiter was writing on a pad. "Shall I bring drinks?"

"Beer," Blair said. "A pint in a china mug."

Hollis and Seeley ordered a bottle of Bordeaux, and Hollis said again, "All the comforts."

"We're not savages," Blair said. He found himself sitting straighter than usual, his shoulders squared as if in reaction to Hollis's slouching, in a jacket that was too heavy for this weather, a tugged-down Old Etonian necktie, a wilted collar. "The waiter's a pious Hindu—teetotal, no meat, no alcohol, but look how efficient he is."

Hearing himself complimented the waiter said, "Thank you, sir," and poured a half inch into Seeley's glass. Seeley sloshed it and sniffed and sipped, then nodded for the waiter to proceed, which he did with panache, the bottle wrapped in a white napkin.

"Ideal fag, what?" Hollis said of the waiter. "In my time the scruffiness of the new fags was unspeakable. And the way they gave themselves airs in their little underworld." He sipped his wine and looked frankly at Blair. "How do you manage here?"

"I don't require a fag. I have an orderly, a bearer, a cook, a sweeper, and for my garden, a mali. And any number of cadets to fetch and carry."

"Do they come in for a thumping now and again?"

"Born servants, sense of duty," Blair said. "Though the occasional striping works wonders."

Hollis said to Seeley, "Do you remember when Blair was beaten for being late to prayers?"

"I do indeed," Seeley said, and to Blair, "You were—what?—rising eighteen?"

"I'm sure I deserved every stripe."

"The anarchist," Hollis said. "And your hated enemy, what was his name—Watts major, was it? You contrived to carve an image of him out of a bar of soap, and stuck pins in it, and mounted it on the bracket below the mirror in your stall."

"I have no memory of Blair doing any such thing," Seeley said.

"It was legendary!" Hollis said.

Two waiters were setting out bowls of consommé, straightening the cutlery, tidying the table, tonging bread rolls onto saucers.

"The crowning achievement was that field day in Surrey, the whole class in the charabanc, Watts major in charge of the rabble," Hollis said. "A boy threw a soda bottle out of the window. As senior boy, Watts major was beaten—Blair's voodoo image worked magic—what a triumph!"

Seeley said, "My recollection is Blair in command in the College Wall Eleven, playing against the Oppidans on Saint Andrew's Day." Seeing Blair roll his eyes and sigh, he went on, "No, Eric, you were magnificent—you kept your head and stopped the rush."

"Tell me, Christopher," Blair said, exasperated with the tedious talk of school. He spooned the last of his soup and said, "What brings you out here?"

"Oxford Union—debating team." Seemingly pleased with the question, Hollis described the itinerary of the team, New Zealand to Australia to the Dutch East Indies, performing before audiences ("packed halls, I may say") against local debating clubs ("some of them rather formidable"). He mentioned the extraordinary food, the hearty portions, the rain in Wellington, the heat in Melbourne, the superb accommodation on the various ships, the warm welcomes—all of it, Blair thought, banal but miles better than old boy memories of Eton.

As Hollis spoke, the main course was served, and the three men, absorbed in eating, fell silent, until Hollis spoke up, seeming to remember, saying, "Seeley, old chum, you don't get much beef at home, you say"—Hollis was chewing as he spoke—vile habit, Blair thought—his knife and fork in his fists.

"The wife's not fond of it," Seeley said, with a glance at Blair, but said nothing more.

"This bit of beef is top hole," Hollis said. "Cor!"

With that word Blair recognized him, saw him clearly. In his rumpled jacket and wilted collar, goggling through his gig-lamps, his spiky center-parted hair, fussing with his food and looking awkward and out of place, he was an H. G. Wells hero, who'd been strapped into a time machine, fitting his feet into the stirrups, and blasted into another era, another landscape. The "Cor!" had done it, the wiffling accent of a lower-middle-class clerk from a drapery shop in a South London suburb, propelled into the unfamiliar future, mingling with another race of men, dazzled at the wonder of it, baffled by the language and manners, blinking at the newness.

"Are you comfortable at your hotel?" Seeley was saying, as Blair smiled.

"Not half!" Hollis exclaimed, poking the frame of his spectacles with one finger to restore them to the bridge of his nose, an annoying gesture Blair remembered from Eton. "Crikey—it's posh."

Yes, Hollis was the clumsy, eager lower-class chap from a scientific romance, discovering himself to be among alien wonders and perplexed to be so far from home.

"Crumbs!" he was saying now to Seeley, perspiring in the heat of the restaurant, unaccustomed to such humidity, in unsuitable clothes, and anxious above all, as Wells's characters always were, about how to travel back to

Earth and the present. "But the sad thing I observed on this tour was how godless some places have become, more intent on music and dress at the moment—this jazz, these flappers, such nonsense—than giving praise to Almighty God. I trust there's greater piety here."

"I'm not much of a churchgoer," Blair said. "As you mentioned, I was caned for missing prayers."

"My clergyman father despairs of me," Seeley said.

"I've brought some pamphlets with me," Hollis said. "Think of your immortal soul."

"I fully intend to," Blair said, pushing the remains of his game pie aside and lighting a cigarette. "How long will you be in Rangoon, Christopher?"

"Long enough for us to meet again—perhaps for tea?"

Seeley said, "My wife and I are going to Mandalay tomorrow—what a pity we won't be able to see you."

"Regrettable. What about you, Eric?"

"Tea—ripping. I'm not sure of my schedule. The governor's threatening a visit. I'll send my boy to leave a message for you at the Strand. Perhaps tea at my club."

Governor, boy, club—the words were deliberate and slightly haughty: Blair wanted to impress on Hollis in his time machine that he was among beings unlike his own Oxford Union junketing self, and most of all he did not want Hollis to know him at all, his misgivings, his failures.

When he saw him two days later in the lobby of the Gymkhana Club, Blair remembered Hollis in the study hall at Eton, his peculiar posture, his arm twisted behind his head, his hand clutching his untidy hair, his legs crossed, as he frowned at a book on his lap, and then the bother with his slipping-down spectacles, his aiming a finger at them and restoring them to the bridge of his nose. Why were such repetitive human acts so irksome to watch?

Hollis had arrived early in the same rumpled jacket and wrinkled Oxford bags and scuffed shoes, his hot face glowing with perspiration that thickened his hair—pale, preoccupied, far from home, sitting under the mounted heads of a tiger, a brown bear, a musk deer, and several stags with racks of antlers. He looked miserable. His posture, his clothes, the expression on his face marked him out as someone who did not belong.

All this Blair saw through the glass in the entrance door, where he'd paused to study him. He wished he hadn't agreed to this, but Seeley was away, Hollis was at a loose end—no debating teams in colonial Rangoon, nothing at all in the Raj a fit subject for debate. It would have been churl-

ish for Blair to turn his back on him. Yet the pomposity at Anderson's—
"Behold the Burma sahib!"—had rankled. Blair hated to be singled out, and
this mockery was of the facetious schoolboy sort, for Seeley's amusement.
Good for Seeley not to have piled on, but then Seeley had his secrets, too.

Seeing Blair enter, Hollis came alive, untangled his arms and legs, wiped
his hands on his trousers, and tipped himself out of his armchair.

"Eric!" His tone was imploring, he looked so relieved, as though he was
being rescued.

"How do you stand this infernal heat?" he said as a greeting.

"There's generally a breeze in the afternoon—but, here, let me sign you
in, have a look at the taxidermy, then I'll show you a marvelous invention."
Blair crossed to the stand holding the open visitors' book and made a business of entering Hollis's name, enjoying keeping Hollis waiting. Then he
said, "In there"—and pointed to the door to the Smoking Room, which he
opened—"after you."

As they entered, an elderly Indian man in a khaki jacket, barefoot, wearing a tight white turban and white sash, stood at attention, saluting.

"Our punkah wallah," Blair said.

The man snatched at a woven cord and pulled hard, setting into motion
a thick fringed cloth suspended from the ceiling like a limp pennant, stirring the stale smoky air in the room, dust motes dancing in the shaft of
light from the window.

Blair dragged a chair beneath it and gestured for Hollis to sit.

"Much better," Hollis said. "I've only read about these in books. There's
an electrical fan in my room at the Strand Hotel."

"This punkah is a jolly sight more efficient, and cheaper," Blair said.
"Shall I order tea?"

"Smashing."

Blair rang for the bearer, the tea was served and placed on the table
under the punkah sweeping back and forth above them, Blair on one side,
Hollis on the other—Hollis patting his hair that was being ruffled by the
breeze from the punkah.

"You're looking splendid," Hollis said.

Blair had considered wearing his linen suit and school tie, but thought
better of it, believing it might seem he was placating Hollis, putting him on
an equal old boy footing, when what he intended was to patronize him, to
wrong-foot him by wearing his full-dress uniform.

This had the desired effect of subduing Hollis; he didn't say "Behold"
now—he had no one to say it to—and he looked properly respectful, if a
bit bewildered.

"I hardly expected to find you in frogged liveries."

Hollis glanced at a shelf of silver urns—gymkhana trophies; and at the far wall, a row of portraits, scowling men in side-whiskers, and as though for relief, he turned his face upward at the punkah swishing back and forth, scattering the dust motes. He took a gulp of the moving air, as though to restore himself.

"Or among all this trumpery."

"Welcome to the Raj, Hollis."

"What makes it so rum is that you seem to savor it. I recall how you resented touching your cap when a master walked past at school?" Hollis was still patting the blown feathers of his hair. "'I shan't,' you said. 'I won't.'"

Blair raised his cup and sipped. "I was an odious little snob."

"Yet I daresay you do a fair amount of saluting in your present position, not so?"

Hollis spoke in the manner of a debater—*little tick,* Blair thought.

"Aren't we a little crusty," Blair said, with a sneer, and then, "I give, and receive, salutes."

"How unlike the sixth form, Blair."

"This isn't the sixth form, Christopher. It's an outpost of the British Empire, as I said. The whole of it rests upon discipline the pansy Left will never understand. I'm quite happy to submit to the occasional salute if it means the preservation of good order. And I expect my men to do the same."

Interrupting, Hollis said, "You flatly refused to sing jingo songs after the Armistice."

"That was a bloody war. And I was a bloody fool. I've met many men here—and natives, too—who fought their guts out."

Hollis looked puzzled, and he smiled in bewilderment, leaning away from Blair who was sizing him up. He said, "I never thought I'd see you in uniform."

"It's part of my job."

"You look like a tram driver. What exactly does your job entail?"

"Supervision, keeping the peace, cracking skulls when necessary, making arrests, charge-sheeting dacoits the likes of which you can hardly imagine." Blair poured himself more tea as he spoke. "Following orders, for king and country."

"In other words, you've embraced the empire, holus-bolus."

"If you like," Blair said and smiled at what was probably a debater's expression, *holus-bolus.*

"What happened to *non serviam*?" But Hollis didn't wait for a reply. "Some anarchist you turned out to be."

Blair tapped a cigarette out of his silver case and lit it and puffed, eyeing Hollis with a frown, deliberately keeping him waiting. Finally he said, "I distinctly recall you were a zealous atheist."

"I found my faith," Hollis said quickly.

"Perhaps I did as well."

"King and country—really!"

"The despotic pope in Rome, Hollis, and you, *flagellum Dei*?"

"I wish to save my soul."

"I'm now thinking of Butler," Blair said. "How does it go? 'I find the nicest and best people generally profess no religion at all, but are ready to like the best men of all religions.'"

"Eric Blair, still mugging up on old Sam Butler!"

Blair wanted to hit him, as he would smack an insolent cadet. But instead he leaned toward him and said, "I won't question your beliefs. And if you had the slightest notion of what goes on here I don't think you'd question my beliefs. Murder, Hollis. I've seen rape victims—mere children—set on fire. The thievery is epic. We have a crime season like you have a season of daffodils. We have masses of monks denouncing the king."

Hollis seized on that, saying, "Can you blame them?"

"Yes, I can bloody well blame them—for that, for their treasonable speeches and sniggering insolence." Blair had begun to shout—he saw Hollis wince—and he realized he was not parrying questions anymore but was genuinely angry. "Monks are the worst—a flaming menace, and a serious threat to good order."

"Maybe they heartily resent being exploited."

"What is this, one of your debating topics—'Motion: Do we need an empire?'" Before Hollis could reply, Blair went on, "'Exploited' my arse. They have the protection of the Raj and all its institutions. They're jolly lucky. This benighted province would be chaos without them—look at the tyranny under Thibaw!"

"What rights do natives have here? What rights does that man have?" Hollis said, indicating the punkah wallah, who smiled and nodded and went on dragging at the cord. "He can't vote, he can't choose his leaders, he's excluded from most offices—including, I imagine, this club as a member."

"That man has a job and all the rights he needs," Blair said. "Natives have their own clubs. How many barrow boys in London are members of the Athenaeum?"

Hollis wagged his head and recited in a lilting tone, "Libbaty's a kind of thing that don't agree with niggers."

"You're awfully crass and predictable for an Oxford debater, quoting that Yank poet to me," Blair said.

"And you're extraordinarily phlegmatic." Hollis held up his hand, his palm facing Blair, because Blair had begun to protest. "It's just that I'm surprised to hear this from you, of all people."

Hollis wasn't cross, he was sad and bewildered, more than ever like the chap in the Wells romance who finds himself fretting in an alien landscape, outside time, murmuring *Crumbs!*

In a cold, even voice, Blair said, "I repeat. You have no idea what life is like here, my friend. Don't presume."

"Tigers," Hollis said, perhaps thinking of the mounted head he'd seen in the foyer. "And the white man's burden."

Blair said with scorn, his lip curling, "Leeches. Ticks. Sandflies. Snakes."

Hollis looked cowed, taken aback by Blair's nagging at him. He buttered a scone and heaped it with jam, not noticing that, gripping it, he'd spilled crumbs on his jacket front and his trousers. He chewed slowly, giving himself a frown of indecision and, when he swallowed, a look of defeat.

"There's a rotten sadness to it, as well," Blair said and thought of what Swann at Myaungmya had once said to him, then spoke again. "It is the poor who rob the poor."

"A desolate thought."

"What of Connolly?" Blair asked, to change the subject.

"Full of judgments," Hollis said. "The principal one is that the art of getting on at school depends on a mixture of enthusiasm and moral cowardice and social sense. The necessary apelike virtues. I'm rather more concerned with Seeley. He seemed so evasive."

"Seeley's a good egg."

"Married not long ago." Hollis continued to nibble at his scone, as he nibbled at this subject. "So he told me." He chewed, looking hungry, the flakes of his scone still sprinkling his lapels. "Never met the missus."

"The missus," said Blair, echoing the word in the same tone to mock him, "the missus is a native." He stared, seeing Hollis look up from his scone. "Hindu."

Hollis swallowed and instead of eating the rest of the scone put the last pinch of it onto his plate. Seeming astonished, he did not reply at once, but finally said, "Good heavens."

"Thus, not a consumer of beef. On the contrary, a worshipper of the sacred cow."

"Seeley married a native?"

Blair said, "The crimes of Clapham are chaste in Martaban." Still, Hollis said nothing. Blair added, "I've been to Martaban—decidedly pleasant."

As they prepared to leave, the Smoking Room door was flung open, McPake holding it to allow another man to enter—a florid-faced and heavily mustached man in uniform Blair recognized as Sergeant Sholto Haggan.

"Lofty!" he cried, seeing Blair.

"This is my friend Hollis, visiting from London."

"Aye," Haggan said. "I might have known. You're looking a bit stunned, laddie."

There was something plucky and theatrical about the two of them, old and young, both mustached, in uniform, lighting cheroots as soon as the door slammed shut, the smoke eddying past the folds of the slowly swinging punkah.

Neither of them spoke again but they both laughed, as though sharing a joke, glancing at Hollis as they did so, the pale, perspiring visitor in rumpled clothes backing away from the three men in uniform who were regarding him with mockery, Blair's gaze—"phlegmatic," he hoped—the set of his lips in a pitying smile, as though at an imposter.

THE PANOPTICON AT INSEIN

The teasing mention of Martaban to Hollis now seemed eerily premonitory, because not long after that—a few days—Blair received a cable from Frank Limouzin: SAD NEWS STOP YOUR GRANDMOTHER DIED TODAY STOP FUNERAL MONDAY FRANK. And on the Sunday he found himself at Martaban Station, just arrived, greeted by Frank in a black suit and tie, black armband, looking lugubrious, gasping in the heat.

But after the ferry to Battery Point, in the gharry, Frank seemed relieved and even impulsively chatty—"East wind from the hills, cool things down, daresay a spell of fine weather, fancy a pastille?"—and offered Blair a yellow lozenge from an open tin. Later at the wake, Frank was fretful again, burdened and breathless, as grieving people often are, exhausting himself, needing tediously to reassure other mourners that he was holding up. He kept repeating, "Eighty-two, she had good innings, smoked till the end"—turning aside, to get away—"and this is her grandson, Eric, big bug in the police."

Blair did not know any of them apart from Aimee and Kathleen and Mah Hlim, who stood in a receiving line, acknowledging the mourners, who murmured their condolences. But there were few mourners, less than a dozen, none Burmese, none Indian, all of them aged.

"Mum was active in the community, but that's past tense—she outlived all her friends," Frank said, seeming to explain the small number of mourners.

At the funeral, Blair sat with the family in the front pew at St. Matthew's, with Aimee and Kathleen, tall and pale between the dusky half-castes, while Frank sang full-throated, "O God Our Help in Ages Past," Mah Hlim squinting silently at the altar, looking buffeted, as though facing a high wind.

The Reverend MacIntosh read a psalm and delivered a bleak homily, calling Therese Limouzin "the salt of the earth," though mispronouncing the family name, making it sound like the automobile, which made Blair cough into his hand to cover his laughter.

Afterward, tea and funeral baked meats for the mourners at Frank's bungalow, Blair realizing midway through it, covertly consulting his pocket watch, that he still had time to catch the night train back to Rangoon from Martaban.

"I look forward to coming back," he said to Frank at the wharf, hoping his lack of sincerity didn't show. It seemed incredible to him that these people were his family—irregular marriages, down on their luck owing to a fall in prices (they'd taken a chance on the rice crop but hadn't counted on Indian competition), Frank's timber business failing, the family living in a dimming twilight, gripped by the same paralysis as their fellow colonials, complaining of their lot but incapable of relocating to England, a place none of them knew, which was more foreign than China. And Aimee and Kathleen were homegrown misfits, not welcome anywhere.

"Big hullabaloo," McPake said in a dark voice in the mess when Blair entered, still dazed from his sleepless night in the train, but keeping his grandmother's funeral a secret—how could he possibly explain?

"Trouble?"

"A right fankle, Eric. Eighteen of them broke through the perimeter, shouting, singing."

"Dacoits singing?" Blair peered at McPake, but McPake only frowned. "What—ragging about?"

"Not dacoits—students, some wee monks, all sort of political badmashes, screaming their guts out against Burmah Oil and the empire. 'Ga hame! Ga hame!'"

Hearing McPake mimic the monks in a Glasgow accent made him smile.

"It's nae funny, Blair. Comstock's beside himself."

"Angry?"

"Crabbit, aye—he blew me up. And faulted you for nae being on duty."

"I was attending a funeral, Angus. Why didn't he blame you?"

"Because I made the arrests, didn't I? I gave the lot of them a thick ear."

"You did it alone?"

"Why not?" He gave Blair the sullen brassy stare that went with his usual whoppers. "They're all in lockup now, licking their wounds."

"What are the charges?"

"Causing an affray, endangering public safety, uttering menaces." McPake stroked his mustache, and Blair was admiring as always at the brute's rough manner in great contrast to his smart uniform, his gleaming Sam Browne belt, his polished boots, the gloves he often wore over his hairy hands, his baton. "Comstock's been asking for ye. Consider paying the chief a visit, lad."

Blair went directly to the superintendent's office, and when Comstock greeted him with, "Ah, the wandering minstrel," he knew it was a reference to his drunken singing at Meldrum's, as well as his unexplained absence. But Comstock was intent in a book, not looking up at Blair.

"I was required at a funeral, sir," Blair said, loud because the man seemed to be ignoring him.

"I find it tedious to listen to excuses."

Comstock was licking his thumb and turning pages in what looked like a lawbook that might have been the Penal Code—it was fat, with the heft of a bible, and a mass of fine print.

"I understand the intruders have been rounded up."

Now Comstock glared at him from behind the wide desk, the book open before him, and said, "But how did these monkeys manage to climb through the fence in the first instance?"

"I gather they surprised the men on duty."

"Your men, Blair."

"Some of them are dogsbodies, I'm afraid."

"Dogsbodies," Comstock said with contempt. "A commander's complaint of inept guards is in reality a confession of faulty foresight. The conclusion is inescapable. You are responsible for this balls-up, Blair."

"I'm sure that needs to be said, sir."

Tapping the pages of the book—it had to be the Penal Code—he said, "They'll be tried for various offenses in the coming days. They will be—all of them—found guilty. They will be sent forthwith to Insein Prison. You will escort them."

"Very good, sir."

"You will not be returning to Syriam. I'm transferring you to Insein. You will be going with them. And I pray that you make a better job of it there than you've done here."

Blair began to speak, asking for details, but Comstock snorted, cutting him off, looking bored, and dragged the thick book toward him again, pinching up a page, speaking to its dense print.

"Dismissed."

Insein was not far, twelve miles or less by train from Rangoon Station, but because of the number of prisoners it was necessary to send them in relays, six at a time, under guard, on the ferry, and thence in closed vans to the main station. The fettered prisoners were old and young, monks in robes, students in school uniforms, working men in lungyis, and two clerks in white suits—the suits showing signs of struggle, tears and stains. They chanted, they shouted slogans, they stamped in their chains, they swore at the Indian guards, calling out "*Kalar!*"—the abusive word.

Blair arrived with the last group and all his belongings, his trunk, his boxes of books, and two large circular baskets, his ducks in one, chickens in the other, his cat tangled in a string bag. And when at last they all boarded the train—prisoners and guards and Blair and his cat—in the reserved carriage, Blair felt himself like a prisoner, being punished, sentenced to an indeterminate period of time to Insein Prison.

"I was expecting the villains but not the livestock," the prison superintendent said at Insein, greeting Blair, as the Indian guards marched the prisoners along the platform.

Blair stood and watched with the man, the guards ordering the prisoners to sit while two horse-drawn wagons with high sides and wooden benches clattered toward the station gate. The prisoners shuffled up a ramp into the wagons—their ankles still fettered, the shackles clanking—and they sat on the benches, their heads bowed against the dust raised by the hooves and the wheels. Up they went on Commissioner's Road, the short distance to the arch of the Victorian entryway, stopping before the gate. The arch was decorated, fluted on its sides, sculpted with palmettes on panels, and petals lifted upward like tongues, the cupola above its keystone dated 1887. But its ornaments were less impressive to Blair than its thickness and its solidity. He thought, *This prison will last for two hundred years and will always be full to capacity.*

Just then, nearby, a rooster stretched its neck and screamed, rousing the hens to squawk.

"A few of my animals," Blair said, seeing his baskets on a cart shifting with the furious birds. "Not to worry. They're well behaved. Fresh eggs, sir—and this cat's more than equal to any rat."

But the man was not listening; he was staring at Blair, his mustache twitching, a sneerlike smile on his face, of derision, a kind of triumph, as though having cornered his prey.

"Our Etonian."

And now Blair remembered, the dinner guest from the *Herefordshire*, the Scot, whose name escaped him, but it was certainly him, eagle nosed, mustached, pipe-smoking, contemptuous, blimpish and bluff.

"Ah, yes," Blair said. "You are—"

"Captain Peddy-Wilmot," the man said. "Come this way, I'll show you to your quarters."

He sounded resentful, blaming Blair for some obscure wrong, as though the captain knew every detail of Blair's failures—his lapses in Myaungmya and Twante, his secret doubts, his covert visits to Monkey Point, his being cheeked by the schoolboys at Pagoda Road, all of Comstock's merciless bollockings.

Supairvision, supairvision, supairvision—that was the man. And there was a toothy wife, a burra memsahib.

Blair should have known they'd meet again—in part because Burma was a community of white sahibs, and it was in the nature for the sahibs to interact and share what they knew. But he thought of the sahib log with detachment, as a writer, not as a loyal Burma sahib, and he concluded that it was part of life's design, obscure to a schoolboy but in adulthood unfolding without remorse, episode after episode, and why? Because actions always had consequences, and consequences were the drivers of plots. Robinson's downfall was foretold in an opium den, Blair's grandmother Limouzin's death was inescapable, and thus his presence in Moulmein; his transfer here was result of his failures in Syriam. The empire was not large, it was a closed and clubby system, and in time, shuttling back and forth in its narrowness, all sahibs ended up entangled, just like this, Blair and the inevitable Peddy-Wilmot. It was not apparent at first, but life had a plot, and there was always another twist, and he thought, *Whatever next?*

The imprisoned feeling he'd had among the foul-smelling men and boys, shackled on the train, returned to Blair that night in his bungalow, his chickens in the tree boughs, his ducks sheltering against its trunk, the cat asleep on the sofa, as he sat smoking in his rattan lounge chair, before he'd risen to light the lamps. The house was unadorned, simple sticks of government-issue furniture, and in the darkness just after sunset he realized he was near enough to the Hlaing River for the hum of the mud and the mangroves to penetrate his parlor.

He was a prisoner like his prisoners; he'd been sent like those men for an indeterminate period. He was being punished, serving a sentence, because he was guilty—of what, he had no idea. Perhaps, by some political witchery of surveillance they had discovered the rebellion in the heart of his other self, the hatred he felt every day when he woke from sleep, and remembered he was in Burma, and rose to go to work, to issue his first orders. It was a hatred he so yearned to conceal he might have seemed secretive—his cunning showing in his anxious eyes. He had been successful in convincing Hollis of his loyalty to the sahib log, but his superiors in the police were shrewder and more experienced men in the ways of backsliders. They were stalwarts of the Raj, who knew a doubter when they saw one.

Or was it something else, something simpler? In his first week at Insein, Blair familiarized himself with the odd design of the prison, a round structure, its cell blocks at the periphery, its central hub a watchtower connected to its circular edge by corridors like spokes in a wheel. From a bird's point of view Insein Prison was in every respect a cart wheel sunk in the Burma dust. Its bleak cells were crowded with sullen men in grubby lungyis and skullcaps, squatting on the earthen floor or seated on benches, the more dangerous and violent prisoners confined one or two to a cell, in chains, the trusty men in the laundry or kitchen. It was an awful place smelling of shit and black beetles, a doss-house with barred windows, a lunatic asylum judging from the shrieks and squawks. A fanciful design for a prison, but without a scrap of privacy; in reality a human zoo.

Assigned to General Stores, the inventory of goods and provisions— but his men did the donkeywork—Blair rarely saw any prisoners unless he wished to. Being curious, disapproving of the conditions, he strolled the perimeter in his free time, glad not to be a guard.

He'd hired a cook and a bearer for his bungalow, two Karen Christians— men, more's the pity, but he had resolved to be above suspicion. One afternoon, Peddy-Wilmot's houseboy brought a card over, the bearer taking charge of it, presenting it to Blair at lunch.

"Memsahib send *thakin* chitty."

An invitation to tea, three days hence, harmless enough, and it would put him in bad odor with the captain if he made excuses. Blair accepted— the houseboy delivering his card by return. On the appointed afternoon, he was met by the woman he vaguely recognized from the captain's table on the *Herefordshire*, a freckled somewhat yellowish burra memsahib in a long dress with loose sleeves, peering at him hungrily, showing her teeth, saying, "A Scottish welcome, Mr. Blair—Blair is Scots, of course."

"My father claimed it to be English."

"John Blair was chaplain to our national hero, Sir William Wallace."

"I was not aware of that." Another inconvenient Blair, Scotsman and God-botherer—good lord. "Fascinating."

"You'll not want any supper later," she said as she described the items on the sideboard for the tea—meat pies and griddle scones, ox tongue and sticky cakes. "And tatties!"

"Looks ripping."

"Our Muriel made the jam!"

At first he took this to mean the scurrying servant, a Burmese woman in an apron setting out cups on the tea table, and he almost thanked her, but he was glad he'd hesitated—anyway, one never thanked servants—when he saw a girl of twenty, perhaps more, sitting on a chair opposite who must have been Muriel—because servants never sat—looking demure, hands folded on her lap, fingers laced, as her mother poured tea.

Now he remembered more, being summoned to the captain's table, the talk of the war, the sinking of a ship off Colombo, his being interrogated by the Peddy-Wilmots about Eton and pressed for details about his father's job in India. They had mentioned their daughter. And there was that long-ago note that had been delivered to him in Twante, inviting him to tea, beginning, *Should you find your good self in Rangoon . . .*

He'd failed; he'd been expected to take an interest in Muriel, but here she was, still unmarried, still at home, her parents resenting their having to find a suitable husband for her, blaming Blair for being casual, appealing to him once again.

Muriel's hair was fashionably bobbed, cut short and smoothed, giving her a shiny helmet. Her dress was long, patterned with flowers, but her arms were bare and seemed so white set off by the dark dress. She wore high-heeled shoes, and sat compactly, her feet together, her hands on her knees now, looking expectant, as though awaiting a summons.

"Charmed," she said when her mother introduced her, the mother adding, "And do call me Edith." But Muriel said nothing more—she blinked, she smiled, and Blair felt a pang for her, because he, too, knew what it was like to sit, seeming to await a summons—and for what?

The other guest—Edith called her "Our good neighbor, Mrs. Morwen Jellicoe"—was more conversational, even voluble. "Old Etonian," she said. "I take you to be a reader" and offered that she'd recently finished *On a Chinese Screen.*

Blair was reassured, jolted by a stab of happiness, as though meeting someone who spoke a secret dialect they shared, a kindred soul, a believer in books. And before he said more, Mrs. Jellicoe was elaborating on Maugham.

"I met him at the Pegu Club in '22 when he passed through Rangoon—hideous stammer, hardly understood a bally word he said. A most unprepossessing soul."

"His writing is like that, too, which is something I admire."

"How so?"

"Samuel Butler says that a man's style in his writing should be like his dress, attracting as little attention as possible."

"That's jolly good," Mrs. Jellicoe said. "But old Nancy Maugham had a chum—handsome chap, frightfully social, who seemed to like the bottle. Oh, well, who doesn't?"

She was provocative, teasing, pretty, late twenties perhaps, gaunt and rather bony, slender with black hair bobbed so close to her head it passed for an Eton crop, a chalky face that intensified the darkness of that hair, reddened lips, blue eyes—he took her coloring to be Cornish. She seemed tall, though that may have been the effect of her black high-buttoned shoes. And she smoked, a cigarette in a carved ivory holder she held in her small white teeth.

She had opinions about suffrage—"Why shouldn't we have the vote?"—and said she liked to gamble at the racecourse in Rangoon—"Who doesn't love a flutter?"

Blair took her to be unmarried, or a widow—the black dress, something in her reckless talk—but when Edith mentioned that her husband, Alec, was sorry he couldn't be at the tea, Mrs. Jellicoe said, "Nor mine—Humphrey's in timber, and he's hideously busy. But he knows I'm well occupied as Muriel's chaperone."

"Do you find there are many amusements here?"

"Jolly few, as Muriel will attest. You'll see, to your sorrow, Mr. Blair!"

Muriel smiled and nodded and twisted her fingers.

"We take refuge in books."

Mrs. Jellicoe was confident and bright, even in the way she sat, her legs crossed, kicking one leg, showing her ankle and the lacy fringe of her petticoat, as she bounced her beckoning shoe.

"I'm sure there are larks."

"Oh, yes," Mrs. Jellicoe said. "Balls in the country! Balls in the country!"

Blair was surprised to find he'd enjoyed the tea, and when Edith said, "We hope to see you again in future"—which seemed a signal that tea was at an end, his cue to leave—he found himself thanking them all with a sincerity that was new to him and not fraudulent. Walking back to his bungalow at dusk through the jasmine that was just beginning to flower in the shadows of the rising darkness, all he could think of was the ripple of the flesh-colored silk and lace petticoat brushing her ankles at the hem of Mrs. Jellicoe's long dress.

Stores and provisions—a merchant's work—and supervising the warehouse kept Blair apart from the prison. Under the pretense of running an errand, he still made visits, but never for long, and always avoiding the hostile gaze of prisoners, appalled by their conditions. He was content in his bungalow, his chickens roamed free, and after he hired a mali to tend the garden, the man dug a pit behind the bungalow that he filled with water for the ducks.

He wondered when he'd see Captain Peddy-Wilmot again, and that thought seemed premonitory, too, because very soon afterward the man showed up without prior notice at the warehouse. Blair was glad to be found at his desk. "Thought I'd pay you a visit," the captain said, but for the man who insisted on "supairvision" at all times, it was to carry out an informal inspection.

Was he aggrieved that Blair showed no interest in Muriel? Probably not—Blair had the sense that the captain disapproved of him for being a toff. Perhaps it was a father's despair that no man had so far showed an interest in his daughter. All Blair remembered from the tea was the spiky clever Mrs. Jellicoe, her ivory cigarette holder in her teeth, the tantalizing scrap of lace on her petticoat, and her singsong "Balls in the country."

There were more inspections by the captain under the pretense of casual visits. On one of them, Blair said to Peddy-Wilmot, "I'm quite content here, but I must say I'm curious to have a dekko at the prison."

"To what end, Blair?"

"Over the past several years I've sent a fair number of men here. One wonders what's become of them."

"Any lag in particular?"

Affecting to be casual, but he'd often thought of the man, sometimes feeling anguish, recalling his small terrified face, his helplessness in chains, Blair said, "Oh, a chap from Myaungmya in my time there in '24, my first serious case. Convicted of murder in the court in Bassein. Hacked his land-lord to death."

"One of yours, was he?"

"Weedy little chap," Blair said, ashamed of saying it so dismissively of the poor desperate man, facing eviction from his mean hut by the greedy landlord, like a peasant in a Russian tale of oppression.

"You won't find him here."

"Shifted elsewhere?"

"Hanged."

His head slightly tilted, Peddy-Wilmot seemed fascinated by the look of horror on Blair's face, horror changing to pity, softening to grief, Blair unable to keep his lips from trembling.

"Buddhist monk from Twante," Blair said to divert Peddy-Wilmot's scrutiny. "Big man at the monastery, they called Sayadaw Wirathu—charge of sedition."

"That black bastard's here right enough, with his cohort of poongees, chanting and moaning and trying to put the wind up. They've made a right little monastery of their cell."

"Various rapists, arsonists, dacoits," Blair said. "I've got their names in my notes. Just wondering what became of them."

"What became of them," Peddy-Wilmot said, "was shackles and confinement and a good deal of enforced silence in the hole. We don't encourage chuntering. The monks are useless, but some of the others are handy in the workhouse, sewing gunnysacks. Give me the names—by all means pay them a social call."

It was not the policeman Blair but his other self, the restless inquisitor, the doubter, the contrarian, who consulted his diary and copied out the names, and next to each name the man's offense, from the murderer in his first month in Myaungmya to the most recent arrests, the eighteen men and boys whom he'd escorted to Insein. There were thirty-seven altogether, the most serious crimes, though now he knew the landlord's murderer had been executed.

"Observe the ingenious design of this prison—it's a modern marvel, really," Peddy-Wilmot said, on the day he accompanied Blair to the cells of the men he'd indicated. "Circular, see"—*sair-cular*—"inspired by Jeremy Bentham. Eton chap like yourself ought to know Bentham."

"I believe he called for the abolition of hanging," Blair said.

"That's just silliness. It's the gallows that keeps the empire safe. He was on firmer ground with this—what you might term a panopticon. A single guard, there"—Paddy-Wilmot raised his baton to the watchtower—"can monitor all the inmates from that central tower."

"Panopticon," Blair said. "Greek."

"I'm sure you're mistaken."

"It means 'all-seeing.'"

"Isn't education a wonderful thing," Peddy-Wilmot said sourly. "Your pongee is in the next terrace."

"*Saitpain*," Sayadaw Wirathu said when he saw Blair approaching his cell. The monk was sitting upright at the center of a group of kneeling monks, holding forth in what might have been a session of spiritual instruction, or maybe a political harangue. When he spoke again, the kneeling monks laughed. He repeated the words, "*Myint-thaw-thit-pin*."

"Blighter seems to remember you."

"He's chaffing me."

"How so?"

"Calling me 'Tall Tree,'" Blair said. "His idea of a joke. Ragging me for my height. Burmese are quite keen on nicknames."

"They can laugh all they want. They'll be here for donkey's years, if I have anything to say about it."

Staring at the *sayadaw,* now looking much older, his face paler, like yellowed parchment, his sunken eyes ringed with dark pouches, Blair remembered his sedition, the accusations, denouncing the Raj, rubbishing the king and the British—*We are their slaves.* If anything he looked more aggrieved, but now he had passionate adherents, the dozen or so younger monks in his cell.

"*Ye-thar,*" the *sayadaw* said and turned his head and spat. Policeman.

"He's got five more years. That'll cure him of his nonsense, what?"

Blair nodded and moved on, and he thought, *Never.*

"They have food, they have tea, they have clean straw in their mattresses, they're a sight better off than many on the outside—yet they go on grousing," Peddy-Wilmot said. "Your very own badmashes," he added as though holding Blair responsible for their complaining.

The eighteen protesters who'd breached the fence at Burmah Oil in Syriam were nearby—most of them young; they looked lonely and frightened and sleepless, crammed into a small cell of one of the prison's spokelike corridors.

"They're political—can't reason with politicals," Peddy-Wilmot said. "They long for the day when Burma has its own king or generalissimo or whatever"—he whacked the bars with his stick, causing the prisoners to wince. "And if that day ever comes, when they have their own native government, they'll be worse off. Probably back here, I daresay, for offending the wogs in charge!"

Blair was pained to see them. How frail they looked, how trapped in their cage, how defiant, many of them no older than sixth formers at Eton, some of whom held the same anticolonial beliefs.

"Notice how they squat," Peddy-Wilmot said. "No white man can sit on his heels in the same attitude as an Oriental."

"Odd, I hadn't noticed," Blair said.

"But a monkey can."

Peddy-Wilmot walked with him to the entrance, but on the way seemed to remember something and gestured to a guard to unlock a heavily barred door he said led to the cell for condemned prisoners. It was far darker, more foul smelling than any of the others, the prisoners chained to the floor, and they sat cross-legged in silence.

"Sahib," one of the men called out.

"Seems to know you, Blair."

Blair recognized him as Mullapoodi, the shopkeeper he'd arrested on one of his last village patrols out of Twante.

"Charged with dousing his wife with paraffin and setting her alight. My inspectors called it dowry murder. Claimed it was an accident, caused by her sari catching fire."

"He'll pay."

But seeing the man, pathetic, imploring, Blair recalled the case, and he was certain Mullapoodi's mother—enraged by the unpaid dowry—had committed the murder; and that her son was protecting her. He remembered the second visit, the mother's plump pitted cheeks, her impassive face in the shop, looking past her customer to sneer at him, his asking his inspector Veeraswami to say in Telegu, *You smell of paraffin.*

Peddy-Wilmot walked Blair to the entrance to the prison, but before he said goodbye he leaned back, taking in the well-shaped archway of the gate, the graceful cupola, and said, "A mill—for grinding rogues honest."

Several days later, Blair went back. He felt you never saw anything clearly until you saw it alone, without interruption. Peddy-Wilmot breathing down his neck and making explanations had prevented him from concentrating on the prisoners and their condition. Recognized at the gatehouse as Peddy-Wilmot's visitor, he was saluted and he walked directly through the prison to the cell holding Sayadaw Wirathu.

This time the monk seemed prepared to lecture Blair. He obviously remembered his arrest—"Where are your Indians?" he called out. Hearing him, the other monks laughed at Blair.

"We are slaves of the British," the *sayadaw* said. "You are stealing our wealth. The British are thieves."

Blair said—lamely, he realized—"We have built schools."

"We have the Buddha. And our pagoda. We have no need of schools." Wirathu then raised his hand to Blair. "You are evil. According to our belief those who have done evil in their lives will spend the rest of their next incarnation in the shape of a rat or a frog or some low animal."

"What will you be?"

"I wish to become a Buddha," the *sayadaw* said. "But there is hope—you can acquire merit. Buy some fish and set them free. Or be like our brother *hypongi* at the bowl."

Blair had not seen the man who was in the far corner of the cell, squatting before a tin basin, stirring the soapy water, removing one bowl after another, wiping them clean and stacking them.

"You can also acquire merit being humble—washing simple bowls."

Of course, become a dishwasher and atone, Blair thought on his way home and laughed at the absurdity of it. Still, he felt he was in debt to Peddy-Wilmot for the favor of allowing him to roam the prison. He wished to show he was willing, he felt obliged for the tea, and he was also quite bored. He sent Edith Peddy-Wilmot a note saying he was available for an outing with Muriel and Mrs. Jellicoe. The response was immediate: yes, a Saturday race meeting at the Rangoon Turf Club, Mrs. Jellicoe acting as chaperone.

Blair met them at Insein Station by the river, both women dressed so well he was ashamed of his old linen suit and the only necktie he owned. Muriel wore a wide-brimmed sunhat, Mrs. Jellicoe a cloche and an ankle-length, long-sleeved dress—a different style, but fetching, watered silk trimmed with lace, yet there was still something sleek and boyish about her.

In the bright sun in her brimless hat, even shaded by her umbrella she seemed older, and she must have been told of Blair's tour of the prison, because at the racecourse she asked what he'd thought of the experience and the inmates.

"In retrospect, I think the politicals were the saddest," he said.

"They deserve to be punished," Muriel said.

Mrs. Jellicoe raised an eyebrow, but said nothing; yet when Muriel rushed to the rail next to the track, urging her horse on, Mrs. Jellicoe said, "It's utter bollocks."

"Their beliefs?"

"No, their incarceration. If I happened to be Burmese, perish the thought, I'd be in there with them."

And then—Muriel still at the rail, howling at her horse—Mrs. Jellicoe positioned her umbrella as a shield, crouching beneath it and placing a gloved hand on Blair's thigh; she squeezed and whispered, "We'd like to see more of you. Muriel and me."

24

THE SYCE

There began a charade, a social round, initiated by Mrs. Jellicoe, at first formal and occasional, then casual and often, Saturday excursions to the Rangoon Turf Club for a flutter, and for the ladies it seemed an excuse to dress up. Or they went for tea at the Insein Club annex, a veranda where women were allowed if escorted by a member—but few male club members ever seemed to appear at this poky place. The Insein Club afternoon teas usually extended to a stroll by the Hlaing River to a particular parapet enclosing a roofed viewing platform, also inconspicuous, rarely visited by any other European from Insein. All these outings were chaperoned by Mrs. Jellicoe, whose role made Blair smile, her lending meaning to the word *duenna* with its suggestion of plotting.

Blair found her agreeable for her modern views, her forthright manner, for her taking charge, and he realized that these excursions were to his taste, not for wooing Muriel, but for the pleasure of being with Mrs. Jellicoe. And he sensed the feeling was mutual, Mrs. Jellicoe using Muriel as a way of chatting with him, about books, about the colonial conventions she said she found ridiculous, about her mockery of the Raj itself. She was someone vaguely out of Kipling (a character who would come to a sticky end for her shocking views), but explicitly out of Lawrence for her frankness.

He had never met a woman in England quite like her, so sure of herself, so contrary, so subtly sexual, so unshockable. He had never been touched so intimately by an Englishwoman like that—her squeeze. He'd blushed, he'd drawn back, but he'd yearned for more.

Mrs. Jellicoe was a reader, she'd been an undergraduate at Oxford—St. Hilda's, she said—but had dropped out to care for her brother, wounded in the war, and married his chum, Humphrey Jellicoe—and, yes, she said she was Cornish, born Morwen Penrose, which explained her dramatic coloring, her blue eyes and black hair and the paleness she somehow preserved here in spite of the roasting sun, a pallor he found so sensual.

Keeping Muriel company was a way of placating the Peddy-Wilmots, the captain especially, Blair's hard-to-please superior, but seeing Muriel deepened his friendship with Mrs. Jellicoe, acting as chaperone—the woman friend he'd always craved to have. In the density of Syriam and Rangoon, among the crowds, his furtive absences had not been noticed: his fellow officer, the soldiers, his guards—all male—had been incurious. But here in Insein, the prison like a fort, the town like a garrison, the compound of staff bungalows and married quarters, he knew he was closely watched. He could not risk slipping out on the train to Rangoon and Monkey Point. And when he did go to the bookshop, Mrs. Jellicoe went with him, Muriel in tow, Blair for books, Muriel for magazines—*Home Chat, Nash's, London Mail, The Queen*—("the shinies" Mrs. Jellicoe called them) that had arrived on the latest ship. Blair would glance at a new issue, and see "All About Coverlets," and his heart sank.

"Tripe," Mrs. Jellicoe said, preferring the *London Illustrated News*. And when Muriel was leafing through a recent issue, or engrossed in "Fashions for Teas," Mrs. Jellicoe became provocative with Blair, encouraging him in his doubts.

"None of the different races here really get on with one another, you see—Burmese can't abide the Indians—but they're united in their hatred of the British," she said. "As for the sahibs and the memsahibs, the plumage and the pomposity—it's theater, you know. Ha! The great British passion, from Willie Shakespeare to Willie Maugham, dressing up and delivering lines and taking bows. But who does the work? The natives, while the sahib log sits and swills gin and pretends to know what they're doing, which is bugger all."

One of her rants ended with, "Never get something done by a European when a native can do it," and another was, "Twelve thousand armed men subduing a population of fourteen million."

Mrs. Jellicoe uttered Blair's secret thoughts aloud, gave voice and meaning to his doubts, and articulated the contradictions in his heart that he had not revealed to anyone, even himself. That other self, the sneak, the rebel, the sensualist—Mrs. Jellicoe seemed to speak for him, the inner man Blair thought of as George.

One day when Muriel was bent over in the train, absorbed in working a buttonhook to fasten her shoe, Mrs. Jellicoe said, "I suppose up-country you had a 'keep.'"

She made the word precious by saying it in a teasing way, the word a burra memsahib might use when referring to a native mistress. When Blair blushed and began to deny it, she went on, "Burmese women—queer little creatures. I saw a lot of them enjoying a picnic. I thought they were all boys. They're a kind of Dutch doll, aren't they?"

The exactitude of her description astonished Blair but he was abashed when he thought of Margaret in Twante. He said, "Chap in my first post had a keep—called her his housegirl, but it was really a chance for a bit of how's-your-father."

"I daresay Humphrey indulges himself in that sort of concubinage," Mrs. Jellicoe said. "And like most men he thinks I don't notice. It absolutely never occurs to a male hypocrite that a woman can be just as hypocritical in ways of satisfying herself."

Blair turned to Muriel, to see if she was listening, but she was still smiling and poking her shoe with her buttonhook.

"Frigging oneself doesn't always do the job, you see," Mrs. Jellicoe said.

That was beyond Lawrence, and it thrilled Blair to hear the dark word spoken aloud by this attractive woman, fragrant with perfume that was like rose petals, sitting sideways in her parlor, her legs crossed, working her foot up and down, her small foot, her pretty shoe, her cigarette holder between her fingers. Muriel gasping with pleasure manipulating her buttonhook, and in the photograph on the sideboard, Humphrey in Moulmein grinning like a fool in a howdah on an elephant.

Blair was shocked but he was pleased, because he hated the prim vulgarity of a coquette but was roused by a woman's recklessness, not that he'd ever witnessed it except from a tart, and they wanted money for it. Mrs. Jellicoe saw he was shocked, and she exploited it, being more explicit, loving the word *buggery*, or *bugger*, and she gloated when Blair blushed. She sometimes touched his leg or the back of his hand and said, "Forgive me—I'm a wicked woman."

Then Muriel would wake from her fussing, or would return from the next room, or from outside where she was dawdling over Mrs. Jellicoe's dog, or stroking her cat, and would say, "What have I missed?"

"I was just about to deal," Mrs. Jellicoe would say, "but I need you to cut the cards."

They played three-handed cribbage, using a special three-sided board for scoring.

"These are my holes," Mrs. Jellicoe said, tapping the board. "I want you to remember that, Eric." He looked away, at a loss for words. She saw he was looking for relief at the photograph of Humphrey on the elephant and asked, "Do you know Moulmein?"

Blair was now comfortable enough with her to disclose that he had relatives there—"My mother's people. Pukka sahibs, the lot of them. Also in timber in a small way."

"Humphrey would know them," Mrs. Jellicoe said, as Muriel scored. "You're pegging my hole, that's awfully sweet of you, Muriel. Or would you rather peg it, Eric?"

They played to sixty-one points, rather than making it a longer game, Mrs. Jellicoe usually pegging out as winner.

"Loser forfeits," she said.

Muriel usually lost, but she said it was the fault of her cards.

"Stand in the corner, close your eyes, count to a hundred."

And when Muriel turned her back and muttered and sighed, Mrs. Jellicoe slipped her hand beneath the card table and touched Blair, and he blushed, not daring to put his hand on hers. Late at night he woke and recalled with delight and confusion her insistent fingers.

On another day she said after the game, "What will your forfeit be, Eric, when the time comes?"

"He can be our prisoner," Muriel said.

"I expect he'd fancy that," Mrs. Jellicoe said. "I'll think of something more punishing."

On some Saturday afternoons, the two women often watched Blair when he played football with the guards, Blair on the side of his fellow officers, the Burmese on the opposing team—the Indians preferred cricket. Blair was an able center forward, and the games were spirited. On the pitch there was a kind of equality, or at least a lack of inhibition, the matches turning physical in a manner Blair perceived as bellicose. Blair was taken advantage of for his loping slowness, the Burmese sprinting in front of him, obstructing him when he kicked.

"That native tripped you," Muriel said.

"Bugger getting his own back," Mrs. Jellicoe said.

But Blair shrugged. "All sports are mock warfare."

Then drinks, or cribbage, and Blair walked with Muriel and Mrs. Jellicoe back to the Peddy-Wilmots, and afterward home, parting with Mrs. Jellicoe at a fork in the path at the compound.

"Fancy another hand of cards tomorrow?"

"I don't mind."

"You might lose, my boy."

She left him with that thought, touching him as she turned away, a little slap that he savored later, thinking, *Whatever next?* But her touch in the path had taken place near a great leggy bush of night-blooming jasmine that filled the soft air and sweetened that memory.

It gave Blair pause to think that she was married and was older than him—but how much? She'd dropped out of St. Hilda's during the war, say 1916, when she was in her second year she said, so if that were the case she was now twenty-eight or twenty-nine. He was twenty-two—not a huge difference. But she had lived in Burma for the past seven years with Humphrey and had made up her mind that the empire was a charade—"A bit like us, pretending to care about Muriel but in reality caring about each other."

"Do you mean that?"

"Isn't Muriel our excuse?"

He loved her for stating plainly their position, though he had no idea how it would end. He told himself he was new at this. But it seemed that he mattered in an important way, for the first time in his life—that he was an essential element in the plot, the sort of romantic entanglement you might find in Kipling or Maugham—amorous deceit in the hot, scented air of a British colony, the ruse of a chaperone. Yet too steamy for those authors, and not Lawrence's love affairs in the midlands. What was unfolding, as far as he knew, was a story that had not yet been written. That was the wonder of it, as well as the promise that it was his own story, an episode in the hidden life of his secret self, that he might himself one day write.

In her idle almost schoolgirlish fashion, always agreeing to an outing, Muriel continued to cooperate—though she preferred the clamor of the Rangoon Turf Club, shopping at Rowe's department store, or seeing a comedy at the Excelsior to the longueurs in the bookshop, or the solitude of watching boats and birds from the upraised platform by the river.

Once, on the platform, looking through her binoculars, Muriel said, "Native men are so queer," and giggled.

"In what way?" Blair said.

"They squat on their hams to do a piddle." Her binoculars were pressed against her eyes.

"Yes, quite extraordinary," Mrs. Jellicoe said and pursed her lips at Blair in mockery.

Muriel was enthusiastic at cribbage, but inept—"I'm bottom, I'm afraid"—her forfeit allowing Mrs. Jellicoe to tap Blair's thigh or pinch his fingers, pinches like promises.

One evening Blair lost. "I'm bottom now."

"You're bum!" Mrs. Jellicoe said.

"Forfeit!" Muriel shrieked. "Shall we make him stand in the corner?"

Yawning, Mrs. Jellicoe said, "It's a bit late. Why don't we revisit this subject next time? I have to think of something rum. Now, I must hurry you home, Muriel."

And so they left Mrs. Jellicoe's bungalow and parted on Commissioner's Road, the two women turning right toward the prison and the superintendent's quarters, Blair continuing for the ten-minute walk to his bungalow, cheered by the sight at dusk of his chickens flapping upward into the boughs of his peepul tree, each one choosing a branch as a roost for the night, the ducks huddled together in the stillness beneath the house, the cat greeting him with a purr at the top of the stairs.

It was the evening mosquito interlude, the hour just at nightfall when it was impossible to sit for any length of time on the veranda. He shut the screen door firmly behind him and, inside, poured himself a whiskey. He sat in his parlor at the side of the house, replaying the events of the day—his reporting for duty at the warehouse, a visit to the prison at noon for lunch at the mess, then off-duty at four to meet Muriel and Mrs. Jellicoe; then cards, and "You're bum!" and "Forfeit!"

And the evening had ended, delightfully ambiguous.

He'd had sandwiches at the cribbage game and Muriel had brought tea cakes, so he wasn't hungry. He poured himself another whiskey and sat in the darkness. Outside the window the moonlight splashed on the leaves of the peepul tree, where the chickens stirred from time to time in the branches with low squawks and a flutter of wings, and he heard the clop and grind of hooves mashing on gravel, probably one of his nearer neighbors back from hacking.

"*Thakin.*"

A shadow in the doorway—his bearer, Tun, with a lantern.

"Sahib come."

Blair muttered at the interruption—he'd been so serene, torpid with drink. And the same thing had happened once before, a brute named Bowling, fetching up after dark, requesting permission to be excused from roll call. A man of forty begging a twenty-two-year-old to bunk off.

"I'll see to him," Blair said.

Tun scuttled to the rear of the house, and Blair heard the sahib on the stairs, as he turned up the wick on the lamp in the parlor. He seized its handle and brought it to the door.

On the other side of the screen he saw a slender smallish man in khaki, a white high-domed helmet and riding breeches, his riding crop upraised in his gloved hand, as though in salute. It was an odd uniform for an after-hours visit—nearly nine—but no odder than Tubby Bowling's, two weeks before, in his kilt and sporran, fresh from some ritual or other, perhaps Masonic, and was Bowling even a Scottish name?

As Blair was about to speak he heard a horse neigh below the veranda, then a low expressive whicker, which explained the sound of hooves on gravel—his gravel—and this fellow's boots and riding crop.

"Yes?" Blair said with a hint of impatience.

The visitor's face was obscured by the shadow of the helmet's brim, but the voice from beneath the brim was dark brown, throaty and confident, and vaguely familiar.

"As your syce, sahib, I just thought of something I want you to do."

After midnight, she donned her disguise again. He loved seeing her dress, transforming herself from a comely naked woman to a handsome young man. And when she'd gone, he lay recalling each detail of her surprising visit—not furious and brief, as most of his other sexual encounters had been; it was at first tentative, their sitting in the darkness of the parlor, talking quietly of their day, and the game of cards, and Muriel, and then in a pause, her saying, "Show me your bedroom." Following him into it, she said, "I expect you'd like me to take this off"—her hacking jacket—and when she did, shaking it away from her shoulders, she sat on the edge of the bed and he pulled at her riding boots, burning as he did so, thinking, *Take this orf.*

"These fettering clothes," she said.

She stood and unfastened the waistband of her breeches and pushed them down with her thumbs and stepped out of them, half naked, still wearing her shirt. She unbuttoned that and let it fall open.

They lay breathing softly, saying nothing in the moon-drenched room until Blair put his mouth near her ear, saying, "I wish this was a meadow. I want to take you in a meadow." He was thinking, *green dusk for dreams, moss for a pillow.*

"We can pretend."

This land without meadows, he thought, resenting the heat and the mud in this month of the rains. But he told her what he was wishing, her pale body lying in green grass on a warm summer afternoon, in a hidden glade in the Thames Valley he'd known as a small boy.

"Yes," she said and dabbled her fingers, flicking open his shirt, chafing his nipples with her fingertips, as though teasing herself.

"What are you playing at?"

"Showing you how."

She arched her back to expose her breasts, presenting them. They were small, they had no weight, but when Blair stroked her nipples they hardened under his touch, and she sighed, encouraging him, "Yes, just like that, lovey."

A lesson in love, he thought, and he took his time, still dazed and half drunk, until he could not wait any longer. He reached and opened the drawer of his bedside table and picked up a small Three Merry Widows tin.

"What's that?"

He pressed it into her hand instead of speaking.

"You can put that away for a start."

Her tone was, on a sudden, that of a strict schoolmistress, and it thrilled him.

"I can take care of myself." She sat up and shrugged, removing her blouse, then flung her leg over him and straddled him, and settling herself astride, added, "Don't you know French letters dull the pleasure?"

Lost for a reply—*I can't keep up with her*—he held her waist, her warm skin, her fragile squirming body, as she lowered herself onto his cockstand—"Yes, yes"—until he was enclosed by her. She rode him, first rising and falling, as though in the saddle on a slow gallop, but then picking up speed, her breath coming quicker, her hands around his neck, holding on and half choking him. He came first, but she said, "Steady on," and still rode him until she gasped and was done, falling forward and laughing with delight.

He must have dozed for a bit after that because when he woke he was startled to find her in his arms and could not remember why or how.

"Let me be your syce." She held his face and kissed him.

She seemed to be printing love on his lips. *My first real kiss.*

"Must be off."

Orf again. She was posh but no burra memsahib. As she'd assured him, she could take care of herself, and what memsahib in Burma ever said that?

Blair watched her dress, he'd never seen a woman dress herself like that. It was an enchantment to witness each stage of it, as she transformed herself from a small naked woman into a regimental syce, breeches, boots, tunic, helmet, and at last standing at attention, severe, brandishing a riding crop.

"At your command, sahib."

He walked her to her horse and just before she mounted she said, as an endearment, "Didn't I tell you? I'm a wicked woman," and laughed in her throat and kissed him again.

Back in his bed, he lay where she had lain, luxuriating in her odors, separating each one in his mind, her hair, her skin, her perfumed breasts, and the slippery tang of her sex, as of a handful of sprats.

25

A HANGING

Blair was happy—he could not remember ever having known such bliss—he was confident, he whistled now, he tended his narrow mustache with care, he was kinder to his men, he joked in Burmese with his cook. Burma was at last bearable, better than bearable, it framed his happiness, it seemed a dream landscape of desire, and Kipling seemed truer than ever. He wrote a few lines of a love poem, unlike any he'd sent to Jacintha, beginning *Grappling with you, the glory of your loins* . . . but he became self-conscious (*loins* was a word from Lawrence) and destroyed the page, burning it in his ashtray. What if someone found out? She was his secret, and the secret made him strong.

In this mood he felt sorry for Muriel, who knew nothing, who trusted him, who seemed so eager to meet, to show him a story in *The Queen*, "I think you might enjoy it, Eric—I thought of you when I read it"—something about Burmese rubies in Queen Victoria's necklace—"rubies protect you from illness and evil."

"Fancy that."

"Maybe you can find one for me, a wee one will do but I'd be ever so chuffed if you found one."

A shiny object to cheer her uncertain heart. Poor, credulous, impressionable Muriel—without the foggiest idea that she was being used, so that he and Mrs. Jellicoe could meet and grapple. On walks, for tea, birdwatching, at race meetings, sometime riding horses near the prison—plodding around the parade ground—then invariably a game of cards, the three-sided cribbage board, Mrs. Jellicoe remarking about pegs and holes.

These outings and games were often a prologue, a promise, a foretaste of pleasure to come, for a visit later in the evening, Mrs. Jellicoe always dressed as a mounted syce, in riding breeches or jodhpurs, full length, with straps under her boot soles. Her clothes, her look of a groom or a young cavalryman, excited Blair.

"I am your obedient syce. Awaiting your command, sahib."

"I know that Kipling story." And when he held her, he said, "You turn discretion into a fine art."

The evenings did not always end in his bedroom. Often she was pressed for time, or Humphrey was back from Moulmein, and she merely stopped by for a drink or what she called a gasper, and they talked about books, about Burma, about Insein.

"Alec is so proud of his prison."

"Well, he might, it's such a marvel of design," she said. "I'm sure you've heard all about the Jeremy Bentham pedigree."

"He was surprised I knew what a panopticon was. But I studied Greek at school, so that was dead easy. Bentham himself was a harder nut. I suppose one's supposed to say 'utilitarian,' then change the subject. Oh, yes, Mill was one of his students."

"I like Bentham for being a simplifier," Mrs. Jellicoe said, removing her cigarette from its holder and stubbing it out in an ashtray. He loved her leaning toward him, her collar falling open, the glimpse of loose silk slipping past her breasts. "Shall we go into the other room? I feel a bit lightheaded. I'd so much prefer to chat to you lying down."

She stripped off her tunic and flung it aside as she entered, then sat on the bed, her legs extended for the ritual of his pulling off her riding boots, and after that tugging off her breeches.

"Knickers," he said.

"Fancy a pair of silk drawers, do you?"

"Mad for them. Please leave them on—for a bit."

He stroked the seams, the soft folds, the lace, he nuzzled it, pressing his face against the softness, thinking, *the silkworm's yellow labors.*

"Hated colonies, Bentham—'emancipate your colonies'—don't stop." She was unbuttoning her shirt as he moaned against her belly. "Hated executions—hangings, severed heads. Even I, poor woman, too thick to understand the byzantine subtleties of a man's world—even I can grasp Bentham's argument. 'The punishment of death, shall it be abolished?' I answer yes."

He had risen to reply but she clasped his head in both hands, pushing down between her parted legs and against her dampened knickers.

"'Shall there be no exception to this rule?' I answer no." And still forcing his head against her. "More, lovey, more."

Knickers, history, sex, the eighteenth century, her smooth belly, her pretty mouth, her boy's bum. *I am in heaven.*

"Peddy-Wilmot's so het up about his panopticon and Bentham, but never for a moment thinking how Bentham would have hated the gallows in his panopticon."

"He hanged one of my chaps, from Myaungmya," Blair said, crawling beside her, embracing her. "Glad I didn't see it." He buried his face in the pillow.

"Don't brood. Touch me."

He counted the times she'd visited—ten, so far, but not enough. Yet each time was pleasurable. He asked her shyly if she minded the danger—what she was risking if she was found out.

"But that's part of the thrill," she said, and touching him, she went on, "This is the other part."

Her visits occurred without warning, sometimes they merely talked.

"Poor Muriel."

"Plummy Peddy-Wilmot might get shirty."

"He's rather a vindictive *pairson*."

"He didn't get on with Humphrey one bit."

But Blair hated mentions of her husband and was glad Humphrey was in Moulmein.

It was now late September, still in the rains, the weather more bearable, so cool some days on waking he imagined he was back in England until he heard the shouts of the mali chopping weeds in the garden with his mamoty, and the sound of the bugle, the marching band on the parade ground, the guards assembled for inspection, the sickly morning light, like yellow tinfoil.

One of those dreary mornings, a bearer handed him an envelope. "Chitty, *thakin*."

A card inside, black ink: *Summoned to Moulmein XX.*

She had left without warning and it was as though part of him had been wrenched away, a vital part of him, his happiness. He felt whittled small by her absence—emptier, sadder than he'd ever known at a parting.

With Mrs. Jellicoe gone, his meetings with Muriel ended. A note left for him at the club by her mother proposed a new chaperone. Rather than face Edith Peddy-Wilmot, whom Mrs. Jellicoe called "Burra Bee-Bee," he wrote a longish letter, pleading overwork and no free afternoons during the week, Sundays requiring him to be in Rangoon. It was lame but she accepted it, probably knowing he had no interest in the daughter—and Alec Peddy-Wilmot was chillier toward him, as though he'd been snubbed.

Blair didn't mind; he was numb to their feelings, desolated by the vanishing of Mrs. Jellicoe. He wished to see no one, immersing himself in the inventory of stores and supplies, and on his visits to the prison proper he gazed through the bars and imagined that he was an inmate like them, unable to leave. He was done with the charade of amusing Muriel. It was Mrs. Jellicoe who managed to make those days bearable, and he reflected on the pleasurable deception of her company, her wit, her willingness, the excitement he felt at her disguise as a handsome syce in boots and breeches. *I'm wicked.*

Writing poetry about it didn't help, and that was the proof he wasn't a poet. He could more easily write a story of a man who'd lost his lover and then in his loneliness shot his dog and hanged himself. His being busy hardly eased his mind. He had many men to carry out his commands. He sat at his desk in the stores warehouse and issued orders, and with time on his hands—freed by a despotic system that only functioned because of the sweat of native servants. The reality of his position appalled him. Now, three years on in Burma, he was seeing the empire with Mrs. Jellicoe's eyes as fraudulent and fiercely despotic, and he was relieved to know that he was not alone in hating it.

Lying alone with her in the dark, damning the British, mocking Peddy-Wilmot ("rather a vindictive *pairson*")—hearing Mrs. Jellicoe disparaging the Raj—all that was more disloyal, more adulterous than their lovemaking. They were a pair of infidels, conspiring in his bungalow, in the shadow of the prison, enemies of the king, more seditious than Sayadaw Wirathu, often decrying the system in the very terms that anticolonial monk had used. While Mrs. Jellicoe snuggled beside him he once said, *What if a whole society was a panopticon, with a tyrant at its center in the watchtower? He would see us—he would see everyone—there would be no privacy.*

Their own privacies were part of their passion. What had bound them together, Blair and Mrs. Jellicoe, was that she knew all his secrets, including the name he'd given to his alter ego, George. It was not Blair but George who was her lover, her fellow conspirator. Blair obeyed orders to soldier on and salute, yet George was bereft.

Because it was over with Muriel he was ashamed to approach her. She now had to accept the fact that he had no romantic interest, that he'd wasted her time. "My parents saw you on your way out, in the *Herefordshire*," she had said to him. "They specially mentioned you and your famous school tie." And now they knew he was a cad and a bounder, and guiltily he wondered whether in some way—because there were so few secrets here—they'd become aware of his dalliance with Mrs. Jellicoe and had put a flea in Humphrey's ear: the reason she'd been summoned to Moulmein. And if they knew, then everyone knew and there was no hope for advancement, and he'd remain a topic of gossip, forever in bad odor.

He missed his nights with Mrs. Jellicoe so badly that out of respect for her he decided not to take the train to Rangoon and visit Monkey Point, to seek out Cha-Cha for solace. It would only make him miserable and feel disloyal. Moreover, he'd discovered a fever pitch of sexuality with Mrs. Jellicoe that was irreplaceable by any other woman, and beyond the delicious wickedness, something a tart could not supply—genuine affection.

In suspense, clinging to his job, a slave to his routine, delegating responsibilities to his men, he was reminded every day that he was a failure, with no future here, and likely the subject of ridicule at the club. To discourage gossip he stayed away from club members. He still played football on the odd Saturdays with the police team and was ruthlessly tackled by the Burmese on the opposing side. He spent his off-hours at his bungalow with this chickens and ducks. Seeing a peddler's dog in distress, he'd bought it from the man, and tethered the thing to a stake in his garden, and sometimes stared at the confined creature panting in the shade of the peepul tree and thought: *I am that dog.* But to take the curse of that thought he named her Flo.

Beadon visited, marveled at the animals ("quite a menagerie") and related news of David Jones, now back in Mandalay and said that he, Jones, was being posted to Twante. Blair did not offer anything about Oliphant: Jones would find out soon enough, probably to his dismay. From his bearing and outlook, Beadon seemed prepared for the long haul, a career in the police. "As for myself," Blair said to him, "only the *bon Dieu* can say." He knew he would not last, but could not imagine what his fate would be if he ever left Burma.

After a month or so, he believed that Muriel had forgiven him for dropping her and that the Peddy-Wilmots were at peace. He returned to the club, he took his dinners there, and some evenings he lingered at the bar for a drink. If there was talk, he didn't hear it, nor even the vibrations of any whispers.

So, seeing Alec Peddy-Wilmot at the club bar one evening, he greeted him with a nod, and Peddy-Wilmot returned it.

"Blair?"

"Sir."

"Join me in a drink."

"Thanks, awfully, sir. Whiskey-soda."

And for a moment he believed he was safe. When the drinks were brought they clinked glasses and sipped, Peddy-Wilmot flicking droplets from the mustache that hid his mouth.

"Eton chap like you must be familiar with a chap called William Marwood."

"Marwood," Blair said, shaking his head. "Doesn't ring a bell."

"Illiterate cobbler from Lincolnshire," Peddy-Wilmot said, smiling across his glass. "He was vexed by bungled hangings. He worked out that to get a fall violent enough to dislocate the spine but not so violent that it tears the head from the body, the length of the rope must be in proportion to the weight of the body."

"Makes sense."

"I'm speaking of short drop versus long drop," Peddy-Wilmot said. "Mind you, it was only an approximate formula. It was perfected by James Berry," and inclined his head and added with pride, "His mother was a MacKenzie, from Dingwall."

"Regrettably, I'm not familiar with James Berry, sir."

"Executioner. Hangman. Pioneer of the long drop." Peddy-Wilmot put his drink down and plucked a card from his pocket the size of a postcard, but with numbers filling one side of it. "What's your weight, Blair?"

"Eleven stone and a bit."

Peddy-Wilmot lifted the card and peered at it. "Six foot six would do the job for you."

"Pardon?"

"The length of the rope, for your hanging—here," Peddy-Wilmot said, handing him the card. "You'll need this."

"Yes?" Blair fingered the card, which was headed *Table of Drops*.

"Task for you, Blair. Supairvision."

"Glad to oblige sir."

"A hanging."

Outside the condemned cell of the prison, the terrace nearest the far exit, Blair saw the man being led out, handcuffed and chained to two of the guards, four Indian warders standing by with Enfields, bayonets fixed. The man was a small weedy Indian, looking newly shaved—evidence from a strange discoloration on his upper lip that he must have had a mustache; his head was shaved, too, giving him a ghoulish skull and with the same sunken eyes of a death's head.

As he passed, Blair saw that it was the shopkeeper, Mullapoodi, the man he'd arrested for his wife's murder—the dowry murder. He had first declared his innocence but finally confessed, though Blair was certain that his mother had committed the crime, as the aggrieved mother-in-law. *Family matters are worst of all, sahib*, Mirza Khan had said, and all the Indian inspectors maintained the mother was guilty.

But Mullapoodi had been convicted of the crime and now looked resigned to his fate, with a strange drugged expression and glazed eyes. But when he saw Blair, he cried out, "Sahib!" and was hauled away by the guards, Blair falling behind, not wishing to meet his gaze.

The procession continued through a rear door of the prison, and under a gateway, and just visible at the far end of a gravel path, a platform, a simple plank stairway leading to a frame, a beam as crosspiece, a noose suspended from the beam—the gallows.

"Come along, Blair!"

It was Peddy-Wilmot, striding beside him and passing him, swishing his stick.

"Your friend ought to have been swinging by now. I say, the prisoners can't get their breakfast until this job's over."

But before Peddy-Wilmot had finished speaking, Blair heard a dog barking—a bark he recognized—and Flo lolloped over to Blair, leaping at him, leaving muddy pawprints on his uniform.

Mullapoodi jerked his head, startled at the insistent barks, and widened his eyes at the dog, as though beholding a weird apparition.

"Who let that bloody brute in here!" Peddy-Wilmot shouted.

"Must have followed me, sir."

Blair called for a guard to give him a belt, which he fastened to Flo's collar, and as he did so, the dog—restrained—barked more fiercely. Mullapoodi quailed again, and then stumbled sideways, but he recovered in something like a dance step, treading neatly past a puddle on the path.

How queer, the condemned man, fearful of the dog, avoiding the puddle, on his way to be hanged. Mullapoodi's hesitation, the fastidiousness of it, his economy of movement, even manacled and chained, became fixed in Blair's mind and preoccupied him as the man was led to the gallows, where the hangman—a white-haired convict in a loose prison uniform—waited, holding what looked like a canvas bag in his hands.

"Adequate rope?"

"The prisoner's nine stone, sir," Blair said. "We're giving him a drop of just under eight feet."

Shaking the canvas sack, the hangman inverted it, hollowing it into a hood, and slipped it over Mullapoodi's head, tugging it close around his neck with laces and knotting them as Blair averted his gaze. When at last Blair looked up, he was relieved that the man could no longer see him. But a strange sound had broken the silence in the damp air of the walled enclosure of the jail yard. It was an insistent gulping shout from the gallows's platform, but muffled by the thickness of the canvas hood.

"Ram! Ram! Ram!"

Mullapoodi chanting, without stopping, pleading with each repetition of the word.

"What the devil is your friend saying?"

Peddy-Wilmot approached Blair for an answer, nudging the dog aside with his stick.

"Calling to his god, sir, I imagine."

"The Almighty?"

"Rama, sir."

Blair glanced up at the hangman, who'd looped the noose over Mullapoodi's hood and seemed unnerved by the chanting, twitching the rope attached to the trap on which Mullapoodi was standing, still calling his god's name. Because the man's breath was confined, the hood swelled with each cry.

Peddy-Wilmot blinked in a peculiar way at the syncopation of the chant, as though keeping count, preparing to arrive at a certain decisive number. Finally, he said, "Blair, give the order. We're holding up breakfast."

"*Chalo!*" Blair shouted.

Mullapoodi's chains rang out as the trap was sprung, and just as suddenly there was silence, except for the dog's soft whimper, as though seeming to know that a man had died, the man's last breath keening in a register only the dog could hear. Blair's hands flew to his face as tears started in his eyes.

"You're neglecting something, Blair."

"Sir?"

"Supairvision," Peddy-Wilmot said. "Inspect your friend, Blair."

Leaving the dog crouched, still whimpering, Blair walked—stumbling a little, his legs like lead—to the open side of the gallows, where the body was slowly revolving, bare feet pointed downward, the chains slack. Blair nodded to a guard, who unfixed his bayonet and poked the body with the muzzle of his rifle.

"He is done, sir."

"Give the order for breakfast to commence," Peddy-Wilmot called out. And turning to Blair, "My word. You look as though you've lost your appetite."

The next time Blair saw Muriel she was walking beside a young officer in the uniform of a Cameron Highlander, an older woman in a sunhat and umbrella trudging just behind them.

Part IV

MOULMEIN

26

PULLED UP

The fragility he felt after the hanging, and the vanishing of Mrs. Jelli-coe, made Blair oblique and evasive, which Peddy-Wilmot seemed to take for insolence and provoked him to go on tormenting him. Blair felt sure he'd hanged an innocent man and would somehow need to atone for it. As for Mrs. Jellicoe, Blair kept his vow to her, resigned himself to celibacy, a gesture he told himself was appropriate and chivalrous—decent, anyway—so that if they should ever meet again he could truthfully say, *This is how much I missed you—no other woman could possibly replace you.*

The tarts at Monkey Point, the women he'd once eagerly sought out, no longer seemed so seductive—even Cha-Cha, whom he called *minthami*, princess. Flattered by the word, in the hot seclusion of her upstairs room she'd often performed for him a shiko, in ceremonial prostration, dropping to the mat before him, clutching his ankles, murmuring promises, declar-ing her obedience. And then would get to her feet, posing in the lungyi she called a *htamein*, patterned and trailing slightly, her *ingyi* blouse that was shaped like downward petals, her embroidered slippers.

Finally with deliberate slowness, removing one article of clothing after another, naming each one, she'd unwrap the lungyi and let it drop, un-doing the side buttons of her blouse, revealing her underbodice—"This *za bawli*"—and kicking away her slippers, then prostrating herself again naked, pleading for him, "*Thakin.*"

It was Burmese theater, a pwe without music, which could never replace the whispers, the touch, the gusto of Mrs. Jellicoe—her gusto most of all, her hot whisper in his ear, *I'm ever so fond of your cockstand, George.*

It was a relief to him that Muriel had a chap, a fellow Jock, a Cameron no less, but this did not mitigate her father's torments. His daughter had been trifled with and humiliated, cast off by Blair. Much worse, Peddy-Wilmot seemed outraged by Blair's sustained interest and perhaps sympathy for the men he'd arrested who had ended up at Insein Prison and still languished in its cells. Blair had been visibly affected by the hanging of Mullapoodi, and Peddy-Wilmot had turned aside and spat when afterward Blair had said, "In point of fact, he's innocent, you know."

"Rot."

"The murder was his mother's doing."

"Where's your proof?"

But there was no use describing the smell of paraffin on the dead woman's body, and none on Mullapoodi, nor the sudden disappearance of his mother. His Indian inspectors—experienced in such matters—convinced him it was the mother's demand for money, resulting in dowry murder, which she'd carried out. Yes, Mullapoodi must have been complicit, but the mother was the instigator, and she was free, her son protecting her. And Blair himself, to his shame, had charge-sheeted the man without investigating the mother.

Then there were the eighteen protesters who'd rushed the perimeter fence at the refinery in Syriam. Seven months later they were still shackled in a cell at Insein, nine grown men and nine students, two of the students no more than fifteen years old, in ill-fitting, too-large prison shirts and trousers, all the protesters Burmese, none of them history sheeters, confined with dacoits and rapists.

Without Mrs. Jellicoe, Blair had time on his hands. On the pretext of carrying out an inspection he walked the prison corridors and found the protesters' cell. Knowing that he could easily be seen from the central watchtower of the panopticon, he pretended to make observations in his notebook, as though in the process of an inventory. But he was too shocked to write. It was a hot afternoon in mid-April, the reek from the cells a thickening fuzz in the still air, the eighteen of them crowded into a single cell, the older men standing, the youths squatting on their heels, all of them eyeing Blair with a mixture of fear and hatred.

He began to address one of the older men in Burmese, but the man interrupted him, replying in English.

"What is it the sahib wishes to know?"

"How are you faring?"

Blair offered the man a cigarette. The man took it with a spasm of gratitude, a little bow that—jerking to attention, throwing his head back—he instantly seemed to regret.

"The guards are beating us, without a reason. Your Indians." He puffed the cigarette, he expelled the smoke, he clarified what he'd said, "Your *kalar*."

Blair admired the man's dignified posture, his standing at attention in the stink and the squalor, stiff-backed, the cigarette in his fingers. He seemed to sneer, then took a puff, expelling the smoke from the side of his mouth.

"The small boys—look." He called to one of them, squatting, pinch-faced, who stood and lifted his shirt and turned aside, so that Blair could see the scars on his back, a lacework of pink welts, half healed, flies settling on them.

"And others here, you can see. They all have wounds."

Blair remembered McPake saying, *I gave the lot of them a thick ear.*

Flicking his fingers at the flies buzzing round his head, and fearing that he might betray to the men the upset he felt, Blair backed away, promising himself that he would file a complaint on behalf of the men. He thought of the wretched monks squatting with the *sayadaw* in that cell, the gray cowed faces of the long-term convicts, the scarred buttocks of the ones who'd been flogged with bamboo, and he remembered the women howling in the Delta when their menfolk were led away in chains. And the condemned man, Mullapoodi—watching him hanged seemed worse than a thousand murders.

Blair went to the office in the annex and had half written the complaint when, to his surprise, Peddy-Wilmot shoved the door open and stood before him, breathing hard. A sudden call like this was always the occasion for a reprimand, but the superintendent seemed more agitated than usual.

"You were observed wandering in the cell blocks, Blair. What exactly was that in aid of?"

Of course, in the all-seeing panopticon privacy was unknown, like the futuristic nightmare of a Wellsian superstate, something out of *The Sleeper Awakes,* the secret police tracking your every movement, the woman Helen saying darkly to the Sleeper, "This city—is a prison. Every city now is a prison." In this imprisoning city, the villains were warders in the watch-tower squealing to the despot, Peddy-Wilmot.

But Blair said crisply, "Doing my duty, sir. Supervision. Curious to note the prisoners' conditions. How the men are being treated."

"Treated with civility."

"Yet they complain of being beaten."

"Beaten?" Peddy-Wilmot tugged at his mustache, a gesture that made him seem even more despotic when it revealed a smile beneath it on his underlip, suggesting the word was preposterous. He repeated, "Beaten?"

"I merely wondered what would provoke a guard to thrash a young skinny schoolboy."

"It would be cheek," Peddy-Wilmot said. He sniffed in a superior way. "And not beaten."

"Not beaten?" In spite of his resolve not to show any emotion, Blair smirked at the obvious lie.

"Slippered rather."

"Slippered, sir?"

"I daresay, you yourself have slippered your bearer, your cook, your syce, from time to time."

Blair hesitated to reply, seeing his hand raised against these very men—and his guards, too, the maddening Indians, the stubborn Burmese—the men crouched and cowering in their misery when he landed the blow or kicked them.

"But never a child," Blair finally said. And he winced, remembering the schoolboys at Pagoda Road Station, one sobbing, another crying out, *Not your business,* the others screeching abuse, how they'd boarded the train with him and barracked him—*Say solly!*—until he'd fled from the carriage.

Peddy-Wilmot was still panting, an effect of his pent-up fury, as he faced Blair who was trapped behind his desk, the half-written complaint on his blotter.

"Do you not know the seriousness of the charges brought against these lawbreakers?" And quickly added, "I reckoned not. These persons violated a section of the Penal Code that makes it a criminal offense to write or say—I emphasize *say*—anything that would inspire hatred or contempt against the British government. Your government, Blair. The one you serve."

In his indignant rage, Peddy-Wilmot became more scolding and Scottish in his speech, with *pairsons* and *sairve.*

"I'm familiar with that section. One twenty-four A," Blair said. "Offenses against the state. But children, sir."

"They are not children. They are enemies of the empire and antagonists of the king. They have been found guilty. They will serve every minute of their sentence."

Another pompous *sairve.* Blair said, "They were unarmed, sir."

"They were rioters. They were seditionists. They caused an affray." Peddy-Wilmot glared, defying Blair to dispute this. "And while we're on the subject of sedition, I need you to effect a transfer."

"Sir?"

"Your friend, that big bug from Twante."

"The *sayadaw.*"

"Quite. He has accumulated quite a following, preaching his poisonous views to the rabble in his cell."

"We can hardly muzzle him, sir."

"But we can place him in purdah. I need you to escort him to Block B."

"The hole, sir? Solitary confinement, sir?"

"That's an order, Blair!"

It was the voice of despotic authority, stern and unequivocal, demanding submission, in the same tone that had ordered Blair to supervise the hanging. And Blair suspected that what lay behind it was Peddy-Wilmot's anger at his high-hatting Muriel. And what else? His being young, his being a Sassenach, his being an Etonian, perhaps. But there was no possibility of refusing. No matter how irrational or wrong or violent, an order had to be obeyed.

"I'll have my men see to it."

"You will see to it personally." *Pairsonally.*

"Very good, sir."

Blair had known in advance that the leave-taking would be emotional, but even so he was not prepared for the scene—the waiting monks clinging to the *sayadaw,* their faces smeared and shining with tears, their shouts of anger as the Indian guards pressed lathis against them to restrain and separate them—but these bamboos were bound with iron rings; the solemn figure of the *sayadaw,* raising his hands in blessing, intoning prayers, looking majestic, exalted in his dignity, allowing the monks to speak for him—screaming abuse—and extending his arms to Blair so that the manacles could be locked on his wrists. And finally straightening, the little man, diminished in size, thinner since his arrest, shuffled on torn and broken sandals, as he was led into the darkness of Block B—a single cell, no window, only a small peephole in the heavy wooden door.

Just before Blair shut the door, the *sayadaw* said, "I am not alone. The Lord Buddha is here with me."

The intention was to humiliate Blair by ordering him to lock the *sayadaw* in the dark hole in Block B, yet it had the opposite effect; it roused his sympathy and inspired in him an affinity with the monk's predicament. He remembered snippets of the *sayadaw*'s speech to the people at the pagoda the evening Blair visited, and Blair found himself agreeing with his objections against the British—heretical objections, but many of them indisputable.

Still, the painful task of transferring the monk was so upsetting, Blair avoided the club, he remained at home when he wasn't at work, he looked for comfort in feeding his chickens and ducks, he took solitary walks with Flo to the river, recalling on those paths the walks he'd taken with Mrs. Jellicoe and Muriel, Mrs. Jellicoe covertly touching his hand as she drew level with him, every touch a promise.

As for following orders, he'd understood from his first days in Mandalay that orders were to be obeyed to the letter, without question. What had not occurred to him then was that orders might be given out of spite, to humiliate and break your spirit, or might make no sense, might arise from the pettiest motives.

But that was before he'd formed an idea of the pukka sahib—someone like Peddy-Wilmot, like Comstock in Syriam, or the order giver that McPake had become. It seemed that the pukka sahib was often a bully and was elevated so far above the native that he had no clear idea of the reality of Burmese life. But there was something more, something worse, something poisonous in the role: the pukka sahib was always a hypocrite.

When he'd escorted the protesters from Syriam to the station in Rangoon and thence to Insein, Blair felt himself to be sentenced to a term at the prison. That sense of being a prisoner himself returned to him. And the feeling was more powerful now. Though he knew the prisoners despised him for his authority over them, they had no way of knowing his predicament, that he too was being punished by his superiors. Despite his objections, he'd followed orders, and yet Peddy-Wilmot had not specifically ordered him to stay away from the cells.

Blair began to see his patrolling the prison, after his warehouse duties, as an expression of his freedom. In this new mood, feeling a perverse brotherhood with the prisoners, he spent those late afternoons listening to their complaints. He sought out the men he'd arrested since arriving in Myaungmya—even the worst of them, the most violent dacoits—to reacquaint himself with them. They were now mostly subdued, they'd lost the ferocity they'd shown when they were captured. They were gaunt, much thinner, pacing their cells like zoo animals. Their hatred for him disfigured their faces, but now and then they responded to his greetings, and one of them in a moment of insight told him what Blair himself was thinking.

"You are in prison with us, sahib!"

It was an Indian, and he used the insulting informal "you," calling him *tum*.

Sayadaw Wirathu said nothing. Moved to a new cell, but alone, a saucer-size hole in the ceiling shed light on him, glowing on his bald head, and gave him a halo. No political slogans—he seemed quieted and more spiritual as he meditated, seeming to Blair like an anchorite, steadfast in mortification, basking but not in holiness. His eyes saw something else. At the pagoda he'd been a ranter, in prison he looked confidently prophetic.

• • •

On one of his turns in the prison Blair stopped at the kitchen where an inmate, one of the trusties, was washing dishes, the man's arms up to his elbows in soapsuds. He was scrubbing tin pots and bowls with a bristly brush, rinsing them in a nearby tub, and tipping them onto a wooden drying rack. The man toiled without any hurry, as though to stately music, a pavane playing in his head, working his brush on the pots, lathering them with creamy soap and then plunging them into the tub, smiling with satisfaction as he did so, as though fashioning a new pot from a froth of bubbles. Blair envied the man's contentment, his obvious pride in this simple satisfying task, and when he saw Blair staring at him he raised his brush in salute, flourishing it as a prestige object, with the swank of a colonel unsheathing and stabbing the sky with his ceremonial sword. As the man laughed at his own impudence and went on scrubbing, Blair thought how he'd seldom seen a happier man at work.

But he suspected that his manner of wandering the prison, observed from the watchtower, might be regarded as an act of defiance. His failure to file any reports of his movements seemed to bear that out, and he knew there would be consequences. So he was prepared for a confrontation when he was handed a chit by Peddy-Wilmot's chaprassi, Rupesh, a stool-arsed Dravidian with a crocodile smile who seemed to take pleasure as the bearer of his boss's aggression against Blair.

The chit said, *See me at once.*

I'm being pulled up, Blair thought. *I'm on the mat.* And when he passed through the outer office Rupesh sat back at his desk and seemed to gloat, showing those teeth.

Blair said, "What's wrong with your arm?"

"Arm, sahib?" Rupesh squirmed in his chair. "Arm is fit, sahib."

"Then use it to salute me."

"Yes, sahib."

"Not one of your slack salutes."

Rupesh brought his hand to his brow, rising awkwardly, bumping his knees against the desk, wagging his head in the Indian affirmative, as Blair walked past him to the end of the corridor, to the door lettered *Superintendent.*

Just as Blair knocked a cry came from inside, "Enter!"

The impatience, the anger in that command conveyed to Blair that his situation was worse than he'd imagined. He was prepared to be buffeted by the furious man. He would hold on, cling to the rail of the pitching vessel, use his sea legs and his silence until the storm passed. He had ceased to regard any reprimand as an indignity—being pulled up was an inevitable consequence of his being unsuited to a job he found more and more distasteful. *Peddy-Wilmot will order me to wash dishes. I shall pick up a scrubbing brush and be delighted.*

"Sit down."

But Peddy-Wilmot himself, chewing his pipestem, was standing at the window, the gateway of the prison visible in the distance but blurred by the risen dust on this hot afternoon, the sun slanting through the haze, making a silhouette of the arch.

When Blair sat, Peddy-Wilmot crept nearer to hover over him. He removed the pipe from his mouth and stabbed it a little like a threat. Beyond his right shoulder a large yellowed panopticon diagram of the prison hung on the wall in a black frame, the design perfectly round and detailed. The lettering was barely legible to Blair at this distance, so it seemed less like an architect's work than iconography of the occult, not a prison footprint but an elaborate oriental mandala, the meaning of which was still a puzzle, yet its mystery held his gaze.

He turned from it to see Peddy-Wilmot's face, its fury giving it a curious pulsing bulge.

"We share a wee bit of history, do we not, Blair?"

"It seems so, sir."

"More than three years since the *Herefordshire*."

All Blair could think was three and a half wasted years, but in his reverie he heard Peddy-Wilmot's characteristic mutter, "What?"

"As you say, sir. Three and a bit."

"And from the moment I clapped eyes on you on that ship I have never been in the least persuaded that you are anything but a slacker." He poked with his pipestem. "A public school wastrel, playing your Eton card to bunk off. What?"

"I am not aware that I have been playing my Eton card, sir. If such a card, indeed, could be said to exist."

"But I am putting it to you that you have done so, and I will not be disabused of it, laddie," Peddy-Wilmot said, lighting his pipe and puffing and speaking into the pipestem.

As Peddy-Wilmot puffed, Blair pinched a cigarette out of his case and said, "Permission to smoke, sir."

"Certainly not. Put that away." He had grimaced on the word *sairtainly,* with the pipe in his teeth, and still spat gusts of smoke. "Edith had hopes, but I told her, 'That lad has no love for the service—no aptitude for police work.' Muriel was persuaded of your good intentions, yet I was unable to convince her that you were a colossal bounder."

Blair sat calmly—except for the gibe about playing an Eton card, every-thing Peddy-Wilmot said was perfectly true. He disliked the service, his heart was not in police work, he'd bluffed Edith Peddy-Wilmot, he'd strung Muriel along, and, yes, he was a bounder. He was not inclined to deny any of it, so he shifted in his chair as Peddy-Wilmot moved back and forth be-fore him; he flexed his fingers and, aching for a smoke, he steeled himself for what was to come.

What tumbled forth was a litany of his failures, some real, some of them concocted, including a misunderstanding with an assistant at Stores, and a misperception by an Indian commanding the watchtower. But what Blair expected, and truly feared, was any mention of Mrs. Jellicoe. He could explain away some of his lapses, but the one with Mrs. Jellicoe was the transgression for which he had no excuse. It seemed to him sitting there being hectored by Peddy-Wilmot—smoke issuing from the man's strangely porous nose making him fiercer—that his dalliance with Mrs. Jellicoe was grounds for being severely reprimanded, if not cashiered. If that was known he was buggered, and it occurred to him that this indiscretion was the reason he'd been summoned, and all the rest of—"Eton card," "bounder"—merely a prologue, teasing him before the delivery of the coup de grâce.

"I was assured by my opposite number, Comstock in Syriam, that you were capable." The captain drew on his pipe and expelled the smoke, this time through clenched teeth. "That you would be my man."

"Sir." Blair yearned for a cigarette, as the room filled with pipe smoke.

"Ever since you arrived at Insein, though, I have felt that you are not my man. And recent events have convinced me of this."

Recent events meant Mrs. Jellicoe. Blair held his fear in his fists, his nails pressing his palms.

After a lengthy pause, intended to intimidate Blair, who was aware of his failures, and who was indeed intimidated, Peddy-Wilmot said, "You've been observed fraternizing with prisoners—politicals. Speaking to them, some of them, in their own language—extraordinary! I am persuaded that you feel these men to be victims of some obscure miscarriage of justice. What's more, that you believe in your callow schoolboy way that the political situation in Rangoon is specially dire."

Because Peddy-Wilmot was glaring at him, as though for an answer, Blair said, "Beg pardon, sir. Is that a question?"

"It is an affirmation, laddie."

"I'm not entirely clear, sir."

Snatching his pipe from his teeth and raking the smoky air with its stem, then aiming it at Blair, he said, "Would it surprise you to know, as a policeman, that there is much greater disruption elsewhere in Burma?"

"Not at all, sir."

"Devious doings?"

"I would not be a bit surprised, sir."

"Moulmein," Peddy-Wilmot said, and it seemed a hammer stroke.

Oh, god, Blair thought. *Mrs. Jellicoe—he knows.*

"Sneaks. Twisters. Mountebanks."

Blair knew his face was flushed with shame and panic, and it gave him a little relief when Peddy-Wilmot turned away from Blair's burning face and reached to his desk to slip a file from his in tray, grimacing with the pipe in his teeth, and frowning as he flipped the file open and scanned it.

"We have intelligence of instances of great disloyalty." He was concentrated on the open file folder as he spoke. "Serious breaches of security."

Not Mrs. Jellicoe then?

"Organizations devoted to the disruptions of civil order."

"Organizations, sir?" Blair said with a gummy tongue.

"Of nationalists. Of monks—*badmashes* leading strikes and riots, indifferent to lathi charges. My friend Ferguson in Moulmein is at his wits' end. His jails are full. There is alarm and despondency in the district. And in your schoolboy estimation you fancy it is dire here." He poked again with his pipe. "It is a great deal worse there."

"In Moulmein, sir?"

"In Moulmein," Peddy-Wilmot said. "Where you are presently being sent, as soon as you sort out your things."

"Yes, sir," Blair said and something odd was happening to his head, a loosening of his scalp, a slippage and itch.

"You are not needed here. I want you out of my sight. You will find Moulmein a test of your mettle."

Blair pressed his lips together to avoid beaming with pleasure, he gripped the arm of his chair, his heart bursting. Moulmein!

"What?"

"Very good, sir."

27

HAPPY ASSOCIATIONS

It was a homecoming of sorts, he knew Moulmein from his Christmas visit to Grandma Limouzin, and later her funeral, his mother's motley family still hanging on in the town. But he gave them no prior notice of his arrival this time, nothing to his parents, either, who would pass the news to them. A conspicuous greeting at the terminus at Martaban was something to be avoided. He knew what effect that would have, his family in the town becoming known to his superiors in the police, or his inevitable membership in the club—his career-blighting relatives, old Frank and his staring Burmese wife, Mah Hlim, their tittering half-caste daughter, Kathleen, or his elderly half Indian great-aunt Aimee. They were colonial residue, the despised Eurasians, unwelcome in British Burma, barred from clubs, jeered at in the bazaar, spat on and subverted, except on the railways where they were dogsbodies. He heard it clearly: *I say, are these, in point of fact, your people, Blair?*

Reflecting on that awkwardness, he flashed to the conviction that they should all have gone home, like his mother in Suffolk, or found another place to live, as his aunt Nellie had done in Paris. They were good old sticks, they might have found footing somewhere in England, Cheltenham perhaps, or Leatherhead, the refuges of Anglo-Indian blimps and dead wood from the empire. But they had foolishly overstayed and lost any position they once had, and worst of all, they were improvident; they'd lost their fortune, the family business, the family pile "Franconia." They'd become conspicuous misfits, and in his uncertainty, new to Moulmein, Blair was ashamed to think he was forced to keep them as his secret.

England did not seem so far away here, on the shore of Moulmein. It was odd how, facing the gleaming Salween River that ran to the nearby sea, savoring the smack of salt air and hearing the hoarse cries of seagulls, Blair had a stronger sense of nearness to home, of Southwold on the Suffolk coast, just below the far horizon—than when he'd been in any of the other posts, good lord, four of them, Myaungmya, Twante, Syriam, Insein—not counting Mandalay—none of them a success, and now Moulmein.

But this same ocean at Iron Wharf in Moulmein lapped against the Palace Pier in Brighton; home was a simple voyage across this water, he could see the way west. It was lighted for him, especially at sunset, the shimmering fish scales of small waves on the surface of the sea, narrowing to a thoroughfare when the lowering sun was squeezed to a dazzling path, the route like a strip of gold leaf ornamenting a pagoda wall, pinky yellow under a clear sky, shining under a jumble of clouds, always at this time of day a band of glowing water that led homeward. It saddened him at dusk when he had to leave the seafront and the sun like a sinking apricot and walk the mile back to the police lines and his bungalow, turning his back on the seaway home.

Mrs. Jellicoe was his other secret. He longed to see her here, to describe to her how it seemed like adultery to be unfaithful to her with a tart; and the delicious irony, how Peddy-Wilmot, to punish him, had sent him to Moulmein. But Blair bided his time. He needed to be careful. The woman was married. Humphrey was here.

This was his third day. On his arrival he'd been met at the Martaban Terminus by the assistant superintendent, a bony-faced man named Mac-Farlane, who'd paid little attention to the steamer trunk but had remarked on Blair's bulky book bag and on the two enormous baskets, chickens in one, ducks in the other. Blair's dog, Flo, had barked at MacFarlane and nibbled at his boot tips.

"I fancy her wee beady eyes," MacFarlane said. A pair of binoculars was slung around his neck. He lifted them and peered at Flo through them.

"Yorkie—excellent ratcatcher. Better than any moggy you can name."

"Moulmein's heaving with vermin. Most of them on two legs." Mac-Farlane scanned the platform. "You'll need three or four coolies"—and he whistled to the porters, Indians with wheelbarrows, who rushed forward shrieking and competing.

On the ferry, MacFarlane used his binoculars to scan the shore, grinning in concentration, making his face ugly.

Blair said, "Keen bird-watcher?"

"Not half," MacFarlane said. "I'm very fond of rambles here as well. There are so many hidden glades." He was scanning and grinning as he spoke. "I usually bring a lunch and spend the day rambling."

"Lunch alfresco."

"Dead easy, too, as I'm a fruitarian."

Something in MacFarlane's manner and this mention of fruitarianism kept Blair from saying, *I do a spot of bird-watching myself.*

MacFarlane said—and still not facing Blair, but rather training his binoculars outward—"I got into it through Boy Scouts. The bird-watching. The diet came a shade later. Moulmein's brilliant for all sorts of fruit. I'm not strict, though!"

Blair wondered what this might mean.

"Some fruitarians only eat what drops naturally from trees!"

A bird-watching, fruit-eating policeman, rambling in the hidden glades of valleys beyond Moulmein: interesting, on the surface of it, better than someone like McPake. And yet Blair was somewhat put off, suspecting MacFarlane of sandals and tight shorts and Nancy opinions. And before they reached the far shore he had a name for him, Fruity MacFarlane.

It was curious how this man, newly arrived in Moulmein himself, in the course of the ferry ride to the jetty, indicated the same sights Uncle Frank had mentioned—Battery Point, the warehouses, the timber yards, the factories, the godowns, and in the gharry, St. Matthew's church and Salween Park, the police headquarters—the same tour, the same emphasis. Blair bore it in silence, pretending to be interested, careful not to reveal that he'd been there before.

"Your bungalow's ready. You're welcome to mess with me until you've hired staff, though you might find the menu a bit tedious—the fruit, I mean."

"You don't eat anything else?"

MacFarlane's beaky nose and sharp chin gave him the profile of a witch in a children's book. He did not look severe, though. He seemed the sort of boy who would have been unmercifully ragged at school, and that roused Blair's sympathy. He knew how cruel schoolboys could be. Maybe that explained MacFarlane's embracing the Boy Scouts.

"Oh, yes. Nuts and seeds of all sorts," MacFarlane explained.

Blair did not dare to speak, fearing he would betray himself with laughter. He was glad when MacFarlane continued to speak.

"The superintendent will want to brief you tomorrow after the staff meeting."

"That would be Major Ferguson, I see in my orders."

"It would indeed," MacFarlane said with a trace of sarcasm, seeming to withhold what he was about to add, a hesitation that hinted Ferguson was daunting.

That hesitation provoked Blair to ask, "How are you finding it here?"

MacFarlane shook his head. "It would be insufferable without my rambles and my birding, and I think the fruit keeps me on course." He pulled at his nose, he looked troubled. "The locals hate us. Bally lot of chancers—they take every opportunity to make our lives a misery. And there's the dacoits, a vicious lot."

"So I've heard."

"It's worse than they say. And there's the weather, bally awful. I've been here a month and it seems to get hotter by the week."

"No bright spots?"

"My rambles. It's lovely to be alone, between one place and another. I'd like to write about it, perhaps a piece for *Blackwoods,* or *The Strand,* something on the order of 'Mysterious Moulmein.' Rock formations. Grottoes. I've found masses of caves." MacFarlane pulled at his nose again. "But if you ask any of the men in the club they'll tell you the tarts, they'll say 'Have a shy' and they'll mention the chee-chees and say they're agreeable." He twisted his lips in disgust. "Not for me, I'm afraid."

Of course not, the carnality was obviously at odds with the man's diet. Seeing him climb back into the gharry, Blair thought: *Fruity MacFarlane.*

And so Blair began once more, starting again in a new bungalow, a new town, new servants, new neighbors, a new boss, new villains, the snakes and ladders of service in the Indian Imperial Police. He sighed and lit a cigarette and coughed its smoke into the still air of his veranda where it drooped and thinned and vanished; and he vowed to avoid messing with Fruity MacFarlane.

And a new climate, Lower Burma, not as steamy as the Delta but in some respects muddier, a hog wallow at low tide; hotter than Rangoon and soon to be hotter still in May and June, but with a sea breeze. That breeze picked up in the afternoon, dispersing the thickened air. And a feature of Lower Burma was the weird quality of diffused light, a subdued and pearly gleam of sunless days under gray skies in humid heat that pressed on his head and blurred his vision.

Blair found some relief in the landscape behind the town and saw the truth of what MacFarlane had said, the pleasure of the glades, the visible ridge in the direction of Siam. He was heartened and uplifted, as always, whenever he saw hills and high ground. There'd been no upland in the Delta or Insein. And so in this narrow coastal town that lay between the mountains and the sea, he was a new boy once more, standing before the full-length mirror in his bungalow, in uniform, making sure he was correct, before setting off for his interview with his superintendent.

Major Ferguson was about forty, a distracted-seeming man whom Blair guessed was a veteran of the war. A photograph on his office wall seemed to bear this out, a young soldier in a tin hat and puttees with a pale shocked face, standing at ease, his hands behind his back, a road of shattered and roofless stone cottages in the distance.

Blair said, "France?"

"Wipers." After a pause—Blair hesitating—Ferguson said, "There's nothing one can say about it that hasn't been said a thousand times already. Ours lasted five months. Verdun went on for three hundred days, the longest battle the world has ever seen. Do you regret you weren't there, lad?"

Blair stammered, saying, "I met an Indian who fought at Ypres."

"India Corps—Ferozepur Brigade fought alongside us. I served in the Connaught Rangers, First Battalion."

"You made it out in one piece, sir."

"Not entirely," Ferguson said and extended his arm, showing Blair his shattered left hand, two fingers missing and the remainder twisted and claw-like. "A wee matter of being shelled to shit by Fritz's fragmentation bombs."

That explained the photograph, Ferguson's hands hidden behind his back, the shocked face. And meeting another veteran of the war, Blair was embarrassed and ashamed, feeling less than a man for not having fought. He hoped Ferguson wouldn't ask, as many did, where he'd spent the war and then sneer when Blair murmured, "School, sir," to avoid admitting Eton.

But Ferguson was holding documents in a file with his good hand, looking them over, saying, "I'd say your progress in the police so far has been"—and he sighed—"patchy."

"Finding my feet, sir."

"You'll need your feet here, Blair. You'll learn." Ferguson was not an obvious Scot but he did say *lairn*. "The villages are unsettled. The monks are a caution. The pongees are cheeky. Smattering of modern ideas. And MacFarlane's too new to handle it—still probationary. You've met him, I believe."

"Fruity MacFarlane."

It had slipped out, the name had stuck in his head, but he'd said it without thinking, seeing MacFarlane's face and binoculars and awkwardness, his pursed lips when he'd said "fruitarian."

And an astonishing thing happened—Ferguson lifted the file and laughed into it—joyous laughter so rare in Blair's years in Burma that he was at first startled and then strangely complimented. And it was not simply laughter, it was also Ferguson trying to check himself, saying, "Oh my word—that's rich, Blair," and put the file down and wiped his eyes, saying, "Fruity MacFarlane, goodness me."

"We had a spot of bother with those monks in Twante," Blair said, to help him settle down.

"You had rabble there—I've seen the reports," Ferguson said, still wiping his eyes, damp from his laughter. "It's rather more organized here. Societies have been formed."

"Pagoda groups, sir. I'm familiar with them."

"No, no," Ferguson said. "Proper nationalist societies." He extracted a photograph from the file, an array of fierce-faced Burmese men, seated cross-legged under a banner in Burmese script.

"*Wunthanu Athin,*" Blair said, his finger on the banner. "Rum name for bolshies."

"You can read that?" Ferguson said, a note of surprise in his voice.

"Happy Association," Blair said. "They don't look very happy."

"They're roughs, of course, and badly misled, a hodgepodge. Old hopes of a deliverer king to replace beastly Thibaw, and new hopes of a sovereign constitution," Ferguson said and gave Blair a grim smile. "These hopes run together in their tiny minds, to confuse and disturb them. And with the crime season coming up you won't be idle."

"I'll do what I can, sir." He was thinking *distairb.*

"That smacks of complacency. I want you to exceed your expectations. Mon is a lovely state. It deserves better than to be at the mercy of a pack of ignorant rustics to create mayhem. Ride them, Blair. Don't cock it up."

"Yes, sir. Bit of stick."

"You'll be on mounted patrol to have a poke around next week, commencing Monday. I suggest you visit the club—meet some of your fellow officers in an informal setting. There's usually a dance band on a Saturday. You'll find it agreeable."

"I'm sure I will, sir."

Another lie. But he couldn't refuse to go. What he remembered of the interview with Ferguson was his eruption in sudden laughter over the name Fruity MacFarlane—it was a plus if one was appreciated as a likable wit, even if it was at MacFarlane's expense. But there was also Ferguson's description of his progress so far in the police, the one word, *patchy.* It was a word his father would have used, but with greater disdain. Ferguson merely seemed puzzled.

It was a Friday afternoon. He'd have the weekend to compose himself, put in an appearance at the club, interview potential staff—he needed a cook, a bearer, someone to look after his chickens and ducks, a mali might do that in addition to the garden. He was not looking to hire a woman who'd become a keep, because at some point his presence would become known to the inquisitive Limouzins, and he hoped most of all in Moulmein to find Mrs. Jellicoe.

Leaving the police headquarters compound, he remembered the timber mills on the embankment—steam sawmills, their yards piled with teak logs, the stables of elephants, many of whom when not working were chained in the outdoor pens, rocking on the pillars of their legs, snatching at bales of grass. How contented they looked, great gray beasts, flapping their ears like punkahs, and seeming to smile. He sought them out, needing to witness their contentment.

Stared at as he passed the shops and the covered bazaar, he became aware that, still in uniform, he was a figure of authority, a target of hostility, dressed as though he was on duty, praying he would not have to intervene in an emergency. That thought impelled him to walk faster, keeping to the shadowy arcades as he descended to Lower Main Road at Mopun, where the mills were situated, fronting the town, the puddled foreshore of the Salween River gleaming silver in the late afternoon.

Though it was near closing time, which was feeding time, at one of the smaller timber yards an elephant was working. A mahout straddled its shoulders, the elephant wrapping the narrower hose of its trunk around a milled teak plank and hoisting it, clamping it to the cradle of its tusks. Its progress was stately and slow as it carried the plank to a pile of them, placing it on top, then steadying it and pushing it with its trunk parallel to the other planks. It seemed so considered, so tidy, such human precision as it gave a last nudge, butting it with the thicker part of its trunk to shove it plumb against the pile.

Blair remembered,

> *. . . elephants a-pilin' teak*
> *In the sludgy, squdgy creak*

"Bloody marvelous," he said softly, lighting a cigarette, watching the elephant plod slowly toward the tumbled planks, to encircle its trunk around another.

"Lord Ganesh." It was a reverent mutter behind him.

Blair turned to see an Indian in a brown suit, wide plus fours and knee socks and a belted jacket and solar topee. The man was smiling, looking anxious but standing his ground. He held a paper parcel before him in two hands, a plump package the shape and size of a cantaloupe. This obscure thing vaguely disturbed Blair—a strange object, a pale cannonball in the hands of a startled Indian.

Seeing Blair's inquisitive gaze, the Indian said, "Pulses, sahib."

"Pulses?"

"Gram, sahib."

"Chickpeas?"

"For elephant. It is sweetmeats to him."

"You're feeding this fellow?"

"When mahout allows. When work is complete. Soon." Though he nodded, Blair did not speak, and so the Indian continued, "Ganesh is auspicious. Starting new endeavors, he gives blessing. He removes obstacles." Still Blair said nothing—what was there to say? "I myself am starting new endeavors. Buying timber for export to Bombay. Teak."

"Timber wallah," Blair said. Uttering the word *deek* had given the man a sudden toothy grin.

"I mean no harm, sahib. I am Mahadev Thackeray."

The man was nervous, blinking as he looked up to Blair. It was Blair's uniform, it was his height, it was his race, and Blair felt he was perceived as a brute, making the small skinny man fearful, the round parcel of chickpeas trembling in his hands, his perspiring fingers staining the paper wrapping.

"Thackeray," Blair said.

"Maharashtra Thackeray," the man said. "Not at all your Mr. Makepeace Thackeray." His widened eyes were glazed with fear as he spoke, and he caught his breath and continued. "Though your Thackeray was born in Calcutta." He gasped again. "Which makes us exceedingly proud."

To calm him, Blair said, "It's good of you, paying a visit to feed the elephant."

"Oh, yes, sahib. To Lord Ganesh. He is eating vegetables. He knows me, though I have been in Moulmein hardly a month. He is so fond of chana I offer."

The elephant had just finished placing another teak plank on the pile and was plodding flat-footed past them on the other side of the fence.

"He is happy," Thackeray said.

"How can you tell—they all seem to smile."

"No, sahib. Observe tail. Wagging tail is happiness. He sees me, he sees pulses. Also, observe trunk."

The elephant had raised its trunk as it had passed them, lifting its tip so that the curled trunk formed the letter S, like the spout of an elegant teapot.

"Elephant is smelling. That is trunk taking air."

"My cigarette smoke."

"Or your body itself, sahib." *Bho-dee.*

The mahout brandished his iron spike as though in greeting to the two watching men, then held it like a dagger and jammed it against the elephant's shoulders, spurring it to another plank.

"Ganesh would be the elephant god."

"Great god, sahib. Remover of obstacles with assistance of *vahana.*"

Blair said, "Vehicle—what vehicle?" and he smiled at the elephant swaying toward the timber stack, a plank balanced on its tusks.

"You are knowing this Hindi word, sahib! I am so happy."

Blair said, "*Main Hindi bolate hain.*"

Thackeray shrieked, raising the package to cover his face in a reflex of apology, and then said, "*Dhanyavad*, sahib! Thank you so much."

"What exactly is his vehicle?"

"Kindly look low down at timber shed. You may see vehicle."

Blair saw a puddle that had gathered at the bottom of a waste pipe but nothing more.

"There, sahib. Just now."

A twitch like a blown leaf, then a cluster of them curling and fattening. Blair said, "Rats."

"Rat is vehicle, sahib. Ganesh is conveyed on rat. Rat is *kouncha.* You may call him *dink.* Or *mooshak.*"

Blair felt faint hearing the Hindi word for "rat" spoken loudly with approval, and in the same moment seeing the awful thing—not one but a jostling throng of them, their snouts in the vile puddle, their pink tails, muddied, hideously maculate.

"Bandicoot rat," Thackeray was saying, "is best vehicle."

Wee-ickle, wee-ickle. Blair had turned away to clear his head. The sight of the rats half choked him with disgust, as the Indian stared at the rats in admiration, extolling their virtues, speaking of the rat as intelligent and resourceful, how he helped Lord Ganesh travel, just as Garuda helped Vishnu move through the heavens. He finished saying, "Many of us have been elephants in previous lives."

With his back to the enclosure—the rats, the elephant, the setting sun— Blair said, "Timber trade—good business?"

"New endeavor, sahib. Exporting to India for tables and chairs. Furniture business. We have poor timber in India, sahib. Burma teak is best quality. Moulmein is best place. I am canvassing firms, sahib, finding prospects. But I am small, sahib."

"Who is big in Moulmein, Mr. Thackeray?"

"Jadwet is big, sahib. Akoojee is big. Bombay Burmah Trading Corporation is biggest of all." He thought a moment, blinking fiercely. "Jadwet has vessels. I have no vessels"—*wessels, wessels*—"I need Lord Ganesh to assist me."

Thackeray had backed away as he spoke, excessively polite in his frightened voice, encumbered by his parcel of chickpeas, without a free hand to gesture, properly. He was thin-faced, slightly absurd in his fuzzy brown suit, his knickerbockers ballooning over his skinny shanks, his shoes mud stained from tramping by the timber yard.

Conscious of his height as always, but more so now, the fear he inspired, his power over the Indian, Blair said, "I daresay you hate we British."

"Not at all, sahib. I admire British. I salute king. British have made India so great."

"They brought business, eh?"

"Business is civilization, sahib."

"This timber yard is a triumph?"

"And rice mills, sawmills. This is Steel Brothers, Bombay Burmah Trading Corporation. Next one is McGregor, the sawmill yonder. Then Jadwet, Akoojee, and more."

"Do you know the Limouzin family?"

"I am not familiar, sahib."

"What about Jellicoe?"

"Mr. Humphrey, sahib. I have been in talks with him. His yard is farther along at the jetty."

"I'm glad we met, Mr. Thackeray," Blair said. "Please give me your card."

28

POLICE WORK

B lair had begun to find contentment in Moulmein, the prettiest town he'd seen so far—was it the influence of Kipling, whose poem was always in his head?—girted by rivers, and the way the sea brimmed against its embankments, embowered by groves of lovely trees, their blessed shade, the somber green of the mango and avocado, the light tints of the towering limbs and twitching leaves of the peepul trees, the neem tree in his garden that Indian boys raided for tooth sticks, the feathery clumps of bamboo, another of his lists—the striped canes, the bluish canes, the black bamboo they called *lako,* the slender shoots of *gracilis,* the Chinese blow-pipe stands, and the tree praised as the Pride of Burma, gorgeous pinky plumes drooping from its boughs.

He had a motorbike now, a Victoria, more powerful than the old Matchless he'd bought in Mandalay. He coursed through the town on it and thought how even the foulest stinking alleys in Moulmein meant something to him, because they were part of his family's past. Beyond the tin roofs of the timber yards and rice mills, the green island of Belu Kyun glowed in the westward expanse of beckoning ocean, the outline broken by the steeple shapes of pagoda spires, each one teasing him with tinkling temple bells. Farther off, dimmed by the heat haze, dark hills contrasted with the glassy faces of winding rivers, and the tender green, like billiard felt, of terraced paddy fields. Away to the north, rising abruptly from the plain, the fantastic needled peaks were honeycombed with caves, some of them sacred, images of Buddha set in interior niches and grottoes, other caves the hideouts of dacoits, or the refuges of desperate homeless wanderers— tribals or hawkers. And at last on the far horizon the limestone ridge, with its rugged outcrop the British dubbed the Duke of York's Nose, for its close resemblance to that beaky aristocrat's profile.

Maybe it wasn't Kipling at all who influenced Blair's impression of Moulmein; maybe his affection had a simpler source, that for the first time in Burma his bungalow was on high ground, and that in another bungalow that was probably not far away lived Mrs. Jellicoe.

He wasn't sure how to send her a note safely—police work was needed. He was certain that at some point he'd encounter her, because Moulmein was so compact. The town was layered from Salween Park at its promontory, sloping past the bazaar and the municipal buildings, to Mopun and the shore, where ships rode at anchor midstream in the river, sampans slipping past them. And tall and unmistakable in the club, he knew he'd be noticed by Mrs. Jellicoe or the Limouzins. He rehearsed his excuse: *My transfer was so sudden I had no time to wire you—and I've been up-country this past while.*

Because Blair was fundamentally truthful, all his excuses sounded lame. But it was true that he'd been on tour for three weeks, the mounted patrol Ferguson had ordered, first exploring the Saddan Cave, then a more distant recce in Amherst to the south, finally the nearer teak forests, and the villages surrounding them. It was more police work, meeting the local headmen, and visiting crime scenes. In the beginning he'd conducted interviews on his own—mostly victims of theft, or the violence of quarrels. But wayside dacoity was common, too, and it pained him to listen to the shamefaced agonies of the parents of raped girls, the wronged girls mute in their misery.

Blair was glad on later days to delegate interviews and apprehensions to his team of subinspectors—three Indians, three Burmese—whose skills he'd come to trust. The rest of his traveling staff included a cook and two bearers, a syce, a bhisti for water, a dhobi for laundry, a dozen men altogether. His subinspectors smoothed the way, kept notes, often translated, and trooped ahead of him. They knew the wooded paths, they knew the villages, and in many cases they knew the criminals, the tough history sheeters and their records of offenses.

Usually they left their vehicles at the trailhead and continued on foot or on horseback in a lengthening column along paths trampled flat by the pounding of heavy-footed elephants; through the wooded valleys, stopping at dak bungalows or in *zayat*s, the guesthouses at timber concessions, and now and then at a Baptist mission. Their progress was enlivened by birdsong; Blair cheered to see a bird of paradise, its rich metallic color glistening in the sun, its two peculiar tail feathers dangling behind it, as it moved through the air, floating rather than flying. In the heat of midday, though, there was silence, and not a bird to be seen.

For several days in a row, wishing to understand logging, Blair walked the forest with woodsmen who, with dahs and axes, were girdling trees. The men were Karen—Christians from the Baptist mission at Daing Win Kwin at the edge of Moulmein. They hacked the bark away from the trunks of the big trees, revealing the pale wood beneath, a wide band of it that doomed the tree.

"We leave. We not chop. Tree die, we take."

"Show me." They escorted Blair the second day to dead trees that were seasoned and upright and felled them while he watched; after felling, they yoked bullocks and harnessed elephants to haul the great trunks away.

These Karen tribesmen did the hard work for the timber companies, and his own men did his work for him—the empire thrived because men like these bore the burden for the sahibs. He was part of the racket and dishonestly relieved knowing he could send his men into a forest village to report on crimes while he sat on the shaded veranda of a dak bungalow reading—he'd returned to Maugham's *On a Chinese Screen*—or writing tosh, or lost in sentimental reveries.

In many of Blair's reveries were his secret self-rehearsed conversations with Mrs. Jellicoe. He longed for her, a heartache that was physical—not loneliness but desire, the hunger of animal lust. He saw a pariah dog trying to mount docile Flo—though from her pungent smell she was probably in heat—but he did not turn away: he was that panting fumbling drooling dog, with the lolling tongue and the chafed red firecracker between his haunches.

You rearranged the furniture in my head, he would say. *I loved it when you showed up and shared it. I got used to it, but without you I forgot what this furniture was for and started tripping over it.*

The reverie left him nerved and agitated, dry mouthed, his face burning, his blood throbbing, a panting frantic dog frenzied in the odor of a bitch's heat. The plain words meant nothing. He wanted to hold her, to bury his face in her neck and perhaps afterward, lying beside her in a sweat, he'd tell her his reverie. And why was it that the particular things she said, wicked wonderful things, stayed with him more vividly than the bumps and struggles of their bodies? Blair knew he might misremember someone's touch, but he never forgot their words, especially Mrs. Jellicoe's. *Frigging,* she'd said, she often said *suck you off,* she loved whispering the word *spunk,* she now and then said *fuck*—words he had never read in a book, and so they were like a magic formula when they were uttered, casting a spell.

"Sahib."

One of Blair's subinspectors—it was Denpo, one of the Burmese—clambered up the veranda's stairs, waking him from his reverie.

"Two men in custody, sahib. Theft of goods. Causing affray."

"Good work. We'll take them back with us."

This was on the Attaran River, trophies to exhibit in Moulmein. Blair saw it as a form of hunting, not the fox hunt that Major Bratby had advocated in Twante, but a more random chase, traipsing along a forest path from village to village, beating the bushes, or like a hunter seeking a stag in the glens with his stalkers.

"We've got to keep these teak forests secure," Ferguson said. "Timber is our bread and butter—oh, I know, there's cotton and rice coming up, but teak is what made Moulmein great."

"Yes, sir."

"I want you to go down to Tenasserim—not now, but soon. That's where the main supply of teak is sourced. I want the roads wide open, all dacoity suppressed. And in the meantime I want you to ride the politicals here."

This was at the club, where Blair wondered, whenever he went, if Mrs. Jellicoe might appear on the arm of Humphrey. Or was one of the men at the bar, at the billiard table, or the skittle alley—hooting, tipsy, telling a joke—Humphrey himself?

On an evening after his return from his patrol, chatting with Ferguson, Blair was buttonholed by MacFarlane, who had seemed friendly enough in the first weeks but had begun to avoid him. He'd been scheduled to go on patrol with Blair but had bunked off, and Blair decided that MacFarlane was a shirker. Yet tonight he seemed insistent to join Blair and Ferguson.

"My round," MacFarlane said.

"I thought you were teetotal," Blair said.

"Cider for me." MacFarlane seemed uneasy yet eager to chat. He ordered the round then said, "I've been meaning to ask, Blair, are you at all fond of games?"

"Up to a point. I get puffed easily."

"It's those rotten fags you smoke."

As though on cue, Blair began to cough, covering his mouth with one hand, holding a cigarette with the other. When his coughing subsided, MacFarlane spoke up.

"Fitba?"

Blair coughed again, to conceal his attempt to translate it and Ferguson explained.

"The police have a braw team."

Ah, yes. Blair smiled. *Football.*

"I played at school, I had a bash at it with the police team at Insein," Blair said, regretting that he'd have to join them on a free afternoon, doing something he disliked, unable to do the one thing he yearned for, to see Mrs. Jellicoe.

Ferguson said, "Fruity's an excellent wing—are you not, Fruity?" and swallowing the last of his pint, said, "See you in the morning, lads."

"That's all your doing, Blair!" MacFarlane said, after Ferguson had gone. "That name—it's going round. I see the men, too, sniggering over it."

In Blair's absence, a matter of weeks, the name he'd given MacFarlane, which he'd accidentally spilled to Ferguson, had been taken up.

"I insist, stop calling me Fruity."

"Leave off," Blair said. "It's just a joke."

"If you stop calling me Fruity, I'll do anything you like. I'll publicly kick any of the men who are sniggering."

"Oh, go kick yourself, Fruity," Blair said, and walked off, smiling.

But in a mood of repentance Blair played on the next three Saturdays, center forward on the Moulmein police team against the Moulmein natives, or lads from the local sports club, with the usual results—tripped by the Burmese, rough tackles, the Burmese often faking an injury or denying they'd laid a hand on the ball.

Blair's police work in locating Mrs. Jellicoe had come to nothing during this time. He had left a note at Thackeray's tiny office in the bazaar but had not received a reply. It was an invitation to tea—not at his house or the club, fraternizing that would be frowned upon, but behind a beaded curtain at a tea stall in the bazaar itself, where his excuse could be that the Indian was one of his informants. And in all the subterfuge that detail had the merit of being true.

Finally he got a reply, not by post but from a runner, a cadaverous Indian man in a turban and dhoti, who met him at the station gate with an envelope—the man had been waiting.

"How did you know this was for me?"

"Your tallness, sahib. Everyone knowing you."

Your tallness—a variation of *Your Highness*—a nice enough title, but another reason to be careful.

Over tea in the seclusion of the bazaar, Thackeray said he'd been delayed in his response because he'd been up-country, visiting a timber concession, and though Blair recognized the excuse as one of his own lame ones and doubted it, Thackeray appeared to be telling the truth. He had been negotiating with several timber firms for logs, and among the agents was "Mr. Humphrey."

"Where is Mr. Humphrey now?"

"Tenasserim side, sahib. With elephants."

"And his family?"

"No family, sahib. Family is here."

"Children?"

"No children, sahib. Memsahib only."

"Where is Mr. Humphrey's house?"

"House is on Upper Main Road. Name on house is Sea View. Ample of deodar trees in garden."

"Tell me, Thackeray," Blair said quickly to distract him from the subject of the house—he feared raising Thackeray's suspicions—"Tell me, my friend, you don't mind meeting me here?"

They shared a small table inside a stifling tearoom that smelled of cat piss and stale cake, the proprietor a young Burmese woman, with an infant in a sling on her back, fussing over a charcoal stove on which a blackened kettle steamed. Outside, beyond the beaded curtains, the hubbub of the bazaar, shouts and shrieks, the screams of roosters, the scuffing of sandals.

"My office just nearby, sahib."

"You understand I can't meet you at the club."

"Club is for sahibs, only."

"That's what I mean."

"I am having my own club. You are not welcome at my club, sahib."

Blair laughed at the man's impudence, but in fact he was being reasonable, forgiving Blair—and the British Raj—in his own terms.

"Arya Samaj," Thackeray said, just as Blair was about to ask. "We have hall and temple." He wagged his head. "You are not welcome."

But *vel-come* seemed a more severe form of the word.

"You people of the Noble Society."

"You are so clever, sahib! You know these words. We are many in the Arya Samaj, but none are sahibs. We have our own code. As you have your code."

Thackeray talked some more, attempting to explain the beliefs of the Noble Society, defending his veneration of Lord Ganesh—"Ganesh is mentioned in Rig Veda, sahib!"—and when he'd finished it seemed he'd forgotten what he'd divulged to Blair about Humphrey Jellicoe's address.

On his blatting bumping Victoria, Blair rode slowly along Upper Main Road, early one morning, soon after his talk with Thackeray. When he came to the bungalow fronted by the large deodars—a fifty-foot cedar blocking the house—he saw a mali under it on a path, sweeping needles, batting them with a brush like a horse's tail. Then he saw the stenciled signboard: *Sea View.*

"Is the sahib at home?" he called out in Hindi.

"Sahib on tour."

"Memsahib?"

"Memsahib taking chota hazri, sahib."

"Give her this," Blair said and handed him a sealed envelope.

Under the letterhead *Government of Burma Office Memorandum*, it read, *My syce is requested any evening*, and under it the address of his bungalow.

A knock came that very night, as Blair sat in the semidarkness of his parlor after dinner, his lamp turned low and set in a corner so as not to attract insects, no other lamps burning, his cook, Gugu, having retired to his quarters behind the bungalow. And what Blair saw at the door was the silhouette of a man who could have been any of his subinspectors, but very like Denpo, and because of that he called out gruffly, "What is it?"

A small voice replied, "Your syce, as you ordered, sahib."

Blair doused the lamp and snatched the door open, and this figure in helmet and khaki jacket and jodhpurs and boots—boots that gave her height—flung herself at him, dropping a bag as she did so. He kicked the door shut and held her as she moaned against his chest.

"What a wonderful surprise. I couldn't wait to see you."

"How did you get here?"

"In a tonga—he's waiting. I can't stay long."

But as she was speaking Blair led her through the darkened parlor to his bedroom and lay down, not seeing much, but hearing her undress, the whisper of her jacket as she pulled her arms from the sleeves, the chafing of her shirt slipping away, and at last the thump of her sitting on the mattress saying, "Help me with my boots."

Her jodhpurs next, and, last, the lisp of her knickers.

And later when they were done, exhausted, side by side breathing hard, slick with sweat, Blair said, "You've rearranged the furniture in my head"—but became breathless and self-conscious and couldn't finish.

"You're sweet but I must go," she said. "I've brought you a present. New book—well, not so new, perhaps, but new to Burma."

She dressed, now by lamplight and whirling moths. As always he loved to see her dressing, the lovely slender black-haired woman, her blue eyes catching the light, stretching naked before picking up her clothes and turning away, becoming a taller young man in a helmet and jacket and boots. In the parlor by the front door she found the bag she'd dropped on entering the house, took a book from it, and handed it to him.

"*Passage to India*," Blair said. "It's been talked about."

He kissed her lightly, and after she'd gone, and he turned up the lamp, sitting in his dressing gown in his armchair, he opened the book and saw a folded note tucked in its pages.

Saddan Cave next Friday at noon.

29

THE SADDAN CAVE

The great advantage of Blair's rank of assistant district commissioner of police in Moulmein was that he was in a position of authority, a Burma sahib indeed, answerable only to Ferguson. Ferguson was in meetings this week at the Secretariat in Rangoon, so Blair presided at the morning staff meeting. He put MacFarlane in charge of the subinspectors and sent Denpo on patrol with a contingent of men to report on political monks in the Happy Associations. And then he ordered tea.

He spent the week, pleasurably, in his office reading the Forster novel, sometimes tapping at a paragraph, at other moments shaking his head. He could tell from the thickened pages and the loosened sewing on the spine that the book had been read before and likely reread. A book was physically altered by having been closely read, and he was aware that he was leaving the marks of his attention on it too. And by the end of the week he knew why Mrs. Jellicoe had chosen to meet at the Saddan Cave.

He'd been there once, but briefly, following his men, because it was a challenge yet at least he knew the way. This time instead of on horseback Blair went on his motorbike, bumping past the Cantonment and through Daing Win Kwin, and a straight road between paddy fields to the village of Naung bin Saik that sat on a bluff above the Attaran River. He left his bike there in the care of the headman and rode the ferry to the far bank, where a gharry took him to the cave.

Mrs. Jellicoe had arrived before him, and she stepped from behind the upright roots of a banyan tree as the gharry approached. She seemed thinner, but that was perhaps an effect of her summer dress—yellow and close-fitting. Her wide-brimmed hat was trimmed with ribbons, and she carried a small hamper that she set down, and an umbrella that she opened as Blair stepped from the gharry.

In the awkwardness of seeing her in daytime after so long, not knowing how to resume, he stammered and said, "You're early."

"My efficient tonga wallah. I sent him away—he'll be back at four. He mustn't see you."

As the gharry creaked and turned, and rolled away, Mrs. Jellicoe twirled her umbrella on her shoulder and used it to hide beneath as he bent to kiss her, hurriedly, without passion, a schoolboy's kiss.

She sensed his nervousness, she said, "You needn't worry. There's no one here in the heat of the day. And it's only ever busy on the weekend."

"I twigged it. Inspired by the novel. The Marabar Caves."

"Clever me. So you read it." She used her umbrella to point to the hamper, saying, "We'll need that—the cave's up the hill."

By the time Blair lifted the hamper and found a way to tuck its handles in the crook of his arm so that he could hold a cigarette in his free hand, Mrs. Jellicoe had started away on the path that rose steeply to the top of the hill, and the cave's mouth.

"Every word of it," he called out as he came near her, but staying behind her, loving the motion of her body moving, making her loose dress shimmy against her curves. "What a queer book. Amazing that someone would spend that long in the dusty middle of India to socialize with natives. To generate so much sympathy. To find them charming and quotable and wise. To care so much."

"You didn't fancy it?" She seemed to dance ahead of him on the sloping path while he labored, breathing hard, having tossed his cigarette aside.

"It's a reasonable job. But Forster seems to believe he can see into the heart of a Muslim or a Hindu, and I don't think that's possible. Natives can scarcely understand each other! He's got his sahibs right, the odious Callendar, the unbending Heaslop. He's good on social awkwardness—the tea party, such a balls-up—wait, please."

Treading the steep path and talking about the book had winded him. He stopped and set the hamper down, and with his hands on his hips he threw his head back to take a deep breath.

"One thing he got right," he said. "The Indian's besetting sin. Maniacal suspiciousness."

"Lots of Heaslops in Burma."

"Forster doesn't really understand him. But I do. 'I'm out here to work—to hold the country by force,' Heaslop says, and asks 'How can we be pleasant? We have more important work to do.' The man's a loyal magistrate, and Forster belittles him for it. I read that and concluded that Forster would belittle me."

They resumed the climb, the path widened, and soon the mouth of the cave was in sight behind the last hillock.

"The natives hate Heaslop, his superiors lean on him," Blair said. "He's wedged between the two. I understand that, too. Forster thinks there are good and bad sahibs, but that's not the issue. The issue is that the empire is despotic, the whole of—plainly self-interested. But the snag is—and he doesn't see this, either—the maharajahs in the petty states are blighters."

"So you weren't impressed?"

"It's the best novel we're likely to get for a while. But he doesn't know what I know. In the police you see the dirty work of empire up close. Forster has never seen a dead man or a dacoit or a rape victim. His India is all about sahibs. It's a sort of prigs' paradise."

"Nor have I seen those atrocities. Does that disqualify me from having a political opinion?"

"Perhaps not," Blair said, still trudging. "His style's a bit showy. And what is one to make of such sentences as 'Like most Orientals, Aziz over-rated hospitality, mistaking it for intimacy.'"

"Surely that's true."

"Not in the least. Hospitality is a duty—intimacy is absent here, and pretty rare in England, too. And I hope I never commit the sin of starting a sentence, 'Like most Orientals.'"

"Your despotic novel will be a smashing success," Mrs. Jellicoe said.

He didn't ask *What novel?* The notion had been in his mind ever since he'd abandoned writing poetry. He laughed, but he thought that was what he loved about her, that was most loving about her, the way she saw into him, to his secret self, the sensual one, who had come to despise authority, who harbored a desire to be a writer—not of poems but of something more straightforward, more ambitious, more Lawrence or Wells than Forster.

Mrs. Jellicoe had collapsed her umbrella. She had walked to the mouth of the cave, calling out "Whoo! Whoo!" and then said, "How disappointing—no echo."

Blair stepped in front of her, instinctively lowering his head, hunching, and walked about twenty feet into the cave. He squinted into the semi-darkness. The air was close and damp, thick with an odor that was sulfurous and foul. He lit a cigarette for relief and kept one hand over his face, seeking the source of the teasing squeaks that resembled the mewing of kittens.

And that was when he saw the bats, hanging from the ceiling just above him, half-hidden, yet his eyes had adjusted to the darkness. A mass of twitching bats, clustered together, jostling their loose wings—and he could only think of them as flying rats, clinging with their claws to the dome of rock.

"No," he said, clutching his face. "This won't do."

Dazzled in the sunlight outside, he stood with Mrs. Jellicoe, surveying the slope beyond the cave.

"Saddan Cave—very famous," Mrs. Jellicoe said.

"With its bats and its bat shit, and its foul smell, it's a truer example of what India is like than Forster's fatuous Marabar Caves," Blair said, and saying so, he imagined a better book, with scruffier sahibs and nastier clubs and surly natives, framed by majestic landscapes—jungle and swamp and river, possessing the menace or the consolation of a character.

This thought led him to walk past the cave to a grove of trees overlooking a grassy hilltop, with a view of the gleaming sea far off to the west.

Mrs. Jellicoe took a folded cloth from the hamper and spread it on the grass. She set out sandwiches on small plates and poured tea from a flask. Blair sat cross-legged, a plate on his lap, eating an egg sandwich, sipping tea, a slight breeze cooling his face, glancing at Mrs. Jellicoe, and past her to the ocean and the afternoon sun.

"Bliss," he said.

When he was finished, he crept close to Mrs. Jellicoe and held her, stroking her shoulders, breathing her perfume.

"You're comely," he said.

"What a love you are for saying that."

"You know what I want."

"Yes, I do. Because I want the same thing." She pinched his nose and held on and laughed.

"That grass is a bed," he said and imagined her lying naked on it.

"It's unwise here—anyone could come along, and see me toss you off. You're blushing."

That *orf* again. "When can I have you?"

"Soon," she said. "Your syce will visit."

They lay together, drowsy, looking upward at the branches of the trees and the flitting birds, the gauzy clouds. Blair subsided into sleep, but soon was nudged.

"Ants, Eric. I'm being bitten."

"I nodded off." He yawned. "No ants in Forster's picnic. No rats in his novel. No corpses."

But Mrs. Jellicoe was gathering the tea things. "My tonga wallah will be here soon. He must not see you. We'll have to take separate ferries."

She packed the hamper, kneeling, her sleeves slipping down to reveal her bare shoulder, the strap of her chemise, a loose lock of hair dangling at her ear—he loved her untidy, a disheveled nymph.

"I didn't know how this day would end," she said as they descended the path. "I think this is right."

"I'll make myself invisible." He crossed to a thickness of bushes and crouched there out of sight until the tonga arrived, the horse's bells jangling, and Mrs. Jellicoe boarded, and soon the bells died away.

Blair found a log to sit on; he smoked and reflected on her saying *Your novel* and smiled to think she'd seen that ambition in him. He did not allow himself to ponder quitting the police, or departing from Burma, but he was keenly aware that a career as a writer was incompatible with policing. No one in the service wrote novels, and that was the weakness of *Passage to India*. Forster saw India as a tripper, someone on holiday, probably a maharajah's houseguest; he only saw surfaces, he had no idea what lay beneath, the grind of the day-to-day. He could describe a tea party or a punkah wallah or a schoolmaster, but it was all guesswork and gush. Forster had no notion of the inner life of empire, which was a great deal worse than he imagined. He had never struck a servant, or seen one struck, he had never witnessed a man hanged, or engaged in the cruelty of club banter, the men rubbishing the natives and one another.

In Forster's mind the club was jolly—he had no idea how vicious it could be; how vicious Indians could be from caste to caste, each man defined by his duty, the sweeper forever a sweeper. His cave was odorless and echoey, it didn't stink of bat shit. The miasma of the bat cave now infected Blair's thinking—he could still smell it. Forster's novel was soft and oblique, his version of empire simply unfair and impolite, as though the tiny mildly discordant town of Chandrapore and its brittle tea parties stood for the whole of India. None of it resembled the beastly empire Blair had come to see—cruel and inhumane, a bloody awful business, where men died miserably of their whippings, and there were two systems of justice—a lenient one for Europeans, a meaner sort for natives. There was no dowry murder in Forster, there was no blood, there were no rats or whores. He did not know the true savagery of the Raj, where sahibs were overlords and natives were drudges and dogsbodies.

At last the gharry rattled in view, the driver calling out, "Sahib!"

Subinspector Denpo was waiting in the outer office the following morning, a logbook on his lap—a Saturday, but Ferguson was expected to arrive in the afternoon. Blair got to his feet and saluted, eager to report on the activities of the Happy Associations.

Over tea in Blair's office, Denpo seemed pleased to have been singled out for the assignment. "It is all in these pages, sir. We have found the names of members. We have their locations. We have portions of speeches. We have recorded many infractions."

But Blair said, "Denpo, what do you know of Saddan Cave?"

"Holy cave, sir. The name is for the Buddha."

"How so?"

"Saddan mean—when Buddha was elephant"—and Denpo hesitated because Blair had started to snort. "In former life," Denpo went on. "Buddha was many animals before he became Buddha, but the elephant is the wisest. Cave named for him."

"For the elephant."

"Yah, for elephant, sir."

She did not come that night, or the next, but within a week there was a knock, so soft that his cook, Gugu, had not heard the arrival and was not roused to meet it. Blair dismissed him and opened the door on the slender young man in uniform.

30

THE IMPOSTER

All through the dog days of June in Moulmein, past another birthday, his twenty-third, Blair's guilt crowded his mind, the humid heat sickening and slowing him, the glare off the water and the metal rooftops burning his eyes. Mrs. Jellicoe had visited three times since the cave, but then there was silence. Had she gone off him? Did her husband know? Blair resisted sending her a note, and there was no other way of safely reaching her. His anxiety over accidentally encountering one of the Limouzins left him in a temper. He found himself shouting "Bloody fool!" at his inspectors, he flexed a bamboo cane and threatened Subinspector Waris Ali Shah with a thrashing, he kicked Gugu for leaving Flo tied up without water in his bowl. He saw fear in the gaze of his men at inspection and thought, *I'm a tyrant,* and he hated himself.

As for the Limouzins, he imagined he'd see them at the worst possible moment, in the bazaar, or in a shop, or at one of the busy arcades—Frank, or much worse, Kathleen or Aimee, would accost him, calling out "Eric!"

He had not dared to send a note to them saying he'd been posted to the town, because—what then? An awkward, meaningless drink with Frank at the club, or an invitation to Sunday service at St. Matthew's, where he'd be compelled to sit in the same pew, in full view of a congregation that might include Ferguson or MacFarlane. It might be tea at the Royal Hotel, among the gawking burra memsahibs. He wished the Limouzins were not in Moulmein; he hated the idea that he was obliged to call on them. Why did they not leave? Didn't they know they had no future here? His parents' letters were forwarded to him from Insein. When he replied to them, he talked about the weather, and his dog, and the books he was reading, and asked for news of his sisters, Marjorie and Avril. He did not mention his debts, he did not allude to his transfer to Moulmein.

His greatest fear, of a chance meeting in a public place, seemed to him a worrying premonition, his fear like a foreboding. And so it happened— another of his anxious previsions proving accurate—outside a cake shop in an arcade near the bazaar. He was supervising an arrest that Ferguson had ordered, of an embezzler who'd absconded with a brick of rupees from the tax department in Rangoon. This clerk, named U Thin, had been seen entering an upstairs office near the cake shop, the office registered in the name of U Thin's cousin. Ferguson had said, "Set your men there. Catch him. Squeeze him. I want him in irons."

Blair had ordered four of his men to the task, while he watched from the shadows, in the shelter of the cake shop's arcade, and when the man was seized, and Blair stepped into the road to supervise the clerk being hoisted into a closed coach, he heard his name screeched.

"Eric!"

Kathleen rushed toward him, but awkwardly, hampered by a cake box she was balancing in her hands, her shawl untangling and dragging in her hurry, a mad look of glee on her sallow teasing face, as Blair turned away from his men.

"I've been meaning to—"

But Kathleen was still shrieking. "You naughty boy—why didn't you tell us you were in Moulmein? Mummy will be so cross! Her birthday is tomorrow—see, I have her cake. You will come, naughty Eric!"

"Rather," he said. "Now I must be off. We have a man to charge-sheet"— and called to his men watching from the coach, "Secure the prisoner!"

But he knew his face was crimson, that what stalled his men in the arrest was the sight of a young Eurasian woman standing with a cake box at the roadside, her shawl at her feet, howling his name at him. Even the prisoner U Thin was gaping with a slight smile at the sahib barracked by a half-blood woman, a common *ka pyar*, screaming his name.

"That is an order!"

The birthday party was jolly, Mah Hlim delighted in her cake, Frank complimented Blair on his transfer and his promotion, Aimee had taken up smoking cheroots, perhaps in homage to Grandma Limouzin. Blair left, repeating his excuses, promising to see more of them and went home, cursing.

MacFarlane asked for a meeting later in the week. He entered Blair's office, shuffling his feet, looking oblique, and as a greeting said, "Good show, Blair, you found yourself a chee-chee."

Though he had vowed not to use the name, Blair found himself in his fury saying, "What is it you want, Fruity?"

It must have been Waris Ali Shah who told MacFarlane about Kathleen, Shah's retaliation for being threatened with a thrashing, the bamboo cane upraised, the Rajput humiliated in front of the Burmese he despised, Denpu and Yaza.

Rebuffed, hating the name Fruity, MacFarlane collapsed in a chair. He put his hands to his face and spoke through his fingers.

"Hang it all, Blair—" But the rest was a buzz of mumbling.

"Speak up, man."

MacFarlane moved his hands from his face to his ears, hooking his fingers on them. "I said, I'll never get off bally probation."

"What gives you that idea?"

"I raised it with Ferguson."

"Yes?"

"He shot me a bitter look."

"And?"

"And pointed to the door."

"Is that all?"

"With his mangled fingers."

MacFarlane sat slumped in his sorrowful posture, saying nothing more, but Blair was so angered by *You found yourself a chee-chee,* he merely glared and was tempted to call him "Fruity" again. He suspected that the young man wanted something from him, and was biding his time until at last, he'd tell him to go away—maybe no words, no "Fruity," maybe point at the door as Ferguson's mangled fingers had done. He was about to do just that when MacFarlane spoke again, this time in an urgent whisper, his long nose narrowing and whitening to gristle in the tension of his misery.

"I don't reckon I'll ever be hard enough."

"Why come to me?"

MacFarlane raised his head and with reddened eyes and trembling lips, he looked across the desk, where Blair sat with his arms folded.

"Because you're hard, Blair."

Blair looked into the man's pleading face, and said, "Hop it, Fruity. I don't have time for this," and watched the young man drag himself to the door.

He paused to say, "No need to get in a wax, Blair."

Hard? He didn't think of himself as hard; he reasoned that he was doing his duty and that involved spells of firmness. The embezzling clerk, U Thin, had cheeked him at the station because he'd seen him with Kathleen, and for that insolence Blair had knocked him about—had MacFarlane meant that? The subinspectors Denpo and Yaza had brought five monks and some ragged peasants chained together in a wagon, a sullen group from a Happy Association. Perhaps MacFarlane had seen their bruised faces, the

manacles cutting into the flesh of their wrists, but had he known they'd resisted arrest and that the peasants had been armed with khanjars and dahs?

No one except Mrs. Jellicoe knew of his disgust for this hateful job, how
his work was turning him into someone he despised, especially when in the
fury of an arrest he found himself grasping a handcuffed monk or a dacoit
by the upper arm and frog-marching the stumbling and squawking man
toward his subinspectors, who backed away, wide-eyed, shocked by his vehemence. Suppressing his disgust, Blair had compensated for his sense of
disloyalty with a mask of a pukka sahib—the mask he'd worn with Hollis
in Rangoon. When someone at the Moulmein Club in his cups said, "Of
course we have no right to be in this sodding country—only we're here,
so for god's sake let's stay here," Blair's reply was, "That needs to be said."
Nor did he flinch when someone—usually an older man—used the beastly
word *nigger*, which happened so often it was taken to be a synonym for
native. To seem plausible Blair stifled his objections and offered no rebuke.
A sahib, no matter his doubts, had to behave like a sahib.

He had doubts—more than doubts, he had antagonisms amounting to
disloyalty. He wondered if his disloyalty had been simmering within him
from the start, since Mandalay, or earlier, since hearing Sergeant Sholto
Haggan's shouts in Rangoon, and the cant of the governor, that talk excusing Dyer of massacring more than a thousand Sikhs in Amritsar, an
abomination sanctioned by the Raj. Certainly, seeing the consequences of
his arrests, the gray scarred buttocks of the prisoners at Insein had shown
him the brutality of his job. Yet his rebellion now ran so deep and was so
dangerous to his prospects he exaggerated his severity. Hollis's questions in
Rangoon had elicited this same bluster. Hollis must have gone away with
the impression of Blair as a model policeman. He couldn't have known
that Blair feared that if his mask should slip ever so slightly, he would be
revealed as an opponent of the Raj. Blair suspected that he might not be
the only one who felt this way, that others must harbor the same doubts.

That man from the Educational Service he'd met in the compartment on
the overnight train to Mandalay, how after some probing questions the man
had seemed safe, and they'd spent the entire night rubbishing their jobs and
damning the empire as despotic and racist, nothing but a racket. Yet they'd
parted at Mandalay in the morning shamefaced and regretful, like an adulterous couple. And why? Because for them it was a job, a town, a province,
an empire of imposters and they had no choice but to pretend to be sahibs.

Blair's solace was Mrs. Jellicoe. She saw into his heart. And he was glad
to think there was an element of corruption in their sneaking and secrecy,
that hugger-mugger, sweating in their lust was a form of rebellion. He

loved that this petite, apparently demure woman could be sensationally foulmouthed, and he had a better memory for her obscenities than the act itself, the words ringing in his ears. He savored her hissing at him, *I want your cock in my mouth*, wicked provocations that possessed a sort of dark magic, a witchery like an incantation, that stupefied him and made him gloat over her power to shock him.

All that, he suppressed. And suppressing it he became his opposite, intolerant and hypocritical, like a lecherous preacher who hides his lechery in scolding. He knew he'd become a scold in issuing orders—that's what MacFarlane meant by "hard." The price of being a sahib in the Raj was subscribing to its beliefs, that natives were inferior, that its despotism was fair, and that sahibs are to be obeyed and never laughed at, that Dyer did his duty. The deepest secret of the Raj was that the higher you rose in the ranks, the less work you had to do, the more men you had under you to take orders. Blair counted on his subinspectors to do his work for him, he depended on MacFarlane who, insecure on probation, was eager to please.

In Mrs. Jellicoe's absence, Blair found solace in his dog and his ducks and chickens. On some afternoons he rode his motorbike to the timber yards to watch the elephants at work, and he often saw Thackeray preparing to feed them—Thackeray who venerated the elephants as protectors and good omens, the living embodiment of Lord Ganesh.

"Sahib," Thackeray called out to Blair, the lonely man pleased to have Blair as a friend, the pair of them at sundown admiring the smiling elephants.

Blair found solace, too, in riding his motorbike to the canebrakes beyond Daing Win Kwin, his Purdey shotgun slung on his shoulder, and firing slugs into the bamboo, shattering the stalks and watching them fall like wickets, target practice that terrified the peasants in the paddy fields.

After the chance encounter with Kathleen, Blair agreed to take tea with her and Frank and Mah Hlim. They said they were proud to know he was keeping them safe, they complained of monks and dacoits, and Kathleen said, "We British are counting on you, Eric," not realizing she was despised by the British and could not show her half-caste face at a club dance. The one safe place for her was at St. Matthew's and even there she was frowned upon. At that tea, Mah Hlim simply stared at him with narrowed eyes and twitched her shawl, and he thought, *My native aunt.*

He could not rid himself of his sense that he was an imposter, and what troubled him was the thought that in order to disguise his disloyalty he'd had to be seen as hard. MacFarlane was wrong, but MacFarlane would never be able to fathom the reason.

In Blair's guarded mood, he spent more time at the club. To stay away would provoke suspicions and he'd be charged with letting the side down. It was whiskey and bad jokes now, the click of billiard balls, the creak of the punkah, and some evenings in the club lounge the gramophone, the sentimental crooning that tore at his heart.

What'll I do
When you are far away
And I am blue
What'll I do?

And he had to slip into the cloakroom to splash water on his face and compose himself, because all he could think of was Mrs. Jellicoe.

That thought was another premonition. One night as he sat with Ferguson he saw her enter on the arm of a stocky somewhat older man in a dinner jacket and white tie, fresh from some sort of official do, his face tanned by the outdoors. And she was elegantly dressed, too, in black, a long gown but tight at the waist, with a flounce at the hem and high crimped sleeves, and a black cloche hat with a narrow upturned brim. The man released her to call to a darts player, who greeted him, "Humphrey, old boy!"

This carried across the room, Mrs. Jellicoe absorbed in plucking and straightening her sleeves in the heat.

"Is there anything wrong, Blair?" Ferguson said.

"I've just remembered that I didn't exercise Flo today. Must run."

And he fled from the room.

In Blair's distress—the punishing job, the imposture, his thinking *I am not that man*—everything that was not related to his work became important to him. He gloried in being greeted by his dog, he had a small pond dug like the one in Insein for his ducks, and he had Gugu make pots of rice so that he could sit and feed them. He set up crates under his house for the hens to use as nesting boxes. And he began to understand why Thackeray spent most early evenings at the timber yards, feeding the elephants, desiring their recognition, a lift, a curling of the trunk. He began to do the same in his way, taking food for the elephants but hardly realizing that in doing so he was seeking to make a friend of the Indian.

On an evening when Thackeray failed to show up, Blair wondered what might have kept the punctual man away. Blair returned the next evening but still Thackeray had not appeared. At last, after four days he saw the Indian, shyly greeting him.

"Thackeray!"

"Sahib."

"I was worried about you."

"My wife is poorly, sahib."

"In Moulmein?"

"Bombay, sahib. I was occupied in cabling. I have been permanent fixture at Post and Telegraph, sending and receiving."

"How is your wife now?"

"Poorly but I hope rallying. That is why you find me here today." He showed Blair his pouch of food. "For Lord Ganesh."

Blair was moved by Thackeray's story—a real man, with real feeling, worried for his wife's health, loyal to her, and alone here, with only the elephant for consolation. The elephant seemed to acknowledge him, and the mahout shouted in welcome as the elephant raised and curled his truck in greeting.

"He says *namaste*."

"The mahout."

"Elephant, sahib. They are so clever. He remembered me. Like you, he wonders why I have been absent. But look"—Thackeray showed his pouch of food—"he knows I am having eatables for him."

They stood, Blair and Thackeray, in the golden glow that lit the delicate standing hairs on the corrugations of the elephant's hide, watching the ponderous animal hoist timbers from the chute at the sawmill and transfer them on his tusks to a neat stack by the gate, to be loaded on the ship moored there, which was also gilded by the late-afternoon sun.

"Lovely animal," Blair said.

"Observe eyes. Examine eyelashes. Sahib, have you ever seen anything so magnificent?"

Blair peered at the amber eye, the tufts of gray lashes, and murmured his appreciation.

"My good wife has such lovely eyes," Thackeray said. He turned away from the elephant, looking tearful. "Eyes are windows to soul."

Blair said, "'To thee I do command my watchful soul, / Ere I let fall the windows of mine eyes.'"

Startled, Thackeray gasped, "Sahib!"

"*Richard the Third*," Blair said. "School production. I played Richmond, for my sins."

"What school, may I make bold to inquire, sahib?"

Blair hesitated then said, "I was at Eton."

"Eton College." Thackeray pressed his hands together, bowing slightly, in a gesture of respect. "I am honored, sahib."

In more than four years, Thackeray was the only person in Burma who had seemed impressed with a mention of his school. But at once Blair regretted it and wished he hadn't divulged it to the Indian. It seemed boastful and snobbish, so he pointed to another elephant, heavily chained at a corner of the timber yard, the poor thing looking agitated, with wild eyes, flailing its trunk.

"That old boy looks stroppy."

"It is bull elephant. Suffering in musth. Trying to break chains. Hungering for female."

Brown syrupy stains seemed to leak from the elephant's temple, giving it the look of a grotesque and disfiguring splash of cosmetic.

"I've heard the word," Blair said. "I've never seen it. Kipling in 'My Lord the Elephant' speaks of 'the elephant in his musth.'"

Thackeray said, "Yes. My lord, the elephant," and pressed his hands together in veneration and bowed, first to the elephant with the teak plank balanced on its tusks, and then at the elephant in the far corner of the yard, tossing its head. And after Thackeray turned back to the working elephant, Blair continued to stare at the trapped and frustrated beast, lurching in its chains.

31

THE MADMAN

A fit of musth, hungry for the female, Blair thought constantly as the weeks passed and he saw no sign of Mrs. Jellicoe. He ached for her. He was mildly tempted by the Moulmein brothels, two of them on a back lane in a slummy district near Coal Shed Jetty in Moulmein South. The area was known for its Chinese gambling parlors and opium dens, but they were so well hidden it was difficult to make arrests, as they shifted from one back room to another. The law stipulated that gamblers had to be caught in the act.

The brothels operated as drinking houses, the girls entertaining clients in upstairs rooms; but as long as they remained orderly—no loud music, no fights—they were not raided. And one of them, Mother Lum's, seemed to Blair—outwardly, at least—as strict as a girls' school, Mother Lum herself less like a mother than a stern headmistress. The girls were not sluttish, they were prim and beautifully dressed, each one crowned with a lavishly wrapped gaungbaung; the girls from the north tattooed on their faces and hands, stipples and petals of blue ink.

And just when he thought he could bear it no longer, an envelope was left for him in his office, printed *Assistant Superintendent E Blair,* and inside was a slip of paper with an address—a house number and street in Dalhousie, a day and time: the following Friday, at six o'clock, among the vice dens in the city's south.

Though it was unsigned, Blair recognized the wide black nib of Mrs. Jellicoe's pen, the ribbon of her script. Not wishing to reveal himself on his motorbike, he hailed a shuttered gharry and asked to be dropped nearby, walking with his head down to the designated road, adjacent to Coal Shed Jetty. He came to a narrow lane, a two-story house set back, half hidden by hedges of mounded frangipani, its sun-heated blossoms heavy with scent.

As he approached the porch he saw a curtain twitch in a side window, and the front door opened, an oldish Burmese woman beckoning and without a word showing him into a corridor, where she paused before a door. He expected a room, but she opened the door to a narrow staircase that led to the upper floor and a familiar fragrance.

Mrs. Jellicoe leaned against a doorjamb—an actress's pose, Blair thought, and pleasingly so—a four-poster bed draped in mosquito net in shadow just visible behind her. Though the blinds had been drawn against the setting sun, the rays flashing through the bamboo chicks picked out stripes of iridescence on the wall. She wore the black long-sleeved gown he had seen at the club and now it seemed as alluring as a nightdress.

"What a lovely frock," was all he could think to say.

She backed into the room, as he entered, shutting the door after him. She kissed him, pressing her jasmine-scented face close to his.

"Take it off me," she said in a small voice. "But slowly."

And then they were entangled, in familiar fury, eager for each other, her breath hot against his ear, her whispered words whipping him to a frenzy.

When she nodded off afterward, he lay on his side and read her face, the sweetness of her features in repose, her long lashes, the surprised circumflex of her eyebrows, her lips—so innocent, slightly parted as she breathed: the same lips that had whispered such wickedness moments ago. There were delicate parentheses on either side of her mouth. He loved the slant of her nose, her slightly receding chin, almost angelic, blameless in her slumber, melting against him.

Yet she was a conspirator with him against the Raj, and he was reminded that she, too, lived her life in Moulmein as an imposter.

She woke and blinked and said, "Must run."

Conspirators woke up quickly.

Thereafter, Blair knew when her husband was away: a note was slipped to him by a peon, and he acted upon it. They continued to meet at the house of the old Burmese woman in Dalhousie, whom Mrs. Jellicoe said had once been a servant, sacked by Humphrey for stealing a trinket. But the old woman's hatred for him kept them safe. "And I go on paying her," Mrs. Jellicoe said.

They seldom mentioned Humphrey, though sometimes Mrs. Jellicoe chanted, "He thinks books are bosh."

"Some books *are* bosh," Blair said. "Some boys' weeklies are ripping."

"You will be a writer," she said, one afternoon, groggy after sex. "You will make your mark."

Blair shrugged but was thankful for her saying that, seeing into his heart as always. He said, "But I read Wells and Maugham and Lawrence, and it seems unattainable."

"You are not them. You are Blair. And I know it will happen." She shifted on the bed, naked, unembarrassed, and faced him. "Because you're a reader, but most of all—essential to being a writer—you're a listener."

With that she slid out of from beneath the mosquito net, heading to the lavatory, and paused at a mirror on the far wall, standing naked before it, her hair wild, her hands on her hips, a rosy glow on her chafed buttocks.

"I look fucked"—and laughed softly.

The cooler weather arrived, and the first rains of the monsoon, the crime season slackening. Blair journeyed to Amherst with a contingent of subinspectors to squelch across sodden fields in single file—the loud downpour falling like rods, Subinspector Hossein behind him holding an umbrella over his head. They were investigating a monastery that was reputed to be political. He was rebuffed by the monks but he loved the forested hills, the enclosed villages, and the simple enduring details of village life that he had noticed in the Delta, women in shawls drawing water from wells like biblical figures and, in ancient postures, carrying clay pots on their shoulders, or filling enormous containers used for rice storage—round, four-foot-high baskets, fattened with the rice harvest, a sign of plenty.

Blair wanted to share these pleasures, and he wished that Mrs. Jellicoe were with him. He missed the days at Insein when he was able to spend whole afternoons with her, strolling along the river with Muriel, or playing cribbage, all their mild deceptions, with the delicious sense that later she would secretly visit him. He loved her company and conversation—"Read Villon, *Le Grand Testament*—'We were two yet had but one heart between us!' Read the new translation of Tolstoy." The trysts in Moulmein were too hurried, and risky, and he feared being found out.

It was a relief to be summoned away from Moulmein, where he often felt he was biding his time, awaiting a message from her—and where life at the club grated on him, his having to be a sahib, his having to listen to the same guff about natives, the same jokes, the same tedious stories. He hated the sight of MacFarlane, and he wished to be away from the Limouzins. So he welcomed the patrols up-country, undeterred by the muddy roads. He depended on his men to smooth the way. As always, they did the work, carried out interviews and collected evidence, and wrestled villains into handcuffs.

One morning in the market town of Hpa-an on the upper Thanlyin River, a Burmese merchant came to him and reported a disturbance in Pabu, the village on the opposite bank.

"What sort of village?"

"Very small, but with big pagoda. A holy place, sahib."

"What sort of disturbance?"

"A madman, sahib."

Blair and four of his men were rowed across the river in the merchant's own boat, a graceful vessel with a prow like a pitcher's spout. On the far bank they were met by frantic villagers and one excited monk.

"It is the devil, sahib," the monk said. "He has fouled the pagoda."

They found the man in a deep wallow at the far side of the village, a hideous sight, naked, coated in mud—a big man, too, his white eyes showing through the mask of his muddy face, and howling curses at the people who surrounded him.

"Seize him, chaps."

But his men didn't move, and when Blair barked the order again, the men stepped back. Seeing the reaction of these policemen, the madman screamed and made as if to rush at them, flinging clods of mud.

"Waris, Hossein—I said take hold of him."

"It is a pig's wallow, sahib," Hossein said with disgust.

Waris made a face. "He has soiled himself."

Hooting at their hesitation, the madman scooped mud and flung it, splashing the subinspectors' uniforms, lifting his knees in a frantic dance and chattering. Now the crowd had backed away, the policemen, too, leaving the madman triumphant in the wallow, gesturing as though defying anyone to arrest him.

The mockery of the villagers, the pleas of the monk, were not directed at the madman—they were screaming at the police, who seemed too timid to subdue the madman. And Blair saw that the utter lack of inhibition of the madman was a kind of power. The mud, too, like armor, like a weapon. The police were helpless to deal with him without wading into waist-high mud to approach him.

"What are they saying?" Blair asked of the chants.

"Coward, sahib."

Blair knew one of the words, "*Waat*"—pig—chanted at him and his men, not at the madman, who heard them and became more animated and repeated the mocking words through the mouth hole in his mud mask.

"It is useless, sahib," Hossein said. "He is doing no harm."

Splashing in the wallow, the madman stayed out of reach. He had the look of a fierce deity from the underworld, gray where the mud had dried on his shoulders and his head, giving his features the crusted appearance of cracked stone, a statue come alive, triumphant.

"Bugger it," Blair said, brushing at the flecks of mud that had spattered his uniform, though still the villagers shouted, all their wrath turned on the policemen, who were still backing away from the naked grinning man, his body thickened with mud.

"We look like bloody fools," Hossein said.

Blair said, "Shut up," but he knew Hossein was right.

They were rowed back in silence across the river to Hpa-an, where the merchant was waiting.

"Five policemen cannot capture one unarmed man," he said.

"It was the mud," Hossein said.

But the merchant spoke to Blair, saying, "Is mud a danger, sahib?"

"The major wants a word," MacFarlane said to Blair the day after they returned. Blair had reported the incident as trivial, but the merchant had sent a note separately, explaining the damage the madman had done to the pagoda, and the failure of Blair and his men to restrain him.

Ferguson was standing in his office when Blair appeared at the door, and what Blair found daunting was the sight of Ferguson using his damaged hand to beckon Blair forward, clawing the air with it, indicating a chair.

"Sit, Blair."

Blair crouched and slid into the chair, Ferguson stepping nearer, still rotating his hand, as though casting a spell.

"I can explain, sir."

"There is nothing to explain. I am in full possession of the facts. You did nothing to restrain a dangerous man. It was a visible failure." He used the pincers of his few fingers to pick up and shake a piece of paper at Blair. "How am I to read this note from the merchant at Hpa-an as anything but a rebuke."

"I take full responsibility, sir."

"Quite right, but I may say you've let the side down."

"I was unsure of the best course to handle it, sir. The man was inaccessible."

Ferguson snapped back, "You might have deployed a rope and harnessed him. You could have ordered one or more of your men to restrain him with a snare. You could have set a perimeter and waited him out—and after a day he would have begged for your attention." Still with his claw, Ferguson patted the pistol holstered on his belt. "You could have shot the idler."

"I see, sir."

"Instead, you left with your tail between your legs." Ferguson walked behind his desk but he did not sit; he stood behind it and spoke in a commanding voice. "What is the greatest threat to order in Burma? It is the natives seeing us as ineffectual, a British policeman looking a fool. And why? Because they will take advantage."

"Sorry, sir."

His face tightening, Ferguson said, "I cannot abide anyone in my command who feels the need to say sorry." Then he turned his back on him. "Get out and do better."

It still seemed trivial. What was it that fueled Ferguson's fear? Blair wondered later. Skinny, naked Gandhi was in the Indian news, calling attention to himself, anticolonial but half mad in his obsessive ostentation and his mysticism. Was it that Ferguson saw in the madman someone like Gandhi who would try to end the empire—the natives rebelling, like a madman in a mud wallow, inaccessible? To deal with them you'd befoul yourself. Simpler to some minds to leave them in the mud, and depart. Yes, the empire was despotic but to leave this land in the hands of someone like Gandhi was insane. Blair never saw Gandhi and his trickery and posturing without thinking, *Rasputin*.

Ferguson was saying he'd failed. In his heart Blair had always felt like a failure, but though he'd lapsed a number of times over the years here, this was the first time he'd faltered in making an arrest and was exposed as a failure. He needed the encouragement of Mrs. Jellicoe more than ever, but weeks passed without a word from her and he guessed that her husband was in town.

A note to her was unwise. Yet he longed for her, and he knew it was a longing that could not be assuaged by a visit to Mother Lum's. Not hearing from Mrs. Jellicoe was a sadness and it coincided with persistent invitations from the Limouzins—to tea, to dinner, to church services, to card games. Blair made excuses, yet he was ashamed rebuffing them and so agreed to some visits. He found himself at meals or at tea with Uncle Frank praising the police, Aimee murmuring, Kathleen saying how proud she was to see cousin Eric in uniform.

"The natives say such frightful things against the government!"

Blair did not reply that most of the objections were justified. He said, "The Happy Associations perhaps. They're determined to make our lives miserable. I wish I knew how to deal with them. I'm at rather a loss."

"Nobble them," Uncle Frank said. "Have you tried that? Get inside."

"I wouldn't know how to nobble them."

"Use your loaf, Eric," Uncle Frank said and tapped his own head.

Another evening wasted, over tea at the Limouzins'. They didn't know they were despised, they still believed in the future of the empire, they clucked over the king; they didn't see that the system was designed to fail for being unfair and overbearing, and that all that was needed was for them to stop believing.

Blair's dog, Flo, was his solace; the mildness of his chickens, the hens fluffing out their wings, and the ducks' wobbly walk also eased his mind. Thackeray was a friend, but what good was an Indian friend in Burma? He could offer Blair nothing, and, worse, it was like a sign of disloyalty to be seen fraternizing with him. And the club that was a refuge to the British seemed unsafe to him. He hesitated spending too much time there for fear they'd find him out, but if he stayed away he appeared disloyal and wasn't playing the game. And so he showed up, he drank, he listened to the idle boasting and the disparaging remarks against natives and wondered if his silence was taken to be opposition.

He perfected the bureaucrat's art of seeming busy, absorbed in paper-work and reports, sending his men out to investigate crimes, not daring to contemplate his future. All this muddle, and still pining for Mrs. Jellicoe, waking at night and lying in the heat that was trapped inside his mosquito net, wondering where she might be and hating the thought of Humphrey.

Knowing how poor he was at doing his job, it amazed Blair to think that anyone trusted him. It seemed proof that the system was deeply flawed. Half the bureaucrats he knew in Burma would have been hard-pressed in England to get a job mending bicycles. How did the empire persist, then? It was the indifference of the majority of natives living in villages, oblivious of government—religion, and ancient superstition and lack of education, allowed the system to flourish. And people like him, unfit to be policemen, pretending to keep order.

Get out and do better, Ferguson had ordered. Yet Blair always knew that he would be found out, and so it happened, in Moulmein, the day of his disgrace.

32

THE SACRIFICE

Blair had known since arriving in Burma, still a boy in his teens—but one in uniform, with access to a gun—that it would happen: that he would fail spectacularly and be disgraced. The day came in Moulmein but was shadowed forth in the most casual way.

He was at the club drinking a brandy with the timber surveyor Laidlaw in the Smoking Room after lunch, Laidlaw describing an upcoming football match, what larks it would be to defeat a team of native policemen, "Wee weedy jossers that cannae kick."

Just then, a servant entered the room, bowing before Blair, saying, "Telephone for sahib."

"Half a mo," Blair said to Laidlaw and went to the office off the foyer where the club telephone was kept. A clerk stood at attention next to the instrument, a black candlestick phone. He presented the earpiece to Blair, then backed away bowing, the soles of his slippers chafing the floor.

"This is Blair. What is it?"

"Subinspector Doshi, Pendon Hill Station, sahib. I wish to report elephant on loose. It is ravaging bazaar. We cannot adequately contain creature. My men believe it to be matter of musth, sir."

"How serious?"

"Perilous, sir. Elephant has destroyed bamboo huts and overturned municipal rubbish van. It is rampageous, sir."

"I'll find a pony and meet you at the bazaar."

"A firearm will be necessary, sir."

"I'll bring a rifle."

As he was speaking, MacFarlane entered the foyer and stood listening. When Blair rang off, MacFarlane said, "Rifle? Can I help?"

"Find me a pony and the Purdey in the locker. We've got an elephant causing ructions."

"That Purdey won't kill him."

"I'm not going to kill him, Fruity! I'm merely going to put the wind up. Now fetch the gun and the pony, there's a good chap."

Blair returned to the Smoking Room and finished his cigarette and his glass of brandy. He promised Laidlaw he'd be at the football match, and by the time he got to the station, MacFarlane was waiting, cradling the Purdey, a syce holding the pony. But Ferguson was with him—MacFarlane had obviously alerted him.

"It's your lookout, Blair," Ferguson said. "I don't want a cock-up this time."

"Yes, sir."

"Solve the problem." Ferguson didn't wait for an answer. He kicked some pebbles from the footpath and went inside.

MacFarlane smiled at that, and handed the rifle over, after Blair was firmly on the saddle, his feet hooked into the stirrups. Blair jammed the rifle into the holster sleeve slung to the pommel.

"Wish me luck," Blair said.

MacFarlane folded his arms, saying nothing. Maddening.

"Fruity."

Pendon Hill Station, located in the southeast quadrant of the town, was a substation of eight men. It offered protection to the bazaar and the community of bamboo huts surrounding it. Beyond it, easterly, was the declivity of a lush valley and open country.

Subinspector Doshi and three constables were waiting outside the station for Blair, their faces dark with concern. Doshi was smaller than the others, but—feet apart, his back straight, a level gaze—with the posture of a leader, his men crouched behind him. He was a finely made Gujarati, with a soft face, long lashes over his watchful brown eyes, an expressive mouth beneath his querying nose, and a truncheon in his gloved hand. When Blair dismounted and handed the reins of the pony to one of the constables, he saw he'd been followed by a crowd of people. They surrounded him, murmuring, as he drew the rifle from its holster.

"Where's the *hathi*?"

"We have lost track, sir," Doshi said. "After he damaged bazaar, he fled, that way"—and the man gestured to a sloping path on the hillside lined with low huts thatched with palm leaves.

Blair shouldered the rifle and set off, Doshi and the constables following him, and behind them the crowd, which Blair now saw numbered over a hundred, trudging and talking excitedly.

"Can you do anything about this mob?"

"Not possible, sir," Doshi said. "They are curious townsfolk, that is all."

At the foot of the hill, the path led to a flatter area of narrow lanes and more huts, built close together, the smoke of cooking fires hanging over them in the still air. Blair chose a lane at random and hearing raised voices ahead he walked quickly toward them, women shrieking in Burmese, "Go away, child! Go away!"

Seeing Blair emerge from a lane they shielded the naked children and pointed to the side of a damaged hut wall where a man lay on his belly, his face twisted to the side, motionless in death, his flesh so raw and red he looked flayed.

"Elephant has done this wickedness," Doshi said.

The dead man was flattened, and it seemed that the weight of the elephant's foot had thrust him deep into the mud; the friction of its skidding footsole stepping away had stripped off his clothes and left him bloody. His raw shoulder muscles were exposed and splashed with mud. He looked sacrificial, his arms extended as though crucified.

Doshi poked one of the constables in the chest with his truncheon and shouted, "Find a suitable dooly for the deceased."

Blair surmised that Doshi was being fierce with the man, making him wince, for the benefit of the sahib.

"And find the blooming elephant while you're at it," Blair said.

"Women are claiming elephant has hastened to the wheat field," a constable said to Blair in a frightened voice. Blair thought, *This man is not afraid of the elephant—he's afraid of me.*

And glancing around he saw that the crowd behind him had swelled and become immense and unruly, filling the lanes, spilling from alleyways, the voices louder now, roused by the sight of the dead man sprawled in the mud, naked and bloody, his face contorted.

"Let's have a dekko," Blair said and walked in the direction the fearful constable had indicated, villagers—men and boys—making way for him, stepping back with solemn formality to give the sahib room.

At the margin of a meadow, beyond the last row of bamboo huts, the elephant stood alone, massive but content. He was absorbed in tearing up bunches of grass and beating these hanks against its knees to clean them of dust before twisting them in his trunk and stuffing them into his mouth. In its snorts and its chewing it seemed famished and fatigued, as though it had just done a day's work, or more likely undergone an ordeal. The dull gleam on its stained cheeks gave it the appearance of having wept.

"Looks decidedly placid," Blair said.

"One can never tell, sir," Doshi said, wagging his head from side to side with certainty. "Musth is there. Anger is there."

Doshi was no longer looking at Blair or the elephant, but instead was glancing around, blinking at the crowd of people hurrying from the village lanes, now fanning out, preparing for a spectacle. The meadow was like a football field, a cricket pitch, a circus ring, dominated by the elephant. Yet the elephant was so intent on eating he seemed indifferent to the jostling talkative people.

"Thousands," Doshi said.

Blair felt them, the invisible force of their mass, their thickening smell in the air, the sour pong of their eager bodies—the pressure of the crowd was palpable. That weight of expectation was a heaviness on his neck and shoulders, and though not touching him they seemed physically to press against him and make him sweat. There was an insistent sharpness of demand in it, too, a hostility that added to its weight.

Feeling isolated and conspicuous, Blair stamped his feet and stretched, tugging the rifle against his chest with a succession of deep breaths, but he could not shake himself loose from their gaze. Every eye was on him, not alarmed but bright with anticipation, in a rowdy festive mood, awaiting the thrill of combat, many of them calling out, emboldened by their numbers, a few of them loudly taunting him, "Sahib! Sahib!"

Holding the rifle, eyeing the enormous elephant, Blair sensed the Purdey as flimsy in his hands, certainly no match for this animal. It was not even loud enough for its report to be heard above the crowd's noise, not enough to scare the elephant. Nor was it lethal: the bullet would just make him mad.

"What rifles do you have at the station?"

"Tiger rifle," Doshi said, "German carbine. Mannlicher."

"Fetch it for me."

"Fetch carbine for the sahib! Be quick about it," Doshi snapped to a constable.

The constable pushed through the crowd as Blair lit a cigarette and watched the elephant tearing at the grass. Blair knew that his every move was noted and remarked upon in whispers by the crowd—his silver cigarette case, his rifle, the match he'd tossed aside. And while the crowd kept its distance, it still confined him, pressing him with its mob murmurs and its mob stink. It was annoying and inconvenient. Had the mob not been there watching him he would have shouldered his rifle and left the matter to be resolved by Doshi and his men, who'd no doubt find the mahout to lead the elephant away to safety.

But I am a Burma sahib, he thought, *and a Burma sahib is an instrument of empire, and meant to take action. And if a Burma sahib does not act decisively he is laughed at—and nothing is worse for a Burma sahib than being ridiculed by a native.* He smiled at the absurdity of his position and saw the elephant as he'd seen the madman in the mud wallow at Pabu by the river, the naked fool defying him, as he heard Ferguson scolding, *You could have shot the idler.*

Were it not for the crowd, Ferguson might have understood his hesitation, his leaving the elephant alone; might have forgiven him for walking away, in a reprieve for a valuable animal. But the crowd wanted taming and no one in that crowd—now many more than a thousand—would have respected the Burma sahib for doing nothing. They would jeer him as he left, they'd pelt him with stones, they'd laugh at his weakness, rejoicing in his disgrace.

In the interval of Blair's waiting for the other rifle, the crowd became louder and more reckless and confident; and in the heat of the afternoon the mass of people emitted a stronger smell, which curled around Blair in foul eddies of sweat-stink that were indistinguishable from hatred.

After fifteen minutes or so—three cigarettes—the constable reappeared, out of breath, with the German carbine and five cartridges. As Blair took the weapon and slid the bolt back a great cheer went up. The elephant, so far unperturbed, stopped snatching at grass and lifted his trunk at the raucous noise and trumpeted.

At that sound of trumpeting, as though obeying an order, Blair executed an about-face, turned to the crowd of people, and aimed his rifle at them. At once a hush descended, the mob silenced except for some scattered anxious mutters, the nearer people backing away from Blair and the gun muzzle.

"They are fearing, sahib," Doshi said.

Blair chucked his cigarette in the grass and spat. "There really is no point."

"But elephant has killed coolie."

"Is that our excuse?" Blair said. "Jolly poor excuse for killing Colonel *Hathi,* if you ask me." He swung round and jerked his rifle at the elephant. "This beautiful beast sacrificed for a Chowringhee coolie."

He had yet to load a cartridge. He worked the bolt again, slipping it back and forth, as though contemplating a decision, and finally took a cartridge from his pocket and pushed it into the chamber. He shrugged and walked forward, waving Doshi off, as though dismissing him. As he made his way on the uneven ground, strolling into the meadow, a hush descended on the crowd. The sudden silence seemed to register with the elephant, as the loud cries had done. Raising its great domed head, it flapped its ears and lifted its trunk, inquiring, sniffing, its pink nostrils dilating at its spout and twitching in inquiry. Then as it straightened and faced Blair it leaned and lurched two steps, heaving its bulk in a mock charge, trumpeting again. But that was bravado—Blair could see fear in its eyes and a tremor of hesitation in its shoulders.

Blair turned his back on the elephant; he aimed his rifle once again at the crowd, where a dozen monks were crouched—shaven headed, clutching their robes, one with prayer beads in his hands, another with a bowl. And scowling at them, Blair struck a pose, as though he was preparing to shoot them—a mock charge of his own. He poked at them with his gun muzzle. It was theater but it had the desired effect, of terrifying them, sending them scuttling backward.

He hated the faces in the crowd at that moment and had a vision of General Dyer at Jallianwala Bagh, giving the command to massacre the mob, and more than a vision—an understanding. Blair imagined himself firing on the insolent mob, it would be so easy—he saw their heads shattered, he saw them running for their lives, he saw blood-soaked clothes, he heard screams. He was for seconds General Dyer, exasperated and at his wits' end, faced with a taunting rabble—until, with a taste of metal in his mouth, and rattled by his murderous impulse, he turned aside and gasped.

The struggle and confusion of the mob facing Blair's rifle caused the elephant to toss its head and plod away, and so Blair walked closer. When the elephant was still, its head upright, seeming to sniff with its probing trunk, Blair took aim. He guessed he was aiming for its brain, a bristly and bumpy spot just in front of its ear.

When he fired, Blair was suddenly blinded and weightless in a great gray blur, deafened by voices, *Buddha was elephant in former life . . . Lord Ganesh the protector . . . Colonel Hathi . . . Humphrey and his elephants . . . musth . . . musth.* He also saw a painted elephant swaying in a village procession, the Feast of Thabaung, majestic in the hauteur of its plodding, worshippers flinging garlands of marigolds at the elephant, a man dressed as a prince in a howdah on its back, its brush of tail swinging behind him as it deposited tawny muffins of straw-bristled dung in the road.

Staggering backward from the kick of the rifle, Blair saw that the elephant was still standing, yet looking old and shocked and senile, beginning to kneel, as though on a command from a mahout. It tottered but it did not fall. Blair shoved another cartridge into the chamber, steadied the rifle again, and aimed for the same spot, now a ragged puncture leaking blood. He fired once more and was deafened anew and briefly dazzled, and when he could see more clearly, the elephant's legs wobbled off plumb and gave out, the misshapen thing collapsed and slumped onto its side, its belly seeming to deflate, its trunk flailing miserably, looking sacrificial in its pathetic gasping.

Walking closer, Blair reloaded and fired again, this time in its chest, releasing a gout of blood that kept flowing like an uncoiling ribbon of red velvet. And when Blair fired his last two cartridges at the wound he caused the blood to spatter his uniform and splash his face. Adjusting his topee, he left bloody fingerprints on its brim.

The loud report of the shots, the crump of the falling elephant, had awed the crowd into silence and sent it farther back. Blair saw that with five deafening shots and a dying elephant he had achieved his objective as a Burma sahib, of subduing the crowd and avoiding looking a fool.

"It is accomplished, sahib," Doshi said, scowling at Blair's bloodied cheeks.

Blair said nothing, but remained staring with his splashed face. He handed Doshi the German carbine and took his Purdey, lifting it to his shoulders, holding it like the crosspiece of a yoke. He walked through the chastened crowd, which parted, making way for him, some of the men holding dahs and baskets, but submissive, awaiting their chance to hack at the elephant's flesh.

His pony was gone—untethered somehow—but it would find its way back to the police stables. Blair walked onward, through the bazaar district the elephant had trampled, and past the overturned rubbish van, but keeping to the middle of the road, heedless of the tongas and rickshaws, the rifle horizontal on his shoulders, now giving him the look of a man crucified, his uniform soaked with blood, his topee stained, blood streaks on his face. He was indifferent to the people backing away—but how they whispered as he plodded on, the blood-spattered sahib, frowning at the glare of the lowering bloodred sun.

He had taken his time in the two-mile walk, through the middle of Moulmein, feeling grim, exhausted by the whole awful business. At the station a small crowd of watchful subinspectors waiting in front stepped away from him. It seemed the particulars of the incident had preceded him. He could read the apprehension in their eyes; someone must have run ahead, or perhaps Doshi had phoned, or one of his constables had brought the news—it was only a short buggy ride from Pendon Hill to the station. Everything was known, and because he had killed a valuable animal, his disgrace was assured.

Ferguson filled the doorway of the vestibule in a posture that was less a welcome than a confrontation, his hands on his hips, his mouth fixed in a sneer that, as Blair approached, altered to a curl of disgust. He took in Blair's bloodstained uniform, his smeared topee, his splashed cheeks, bubbles of blood adhering to his pencil mustache.

Beckoning like a schoolmaster, with upraised fingers, the mangled ones of his bad hand, Ferguson said, "Allow me to disembarrass you of your rifle, sahib."

"And you know what you can do with it."

"Blair!" Ferguson reddened as though he'd been slapped, and he twitched in fury as he grasped the rifle.

Blair pushed past him saying, "Stick it up your arse, Jock."

Part V

KATHA

33

BANISHED

I n that moment, loudly cheeking Ferguson—and his curse had come like a thunderclap—Blair was revealed, he was damned, and there was no going back. He had violated the code of the pukka sahib, for whom free speech was unthinkable. He could drink, he could fornicate, he could rubbish any native—and more than rubbish, he could threaten, he could kick them, bend them over and bamboo them until they howled. But he could never divulge the doubts of his inner thoughts . . . or abuse a superior.

Blair had done it, surprising himself as much as Ferguson in allowing his mask to slip and show that beneath his sahib's pretense he was bolshie. But it had exploded from him, his seeing Ferguson as a tyrant, the embodiment of a despotic system that Blair had come to loathe. And the times he'd been insulted as a "posh" Sassenach still rankled.

It was the elephant, too, the challenge of the poor inconvenient beast, snorting and stuffing his mouth with grass, drooling and shuffling in the corner of the wheat field, the crowd watching, judging him. He'd had to shoot it, to save face, to save Ferguson, to save the Raj, and then had to take the blame. He'd hated the position he'd been put in as a policeman, having failed with the madman, whom Ferguson said he should have shot. Jeered at by the thousand sweating, shouting Burmese, ordered by Ferguson to solve the problem, driven half mad by the yelling, he had two choices— become General Dyer and fire on the mob, or save face by firing on the big soft beast, munching contentedly, exhausted by its spell of musth. He'd shot the peaceful creature in the brain, watched him shiver with the shock of the bullet. In seconds, he'd looked stricken, shrunken, immensely old; he stumbled, and, as Blair had fired again, the animal had finally collapsed. The blood running out of him, that red velvet, had a hideous beauty.

Blair hated the natives screaming at him, he hated the timber merchants for enslaving the elephants, he hated the police, he hated the empire—most of all he hated himself.

• • •

After years of hiding in his uniform, his skeptical eyes concealed by the brim of his topee, practicing an implacable expression, even when he was baited, or witnessing a grotesque injustice, such as the hanging of the innocent Mullapoodi at Insein—after all that, Blair was now as conspicuous and unwelcome as a turd in a punch bowl, chaffed at the office by Fruity MacFarlane, who was delighted to see his superior looking incompetent. He was sneered at by the tradesmen and timber merchants at the club, and even Frank Limouzin sent him a note, *The town's not best pleased by your elephant fiasco but we're here to help if you need us*—pitied by the Limouzins, who were themselves feeling too disgraced to invite him to tea.

And Mrs. Jellicoe—whom he had not seen for almost two months, except at a distance at the club—Mrs. Jellicoe contrived to pay a visit, slipping onto his veranda early one evening a week after his shooting the elephant. She was dressed elegantly, big hat, white gloves, a long cream-colored dress with a ruffled collar and full sleeves and a flounce at the hem where it danced against her buttoned boots. "I'm off to the club"—that meant Humphrey, still in the picture. But the stylish dress was deceptive, her tone was severe, colder than he'd ever known her to be, reminding him that she was an Oxford bluestocking. She said she'd come to warn him.

"Mind, you must take care. That was a massive blunder, Eric. It's inconceivable to me that you didn't foresee the consequences."

He listened, his head down, silenced like a schoolboy scolded by matron, belittled by her saying his name. And she wasn't finished.

"An elephant is valuable. You'd have been forgiven for shooting a coolie—but a working elephant, good lord."

When Blair reached to calm her she drew back. He lit a cigarette. She waved the smoke away.

"You know very well how it's the businessmen who have the last word here. Humphrey's absolutely livid, I can't say I blame him, though the creature wasn't one of his. But these chaps stand together. The sahib log will come after you."

She remained in the doorway, the last light of day glowing through her dress, outlining her slender body, as she spoke from under the shadow of her hat.

Blair groped for a reply but all that came to him was, "Drink? Tea?"

"No, I can't stay—I'm risking a lot to be here as it is. But I need to warn you—stay away from the club. They'll humiliate you, they'll turf you out. I couldn't bear that, but I can't help you. I can't do more than wish you well."

All this time, Blair had stood before her in his odd hunched, punished posture, so that he wouldn't tower over her. She'd ceased to be a scolding matron, she was now mothering him with concern over the menace of forbidding adults, cautioning him like a worldly woman taking charge who seemed so much older in her severity—her gloves in particular, as though she didn't wish to touch him with bare hands.

"Thank you," was all Blair could manage before he began to gag and found himself coughing uncontrollably. Finally, swallowing hard, he said, "We've been lucky, you and I, but I've been so sad. After Insein I never thought I'd see you again."

"You're a love to say so."

He was glad she didn't say his name. She glanced behind her at the driveway, as though nervous that someone might see or hear her, yet perversely she stood in the doorway.

"We've had a good run," he said, and immediately felt a fool for the banality of it. He had no head for endearments.

"Oh, yes, I'll always remember our jolly-up," she said, but he could see no more than the lower part of her face, her small pale chin, her pursed lips—was she smirking? She went on, "Or, more than one—our jolly-ups—heavens, your chest is not half rattling, lovey."

The usual aftermath of his coughing, his lungs bubbling, and her mentioning it was like a cue for more. He held his cigarette away from his face and coughed into his hand.

When he stopped to catch his breath, she said, "I've noticed it before. You've got a chest. And the fruity cough of a much older man." Fixing her hat straight, preparing to go, she said, "Remind me, how old are you?"

"Twenty-three."

"God, I'm such a fool." She smiled in what seemed to him disbelief. He could not see her eyes, but her mouth was expressive. She then slipped off a glove and touched his hand, then gripped his fingers, holding on, warming them. "I haven't the faintest idea what's in store for me, although I'll never be a burra memsahib. But you have a good heart. Take a pull on yourself, and I feel sure you'll be all right. You'll make your mark. It won't be in Burma, though."

"You're sure?"

"I twigged it early on—you're much too fastidious for this lot," she said. She tugged at his fingers. "Please don't forget me."

He stooped to kiss her, but she let go of his fingers and raised her hand to him, repelling him. And she left, calling to someone at the foot of the stairs, a woman croaking a reply, perhaps the old Burmese woman, the former servant, who could be trusted, in the upper room of the house in

Dalhousie, where they'd made love in a four-poster under the iridescence of a sunset on the bedroom wall, and afterward she'd stood naked facing the long mirror—he couldn't bear to remember more.

The visit had pained him. *I can generally bear the separation, but I don't like the leave-taking,* Blair recorded in his notebook, inspired by a line from Butler. He heeded Mrs. Jellicoe's advice and avoided the Moulmein Club after that. He wondered what his fate would be, and he suspected he was doomed, but found the answer within days, Ferguson summoning him to his office by means of a cringing constable with a chit.

"No need to sit down," Ferguson said. "You're being posted to Katha."

"Katha, sir?" He knew the name but could not recall where it was.

"Not the arsehole of the world, Blair. But fifty miles up it. Where you belong. Pack your things and take your bloody farmyard with you. I want you out of here."

"Yes, sir."

But Ferguson was pointing with his mangled crab claw. "Bugger off, Sassenach bum boy."

Blair had regretted that the Limouzins knew of his disgrace; he guessed they were ashamed and had heard of his banishment—there were no secrets in the sahib log. They'd pity him, he was certain they'd avoid him.

So when one of Uncle Frank's servants appeared at Blair's office with a note—an invitation to tea with Frank and Mah Hlim—Blair rehearsed a little speech of apology. And he considered telling them he had not so far revealed to anyone that he was related to them. *You can rest easy on that score,* he'd say.

The next afternoon at Uncle Frank's, Kathleen ran to him on the gravel drive, calling out "Cousin!" And she smacked the sleeve of his tunic. "You bad boy!" She was shivering with excitement, her Burmese eyes dancing. "You are notorious!"

Over tea—just Frank and Kathleen, Mah Hlim was down with a bout of fever—Blair found them welcoming and inquisitive, and not at all displeased. The elephant had belonged to a competitor, good news for Frank, whose faltering timber business had been squeezed by bigger companies.

"Katha," Frank said, peering into the distance, seeing it, looking hopeful. "I know a bit of Katha. Some of my loggers worked there. They have a good opinion of the forests."

He was whispering as though sharing a confidence, yet watchful and eager. Kathleen was rapt, sitting forward on her chair, admiring her reckless cousin, who was the talk of Moulmein. Though she wore a gingham frock, and her hair was bobbed, Blair thought, *Chee-chee, with hairy arms, jowly like her mother, and the same eyes,* and he could smell the coconut oil in her hair.

"I know nothing of the timber," Blair said. "It's a small station. I haven't a clue as to its precise whereabouts."

"Katha's on the river, the teak forests behind it in the hills," Frank said, raising his voice, speaking with confidence. "It's a day's run north of Mandalay on the steamer, rather less by rail."

"They can float the logs," Kathleen said, chipping in. "Isn't it, Papa?"

Frank ignored that and looked suddenly pained. "We're suffering depletion here in the forests. Tenasserim is seriously cleared. The big firms, their up-to-date equipment—steam saws and steam tractors and the newest tackle. Some hills bald as a coot."

"I thought your business had recovered, Uncle."

"It's in a bad way, like the whole blasted country. Twenty-five years it takes for a teak tree to mature. The forests have been replanted but they'll not be ready for donkey's years."

"Being sent to Katha, I'm being punished, you know."

"Look at it as an opportunity, lad."

"Uncle, I'm not a timber merchant."

Uncle Frank sat back, holding his cup of tea before his smile, not drinking, letting it tremble there. The faraway look in his eye of a bit earlier returned; he was squinting with relief at something again, like a man in a pickle, seeing rescuers advancing from afar. Then through barely parted lips he breathed a word, "Katha."

There remained only one more farewell, not to his men who'd lost respect for him, because Major Ferguson had turned his back on him; and there was nothing more to say to Mrs. Jellicoe, though he might put his feelings into a poem that she'd never see. It was Mahadev Thackeray, devotee of Ganesh, to whom he would seek forgiveness.

Blair found him the day before his departure for Katha, at the familiar timber yard where he'd first seen him, and today just as then, the man was wearing a brown belted jacket, plus fours and knee socks and ankle boots, a sack at his feet—food—and he was watching an elephant moving planks from a newly sawn pile to a stack at the loading dock.

"Sahib," Thackeray said when he saw him, but it was only a brief acknowledgment, after which the man looked tearful.

"I've done a terrible thing," Blair said.

Thackeray shook his head sadly as he removed his topee and wiped his face. Blair had never before seen him without his topee. He was bald, his head smooth and shiny-brown like a conker, wiry tufts of hair above his ears, and the earholes themselves oddly hairy.

"You have committed heinous murder, my friend," Thackeray said. "I shudder from pinching lowly ant. But you have slain god."

"I have no excuse."

"I can see sorrow in sahib's eyes. Maybe political system is your excuse. Terrible things have been done in its name." He replaced his topee, he tucked his handkerchief away. "I think of Clive, who was a blighter. And General Dyer, who massacred so many of my people at Jallianwala Bagh. Sahib believed he was doing his duty."

"Dyer was a murderer."

Thackeray emitted a soft gurgle of surprise and licked his lips. "I have never heard a sahib say such a thing."

"Maybe I'm not really a sahib."

"You will bear harshness from your people. Not because elephant is god, but because elephant is worth lakhs of rupees."

"I won't be around much longer to deal with those people. I'm being banished." He sighed. "To Katha."

Thackeray straightened and became alert, nodding slowly. "Yes, it is far distant, but"—he stepped nearer to Blair, as though disclosing a confidence—"there is good timber at Katha."

"I've heard that. You know the place?"

"Yes. It is like Sheen-pagah and Shwe-gu. One of those places where people gather together to keep from starving."

Blair admired the exactness of the description. "Righty-ho."

"But, my friend, there is ample of timber in Katha. I have been there."

"Why didn't you stay and do business there?"

"It was not possible. I had no friend there."

"Maybe you have a friend there now."

Thackeray put his hand over his heart and looked tearful again.

Arriving at Battery Point with a procession of rickshaw pullers dragging at the shafts, the rickshaws filled with his possessions, Blair was not insulted that no one appeared on the jetty to bid him farewell. And across the water, at Martaban Terminus he was spared the indignity of their contempt. He was accompanied by his cook, Gugu, who supervised the baskets of ducks and hens, while Blair held Flo by her leash. One of the duck baskets came to pieces as it was loaded onto the goods van, the fat birds flopping and quacking on the platform, chased and gathered by Gugu and the porters.

Then the shrill whistle and smoke, the first slow chugs, the clang of the couplings, and the train headed north past Pegu Junction, bearing him away from the sea that he'd always thought of as his link to England, the shining waterway from shore to shore. Board a ship from the wharf in Moulmein and it was blue ocean all the way to Tilbury and home.

In the morning he let down the window shutter of his sleeping compartment and saw through a haze of dust thrown up by the train the brown wastes of inland Burma, the scabby bush, the scrub forests and mean villages—women carrying jugs of water, men leading buffaloes, naked children jumping into foul creeks, the real life of Burma, away from the sahib log; ancient and everlasting, indestructible in its simplicity.

All the following day, the train drew him farther from the coast, farther from England than he'd ever been, up-country, banished to oblivion. Over breakfast in the dining car he saw an ornament pinned to the wall mirror at his table, red ribbons, cotton wool, a scattering of sequins, pathetically festive, trembling on the mirror as the train jogged across the rail joints and jumped on the points at junctions. It was a reminder that in two days it would be Christmas, the worst time for an arrival in a distant place, a hated holiday—ghastly jollity, tiresome parties, and knee-drill at church services, among strangers.

He lingered, rocking at his table as though in suspension, in the dining car of the hooting train, doodling in his notebook as he headed north across the December-dry plains of central Burma. He wrote the word *Banished!* in his notebook but nothing more, astonished at his audacity, yet thinking: *It grieved me much to hear the sentence,* a line from Webster, Eton serving him again to frame his thoughts, today the apt *White Devil.* But who was that white devil who'd burst forth snarling at his superior in Moulmein, that rebel who'd insulted Ferguson and the Raj?

The landscape and the sunlight were briefly eclipsed by the smoke-filled sleeve of a tunnel, its darkness and dust offering him a reflection of his face at the window, a brief portrait before the plowed fields flashed again at the glass—though his white face remained as a dazzling afterimage of the upstart. The culprit was that inner man, who'd lurked inside him, the one always tugged by his conscience, grousing silently.

He knew that man: it was the self who'd hidden within him since Mandalay in 1922, the secret self, his real self—not Blair but that other man who'd never accept the police, who'd hated every moment of his colonial captivity, enemy of the sahib log, who'd remembered everything, the way conscience-stricken men were cursed by an accumulation of wrongs they'd committed, the men no one knew, the rebel, the Tory anarchist who'd always dogged him, the conspirator, the poet.

Still at the swaying table he flicked toast crumbs off his open notebook and under *Banished!* began to write.

> *Ordered by the superintendent*
> *To sort out the beastly chore,*
> *His policeman's kit resplendent*
> *I can't take it anymore!*

He crossed everything out but the title, stabbing at it with his pen—tosh. It was awkward, it didn't scan, it was posturing. A poem demanded a certain affected voice, and a deliberate schoolboy struggle to shape it, pompous and orderly. How to put it plainly?

His dog growled at his feet—a steward was passing with a tray. Blair scratched behind Flo's ears to calm her and felt the pressure of Flo's snout, nuzzling and warming his ankle.

Turning to a new page, Blair wrote, *The Last Straw,* and under it, *Flory— John Flory—was summoned by his superintendent and handed a rifle. "There's an elephant in musth causing havoc in the bazaar . . ."*

No. He began again. *John Flory arrived in Burma in 1922.*

His mind was racing as he crossed that out and wrote, *In Lower Burma, John Flory was hated by large numbers of people, not only natives but also by his fellow officers in the police. It was the only time in his life that he'd been important enough for this to happen. For four years he endured it, pretending not to notice, going about his daily tasks, making arrests, listening to complaints at the club about bloody natives and cheeky servants and "Give the bearer of this chit ten lashes." But one morning, he was summoned . . .*

He smiled at the page—fragments, not very good but better than a poem, and he knew he could improve it. It was not a story, it was a gesture, his admitting to himself in the solitude of this train that he'd always wanted to be a writer—a famous writer, he'd sometimes thought, and so he'd confided to Jacintha Buddicom. This scribbled page in the dining car represented a decision. He knew it was the right one, because he felt a sense of release. Writing—just that paragraph—made him happy.

That was the meaning, the intention, behind *Stick it up your arse, Jock.* It was defiance, of course, it was rejection, a shout of rebellion; but it was also an affirmation. He had no future here, he would be a writer, somewhere else. But the writer was hidden now. He had always known there was someone inside him, but now he knew who he was and what he wanted.

Two men stepped from the train to the platform at Katha, Blair and the nameless man within him.

34

I HAVE BEEN HERE BEFORE

W hat luck, Blair, you're bang on time for our Christmas beano at the club tomorrow," Major Eastwood was saying as they walked toward the maidan. Eastwood, beefy and bluff, superintendent of police, was in uniform, shorts and knee socks and topee, thrashing the air with a bamboo swagger stick he had on a wrist thong. His rank, his bearing, his posture, and his age—about thirty—suggested he was another veteran of the war, an unsettling instance of courage that struck at Blair's manhood, diminishing him.

Blair was too abashed to ask Eastwood if he'd fought. He loped slightly behind him, weary from the journey, tugging Flo on a leash—Flo, skittish in the strange place, reluctant, pawing the dust.

"That's the club over there."

Eastwood pointed with his bamboo stick to a one-story building over-hung by tall pyinkado trees, facing the ocherous river that was so slow-moving the only sign of its current were offscourings of detritus, of drifting sticks and cabbagey clumps of water hyacinth that had come loose from rafts of the plants upstream, some of the flotsam swirling in eddies, none of it flowing fast.

"Katha Club, all welcome." Eastwood stood at attention, reviewing the club and the river. Yes, he had fought.

Blair knelt, pretending to adjust Flo's leash, but in fact kneading her neck to soothe her. He was so distracted by Flo's fretfulness he hardly heard.

Eastwood might have taken Blair's silence to be skepticism. "Don't be fooled by its unprepossessing appearance. We've had many a jolly there."

"I don't doubt," Blair said, but he winced at *jolly,* Mrs. Jellicoe's word. When he stood up he turned to look back at the jetty, where Gugu was struggling with his steamer trunk, the boxes of books, the baskets of squawking birds.

"Your chap's showing enterprise," Eastwood said. "And my chaps will lend a hand. They'll scare up a dooly for your fowl, as well. Your quarters aren't far away." He pointed again with his bamboo stick. "That's you up there at the top of the maidan, beyond the white bungalows. Smashing view of the river. And that's the church—Saint George's." Then he laughed a little in hesitation. "As we're close by the club why not share a celebratory drink?"

He led Blair to the squat building beneath the tall trees, and as they entered Blair heard the scratchy sound of a gramophone playing a familiar song.

> *Where did you get that hat*
> *Where did you get that tile?*
> *Isn't it a nobby one,*
> *And just the proper style—*

And a shout of welcome went up when they entered, a drunken hoot from three sweating red-faced men, one in uniform, a fat man with a battered terai hat cocked over one eye.

"Lead on, Macduff," Eastwood said.

I have been here before, Blair thought after Gugu served dinner that night, as he sat smoking on his veranda, a tuktoo quivering on the rail. He was facing the river, paddy fields beyond it, and in the distance a range of low blackish hills, darkening now in the eastern dusk. Tomorrow the sun would rise there, the pitiless Burmese sun. But he was grateful for the cool evening and the call of a bulbul somehow hidden, in a nearby tree, its *peep-peep* like the greeting of an old friend.

Another club—he'd greeted the drinkers, he'd offered to stand them a round, they'd told him their names, he'd forgotten them. But he knew these men, he'd seen them before, in Myaungmya, in Twante, in Syriam, in Insein, Moulmein, and Rangoon, always snagging a seat under the punkah, chaffing each other and being rowdy and testing him with blimpish opinions. *The little monkey says to me* . . . And, *Well, your native's primitive, innit* . . . The Cockney *I had a Eurasian tart in Mandalay—she had a nine-inch tongue and could breathe through her ears. Nothing like a yellowbelly for a first-class rogering* . . .

"Eastwood will do you to wainwrights," said the man in the terai hat. "His job's a bloody doddle. He's got a team of bribe-taking constables and knock-kneed babus doing the dirty work for him. And now he's got you."

"You look an educated lad," another said—Scottish, ginger hair, freckles, winking at him. "Bookish sort, are you?"

Blair smiled and said, "But books don't put you wise to the dangers up-country."

Terai Hat said, "What bloody dangers? No Englishman should ever feel in danger from an Oriental."

"Willy wet-legs, the sodding lot of them," the Cockney said.

"Dacoits abound," Eastwood said.

"Eastwood's great mistake is that he sticks his wee beak into native quarrels. The sahib should always steer clear. It's rather lowering to take an interest." This from the freckled Scot.

"Nature of the job," Eastwood said.

Terai Hat said, "Even to know the rights and wrongs of a native quarrel betrays a lack of prestige. Bloody slackers, what they want is a good bambooing."

"But 'as luck would 'ave it," the Cockney confided to Blair, "you'll not find one of the black bastards in this club." He turned and made a megaphone of his hand and yelled, "Steward, more ice—*jildy!*"

"Here's how!" Terai Hat said, raising a glass.

Disgusted by the talk, Blair had pretended an interest in the photographs on the wall of the lounge, also familiar from other clubs: a man with a rifle, his foot on the head of a dead sprawled tiger; a portrait of the king; a group portrait of smug and overdressed garden party attendees, and above them the usual taxidermy, a dusty sambar skull, a set of bumpy antlers, and a sequence of "Bonzo" pictures. He'd seen them all before. Wandering into the next room—a bronze plate above the door lettered Library, paused by the table where magazines were arranged symmetrically, a fan of *Punch* copies, another of the *Pink 'Un,* of *Blackwoods* and *The Field.*

In an adjacent room a punkah wallah scrambled to his feet as Blair entered, another familiar figure, the club chokra.

"Sahib!" the man cried.

The mildew smell was familiar, the hum of decay from the green felt of the billiard table, the itch in his nose from the dust of cue chalk, the sourness of dartboard cork, the medicinal thickness of furniture polish on the teak chairs and card tables. The creak of the punkah, the slashes of glare in the cracks between the chicks on the window. The same tarnished trophies on the shelf, the same books, but just a few, some novels, E. Phillips Oppenheim, Charlotte M. Yonge, a history of the Mutiny, Nisbet again, a *Burma Gazetteer,* a bible, and some small red leather volumes of Kipling's works, among them a battered *Many Inventions.* Blair remembered Oliphant recommending a story in it, "Love-o'-Women," and slipped it into the pocket of his jacket.

He returned to the bar, and the men.

Terai Hat said, "What are you looking at, lad?"

"Your gramophone," Blair said, improvising. "Its prodigious horn."

But thought, *Dull, boozing, witless porkers.*

Blair allowed himself to be joshed, the usual cracks about his height, another reference to school—they probably knew about Eton, but had they heard of his disgrace in Moulmein, the elephant and Ferguson? Scandalmongering was a club pastime. After a decent interval, he'd made his excuses—"I need to be pushing off"—and walked across the tussocky maidan that was too stony for cricket and dangerous to horses.

Gugu was waiting at his bungalow, another bungalow, much too big for one person, but furnished with the same oddments as all the others, teak armchairs and brass jars from Benares in the parlor, a map of Burma on the wall next to a portrait of the king. In the dining room, a tray in the middle of the long table held a pot of mustard, a bottle of Worcester sauce, a cruet of vinegar, a dish of salt, a jar of pickles, a cup of toothpicks. Two bedrooms, the first with a mosquito net suspended over the bed, the second semiderelict, more like a box room, but with a table that might serve as a desk. The bathroom: a zinc tub, a china bowl for a sink, a small mirror, and another old friend, a tuktoo goggling at him from the windowsill.

Blair had been in this bungalow before, he'd seen that same tray of pickles and toothpicks, he had drunk in that club, he knew those men; and tomorrow he would show up in his uniform at a police station that would be familiar, a jail attached with the usual urinous pong from the earth latrine, the sulfurous stink of piss, the lockup itself a cage of wooden bars, dark and stifling, guarded by an Indian constable armed with an old carbine, and a little distance away the prison, a vast square block, fifty yards on each side, concrete walls, twenty feet high, Indian warders, and prisoners dressed in pajama-like uniforms, small dunce caps on their heads, their legs in irons that clanked when they shifted on their benches.

None of it was new, all of it was either hateful or humdrum. The *dudh* wallah with his pails of milk, the dhobi with his basin of wet clothes, the rickshaw wallah, the club members' wives making *kit-kit,* nagging the servants. It made the Raj seem eternal and immovable. But Blair was also a servant and was obliged to go through the motions. He showed up for the Christmas party at the club, which was more sedate than he'd expected, owing no doubt to the presence of wives—burra memsahibs all, a moderating influence. One of them had flirted with him and asked him to dance with her.

"It's a foxtrot," she said.

In all this familiar tedium the song was new, "Bye Bye Blackbird," and the words moved him.

No one here can love or understand me
Oh what hard luck stories they all hand me

"I don't dance," Blair said. "I'm sure I'd crush you."

"I might fancy a bit of that," she said softly.

"Your, um, husband," Blair stammered as she hugged him.

"Bother him." Her breath was ripe with whiskey.

He got through the dinner, which was unexpectedly lavish, a buffet with a gammon joint, a platter of jellied tongue, a baron of beef on a bloodied trencher, pots of pickled walnuts, plates piled with sausage rolls; and afters: mince pies and a flaming brandy-soaked pudding. He stumbled home to his dog and his cook, and in the ensuing days he searched for something in his life here to make him hopeful.

His chickens and ducks seemed content, Flo had settled down, Gugu was subdued, seeming also to suffer as a fellow alien. And because Gugu was also a stranger here, Blair developed an understanding of the man. Gugu revealed he was not Burmese but a Mogh, from Arakan, whose father had also been a cook, having been taught by Europeans who'd settled beyond the hills in Chittagong. The skills had been passed from father to son, but diminishing and coarsening, with improvisations, because quite simply Gugu did not eat the food he prepared for Blair, but ate Burmese food, which Blair had never liked.

But Gugu was a good influence. Although he was a stranger he made an effort to be congenial, he acquainted himself with the hawkers at the bazaar, he befriended Irrawaddy fishermen who supplied him with a species of bream and smoked fish for Blair's kedgeree, and prawns and rotten fish to make the odious-tasting *ngapi* for himself. Gugu found friends at the staff quarters, and one evening Blair saw him surrounded by attentive men, Gugu seeming to hold their interest with a story—perhaps of the wonders of Moulmein and the glory of the ocean, the great pagoda, the caves filled with Buddha images, or maybe he was talking nonsense.

Another glimpse, but more ambiguous: Gugu conferring with a younger woman who sat smoking a fat cheroot, and seeing Blair, Gugu had leaned and whispered to the woman, but what? Perhaps something on the order of, *That sahib is my thakin,* because the woman had slipped the cheroot from her mouth and turned to gaze at Blair, then whispered back, expelling smoke.

Unexpectedly—because, after all, he was a native and a servant—Gugu became a friend. They were two strangers, new to Katha, though Gugu was the more sociable.

The flowers in Katha were more abundant than in Moulmein or the Delta, familiar flowers from Britain, swaths of English flowers, phlox and larkspur, hollyhocks and petunias, violets by the path, honeysuckle on a trellis, and climbing next to the bungalow roses—fragrant roses. The merit of Katha was that its damp climate favored flowers; yet instead of cheering Blair, the flowers made him homesick.

The other flowers, an anthology of Burmese blooms, had adorned every other bungalow he'd lived in, the bloodred blossoms of the gold mohur trees, purple bougainvillea on thorny branches, frangipanis with creamy stalkless flowers, blown-open hibiscus petals that hardly lasted a day, and dark-veined yellow-green crotons. Lining the walkway to the house were marigolds that Indians wove into garlands, brilliantly gilded, though they gave off a bitter aroma and smelled of cat.

At the station in the days after Christmas and into the New Year, Eastwood remarked that Blair had not returned to the club, and he repeated that he was welcome.

"There's bugger all else to do in Katha."

"I'm planting a garden," Blair said.

"Keen gardener, are you?"

"I'm more interested than I can say."

"I'm woefully ignorant of the local flora," Eastwood said, but casually— he obviously didn't care.

"In Moulmein I had a patch of garden."

Eastwood smiled. "I heard a few piquant details of your time in Moulmein."

Not knowing how to respond to this, Blair found himself growing hot, and he knew he was blushing, thinking of the elephant, and his retort to Ferguson—and what did they know of Mrs. Jellicoe or the half-caste Limouzins? His months in Moulmein had been a chapter of accidents and lonely debaucheries.

"There was always a flap," Blair said. "And always a buzz about it."

"Never mind," Eastwood said, helpfully bluff and dismissive. "Start afresh. Clean slate. If you think I'm on the wrong track, I'll need you to put me right. We're shorthanded here, so I'm counting on you, Blair."

"I'll do my best, sir."

"I've seen your record—mixed results, but I know what you're capable of. Oliphant in Twante gave you full marks. Neville and I were probationary together."

"He was quite the reader."

"And a stickler for order. I'm of the same mind." Eastwood had risen from his desk and gone to the window, facing the direction of the Katha Club. "I do hope you'll join us and muck in. Wraggett and Slattery can be a bit florid, and Selkirk a shade cruel. But still."

Selkirk in the terai hat, the Scotsman who'd said that Eastwood had a team of bribe-taking constables and knock-kneed babus, Wraggett the Cockney, *Nothing like a yellowbelly for a first-class rogering.* Slattery, an Ulsterman, was Freckles—*Bookish sort, are you?* and it must have been Mrs. Wraggett—Mavis—who'd asked Blair to dance at the Christmas party.

"Selkirk's divisional magistrate," Eastwood said. "Policemen and magistrates are natural enemies."

"And the other chaps?"

"Wraggett's in timber, Slattery's a surveyor. And there's ones who show up to collect the English mail once a fortnight, but one way and another they're all of them good value."

Familiar porkers, but what Blair remembered of this conversation was Eastwood's expression, *a few piquant details.* Yet he didn't elaborate, he didn't return to the subject, and he did not dwell on the behavior of the men at the club. He seemed a decent man, his Indian constables respected him, and the two Gurkhas at the station were fiercely loyal, young round-faced men, who seemed eager to use their kukris to carve up a dacoit.

In Blair's first month all these men helped him negotiate the forest paths that linked the rural villages, and it was they who interrogated suspects and wrote the charge sheets for Blair to sign. On the days they led arrested men back to Katha, they allowed Blair to present them to Eastwood, as his trophies.

The patrols proved enough of a distraction to keep Blair from brooding, but on every return to Katha, approaching it from the edge of the teak forest, he always saw the wide greasy river, often passing a long timber raft piloted by a boatman in a fragile hut in the bow; the wood-frame church, the gray walls of the prison, the cemetery filled with snakes in the high untended grass, its tilted tombstones inscribed with the names of European children and adults who'd died there of tropical diseases; and in the distance, the Katha Club in the shade of the pyinkado tree.

He surveyed it and sighed. *Bloody hole.*

After he'd delivered the latest chained suspects he fled to his bungalow and took refuge in a book. These days it was *The Casuarina Tree,* Maugham's recent collection of stories, posted by the book wallah in Rangoon. Blair took a particular interest in "The Outstation," identifying Oliphant and Albee in it. He read the stories slowly, studying the sentences, the way effects were built up without calling attention to themselves, a simplicity and subtlety that he wished to emulate. And often he turned to his notebook and elaborated on his alter ego, John Flory, the secret rebel, lamenting life in his Burmese outpost.

He was pining for England, though he dreaded facing it, as one dreads facing a pretty girl when he is collarless and unshaven. When he left home he had been a boy, a promising boy and handsome in spite of his ridiculous height. Now only five years later he was yellow, thin, drunken, almost middle-aged in habits and appearance. And still, he was pining for England . . .

He clapped the notebook shut and went to bed.

"Club?" Eastwood often said after work.

"Gippy tummy," Blair might reply, or, "Maybe tomorrow."

He couldn't continue making excuses, though, so he sometimes showed up at the hateful place and endured the banter and listened to Selkirk disparaging the riffraff he had to sentence, and Wraggett's talks of his last leave in Rangoon among the yellowbellies and Eurasian tarts, or Slattery's insincere disparagement of the Raj: "It's finished, Blair. Time we cleared out of it and left these sods to their own devices." But in his heart Slattery knew he was a pukka sahib—they all were—and would never leave.

Blair pretended he was a pukka sahib, but he lived in books, and he longed to be in his bungalow, losing himself in a Maugham story or in his battered copy of Samuel Butler's *Notebooks.* And in his grimmest moments, as he sat writing late at night, after the club, he thought *perhaps something overheard by John Flory,* finding himself reproducing rants from the grousing men, setting them down verbatim. He couldn't improve on them, it eased his mind to write them, he was making a record of them, creating something all his own, and in so doing experienced a distinct improvement in his mood. He knew it was a conceit, but fiction was joyful for making sense of the world—it was the joy he'd felt at school swapping poems with Connolly. He was exhilarated by writing. There was no other exhilaration to be had at Katha.

Gugu seemed to see his mood differently. When Blair was seated in the parlor reading, or writing at his desk in the back room, Gugu usually approached, bowing in an elaborate shiko and asking if the *thakin* wished for a drink, or *myape*—peanuts—of which Blair was fond, or was he hungry— had he any order to give?

Gugu couldn't read, so he took Blair to be lonely; he saw a kind of sad brooding in Blair's motionless solitary act of reading, his utter stillness in writing, scratching on sheets of paper and sometimes crumpling them or tearing them to pieces, tossing them in the basket at his feet. It looked like sorrow, it seemed at times like frustration: Gugu was unused to seeing a man sunk in his own company, without an obvious friend. Burmese were sociable, they laughed together, they sought each other out, they talked, they sang. They didn't read. A book to an illiterate was dark magic, something somber; it silenced you, it immobilized you, it cast a spell and kept you apart from other people.

One evening Blair remembered the Kipling collection of stories, *Many Inventions*, he'd purloined from the Katha Club library, the one with the story that Oliphant had recommended, "Love-o'-Women," an absurd, or at least off-putting, title. He turned to the story.

"The horror, the confusion [he read], and the separation of the murderer from his comrades were all over before I came. There remained only on the barrack-square the blood of man calling from the ground. The hot sun had dried it to a dusky goldbeater-skin film, cracked lozenge-wise by the heat; and as the wind rose, each lozenge, rising a little, curled up at the edges as if it were a dumb tongue. Then a heavier gust blew all away downwind in grains of dark colored dust. It was too hot to stand in the sunshine before breakfast. The men were in barracks talking the matter over. A knot of soldiers' wives stood by one of the entrances to the married quarters, while inside a woman shrieked and raved with wicked filthy words."

Ripping, he thought, but reading on he saw it was the blood of a man shot by the enraged husband of a woman whose lover was that dead man. He could only think of Humphrey Jellicoe as the killer, and his own blood on the barrack-square, and Mrs. Jellicoe shrieking and raving afterward with wicked filthy words.

In the first weeks of February, the days growing warmer, Blair sometimes stopped at the club for a drink after work, lingering until he was tight as a tick, because only alcohol made the club bearable. On one of those evenings—just at sunset—walking home from the club, Blair saw Gugu feeding the chickens and ducks accompanied by a young woman. She was not dressed for such a chore. She wore a brilliant blue lungyi, and her pure white *ingyi* blouse had frilled sleeves and a pleated collar. She had the feline face of a child—the doll face that Mrs. Jellicoe had remarked upon: *They're a kind of Dutch doll, aren't they?* This one's hair was thick, lustrous, piled behind and fixed with a silver pin that had spidery filigree on its end. When she sprinkled feed to the chickens, flinging her arm out, the bangles on her wrist tinkled beautifully, like distant temple bells. She fed the bustling birds with the delicate hand gestures he'd seen on dancers at a pwe.

"You have a helper."

"This Mee Hla."

Blair had spoken in English out of caution, but hearing her name the young woman clasped her hands before her and bowed.

"*Thakin.*"

"Your friend?" Blair said to Gugu.

"Mother my friend."

Before Blair could answer, Flo rushed from the upper veranda and stumbled down the stairs, trotting to Blair to be petted, brushing against his leg, panting for attention. This made Mee Hla laugh and clap her hands, and the dog seemed to take this for a command and ambled to her. Mee Hla stooped and clapped her hands again, as Flo frolicked at her feet, allowing her to scratch her neck—more music from the bangles on her pretty wrists. Flo yapped at her, and she knelt and hugged the dog, a puppy like herself, fearless and full of affection.

"Do we pay her?"

"Pay mother."

He knew that Gugu was offering Mee Hla as a keep, taking pity on him for his loneliness. But Blair did not act upon it. She apparently lived nearby and lingered near Gugu's small house each evening, Blair greeting her as he returned from the station. Often she was playing with Flo, who'd taken to her. Blair was touched by Mee Hla's tenderness with Flo, her laughter as the dog shook in excitement; she'd toss her head with pleasure at being scratched and then would roll over kicking her legs, inviting Mee Hla to rub her belly.

Blair noticed several things about the pretty young woman. Each day she wore a different gaungbaung, the head wrap so prized by Burmese women. Mee Hla had a yellow one, a pink one, a blue one to match her silk lungyi, a red one, and more. She had a way of tying them that made her seem tall, like a princess wearing a crown, the end of the wrap twisted upright in a flourish. Another thing: like a dancer in a pwe, she wore makeup, reddened lips, slightly rouged cheeks, a bluish enhancement around her eyes.

And when Mee Hla caught Blair's eye she always pressed her small hands together, her painted nails like beautiful claws, and bowed.

"*Thakin.*"

It pained him to walk away. At dusk on one of those evenings, tight after drinking at the club, he greeted her and began to mount the stairs to his veranda, but he felt a pang and paused. He was weakening, his palms damp as he clung to the handrail. His throat constricted, a kind of hunger—yet this feeling was familiar, too, the tremble of anticipation, the taste of desire—nerves—like the onset of a fever, for which there was only one cure.

He had not had a woman since Moulmein, the last time with Mrs. Jellicoe, memorable for the black knickers concealed beneath her disguise, a stable boy syce, but vivid most of all for her talk, because it was her talk when they made love that stayed with him, her urgent words more than the act in the dim light of the room, slipping her hand into her knickers and lying on the bed before him.

I want you to watch me frig myself.

"Come," he said now, insistently, in English.

Flo then ran to him, yapping.

Mee Hla had smiled in confusion.

"*Lar,*" he said, with a catch in his throat. "*Dekolar par.*"

She understood *Come here* but still seemed to hesitate. Her fragrance reached him from eight feet away.

"*A-khu,*" he said. Now.

She was a pale sliver of a woman, hardly a woman, her doe skin luminous in the half light of dusk. She raised her hand to touch the fabric of her head wrap—it was the red one this evening—and her bangles slipped to the crook of her arm where they gathered and clinked.

"*Kye-zu-pyu-bi.*" He struggled a little with the word. He had seldom found an occasion in Burma to use the word *please*. But in that same instant, Mee Hla stirring the air, hurrying to him, he got another whiff of her fragrance, a dizzying sweetness of sandalwood.

35

OUTSIDERS

Blair chuckled to think that somehow, in what he regarded as his life of
lies, the addition of Mee Hla as his keep—another deception—gave
a sort of civilized order to his routine. Made him happy, of course, but
now with more to conceal he was obliged to visit the Katha Club more
often. If he didn't, if he stayed away, they'd accuse him of being secretive,
they'd tease him, they'd probe and pester in their oafish senior schoolboy
way. So his life as a sahib in Katha was complete and plausible, and as for
his secret self, the aspiring writer, the skeptic, the notetaker, every opinion
he had was blasphemous.

He'd been cast into the outer darkness of this small Burma station,
wishing—though he didn't know how—to extricate himself from the police, from Burma, from the oppression. He wondered if his efforts at writing
were worth anything. He lacked the spark of courage it took to speak his
mind to the blimps at the club, nor could he refuse the more brutal orders
Eastwood gave him, chaining men to stanchions, turning them over to his
men to be beaten or viciously interrogated. He was aware that he was part
of a tyranny, and he had enough Greek to know that the word *martyr* indicated a man who had knowledge from personal observation—the word
meant "witness."

He justified his silence by reasoning that he would remember everything; that however amateurish his writing, at least it was the truth of the
Raj—not the social slights and pomposities of silly-ass tea parties or junkets
gone wrong in the Forster book. Had Forster seen anyone hanged? Blair
would write of the savagery of the police, the terrified eyes of prisoners, the
howls of women widowed by dacoits, the foulmouthed porkers at the club.
He would never forget; and someday he'd have a tale to tell, of what he'd
witnessed in his miserable martyrdom.

Mee Hla, submissive and sweet, was the stock figure in the life of a colonial bachelor, yet it calmed him to know that she was waiting for him
at home, probably amusing herself with Flo, or dabbing her face with the

yellow paste she made from the bark of the thanaka tree, the pastime of many Burmese women, smearing her cheeks to protect herself from the Katha sun, giving herself a mask, smiling at her face in the little mirror she carried in her shoulder bag.

Meinm, Gugu called her—woman—clucking at her for her idleness. But she hissed back at him, because she thought of herself as *bo-kadaw,* the white man's wife. And she swanked before Gugu, displaying the bangles Blair had bought her at the Indian shop, the kitten he'd given her, a silk shawl from the bazaar, proof of her position in the household, lover of the *thakin.*

Blair was careful not to make promises, he restrained himself in his endearments—"*Ngar kyaung,*" my cat, he whispered—he didn't want to delude her with hope. His farewell to Margaret in Twante had shaken him and he couldn't bear to think where the poor woman was now, because she was a childless widow, and a childless widow had no status in Burma. He had no idea what his own future might be. Yet Mee Hla mattered more to him than he could say. In his wisdom, Gugu had known what a difference she'd make—clever man, he must have noticed how the visits of Mrs. Jellicoe has cheered up the *thakin.* And it seemed that Gugu, too, had a woman in his hut at the back of the bungalow. Blair delighted in their laughter. Gugu the Mogh from Arakan, an outsider in Katha, and Mee Hla, a Tai from distant Taunggyi in the Shan States, and Blair as well—outsiders all.

As time passed, the club became a greater torment for Blair, trying his patience to the point where most evenings, after all the talk and drink, he thought: *I must get out of this room quickly, or I'll punch one of these porkers in the face and smash the furniture.* Wraggett sang songs of insane filthiness, Selkirk boasted of men he'd sent to the gallows, Slattery told tedious jokes. Occasionally a bit of banter degenerated into a shouting match, often on tribal lines.

"Bloody Scots bastard," Wraggett said.

"We invented the steam engine—James Watt. We invented the telephone. By god we gave the world the bicycle—step forward, Kirkpatrick MacMillan."

"Dinnae forget the rubberized Mackintosh," Selkirk said. "Think what a blessing that became."

For several weeks, Slattery was dazzled by Selkirk's niece, Elizabeth, visiting Katha on her way to Australia. She was twenty-two, her blue eyes framed by mascara, but with a cherubic schoolgirl's face, wearing the latest fashion from London, a pale green, knee-length dress with a shawl for a collar and a cloche hat that sat close to her head like a helmet. She was stylish and pretty, but an odd figure in Katha, a town of men and women clad in lungyis, and where even the memsahibs' dresses were still ankle-length.

"Legs!" Wraggett said. "It's a bleeding revelation in Burma. And she's got muck on her mince pies."

"A flapper," Selkirk explained.

"Oh, right," Wraggett said, but when Selkirk was out of earshot, he muttered, "A tart."

But Slattery was besotted. "You want a proper topee," he said and offered her one.

Elizabeth laughed and said, "I'm sure I'd look perfectly ridiculous in that."

"The sun here can do serious brain damage," Slattery said.

She began to use a silk Chinese parasol, another oddity in Katha, where wide black Indian-made umbrellas were preferred.

Proof of Slattery's seriousness in his wooing was that he now shaved every day, he dressed with more care, and he took pains to show Elizabeth the town—the market, the pagoda, a pwe performance by the river.

"What do you reckon of our bit of the country?" Wraggett asked when she came to the club. "Not half bad, eh?"

"It's perfectly beastly!" She lost all her beauty in her toothy laugh.

But Slattery was not deterred. He promised her a leopard skin, he said he knew a chetty in town who had access to rubies. Elizabeth allowed him to dance with her to the gramophone—"Bye Bye Blackbird" again—and she accepted the leopard skin, though complained that it was badly cured. "It's stiff as a board. What on earth am I to do with it?"

Smitten, Slattery was revealed as lonely, helplessly craving companionship. That wasn't unusual: Blair had been lonely himself. But he was struck by how shallow the Scots lass was, and how young, knowing nothing of the country and seemed only at ease when she was disparaging the Burmese as dirty, mocking their food and naked children.

"Bit of a martinet," Eastwood said.

Blair said, "She'll make a perfect burra memsahib."

The little drama played out, Slattery doglike, trotting after her, Elizabeth twirling her parasol and twitching her pretty bottom in her short tight-fitting dress. Slattery's effort to woo her was the talk of the club—how he accompanied her to church, how he found her a horse to ride, and a pea-size ruby from the chetty. How he stopped swearing and moderated his drinking and affected a cravat.

But one day, without warning, Elizabeth left Katha on the Irrawaddy Flotilla Company steamer to Mandalay, bound for Rangoon, shipping onward to Australia. And Slattery looked bereft for weeks afterward, gaunt, so depressed as to seem suicidal, unshaven and foulmouthed in his humiliation pretending to be defiant but still sad.

"You've come back to us," Wraggett said. "You'll always find a welcome here, mate."

It touched Blair to see their compassion for Slattery, and it was odd for such a man who seemed a brute at times to reveal himself as so fragile, rebuffed by this chit of a frivolous girl, who'd breezed through Katha showing her bare legs. Even her uncle, gouty old Selkirk, was sympathetic, bucking Slattery up with whiskey while avoiding any criticism of Elizabeth, whom Wraggett referred to under his breath as "the bint" and "the bitch." Slattery's gloom persisted; it was like an illness—he was hollow-eyed and wounded. Blair said nothing—he had no small talk—but he gave thanks for Mee Hla, who was happy with her kitten and the occasional bangle and in the throes of passion, as he knelt over her, thrusting, she moaned, "*Aahkyit, aahkyit, aahkyit*"—love, love, love.

He tried to be congenial at the club, yet Blair remained an outsider, a Sassenach to the Scotsmen, a toff to Wraggett. He was not surprised—he'd never fitted in, and though he played the game he felt sure his skepticism showed. And there was his age, he was still only twenty-three, the youngest man in the police. He was also certain there were whispers of Eton, and the piquant details of Moulmein that Eastwood had hinted at.

What maddened him at the club was the way in which, as the men grew more familiar and matey, they became ruder and more abusive, abandoning any pretense of politeness—shouted into his face and teased. They could not have known the whole of his Moulmein disgrace but they knew enough to make him miserable, and it was all the worse for being inaccurate. They didn't seem to know exactly what he'd said to Ferguson but they quoted what Ferguson had said to him. "Bloody Sassenach bum boy" became a club catchphrase for Blair.

But his secret self was a watchful spy, and it was a relief, an unburdening, to write down what they said. They might know about Moulmein, they perhaps had glimpses of Mee Hla, but they had not the slightest idea of Blair's writing, and these oafs could never know how they were folded into fiction. Writing was a form of transformation, it took the sting out of their slights, because John Flory was the whipping boy, not Blair Sahib. The freshness he felt in writing was a renewal, a purification—happiness—and he was continually reminded how his earliest ambition had been to be a writer. How odd that this wish was stimulated in this bloody hole, the small town by the river, so far from home. Or was it not a paradox at all, that in this bloody hole he at last had something true of the empire to write about?

And he was stimulated in his writing by his reading. He'd finished Maugham's *Casuarina Tree* and returned to Jack London, not the stories but *People of the Abyss*. He'd missed a great deal on his first reading and now saw that Jack London, an outsider, had succeeded in penetrating the East End by disguising himself, exchanging his gray traveling suit in a pawnshop, swapping it for ragged clothes, and in that way found lodging and companionship with the tramps at the spike. *I should like to see a spike,* Blair thought. *I'd be happy in a doss-house or among hop pickers,* and he read, *The street folk, who have been driven away from the soil, are called back to it again . . . not as prodigals, but as outcasts and pariahs.*

The American had had a plan. His scheme was to sink into the misery of down-and-outs. *I went down into the under-world of London with an attitude of mind which I may best liken to that of an explorer.*

To Blair those filthy lanes and backstreets of Whitechapel were more foreign to him than the swamps of the Delta, or the back alleys of Moulmein. "Explorer" was wonderful. Blair saw himself in the word; it offered hope, it gave him a notion. He sat back on his veranda chair and imagined himself with the freedom of a tramp, on the bummel, having exchanged his good clothes for rags, loitering at the spike, traipsing from job to job, tapping passersby for handouts, smoking black shag, and picking hops. Jack London had plotted the journey and offered a ready-made scheme. It was a descent into the netherworld of George Gissing, a greater challenge being powerless in the abyss of the East End than idling in this Burmese bungalow, drilling his constables, returning each night to Gugu's food and Mee Hla's caresses. Being a tramp was a proper vocation and a refuge, his life in Burma turned upside-down. It might serve to undo the guilty feelings he'd lived with since Mandalay.

People of the Abyss was dated 1903. What had changed in the slums and the hop fields in the intervening twenty-three years? He could find out, he saw another book he might write. He was ashamed of this bungalow, he hated the club, he yearned for atonement, for expiation in a doss-house.

And London had also written, *The political machine known as the British Empire is running down. In the hands of its management it is losing momentum every day.*

Blair had a glimpse of himself walking quickly away in old clothes and vanishing into a crowd of men who took no notice of him.

• • •

It helped that Eastwood was shorthanded, that Blair was able to leave Katha for a week or two at a time with his men, on patrol, upriver in the steam launch, or on horseback in the teak forests, visiting villages that had been plundered by dacoits. Anticolonial feeling was stronger in Rangoon and Moulmein, but Katha was a backwater—literally so, for the way it fronted a lagoonlike portion of the river, the current driven backward, swirling in bubbling eddies, where women at the embankment washed clothes, beating them clean on boulders and hanging them on bushes and mangrove roots to dry.

Even so, seditious pamphlets traveled upriver from Mandalay, and one day Eastwood told Blair that the riverside town of Moedar, a day's voyage north from Katha, was rumored to be the site of agitators.

"How grim?" Blair asked.

"One of those so-called Happy Associations, bloody nuisance."

"Masses of them in Moulmein. We sorted them out," Blair said with his pukka mask on. "Bit of rough justice did the trick."

"Make some arrests. Come down on them hard. Flog a chicken to scare the monkeys."

Blair was glad to have another excuse to leave Katha, and to travel in a new direction. And he was touched when, as he left his bungalow, Mee Hla clung to him and pressed her face to his, a formal farewell for the first time, taking an adoring whiff of his cheek, in the Burmese way, inhaling his essence.

"My little kitten," he whispered.

Rather than taking Burmese subinspectors, whom he suspected might be sympathetic to the Happy Associations, all of their members Burmese malcontents, he ordered two of his Indians, Punch Chatterjee and Chandra Bose, to come with him, Chatterjee to pilot the boat, and Ganju, the Gurkha he considered half barbarous, to stand guard at the bow.

Moedar was an overgrown village, a one-story sprawl, a timber depot. It had no clinic or police station or school, and only a rough open-sided shed that served as a market. Drawing near the dock at its embankment Blair saw a dead buffalo floating, its legs upraised, black-winged kites circling its bloated belly and darting at it, piercing the thing with their beaks. Yet the dock was new and impressively wide, an example of the greedy enterprise of the empire, the only amenity in the town, a superior jetty with a crane, to serve the interests of the timber companies.

Chatterjee, who had toured the town before, pointed out the just-visible pagoda, the tiled roof of a monastery, and a nearby nondescript flat-roofed building he said was a hostel for dockworkers.

"Kachin men," Chatterjee said.

From upriver: more outsiders.

"We'll have a look there," Blair said. "Let's march."

Ganju the bullheaded Gurkha led the way, grinding the pebbly earth with his boots, Blair and the two Bengalis behind him. Seeing them approach, a man shrieked from a hostel window and the front door was slammed shut, the thud of a bar banging in clamps behind it, with muffled squawks of frightened men.

These sounds excited Blair's men, who looked at him eagerly and when he nodded, Ganju stepped to the doorway and raised his rifle butt and hammered the door. The first blow shook it, the next one splintered it, the bar cracking apart.

It was revealed to be like a rabbit warren, the men inside scampering to the dark recesses of the interior, chased by Blair's men, while Blair himself remained outside to smoke. The subinspectors easily caught a man each, whom they presented to Blair. They reentered the hostel and returned with more. The men were handcuffed and chained together and made to squat outside near a pile of torn-open coconut husks, where hens were pecking and strutting.

"Search the rooms," Blair said.

After his subinspectors had gone, Blair walked over to the men in their chains, some sprawled, some squatting. They were cowed and fearful, unsure of their fate, yet facing them Blair sensed an affinity with them in their confinement, fettered and uncertain. As Kachins from the far north, they were aliens here, poorly paid laborers, Jingpo speakers, who barely understood Burmese, Moedar beyond the limit of their tribal world.

Two of the men, one old, one young, were chained together. They murmured urgently in Jingpo as Blair knelt before them.

Blair said softly, in an urgent confiding whisper, "I don't belong here."

They blinked at his English words, as though hearing strange music, and when he got to his feet and stepped back, they smiled, perhaps in relief, and relaxed in their chains. Blair turned away to light another cigarette.

"Propaganda," Chatterjee said after half an hour of ransacking the bags and crates in the rooms. He showed Blair a stack of yellowed pamphlets, poorly printed—smudged and torn. The ink had soaked into the paper and blurred many of the words, though Blair could read enough to see that they were tracts against the Raj, and one of them demanded the return of the king.

"They haven't heard the news," Blair said. "Thibaw died ten years ago."

"But this literature is inflammatory, sir," Bose said. "This is like infection. Body politic going septic."

Blair smiled at Bose blobbing his lips on *body politic*. He said, "Only if they can read. And I doubt they can."

"Others will read for them. Monks will do so. Headman of this place—the *thugyi* can read."

The titles of the pamphlets in large print were easier to read than the texts. They called for action and rebellion and the defeat of the British, and the crude illustrations were more explicit—big-nosed soldiers bayoneting men in lungyis or flogging stick figures on all fours. A stool had been found for Blair to sit on and as he read, Ganju began kicking one of the chained men.

"Stop playing about," Blair called out.

"He resisting, sir."

"Wouldn't you resist if someone handcuffed you for no bloody reason?"

But the handcuffed men were not defiant, they were fearful, with pinched peasant faces. Their lungyis twisted around their skinny legs, yet their arms were hard and sinewy from their labor on the docks and in the teak forest. They'd paddled downriver from Kachin here in canoes and sampans, leaving wives and children behind, to girdle trees and hack them down, and haul the logs to the river; they were worker ants for the empire, wage slaves of the timber companies.

"Release these men," Blair said.

With an armful of ragged pamphlets, Chatterjee said, "Shall we log literature as evidence, sir?"

"That's not literature. It has no evidentiary value."

"Appearing to be inflammatory, sahib."

"It's bumf."

"Sahib?"

"Bum fodder. Hand it back."

The Kachin men—timber cutters, dockworkers, despised peasants—were bewildered by the care with which the Gurkha, Ganju, who'd been so fierce up to now, knelt to unlock the handcuffs. The men still squatted confined.

"They are undergirded," Bose said. "Observe chains."

The chains were stripped away. The men stood, chafing their wrists, as Blair apologized for breaking down the hostel door. He gave them a wad of folded-over rupees to pay for its repair.

On the voyage downriver, back to Katha, Chatterjee at the wheel, Bose cross-legged by the wheelhouse, Ganju impassive at the bow, all of them were confused by what had happened and somewhat fearful. Blair knew how a fickle superior is more disturbing to his men than a brutish boss. They could not read him. Early on, Chatterjee had said his village was in Bengal, "Near Motihari." Blair resisted saying, *I was born there*. It seemed a condemnation.

He sat in the stern, his back to the men. He was watching Moedar recede and finally vanish behind a bend in the river.

Like an infection, Punch Chatterjee had said of the pamphlets. The memory of it made Blair smile as broadly as Bose saying, *undergirded*. Probably true—good.

"And our friends in Moedar?" Eastwood said, greeting Blair on his return.

"Coolies living in a filthy kennel," Blair said.

"The timber chaps mentioned they were bolshie."

"Schoolboy games, sir. Rather a nonsense."

"Did you find the *thugyi*?"

"Weedy little sod. Daft as a brush."

"We'd had word of unrest. Of pamphlets."

"It passes belief," Blair said. "You cannot overestimate their childishness. It is fathomless."

There came another outsider, unexpected yet familiar and welcome, a man Blair could confide in as a friend, though it had to be a lopsided friendship. A sahib's friend who was a native, not his social equal, was a disagreeable thing to other sahibs.

It was heralded by a letter, an appeal, two sheets of paper, graceful colonial copperplate, a good fist. It was fluent and without a blot, so it must have been rewritten and recopied, signed with a flourish *Mahadev Thackeray*.

Esteemed Sahib, it began. *It is my earnest wish that your good self finds Katha to your liking, and is prospering accordingly . . .*

It went on in this vein for the first page, and Blair was certain that its laborious bonhomie was prologue to what would be a request for a favor. He'd found that the more florid the flattery from one of his Indians, the greater the demand. This proved to be the case, for on the second page Thackeray came to the point.

It is my intention to visit Katha on timber business and I harbor the fond desire to see you there.

Blair remembered telling him, *Maybe you have a friend there now.*

One made those insincere promises to give emotion to a final farewell. The words had slipped out easily and made Thackeray tearful. Blair had never expected to see the man again. Yet he'd given his word. He wasn't worried. He'd wished for a friend, but he had not expected the friend to be a native.

Perhaps the fifteenth of this month, Thackeray had written in a postscript.

Blair looked at the date of the letter. He'd sent it three weeks ago. It had obviously been delayed. Today was the seventeenth.

Of the two rest houses in Katha, only one was Indian owned, Saraswattee Lodge, adjacent to the market. Blair pocketed the letter and walked across the maidan to Saraswattee Lodge and found Thackeray—brown suit, plus fours—on the veranda, lifting his topee in greeting.

36

BYE BYE BLACKBIRD

T hackeray seemed so improbable here this cloudy February day, a damp chill drifting from the river. It was hard for Blair to imagine this same man away from the golden afternoon at the shoreline timber yard at Moulmein, where he'd looked longingly at a toiling elephant, awaiting a chance to offer him food. *It is sweetmeats to him.*

Improbable, and spectral. He was thinner, his jacket hung loosely on his bony shoulders, he was gaunt, glassy-eyed from the journey, perhaps weakened but more intense, his beaky nose, his close-set eyes, strangely single-minded in his stare, like a bird on a branch searching for something below him to peck at.

Weary from his day's work, Blair was put off by Thackeray's air of high emotion. He seemed nervy, and that was a concern—Indian prisoners with stares like that sometimes howled, and it took three men to grapple and subdue them. Blair did not feel equal to Thackeray today, what he suspected might be an outpouring of anguish and a demand for attention.

He was rehearsing an excuse to leave early as Thackeray with a thin smile and a soft controlled voice said, "I have brought gift, sahib."

He slipped his hand into the pocket of his brown belted Norfolk jacket—he was, as always, dressed as though for golf—and drew out a small cloth bundle, knotted at the top. Using both hands he formally offered this in a propitiating gesture across the veranda rail.

Blair did not accept it at once. He turned to see whether anyone passing by noticed him, and he only then walked up the stairs to where Thackeray was standing and took it, bobbling it a bit because, though smallish, it was heavier and bulkier than he'd expected, a chunk of lumpy metal inside the loose cloth. He turned again to survey the road and was glad it was late in the day, the market closed, just a few women sweeping the stalls with sheaves of grass brooms, a man tending a fire of smoking rubbish, poking it with a fire-blackened mamoty.

Seating himself on a veranda bench, Blair picked open the bundle and a bright brass object swaddled in the cloth came loose.

"Ganesh," Blair said. "And this lovely fabric."

"Fabric is khadi, sahib. Homespun with dobby loom, charka, as the Mahatma preaches. Image of Ganesh appropriate to occasion."

The Burma police had been alerted to the Swadeshi movement of the pest Gandhi, whom Blair thought of as the Indian Rasputin. Handloomed cloth was a political statement, meaning Thackeray was possibly a follower. But Blair said nothing.

"Because of my unfortunate elephant affair in Moulmein."

"Not at all, sahib. Because Ganesh is lord of new endeavors. He will be your protector here." Thackeray touched the potbelly of the small seated elephant, the brass glinting like gold from a ray piercing the slash in a cloud, the last of the sun. As Blair held it, Thackeray seemed in the same tender gesture to be touching Blair's hand. He ungummed his tongue, he said, "*Ekdanta.*"

"One tooth."

"You are so remarkable, sahib, for knowing."

Blair became shy and fidgeted on the bench and wondered again how to frame an excuse to leave.

"Will you take tea, sahib? We have cakes and eatables."

"Thank you for this. I really must push off. I have to tidy my office—I came here as soon as I got your letter. But let's meet again in a day or two."

At this Thackeray stiffened and fixed his gaze on Blair—reddened eyes, bony face—as Blair had feared.

"It is matter of highest importance that we meet without delay, sahib. I have much to tell you."

This, Blair felt, was a preamble for Thackeray to ask a favor. He stood up and backed away, still reassuring him. "Yes," he said, "soon. I'll leave a message for you here." He weighed the brass Ganesh in his hand, exhibiting it like a trophy. "Thank you."

Leaving, tugging the brim of his topee down, swinging his head to the left and right as he crossed the road he felt as though he was taking leave of an adultery, the sense he always had had when parting from Mrs. Jellicoe, anxious uncertainty, of disgraceful hugger-mugger, wondering whether he'd been seen or overheard.

The guilty feeling stayed with him, Thackeray on his mind for the next few days, in the office with Eastwood, at the club with the drunken members playing darts—a member he hadn't met before, named Wigney, who'd come to collect the English mail, who'd called him "Lofty." It was the feeling he had with Mee Hla in his life, the awkwardness of such a secret seeming like unfinished business.

Yet on another level he wanted to help, to listen to Thackeray, who looked adrift in this remote place, so unlike the confident man in Moulmein. Blair had power, the prestige of his uniform, his imposing bungalow, the obedience of his men—and what protection did this skinny solitary man have? The uncertainty of being a despised Indian in a Burmese town, looking friendless, needing—what? Someone to unburden himself to. Blair sighed at the notion, because he too longed to unburden himself.

Thackeray stayed on his mind, preoccupying him, and he was ashamed when, naked, resting on her elbow, Mee Hla caught sight of the Ganesh statue on the side table beside his bed, sucked her teeth in reflection, then laughed and poked at it with an enameled fingernail.

"*Sin*," she said in a mocking voice—elephant. "What coolie woman gave this to you?"

"I bought it at the market," Blair said, and thought: *Why am I lying about this to this little woman?* Then answered, *To keep the peace.* He knew how violently Burmese hated Indians.

"I think an Indian whore made a present of it to you."

"Don't be silly." He embraced her, and she seemed to grow smaller in his arms.

When she put her mouth to his ear, Blair expected an endearment, her hot breath, the whisper of it, the heat of it promising words of desire. She often said in a soft voice, "Take me, take me," because she was too shy to face him and say it outright, though he wished she would. She was still breathing, warming his ear.

Finally, swallowing, she said, "If it is a woman, I will find her and beat her like a bad dog."

That shocked him; he'd never heard Mee Hla speak that way before, and perhaps it was because she suspected he was lying.

Indeed, he *was* lying, and why? Because he was keeping Thackeray his secret.

And later when Gugu commented on the Ganesh, pretending to dust it as an excuse to offer an opinion, Blair said, "It's an elephant god. An Indian man gave it to me as a present."

Gugu said in a superior way, "We have Lord Buddha. We have his wisdom. We have no need of gods or animals."

Blair remained tense with the certainty that Thackeray was waiting for him to call—tense because he felt it would complicate his life. Yet that was craven, he'd encouraged him, he'd offered his friendship, he'd accepted the present of the Ganesh—and in Burma a present was always a down payment on a serious request. He'd promised to return to Saraswattee Lodge for tea. He had to keep his word. Treating a native as an equal went against the code of the pukka sahib, and so when he sent the message—Punch Chatterjee conveyed it—he knew he was violating something sacred. But the feeling of rebellion made him shrug, as though an inner voice was saying to the sahib log, *Take that, porker.*

Thackeray himself must have realized how such a meeting would seem to a passerby, for instead of the tea things set out on the veranda table at Saraswattee Lodge, they were arranged on a low table in the parlor, a stuffy room hung with dusty curtains and the mingled smells of syrupy incense fumes and decaying carpet. With the curtains drawn the room had a shuttered atmosphere of secrecy, something conspiratorial in its shadows.

"Bung your coat there," Thackeray said. "So good of you to pop in."

He looked rested, more composed than at the previous meeting, and Blair was somewhat reassured. He'd feared he might find an angry man with blazing eyes, but here was Thackeray in a newly pressed jacket, his bald brown conker-smooth head gleaming by lamplight, calmly pouring tea and remarking on the weather.

"Katha is good climate—clement, I should say. Mild in daytime, cool in night. Not at all like overheated Moulmein. No need of punkah here."

"And yet there is a punkah wallah at the club."

Thackeray straightened and stared, as though seeing the words in the air, illuminated and dancing between the two men, glowing in a smoky echo, and then before they could be verified, vanishing, winking away.

Blair wondered what it was that had seized Thackeray's attention, and almost asked, but he didn't want to embarrass the man. He said, "It's generally cool here, though I suppose it'll be hot in May, just before the rains. But you're right. We're far from Moulmein."

The words were wrung from him. How he hated small talk.

"The journey was acceptable. Overnight to Mandalay, and then branch line. I wish I could have come sooner."

"Maybe you should have."

"But you were not here."

Blair was oppressed by his putting it that way. He said, "You're in the timber trade. You'll find plenty of good timber around here."

"Yes, that is one of my objectives. But I am also fleeing Moulmein, where I am the innocent victim of malicious gossip."

"Who would have the cheek to gossip about you?"

"Not an English gentleman, but only a Burmese blighter."

Thackeray began stirring his tea, and Blair could see the man's agitation of mind in the way he worked his spoon, clinking it against the china cup. He was certain he'd been right: the man had something on his mind, a plot against him.

"Anonymous letters in *Burmese Patriot* newspaper, accusing me of disloyalty. Blackening my good name. I have become object of scorn."

"A Burmese?"

"One man, Po Kyin. Also timber merchant himself and my chief competitor."

"But there are so many timber merchants in Moulmein. Even my uncle—" And stopped himself.

"Your uncle, sahib?"

It had slipped out, he hadn't meant to say it, but it was too late. He could not go back, he could not deny it. He said, "Frank Limouzin. He has a godown near the main jetty."

"I know this sahib," Thackeray said with mild surprise that bordered on awe.

"I'm sure all you timber chaps are acquainted."

"But Limouzin Sahib"—he pronounced it *Limoujeen*—"his good wife is Burmese. He is the only one I know with such a wife. He is truly your uncle, sahib?"

"My mother's brother," Blair said, hiding his regret by averting his eyes, tapping a cigarette on his case and lighting it.

Thackeray beamed with the knowledge and turned his soft eyes on Blair with a fondness that Blair found embarrassing.

"And his lovely daughter."

"That would be my cousin, Kathleen."

"How charming for you. A good family and well known in timber business. We have exchanged communications from time to time."

"You're friends with Frank?"

"Let me put it to you we have common concern—decline of teak forests adjacent to Moulmein. Tenasserim is cut to pieces. Business is not what it was."

"There's plenty of teak here. I was upriver a few weeks ago, a timber depot, Moedar. Stacked with logs. Bloody great forests behind it."

"Ah, that is one of the reasons I am here."

"What's the other reason?"

"As I said, I am being vilified by Po Kyin. Bullied like boy at school."

"Because of timber?"

"Because of club. The new edict. You are not aware?"—Blair was shrugging, still smoking—"It has been officially gazetted. That European clubs are being enjoined to admit natives as members. Po Kyin wished to join Moulmein Club. He knew also of my desire, so he initiated a campaign to impugn my character."

Blair sat back and said, "You told me in Moulmein that you were a member of Arya Samaj with your Indian mates, and that it was all you wanted."

"Sahib, that was before the timber trade went bad," Thackeray said, grieving. "There is no prestige in Arya Samaj. But it is invaluable to belong to Moulmein Club. I saw that if I became member, how different that would be to my position. Po Kyin resented my wish to put my name forward. He knew club would not admit two natives, and so he published letters against me, raising question of loyalty."

"What proof does he have?"

"No proof, but accusation is proof enough. As policeman sahib in Burma, do you not know this?"

Blair shook his head, dodging the question. He remembered how at the Katha Club, someone—Selkirk, was it?—had said something to the effect, *Never get involved in a native quarrel*—and here he was listening and being asked to comment on the particulars of Thackeray's grievances with a Burmese.

"As sahib, you cannot know what prestige it gives to an Indian merchant to be member of European club. In club he is almost European. No calumny can touch that."

Thackeray spoke with indignation and Blair smiled at his assertiveness, his wormlike pride.

"Prestige is everything in Burma," Thackeray said. "If my standing is good, I can carry my business forward."

"In Moulmein?"

"No, sahib. Here in Katha. I have removed myself from Po Kyin. I don't fear him. I wish to be member of Katha Club."

It was just as Blair feared, the awkwardness of Thackeray asking a favor that would compromise him at the club. He had not heard of the directive to admit a native as a member, but if it happened to be true—Eastwood would have the *Gazette*—he could use that as a reason. *Nothing provocative on my part,* he'd argue—*I'm only following the recommendation of a government paper-chewer in Rangoon.*

Blair drank more tea, he sampled a cake and brushed crumbs from his lap. Then he said, "The club is no fun—frankly, it's a bore. I can hardly stand it. The members are drunk most of the time. They're rowdy. My superintendent is a good old stick, but the rest of them are odious. They seem to represent the worst of the empire."

"You mean bluff and bluster, sahib?"

"I mean moral squalor," Blair said. "It's a racket, it's a despotism, Thackeray. And the real backbone of the despotism is the army and the police—that would be me, your Burma sahib, Assistant Superintendent Blair. Can you imagine how that makes me feel? I'm the iron heel."

"You are a good man, sahib," Thackeray said. "I know I am asking favor, but I have nothing else."

"But the club—"

Thackeray became confidential, sharing a secret, saying, "Membership is all I desire. Even if I were elected, I should not of course ever presume to visit club."

"Not visit?"

"Goodness, no. I would not force myself upon European gentlemen. I would simply pay subscription. That is high enough privilege for Mahadev Thackeray."

"I'll make inquiries," Blair said. "If that is in the *Gazette* as you say, the members will know about it. And I'll put your name forward."

"So kind of you, sahib."

"But I'm curious—Thackeray, like the writer?"

"Written as such, but properly it is Thakre"—and he spelled it—"Marathi name. We have improved it. It is a notable family not in rupees but in caste. Middle initial is K for Keshav."

"Mind you, I can't promise you'll be elected."

Thackeray's eyes filled with tears like the liquid eyes of Flo when Blair held her head and crooned at her. "I am not surprised you are nephew of estimable Sahib Limoujeen. Like them, you have embraced Burma."

Blair recoiled, alarmed that the man would hug him—he seemed to be inclined that way, as he had gotten to his feet, had raised his arms. But when Blair stood up, knocking his head on the lamp suspended over the table, it was as though he'd taken command, and the small Indian retreated, bowing, murmuring his thanks.

On his way home, crossing the maidan, Blair could not help laughing. He had committed himself to proposing Thackeray for the club! The prospect would have appalled him in Moulmein, but here in Katha it exhilarated him. And it was something to write down, the Burmese merchant Po Kyin blackening Thackeray's name by writing scurrilous letters to the *Burmese Patriot*—something more for his book.

• • •

General meetings of the Katha Club were held once a month. Blair had missed the December meeting, having arrived too late; and he'd been on patrol at the time of the January meeting, held on Burns Night. He'd heard from Eastwood that it had been rowdy, but "Your absence was noted." The February meeting would be held in a week's time.

He pondered for days beforehand to contrive the best way of proposing Thackeray. Eastwood had been to Rangoon after Christmas to meet the inspector general of police at the Secretariat. He'd mentioned at the time that they'd lunched at the Pegu Club. Blair had replied, "I was a member of the Gymkhana—mate of mine proposed me"—McPake, the pukka sahib, the oaf, the bully, the wog basher—"we were probationary in '22."

"Memorable year—Royal Tour," Eastwood said. "Prince of Wales and Lord Mountbatten. I was part of the security detail. It was my privilege to salute His Royal Highness outside the pandal at Rangoon University. My chaps were suitably impressed."

"I watched from a distance in Mandalay."

"Prince Edward will make a great king."

"Undoubtedly."

Now—after the Thackeray tea—Blair reminded Eastwood of his recent visit to Rangoon, and the Pegu Club.

"I'm led to understand that some clubs have admitted natives as members—a new edict."

"Didn't see any black faces myself, but, yes, there was a directive," Eastwood said. "Officials of gazette rank and some others are acceptable. Dogsbodies. Box wallahs."

"What would make them acceptable?"

"House trained, one would imagine."

"No betel juice."

"No betel juice, Blair!"

Blair said no more, he mulled it over, and at morning assembly, in meetings and parades he found himself assessing his men and finding much to admire, their pride in their work, their close attention to their uniforms. Polished buttons, gleaming boots, pressed shorts: he seldom had to blow them up for an infraction. The way they spoke showed effort, Bose saying *body politic* and *They are undergirded, sahib.* Watching some parades, the skirl of bagpipes, the rattle of the snare drums, his spirits soared and all his doubts about the Raj were put on hold. These men and their music were the pride of the empire, the keepers of law and order, marching in a blustering oompahing band for the king, carrying the colors, the Gurkha flashing his dagger, stouthearted men, and—for the length of time the music played in the march-past, bagpipes and bugles and drums—he was recalling Kipling and proud to be part of this unit, to command them. Natives could be tedious, but they deserved respect as men.

Thackeray, too, a decent chap. Why not?

"Lay out my dress uniform," Blair said to Gugu.

Not only did Gugu brush the uniform and press it and arrange each garment on the bed, he also attended Blair, dressing him: his tunic with frogged buttons, his striped trousers with straps under his boots that always gave him a feeling of command, his spiked helmet. And Mee Hla, who was allowed to watch, said, "My *thakin*, Burma sahib."

"On parade, guv?" Wraggett said, when Blair entered the club.

"Just came from an inspection," Blair said—not true, but the Cockney was impressed in spite of his gibe.

Seeing Blair formally dressed, Eastwood said, "Lead on, Macduff."

Selkirk chaired the meeting in the dining room, the club chokra having shoved the tables against the wall and lined up the chairs in rows. Slattery was seated with Wraggett, Eastwood with Blair, and the oaf Wigney who'd called Blair Lofty was at the back with four men Blair had never seen before, who'd come to Katha on the train from up-country Bhamo especially for the general meeting.

The four men were silent and sunburnt, looking uncomfortable in tweed jackets and argyle neckties, one with corduroy breeches, another in a kilt. Their hands were thick and dark and bruised, tougher than the hands of anyone else in the club, the hard meaty hands of workingmen. Seeing them, the yellow nails, the lumpy fingers, Blair looked down at his own and was abashed by their pallor, their softness, his slender tobacco-stained fingers.

Selkirk worked through the agenda. He was coarse in his drinking, but sober and so methodical chairing the meeting, Blair concluded that Selkirk had to be a decent judge. He was patient, too, though at one of Wraggett's outbursts he said evenly, "Keep your shirt on, Francis."

At last, Selkirk said, "Call for new members."

One of the men in the row of timber workers raised his hand. "Aye, we've a new arrival in Bhamo station, up from Rangoon. Baird by name. I'd like to propose him. He's in camp at the moment."

"Set down his name, by all means."

The man got to his feet—he was the one in the kilt—and he walked to the notice board where a pencil was attached to a string. He leaned and wrote the name under the inked heading, *New Members*.

Wraggett said, "Another Jock."

"D'ye have a wee objection, Francis?" the man in the kilt said as he passed Wraggett on his way to his chair.

"I've nothing against Burns Night," Wraggett said. "It's just that we Londoners are thin on the ground." He had turned to face the Scotsman and now noticed Blair. "Might you be a Londoner, lad?"

"Can't claim that—my folks live in Suffolk," Blair said. Wraggett began another outburst, but Blair interrupted him saying, "I'm proposing a new member."

"Inscribe his name," Selkirk said.

Blair stood, and striding to the notice board he was aware that his dress uniform was noted. He might have been mocked for it were it not for the presence of Eastwood, beaming at the sight of his assistant superintendent, looking elegant, his boots and buttons gleaming, his spiked helmet under his arm. And a further flourish: Blair had let his mustache grow, and until tonight he'd left it thick, but before he'd dressed he'd trimmed it, and his pencil mustache was restored, a thin line of stubble just above his upper lip that gave him a severe look of maturity.

As Blair wrote the name, Selkirk said, "I cannae make it out, lad."

"My man," Blair said, still writing, "is Mr. M. K. Thackeray, new to Katha."

"Was there not a writer of that ilk?" Selkirk said.

"William Makepeace Thackeray," Blair said. "To be precise, he was born in Calcutta. His father had a house in Chowringhee." He turned to the attentive men in the chairs. "Author of *Vanity Fair.*"

"You're raising the tone of the club," Slattery said.

"One of your Eton chaps?" Selkirk said.

"His bum boy," Wraggett said.

The five men, Wigney and the others, the timber workers, who sat together, seemed taken aback at the jeering. They looked sourly at Wraggett and Slattery, pityingly at Blair, who showed no emotion, facing forward, his eyes on Selkirk.

"If there's no other business, I'll call this meeting adjourned," he said. "I suggest these candidates be invited for interviews at the earliest date possible. Gentlemen?"

The meeting ended, the men headed to the bar, and Blair slipped quickly out, repelled by the thought that if he stayed he'd have to speak even a few words in a civil tone to these porkers.

The interviews were set for the following week. Blair visited Thackeray at Saraswattee Lodge just beforehand, to prepare him, but all he could think of to say was, "They'll want to know a bit about you. There are bound to be questions and, I daresay, some objections."

In the nasal insistence, a kind of fluting, that was familiar to Blair when Thackeray was being firm, Thackeray said, "I will maintain that I will pay subscription but will not attend club. Membership only. I will not presume."

"Jolly good."

Walking from the Saraswattee to the club Blair felt he was marching into battle, that Thackeray was not a soldier but a weapon. It had gone dark, and the loud noises echoing from the open windows suggested that drinking had been in progress since sundown.

"Bye Bye Blackbird" was playing on the gramophone, and Wraggett could be heard shouting the words. Blair hated the sound of drunken men, the idiocy, the oafishness, one shouter contending with another, like the stirrings of a mob, something animal in it, and when he heard them, he feared for Thackeray.

He said, "Are you certain you want to go through with this?"

"It will mean so much. Prestige is everything."

They were on the veranda now, passing into the foyer, the voices louder, the gramophone still playing "Bye Bye Blackbird."

Blair closed his eyes as though in prayer and took a deep breath, then pushed the door open. *I'll be home late tonight . . .*

"Here we go."

After the darkness of the veranda and the gloom of the foyer, the bright lamps in the room dazzled the two men, Blair in his dress uniform, Thackeray in his brown suit behind him, clutching his tweed golfing cap, his bald brown head gleaming. There was a hush, the music slowing to a groan, the gramophone running down, *Blackbird, bye bye . . .* And finally dying, leaving the room silent, the men at the bar staring, wide-eyed.

Blair coughed a little, then said, "I'd like to introduce my candidate, Mr. M. K. Thackeray."

No one spoke, somehow the music—not the tune but the words—hung in the air as a dusty echo. A man at the back cleared his throat. There came a whispered word, but audible enough for all to hear.

"Nigger."

Then a shout, "What are you playing at, Blair?"

37

THE SECRET SHARER

I fear I was a bit previous," Thackeray said, gasping with embarrassment. "I should not have presumed. Please forgive me, sahib."

They were at the edge of the maidan, bathed in moonglow, minutes after the fiasco at the club, the beastly word, followed by the shout. Yet Thackeray was a study in abject atonement, and Blair was pleading with him to stop apologizing.

Blair had hesitated in the meeting room at first, glaring daggers at the other members, then clapping on his helmet and tugging the chin strap into place, and finally executing a smart about-face, pushing the door open and slamming it on the howls. The two men had slipped into the night, Thackeray begging for forgiveness.

Soon Thackeray was hopping in misery in the moonlight, grief-stricken in his moaning as he crossed the maidan, and Blair marched uphill to his home, taking angry strides. He poured himself a drink and sat on the veranda, still in his uniform, studying the twitching of the familiar tuktoo on the rail, and beyond it a constellation of twinkling fireflies. In the moonlight the whole of Katha looked metallic.

There was a soft tap at the door—Gugu. "The woman is here, *thakin*."

Then the screen door ajar, Mee Hla peering around it, her hair piled high and fixed with a pin like a gilded dirk through her topknot, her lips reddened.

Blair said, "Not tonight."

She stamped her foot. The tucktoo skittered away.

In the morning, Eastwood was waiting in Blair's office, frowning in concern. He said, "It's not often I agree with our friend Wraggett, and granted he was fuddled with gin, but honestly, Blair, what are you playing at?"

So it was Wraggett who'd shouted that.

"Was it a wheeze, Blair?"

"It wasn't a wheeze. It seemed a reasonable request."

"Letting the side down?"

"Gymkhana Club in Rangoon admitted two natives. I daresay Pegu will do the same. I don't see the harm."

"It came as rather a shock. You might have had the decency to forewarn the others."

"Are those brutes so easily offended? I should have thought they'd be equal to it. That man Thackeray had no intention of participating in the club. All he wished for was membership, paying his subscription and staying away."

Eastwood massaged his chin in bewilderment. "What an extraordinary idea."

"No. He knew he wasn't wanted. But the edict was gazetted. He was looking for a tiny bit of prestige."

"I expect he was rather put out."

"Not at all. He apologized to me."

Eastwood appeared to sympathize, but for all his fair-mindedness he was of the sahib log; he knew his place, he couldn't extend his hand to a native, nor side with Blair.

"It won't do, Blair."

But somehow Blair's subinspectors knew, the servants at the club must have talked, and his Indian constables were unusually responsive that morning, Punch Chatterjee especially. He had once taken a note to Thackeray at the Saraswattee Lodge, so he was in the know, but he was safe. Blair sent him with another note.

Blair returned to Saraswattee Lodge, in the parlor that hummed with dust and cat hair, the curtains drawn. He sat, slumped over, staring into a glass of gin, averting his eyes from a dented cuspidor beneath the teak table on which Thackeray had set out another elaborate tea—dishes of cakes, a tray of drinks, a soda siphon. The man was still apologizing, his face crumpled and sleepless.

Blair said, "It's over. It's not your fault. You've just witnessed firsthand the breathtaking hypocrisy of the Raj."

It was supposed to have been so simple. Blair would offer this one favor, proposing Thackeray for membership and be done with it; Thackeray could then swank in the knowledge that he was a member of the Katha Club, believing he had gained in prestige. But the rejection, the man audibly blackballed with the beastly word, had changed matters. It had drawn the two men together. After that humiliation, Blair could not bear to abandon him.

It was one thing to bully a nameless prisoner, or manhandle a goonda, or cuff an obstinate dacoit—that was the nature of the dismal job. Bair had often written home saying, *Living and working among Orientals would try the temper of a saint. One wants to smash their sneering faces. I often think the greatest joy in the world would be to drive a bayonet into a Buddhist priest's guts.* His father had written back, *Hear! Hear!, Eric.*

But this was Mahadev Thackeray, a decent man, about thirty, with a sick wife, playing by the rules, loyal to the British Crown, law-abiding, wishing only for nominal membership in the club to improve his chances in the timber trade. Didn't the Raj want to promote the idea of encouraging native participation in commerce, for the greater good?

"They're the ones who should be apologizing," Blair said. "Not you. The fact is they are uncommonly stupid. I can't imagine why you'd even want to associate with them." He sipped his glass of gin. "As for me, I don't have a choice."

"You must not speak so, sahib, abusing the sahibs. They are salt of earth. Consider admirable things they have accomplished—Clive was a blighter but a great administrator. And Warren Hastings, Dalhousie, Curzon—consider how noble a type is the English gentleman. Their loyalty to one another. Even those of your fellow members, whose manner is unfortunate—some Englishmen are arrogant, I concede—but they have sterling qualities we Orientals lack. Beneath their rough exterior, their hearts are of gold."

"Thackeray, they insulted you. They blackballed you."

"It is likely that I failed to measure up. That they believe me to be *shok-tae.*"

"Untrustworthy? No. They're living a lie."

"With the greatest respect, 'living lie' is cliché."

Blair was shaking his head. He said, "The lie is that we're here to uplift our black brothers instead of to rob them. It's a natural lie. But it corrupts us in ways you can't imagine. There's an everlasting sense of being a scoundrel and a liar that torments us and drives us to justify ourselves night and day. It's at the bottom of half our beastliness to the natives."

Thackeray said, "The weakness of your argument, sahib, appears to be that you are not a scoundrel."

"How can you make out that we are in this country for any purpose except to steal?"

"It is trade, sahib. Could the Burmese here trade for themselves? Can they make machinery, or ships, railways, or roads? They are helpless without you. And whilst businessmen develop the resources of country, your officials are civilizing us and keeping us safe. It is a magnificent record of self-sacrifice."

"You were better off before."

"Bosh—forgive me, sahib, for saying so. Consider Burma in the days of Thibaw, with dirt and torture and ignorance. Now look around you. Look at the clinic, the school, your police station. It is modern progress."

"I don't deny it," Blair said. "But consider this—these great institutions are run by scoundrels."

"You are mistaken, sahib. You are a good man, sitting with me as friend. So I was blackballed at the club. But you risked the wrath of your fellow members to support my application. You have no idea what that means to me."

"I'm ashamed," Blair said, sipping his drink. "I failed."

"Not at all. I gained in prestige."

"How so?"

Thackeray leaned toward him, softly nodding, the light catching the shine of his conker baldness, giving his posture drama. "The mere fact that you are known to be my friend benefits me more than you can imagine."

Blair was too moved to reply to this. He swirled the last of his gin in his glass, then drank it in a gulp.

"I have drunk and seen the spider," he said, slurring the words, realizing he was tight.

Thackeray wobbled his head from side to side, as though he understood. But he had no idea, nor could Blair explain how he was still ashamed, how profoundly he hated what he had become.

His tongue was thick in his mouth, as he said, "Almost five years here, and what I've found is that to rule over barbarians you've got to become a barbarian yourself."

"I assure you, sahib, we are neither of us barbarians."

Blair was still holding his empty glass, the thing warm and slippery in his hand. He considered pouring himself another drink, then thought, *One more and I'll begin ranting*. Already he felt he'd said too much. When had he spoken this way before, except to Mrs. Jellicoe, in the darkness and seclusion of a bedroom?

"I can run you up to Moedar," he said. "It's rich in teak, and no one in Katha will volunteer to take you. The timber workers are browned off with the logging companies. If you play fair, you'll have those men on your side."

It was easy enough to create a pretext for returning to Moedar. Maybe another dekko at the Happy Association to update his report, Blair suggested to Eastwood.

"And Chatterjee's mentioned badmashes stirring up trouble." Blair, a terrible liar, was astonished at own audacity. "Nip it in the bud."

This pleased Eastwood, Blair showing initiative.

"You know the Burmese by now," Eastwood said. "Insurrection is a public duty."

"I'll need the launch."

"Bon voyage, my boy."

They left before dawn, Thackeray slipping down the gangway, looking nervous, carrying a bundle—his luggage. The three Hindu subinspectors were pleased to see another Indian on board, perhaps a Brahmin—and they were deferential, seeing him in a brown suit and plus fours rather than a kurta or shalwar kameez, or much worse, the dhoti they'd come to see as a ragged nappy. Ganju took up his place at the bow, Punch Chatterjee at the wheel, Bose in the cuddy making tea, which he served to Thackeray who sat with his knees together on a crate under an awning. Blair at the stern leaned on the gunwale, smoking and fanning mosquitoes away.

They chugged upstream, leaving Katha behind in darkness. Blair remembered his river trip years ago to Myaungmya through the narrow creeks and canals of the Delta, distant fingers of this same river, when everything he saw was nameless and strange and alienating. But the river had become familiar; it figured as strongly in Blair's mind as the face of any person he'd known in the country. It revealed itself as dawn seeped slowly from beyond the east bank, a glow in the sky and then the first flare of sun piercing the horizon, rising over the paddy fields, picking out the mangroves and the parasols of nipa palms. Weaver birds in canebrakes took flight at the sound of the engine, a pair of cormorants skidded across the water, flapping fiercely, a black-headed ibis cowered under a mudbank. Farther on, a stork in the shallows stabbed its swordlike beak downward for a fish—a painted stork, white headed, its black wings like epaulettes, a fabulous strutting bird out of Lear's *Book of Nonsense*.

For the pukka sahib and the club member and the city merchant, this aspect of Burma was an enormous vacancy. Yet for Blair it was vibrant, shimmering with life, his only solace. Whenever he withdrew from other people, finding himself adrift in such a landscape, he was content. He thought, *One day, when I'm far away from here, this is what I'll remember, the soft and plodding land, the feathery palms, the sinuous creeks, the squawks and screams of its birds, delicate blossoms flourishing in its heat, the sweetish odors of its foliage, all of it somehow reflecting its people—the land's unassertive sensuality.*

He lit another cigarette, he sipped his tea; it was still early, still cool, a haze of golden light fizzing with insects, fish jumping with a plop, and in the reaches out of the swifter river current thick carpets of water lilies, the crimson lotus, no people—an Eden, its watery odors swimming around his head. What was unfamiliar, unexpected, was his mood. He quizzed himself, and finally smiled. *I am happy.*

Even so, he was cautioned, remembering his misery in Katha, and thought, *Look thy last on all things lovely, every hour.*

Thackeray took the tray from Chandra Bose and served Blair another cup of tea.

"Lotuses," Blair said.

Scowling into the bright sun, Thackeray said, "Sacred lotus flower. They are cooking it, the natives. Lotus root, sahib, it is eatable."

Then Thackeray returned to sit under the awning and chatted with Bose, who crouched in the Indian way on his haunches, close both to Thackeray and sometimes calling out to Blair when he saw another bird. Laughing a little, Blair thought, *I have never done this. My men have served me well, but I have never sat with them, chuntering.* They ate together, a tiffin of rice and vegetable stew. Bose opened tins of custard, and they talked, Blair thinking, *But I scarcely know these men.*

In the early afternoon, the low profile of Moedar appeared far off, reflected in the river—its spindly crane, its sheds. The clank of its machinery, the rattle of carts on rails, the jawing of a steam saw were audible from a distance, and finally the derangement of the engines and the stink of fuel shook the magic from the golden day.

Approaching the jetty, the boat slowed and Ganju raised his carbine and called out, "Police!"

The six men in ragged puggarees on the jetty looked alarmed but held out their hands for the mooring lines flung by Bose, and the men gestured with fumbling salutes, as the boat was fastened, its passengers stepping off, yawning and stretching.

Blair sent his men to interview workers at the hostel and in the timber yards, Thackeray wandered away on his own, vanishing among the machinery and the stacks of logs in the direction of Moedar proper, which was a single rutted road lined with shop houses, lying parallel to the river. Blair knew those shops, their shelves of cooking oil and flour and amber bricks of jaggery, cigarettes, matches, and tins of condensed milk, bolts of cloth, or the other shops hung with chains, hand tools on shelves, coils of fencing wire, an array of padlocks, and dusty bronze hinges and hasps, piled next to rusted axe heads and ironmongery.

He returned to the boat alone, seated himself in the stern, and wished he'd brought a book. He tried to recapture the serenity he'd felt in the morning on the river. He closed his eyes, but it was no good. Wherever there were people in Burma there was blight and crime and stink.

Blair smoked and dozed, and in the late afternoon Thackeray called "Sahib!" from the jetty. He was accompanied by a small skinny man in a gauzy dhoti and white headcloth and sandals, a string bag slung over his shoulder.

"This is Pramod," Thackeray said. "It is my good fortune to meet him. He is Marathi man, as well."

"Would that be your luggage?" Blair said, of the string bag.

"It is ledger, sahib," Pramod said, bringing out a book from the bag. He wagged his head. He knew he was being teased. "It is accounts book."

"He is shroff here," Thackeray said. "You know shroff, sahib?"

Hearing the word the man beamed and pressed his palms together, bringing his hands to his face.

"Banker?" Blair said. "Moneylender? Paymaster?"

"All such, sahib," Thackeray said. "And more."

"We don't have space for another passenger," Blair said, envisaging their arrival at Katha, perhaps met by Eastwood, who'd complain, and jeer, something like, *Pleasure trippers, Blair?* It was forbidden to take civilian passengers unless they were under arrest. Blair's idea was to sneak Thackeray back ashore some distance upriver from Katha.

"I shall stop here for some days," Thackeray said and asked for his cloth bundle. "With Pramod-ji, my Marathi brother."

After they'd gone, Blair sat and smoked, and when the mosquitoes came alive at dusk he crawled into the cabin, which was screened, like the meat safe in the launch at Myaungmya. The Indians slept on deck, the Gurkha Ganju dozing at the bow, and at first light they cast off. Blair stirred then went back to sleep, until Bose woke him with a cup of tea and a banana.

Sailing downriver to Katha, Blair remembered how Thackeray had been startled at the club, twisting his cloth cap in his hands, his bald head gleaming, and weepy afterward. Now this, landing on his feet, with a friend in Moedar. He was glad for the man and relieved that Thackeray had found his own way, because it was so vexing to have a native for a friend.

A book by Conrad that Blair had brought from England, '*Twixt Land and Sea,* recommended by Connolly, was a collection of three stories, two disappointing tales and a masterpiece, "The Secret Sharer." He'd read it on the *Herefordshire,* reread it in Mandalay and Myaungmya, and had wondered, *Will I ever meet a fugitive, falsely accused, and risking my reputation, rescue him, hide him, then release him to freedom, as the captain did with the accused reprobate Leggatt in the eastern sea off Koh-ring?*

Now he knew. Thackeray was that man. He'd been slandered by a Burmese merchant in Moulmein, he'd fled to Katha, he was foundering, at sea, and Blair had extended the hand of friendship. Like the captain in the story, Blair had met him covertly. He was Blair's secret, and in some respects—like Leggatt—Blair's counterpart. *My double?* he wondered. The words *my double* were used repeatedly in the story. The blackballing at the club had brought them close, Blair unburdening himself to him, and on the pretext of investigating sedition and badmashes in Moedar, he'd sailed up the river and set him free, to strike out for a new destiny.

Blair was gladdened by the experience, and in the course of it felt he was himself freed. In his talks with Thackeray he'd been truthful, more forceful than he had with Mrs. Jellicoe, damning the empire, rubbishing the club, speaking his mind in a way he had not done in almost five years.

It was the hidden man, the cautious man, the secret writer, the diarist, the notetaker, who'd come clean—and by the way, helping this lost soul, a secret sharer, becoming freer by revealing himself. Thackeray had been inconvenient, but at last in conspiring, Blair had allowed that inner man to act. He had never before exposed himself so completely as a rebel and risk-taker. *I didn't know I had it in me,* he thought. *That's the man I want to be.*

As the weather grew warmer, the air thickening with humidity and the smell rising from the river, the club members cursed the heat and used it as an excuse to drink. "Brings out the mosquitoes!" they cried. Blair scoffed, because it was nothing like the Delta where mosquitoes in the early morning had risen in whirring clouds and thickened around his head and flown into his nose and mouth. "The heat's a caution," Slattery said. "Mind you, there'll be fever." Not long afterward Wraggett went down with dengue fever.

"You'll likely catch it," Slattery said. "All it needs is for a mozzie to bite Wraggett and then bite you."

"'Mark but this flea,'" Blair said, with an upraised finger. "'It sucked me first, and now sucks thee.'"

"Bloody nonsense," Slattery said. "Where's your bum boy, that native?"

"He was as hairless as a cheese!" Wraggett said, and then he growled. "We're the last club in Burma to hold out against natives. It'll never happen—there'll never be a black face in here."

They hadn't forgiven him for proposing Thackeray. Blair was glad of that: wanting them to remember was part of his rebellion. He still went to the club from time to time, because staying away suggested he had something to hide, a secret life, perhaps something disgraceful. He was well aware that he'd shown his hand—and no sahib trusted a man who'd befriended a native. And they didn't know the whole of it, that he'd benefited Thackeray, who was prospering in Moedar. He often wrote letters to Blair, his handwriting was beautiful, he said he had partnered with the shroff Pramod. *I am proceeding from strength to strength, Sahib.*

Now it was Blair who was *shok tae*—not to be trusted. Never mind, he had chickens and ducks, his dog, Flo, the ratcatcher. He had Gugu, he had Mee Hla, and a greater contentment than he'd known anywhere else in Burma. In his heart he was a traitor, making notes, keeping a diary, filling out his portrait of John Flory, who was not a policeman but a timber merchant, making money off the backs of peasants, lonely, a bitter club member, a fornicator, an amiable enough drunk but screaming inside. Flory, too, had an Indian friend, a doctor named Veraswami.

In those days and nights of writing about Flory on government notepaper he'd pinched from the station, Blair renewed the pleasure, the release, of using the embarrassments and stupidities of the club—removing them from his mind by recasting them as fiction, creating something new and worthy out of such unpromising material. It was coarser than Forster, more explicit than Maugham, but it was truer. *I have seen a man humiliated, I have seen a man hanged, I have ordered a prisoner flogged till he bled. The empire is not a tea party or an echoing cave.*

He'd seen, in some villages, pious peasants egged on by donors, erecting a new pagoda for merit. They labored in a muddle of sticks and stones, using the rough material to make it, working slowly, giving it height and shape, fashioning it to look like the sacred hill it mimicked, and when it was formed, coating it with plaster and smoothing it, and at last applying patches of gold leaf.

Writing was like that. Words were sticks and stones, the narrative was a symmetrical edifice, and if it was good it was golden.

Blair wrote to Thackeray and eagerly awaited his replies, cheering the man in his success, feeling that Thackeray had discovered a greater freedom and prestige in his timber business in Moedar than would ever have been possible in Moulmein or Katha. Letters from Thackeray were welcome, because the English mail was slow. In any case, Blair found that he had very little of consequence to report to his parents, and their letters could be a burden, especially their questions, their implied expectations, his father's tedious reminiscences of the Opium Department.

A letter arrived one day, addressed in unfamiliar handwriting, a Burmese stamp on it, two annas, the king wearing a domed crown set in a pink cartouche. Studying the envelope on this hot day just before the rains, Blair took it to be a bad omen when a drop of perspiration from the tip of his nose plopped onto it, puddling the ink to a veiny blot. He suspected it was from Mrs. Jellicoe—something about Humphrey.

He knifed it open and without reading it looked at the signature.

Uncle Frank.

38

THE LETTER

My dear Eric,

We pray you're keeping well. The only snag at our end is Mah Hlim down with a nasty bout of fever, but Kathleen is in the pink.
    We arrived in Mandalay a fortnight ago, beating the bushes for custom (pickings are a trifle thin in dear old Moulmein) and I recall your mentioning being posted to Katha, not far from where I'm penning this—

Blair stopped reading. He dreaded what was coming and averted his eyes. He folded the sheet of notepaper and turned it over, flattening its creases with the meat of his palm, wishing it away. Then he lit a cigarette to calm himself and glared at the folded paper and blew smoke on it. Flicking it open with an impatient finger he saw what he feared.

    . . . pay you a little call.

He groaned and left his office, hoping that legging it across the maidan would help in inspiring a convincing excuse for discouraging Frank in his visit. Walking with this on his mind, he began to see Katha with Uncle Frank's eyes—the tussocky maidan littered with stones, eroded in runnels from the rain, crisscrossed with footpaths, unsuitable for any sport, vastly inferior to the grassy maidan in Moulmein. Katha had nothing to offer but the forbidding divisional jail, the gray prison, the club and its louts, the wooden church and its neglected brasses, his bungalow at the top of the hill, the shadow of Mee Hla.
    Blair had never been more aware of being an alien in this negligible place, where he'd been banished—of being a different person, a man whom

Frank had never really known, mocked at the club, going through the motions of his dreary job, turning a blind eye to the nationalists, disillusioned, a stranger.

He had changed in the years since Syriam, when Frank had first seen him, that visit to his grandmother's in Moulmein. He'd been bewildered then, he was disgusted now, feeling a bitterness he could not express. This was reflected in his physical state, greatly changed since Syriam, altered as well in the months since Moulmein. He was thinner, sallow, his face lined, his eyes duller and disappointed, his pencil mustache that had seemed an affectation, a helpless gesture of concealment, stained from smoking. His cough had worsened to a choking howl.

Frank had bade him a brief farewell in Moulmein three months ago, yet might scarcely recognize him now. Blair hardly recognized himself, insulting his face in the shaving mirror each morning, thinking, *Who are you and what do you want?*

Sometimes he'd hunted dacoits and ambushed them on jungle paths, isolated and defiant: they were nameless and unknowable. But there were others—arsonists, rapists, village pilferers, chancers, and dodgers he'd arrested, pushing into their huts, and he'd shrink at their children bawling, the wives screaming abuse, or at the glimpse of a lame elder crouched on a mat, or the remains of a sad gray meal, a foul bowl of noodles in the squalid room stinking of rags; he'd feel pity mingled with contempt.

He couldn't allow Frank to see him that way in Katha, a fox in his lair, so different from the enigmatic man he'd seen in Moulmein, "a big bug in the police." Frank would not be impressed. He'd be confused, feel vaguely unwelcome as one does among strangers, regretting he'd come. He'd see the sorry face, the evasive eyes, of a failure.

Odd, Blair thought, how he'd been so candid with Thackeray, baring his soul, denouncing the empire—the Englishman bitterly anti-English, the Indian fanatically loyal; and yet he did not dare speak his mind to his uncle, who'd be shocked, who'd report these heresies to his sister Ida, Blair's mother, another person from whom he'd hidden. And he knew he was the despair of his father, Subdeputy Opium Agent, Grade 4 (Ret'd).

Uncle Frank must not visit. Mah Hlim's nasty bout of fever gave Blair an idea: he, too, was down with a nasty bout of fever. Laid up, he was in no position to entertain visitors.

He hurried back to his office and passing Chatterjee, he asked not to be disturbed. He drafted a letter that was apologetic and he hoped persuasive. Just to be sure, he recopied it, to strike the right note of regret, emphasizing his fever, adding, *Perhaps some future date?* He was copying it a third time when Chatterjee appeared at his office door, lowering himself, palms together, in a cringing shiko, offering on a saucer a yellow *Imperial Wireless* envelope.

"Not to disturb, sahib. But cable is marked urgent."

Blair put out his hand for the saucer, and when Chatterjee withdrew he tore open the envelope, a terse cable: *Leaving Mandalay tonight. Arriving Thursday. Frank.*

Blair cursed and crumpled his craven letter. Frank could not be found by post or cable. He was unreachable now. And there was another question: Who exactly was coming? If Mah Hlim was down with fever, did this mean that Frank was coming alone? But if Kathleen was "in the pink" perhaps that meant she was with him. *We arrived in Mandalay a fortnight ago*, he'd said in his letter. Who was *we*?

Blair brooded over dinner, remembering how, when he'd been selected for training in the Burma police, his mother had said, *Granny's in Moulmein—some of my people are still there. Frank's in timber.* He'd been vaguely curious to see his relatives, who'd lived in the town since the 1850s. His mother, raised there, had often reminisced about the weather, the festivals, her amah, the richness of their mansion, "Franconia," as she sat in her poky parlor in Southwold, dogcarts rattling past the window to the seafront. *We had a carriage house, we had a syce, we had stables.* Blair thought knowing his Moulmein relatives, he'd know himself better. And so he'd sought them out; but it had not gone well. They seemed baffled by him, a lowly probationary policeman, guarding Burmah Oil in Syriam. And he'd been disappointed by them; once prosperous, they'd lost Franconia, they were down on their luck, in and out of timber, miscalculating in rice, and after all her years in Burma, Grandma who'd gone native in every other way (shawl, gown, slippers, cheroot) still did not know a word of Burmese.

Until he'd met them Blair hadn't given much thought to their irregular marriages. But it had not taken him long to understand the contempt that Europeans and Burmese alike felt for such pairings as William and Sooma's, Frank and Mah Hlim's, and the derision for their offspring. Half-castes were hated, they had no status; most of the tarts in Burma were chee-chees, a word Blair came to loathe. Whenever someone made a disparaging reference— "that yellowbelly, Chutney Mary"—Blair was pained, and he was ashamed of being ashamed. Most Europeans merely teased and excluded them; the Burmese were fierce in their disdain for the *ka-pyar*, the half blood, or the *thwe-hnaw*, mixed-blood. The Burmese denounced Indians as intruders and parasites, but they despised mixed-bloods as mongrels.

Arriving Thursday . . .

Today was Tuesday, Mandalay was not far, a day's journey by train to Naba, then the branch line or a motorcar to Katha. Perhaps they were stopping the night in Naba, or were they availing themselves of the Irrawaddy Flotilla Company steamer on its weekly run?

He had a day to prepare. He was still dawdling over his dinner, toying with Gugu's kedgeree, gulping whiskey, and cursing Frank's unhelpful cable that lay beside his plate, splashed by his meal, stained by the base of his whiskey tumbler, the watermark of a sodden circle soaking the paper. The message now seemed imperious and presumptuous.

Thinking of his family, the expression *ka-pyar* spoken with derision by a Burmese put him in mind of Mee Hla—lovely, inconvenient Mee Hla.

"Where is the woman?" he asked when Gugu came to clear the plates.

"Waiting for you, *thakin.*"

She must have heard, because the sounds of her stirring on the veranda were unmistakable, the creak of the rattan chair as she squirmed in it, the scuff of her slippers on the plank floor, her kissing sound to calm the cat.

Blair rose from the table to meet her. He never ate with her, he felt awkward having her so near him at his meal. She bowed when she saw him, touching her pink head wrap—beautiful as a lotus bud—and she backed into the shadow of the veranda, Blair following.

"*Thakin.*" She breathed the word sweetly, affecting an exaggerated tone of reverence for the master.

The cushion of the rattan deck chair had been warmed by her having rested against it, Blair felt the heat of her body on it. Mee Hla crouched at his feet, her head resting on his knee, tracing with her fingers on his thigh, and settling against his legs like a cat, a lisp of her silk lungyi as she shifted to squirm close, a scrape of her starched linen blouse on the roughness of his khaki drill shorts. The fragrance of a gardenia tucked in her headcloth reached him. He touched her, smoothing what he took to be silk. It was her fine skin.

"My little cat."

"Why do you make your little cat wait? I wait all day for the *thakin* to call me."

She was pretending to pout, she enjoyed putting him in the wrong, so that he would beg to be forgiven, pretending himself, playing his role in a little love drama. It was the sort of back-and-forth he'd seen in a pwe performance, with music, the affectionate combat of two lovers—a game, verbal foreplay, teasing with a minimum of touching.

"I'm calling you now."

"Tell me that you missed me."

"I have something to discuss with you."

"First tell me that you missed your *bo-kadaw*."

Calling herself his wife alarmed him, and though it was just an expression that many of the keeps used—Margaret in Twante had once gasped it into his ear in the frenzy of their lovemaking—it implied a formal role and a responsibility he could not accept.

Nevertheless, he said, "I missed you."

"Your *bo-kadaw*."

"Listen to me," he said, growing impatient. "My uncle is coming from Mandalay. He's traveled all the way from Moulmein to see me. He's staying here for a while."

"I will be kind to him," Mee Hla said.

"No. For the week, starting tomorrow, you must go to your mother."

"You are ashamed of your *bo-kadaw*."

"No, no"—he heard himself insincerely protesting. In fact, Mee Hla had it exactly right: she suspected she was inconvenient, that he was trifling with her, taking her for granted. He remembered Swann, showing the gap in his front teeth, saying of a keep, *She'll ply your shoulders with a sponge in your bath*. He'd become that man.

But the prospect of Uncle Frank, or any European in Katha, observing Mee Hla with him—the Englishman with his native keep—that was a worry. She had to be Blair's secret.

"You are sending me away."

She twigged precisely the conflict and the hypocrisy. He had learned as a policeman that Burmese peasants, especially the more devious ones, could be maddeningly shrewd—"Canny little sods," McPake called them, half in admiration, half in anger. Blair could not deceive Mee Hla, crouched on the floor, purring in suspicion against his legs.

"I have a bangle for you."

He took it from his pocket. She raised her hand, fingers together, as though swearing an oath, and he slipped it over her fingers and let it drop, as it clinked upon the others gathered at her elbow.

"*Pite-san pay like*," she said. "Give me money. My mother will want money."

Blair's nerves were fraying, he was dizzy with drink. He'd expected resistance—she had all the mulish stubbornness he'd come to see in many Burmese—but this was becoming a tedious negotiation.

He felt for his wallet, he pulled some rupees from it, he pressed them into her foraging fingers.

"How much?"

"It's too dark to see. It's enough."

"Now I want to give you something, *thakin*."

"It's late," he said. "I drank too much."

"If I go away, I want to take a memory with me."

"What memory?"

She touched him where he was tender and lightly squeezed, as though caressing a small animal, rousing it to affection.

Blair was reminded of the sinking feeling he'd had at Eton whenever his parents wrote to say they'd be in London on the Sunday to visit him at college, taking the train, and would he kindly meet him at the Windsor-Eton Riverside Station?

He'd sneak alone to the station, buy a platform ticket, and hide behind the newsagent's kiosk until the train drew in. Then he'd hurry them through the barrier and up the high road to Castle Tea Rooms at the end of a mews, fearing the whole time he'd meet a fellow student or a master, appalled by his mother's old coat, her hat like an overturned bucket, his father's scornful stride and sidelong looks—"Chap wants a short back and sides, if you ask me"—ashamed of them for what they revealed of him, and as always ashamed of his shame. Then, excruciating, the stroll around Agars Plough, the questions, the glimpses of other boys, other parents, and a knot in his stomach until he put them on the train once more and scuttled away.

"I have a visitor coming tomorrow," he told Eastwood lightly, hoping to conceal his anxiety.

"Our Indian friend?" Eastwood said, twitting him. There was no malice in the man but he shared the resentment of the others in the club of having been ambushed by Thackeray. Still, he'd had the decency to put a flea in Wraggett's ear for calling Thackeray "a bottle-arsed babu."

Blair said, "No. But it would help if I were put on light duties. I'll need to squire the chap around, as it were."

He could have said, *My uncle from Moulmein—born there—good family, decent businessman, keen cricketer, my mother's older brother.*

But then Eastwood would know him, and he did not want to be known.

"I have a fair idea of what it's like to have visitors in Katha," Eastwood said. "A dekko at the church, a shufti at the bazaar, a squint at the pagoda—it's got a few interesting old bits. Then a chotapeg at the club. Apart from that there's fuck all else to do."

• • •

Unable to sleep, Blair lit his lantern and opened *People of the Abyss,* and smoked, but the notion of his uncle about to descend kept him from reading consecutive paragraphs. He'd get to the end of one and brood over Frank's arrival, and he'd invent excuses for his having to leave Katha soon. *Spot of bother at Indaw—pirates on the ruddy lake. I'm needed there but I can drop you at Naba on the way, what?*

His feeble excuses left him wretched, and the feeling of wretchedness reminded him of his accumulated abuses, dumping Margaret, jilting Muriel Peddy-Wilmot, failing in Syriam when the fence was breached, watching Mullapoodi hanged, shooting the helpless elephant, romancing Mrs. Jellicoe, proposing Thackeray at the club when he knew the man would be mocked and blackballed. He had a weakness for making lists—of Hindi and Burmese words, of books he'd read, of trees and flowers and birds; and now this—a litany of his failures.

He closed the book though he retained an image of Jack London pulsing on the page and in the East End, indistinguishable from the tramps in his old clothes, a free man in his anonymity, vanishing in a crowd of poor people. That was the ideal—to vanish. If only he could evaporate now.

At dawn, having dozed a little, he again saw everything with Frank's eyes: his ducks, his chickens, his dog, the veranda rail that needed a repair, the mass of bilious yellow croton leaves. He could not rid his mind of the visit, which was an intrusion, and he kept murmuring his excuse, *Spot of bother at Indaw . . .*

Motorcars from Naba usually dropped their passengers at the market forecourt; and the jetty was beneath it, where the steamer called. So Blair walked to the market after breakfast and found a bench under a peepul tree, near which hawkers were setting out baskets and piling mangoes on mats. He studied them, men and women, who were powerless and without pretensions or artifice, Burmese who loved their families and doted on their children and admired their uncles and aunties. He envied them in their simplicity and decency. They were home. They were better than him.

He sat, he smoked, he sweated, and toward noon a Ford motorcar rolled slowly past him and parked near the cabstand at the market. The rear side door swung open—Frank—but he stretched and spoke to someone inside and stepped back to allow that other person to alight: dusky Kathleen.

39

EASTER WEEKEND

They'd finished lunch, one of Gugu's mongrel meals—pickled chicken, burnt brinjal, fried rice, slimy bhindi—and for afters he'd served bowls of yellow trembling custard he'd made from a tin of powder.

"We too are very fond of Bird's Custard," Kathleen had said. "Cook makes delicious *doodh keri*." Filling the silence she added, "Mango custard."

And there was more silence.

Now it was midafternoon and they were reclining on the veranda deck chairs, Frank and Blair smoking, Kathleen busying herself with needlepoint—a Christian cross entwined with a thorny vine of red roses. It was as though they were digesting the awkward conversation at lunch as much as the stodgy food—Kathleen's odd interjections, and Frank's monologuing, because Blair had sat silent and apprehensive, thinking, *Whatever will I do with them?*

"You've got masses to be proud of, Eric," Frank had begun. "Imagine your grandfather, old Francis Limouzin, fetching up in Burma from some kiss-me-arse place in France all those years ago, just after the Mutiny I believe, or a shade later, barely spoke a word of English, so they say, hardly two annas to rub together, and—presto—makes a go of it, pukka sahib. Gets his feet under the table, dives into timber, acts as agent at a top-hole shipping firm, acquires a reputation as a shipwright, builds some boats of modest tonnage, then lets fly and buys a bloody shipyard!"

Sunk in gloom, Blair let him continue, and Frank had the ability to talk as well as eat, using his knife and fork to gesture—he used them as he described his father's shipbuilding, the knife and fork as a shipwright's tools.

"Whacking great ships—he's launching proper vessels into the Salween, employing hundreds of coolies and roustabouts and babu mistries, and now it's Francis commanding the shipwrights—what?"

"Quite." Blair saw his grandfather, the pukka sahib, astride a gantry, lording it over the coolies and carpenters. "That's got to be said."

"His designer chap—marine architect, so called—sketched plans for

Franconia. I wish you could have seen the inside, Eric, it was absolutely marvelous. The cabinets, the fixtures and fittings, exquisite paneling, nothing shoddy or sham, no gimcrackery, only the best for Francis—polished teak and a grand staircase. The kind of cabinetry you'd find on a ship of the line, the sort of blooming great cutter they finished the year of the Jubilee—'97—I remember it well, the speech by the chief minister of Moulmein Division, how his lady wife climbed to the top of the scaffold!"

His knife became the scaffold, his fork the wife.

"Climbing just so, to the roar of the crowd as she held the bottle of Champagne like a cricket bat and set to with that willow, smashing it for a six on the bow, the cheers as they unchained it to groan down the slip way, christened *The British Queen*. I was proud as punch, the whole family watching, pennants flying, the band playing—imagine, Eric, your grandfather's work!"

Blair's gloom had deepened, as Uncle Frank added detail upon detail—the celebration tea, the fizzing rockets, the bang of crackers, the sampans gathered round the ship's hull, their pennants, their bands, the native instruments, flags and cymbals, the grandeur of the launch. Yet all he could see in this memory were the shipwrights and carpenters and babu mistries, dark-skinned coolies and chokras, nameless barefoot men, who'd toiled for a year on the ship for a handful of rupees.

"That's your heritage, Eric."

Though he'd meant it as praise he could not have uttered anything more hurtful. Blair said nothing more until, on the veranda, he remembered the monologue and asked, "Were there many ships after *The British Queen*?"

Uncle Frank puffed his pipe and peered through his own smoke and said, "Not of those precise dimensions. The Scottish firms took over. They'd been building stout vessels on the Clyde and knew a thing or two. They found it cheaper to build here with local chaps."

"And what did grandfather do then?"

"He was French, wasn't he? He wasn't as canny as the Scots. He went back into timber, but it didn't pay half as well." Frank puffed, blowing smoke, seeming to read its wisps like cursive script. "After a bit we lost Franconia and moved down the hill."

And so what Frank had intended as a glorious account of empire was a history of failure, the self-serving parasitical role the Limouzin family had played in the racket of the Raj. But Uncle Frank was oblivious of this. Tamping his pipe he said, "Nellie in Paris, Ida in England, you at Eton, and now a big bug in the police. Makes one ever so proud."

Glancing up from her needlepoint, Kathleen said, "Eric, do you have a gramophone?"

"Sadly, no."

"I expect there's one at the club. I'm awfully fond of listening to gramophone records."

"The club's rather a bore," Blair said, alarmed at her suggestion, imagining the tepid welcome she'd receive from the likes of Wraggett and Slattery, their surprise at seeing a chee-chee enter as Blair's guest, as bad a disgrace as the Thackeray business, Blair's stammering introduction, *My cousin Kathleen from Moulmein.*

Over lunch he'd studied her smooth sallow Eurasian features, her broad not-quite-European nose, her surprised eyes and mousy hair, her slim figure in an English dress. She was no beauty but she was cheerful, spirited. That counted for a lot and gave her a vitality that made her attractive. It saddened him to think how half-castes were regarded in Burma, relegated to clerking jobs, or flunkies on the railways, and those were always men. There was no place for her here; truth to tell, there was no place for her in England, either.

"I should like to see something of your Katha," she said.

"Rather warm for that at the moment," Blair said, his anxiety returning. "We could take a tonga later for a bit of sightseeing, have a dekko at the market, a squint at the pagoda."

"One must not enter a pagoda," she said. "It will do you harm. But merely to look—that would be smashing."

A closed tonga, the curtains drawn, clopping from sight to sight in the semidarkness of a Katha dusk. That might be safe.

"Teak trade—fickle business," Uncle Frank said. He wasn't listening. He seemed, wreathed in smoke, to be pondering the reduced fortunes of his father, and his own struggles in timber. "Maybe regain a kind of solvency with fresh supplies." Or was he commenting on his visit here? "When mother died, I fancied I might come into a bit of money."

He halted there, puffing vehemently, so Blair said, "And did you?"

"Not a sausage," Uncle Frank said. "More's the pity, I inherited mother's debts and Aimee got the house." He pondered this, and then flapping his hand, he cleared the smoke away from his face and revealed a smile. "So I was overjoyed to hear from your friend Thackeray."

"Thackeray?" Blair squawked the name so hard he began coughing.

"Queer, isn't it? Normally the timber trade is very hush-hush. But Thackeray put me wise to prospects here. I suppose it was a way of thanking you—he said you'd done him a good turn."

"I had no idea," Blair said, gagging—his throat ached from coughing. Thackeray, the grateful Indian, had wished his uncle upon him.

They dozed, and then it was evening—too late, Blair said, to venture out: the market would be closed, the pagoda mobbed, mosquitoes were fierce after sunset, nothing to see.

"What do you normally do of an evening, Eric?" Uncle Frank said.

I brood, I drink, I read, I ponder John Flory. I drag myself to the club and endure insults, and at last I stumble home and make love to my keep, holding her like a drowning man, clinging to her for her buoyancy, and then I brood again.

"I read books," Blair said, and he detected a distinct stiffening of Frank on the word *books*. So he added, "Cards—I play cards."

"I'm very fond of a hand of cards," Kathleen said.

"Or dice. Three-handed Cross and Anchor. I played it a bit in the Delta."

At Kathleen's urging Blair brought out the card table and passed the deck of cards to Frank, to deal. Then he set out glasses and uncorked a bottle of gin.

"Lips that touch liquor shall never touch mine," Kathleen said, looking up from her needlepoint.

They played Crown and Anchor, Blair sneaking glances at his pocket watch, which grew blurry as he became drunker, and later, after they'd gone to their rooms, Blair lay in bed, thinking, *I've got through one day,* a little victory, and began to worry about the next day, Friday. *What shall I do tomorrow?*

He lay awake half the night and when he woke he realized he'd overslept, and only then remembered Frank and Kathleen. He dressed hurriedly and rushed to the dining room where Frank was spreading marmalade on toast, a yolk-smeared plate in front of him.

"Overslept," Blair said. "So sorry. You must have been up for hours."

"Not me—Kathleen's the early riser. She was up with the lark."

"Do you know, Uncle Frank, there are larks here in Katha? The bush lark, lovely little creature"—Frank chewed his toast, the regularity of his chewing without swallowing seeming to indicate boredom. "Is she in her room, then, Kathleen?"

Now Frank swallowed, his chest heaving. "Believe she went out."

"*Out?*" Blair could not disguise his tone of panic. "Out *where?*"

"Oh"—Frank took another bite of toast, licking marmalade from his lips and then from the tip of his thumb—"you know, bit of a stroll, I imagine."

"A *stroll?* There's nowhere to stroll. No one strolls here."

"The town, I reckon—down the hill, past that waste ground."

"The waste ground is the maidan."

"Fancy that for a sticky wicket."

"I must go fetch her."

"She'll find her way back."

"It's not that. You're up-country, uncle. This isn't Moulmein. Badmashes abound. We've had dacoity attacks near the jetty. They flee in boats."

Uncle Frank put his toast down and licked his thumb again. "I had no idea."

Blair flew to the veranda and peered out, past the gravel drive, where the mali was resting on the handle of his mamoty, and through the trees, he saw Kathleen walking toward the house, taking long schoolgirl strides, Flo frolicking beside her.

"Where have you been?" Blair asked when she got to the top of the veranda stairs.

"Out and about," she said airily. "I've been up for hours."

"Did you see anyone?"

"What a funny question. I saw shoals of people. Natives are always up early, you know, fetching and carrying."

"I mean to say, were you inconvenienced in any way?"

"Inconvenienced—not at all. Your friendly puppy accompanied me the whole way."

"Flo—good dog," he said, and he saw Kathleen wandering the town. Anyone who saw her with Flo would know where she lived—Blair's dog. Kathleen was not known in town, there were few half-castes in Katha—Cecil a clerk at the Irrawaddy Flotilla Company office near the jetty, Samuel an accountant at Imperial Wireless, Malcolm an orderly at the prison. Kathleen would not have noticed anyone in particular. But everyone would have seen her and remarked on the dog.

"You seem in rather a wax, Eric."

"I want you to be safe."

"I'm quite safe, silly. I saw the market. I was hoping you'd take me back there and explain some of the fish."

Blair hated leaving the house with them, hated walking down the hill; he risked being seen by someone from the club, or one of his subinspectors, or a burra memsahib like Mavis Wraggett. A Burmese might spit betel juice on Kathleen's daring frock—her legs showing—with a cry, "*Ka-pyar!*" or worse. He was glad Kathleen had taken his suggestion to bring an umbrella, hoping that would help conceal her.

They made it to the market by the river without incident, yet Blair felt conspicuous and tried to nudge Kathleen away from the footpath, out of the revealing sunshine.

"It's not my idea of a bazaar," Kathleen said. "It's nothing like Moulmein. It's like a cattle pen, really. Horribly dirty."

"River's a sight," Frank said. "But those sampans—they do the same in Moulmein, paint eyes on the bow. I suppose it's for—what—luck?"

"A boat is like a living thing to them. It needs eyes to find its way. The ancient Egyptians, the Greeks, the Phoenician triremes—"

But Frank wasn't listening, Kathleen had grasped his arm. "Look, Daddy!"

It was a monkey, stiff in death, lying on its back, a naked pinched face and the rest of it covered in thick black fur.

Kathleen cried out, "It looks like a child in winceyette pajamas!"

"I think this one's called a colobus monkey," Blair said. "They catch them in the mountains."

"Whatever for?"

"Meat, fur, bones. They value the paws as amulets."

"It's covered in bluebottles."

"There's a wonderful story. 'The Monkey's Paw'—"

"Those women," Frank said. "I've heard of them but I've never actually seen one."

They were giraffe-necked women, brass neck-rings rising from their shoulders, their heads wrapped like nuns, their earlobes pierced with small gems.

"Palaung women, from the Shan states," Blair said. "It's their idea of feminine—"

"Look!" Kathleen said and walked where a man and his son were juggling eggs.

They were so intent on looking they had no idea they were being observed—Kathleen being closely watched, singled out for her Eurasian face and bare legs and floppy garden hat. She was unaware that she was poking passersby with the edges of her umbrella. They struggled past the stalls, bumped by marketgoers, shouted at by hawkers, a reek of dried fish in the air. A snake seller pinched the head of a viper, allowing it to wrap itself around his arm, and grinned at them with black teeth when they drew away. Piles of coconuts, stacks of mangoes, bolts of cloth on counters; eviscerated chickens, knotted coils of dying eels, and plucked carcasses of ducks—shiny, looking lacquered—strung up by their feet.

"I'll get something for tonight," Blair said, passing a butcher's slab of pigs' heads and trotters, bleeding bellies. "Gugu does a passable pork curry."

"No meat for me," Kathleen said.

"You ate chicken yesterday."

"Today is Good Friday."

"I'd quite forgotten."

"No meat," Kathleen said and stamped her foot.

Frank made a whinnying noise in his sinuses. He said, "I'm not fussed."

"Gugu does a decent egg curry as well."

"Not that fond of gussied-up eggs," Frank said.

This must be what it's like to have small children, Blair thought, as he steered them out of the market and into a side road, all the while looking round to note the reactions of passersby. Most paid no attention but now and then Blair recognized looks of disdain, and once a man called out "Sahib," an Indian who recognized him as a policeman.

They stood in the sun, covering their faces against the risen dust of the tongas, gaily painted, with clattering wheels, and that was when, as Blair feared, a young man passed Kathleen and spat a gout of betel juice on her dress, leaving a streak like a bloodstain on her shoulder. And when she shrieked and people stopped to stare they, too, seemed to take it for blood.

"*Kun-yar,*" Blair said, referring to the quid of betel in the man's mouth, and the onlookers laughed at the stain, at Blair's pronouncing the word like a sahib, the way he gripped the sobbing half-caste woman and bundled her into a tonga.

Back home Kathleen sat compactly, as though wounded, in an armchair in the hot dusty parlor, holding her needlepoint hoop—the half-stitched cross, the rose vine twirled around it. She lowered her head and spoke into her knees, "Beastly, how can they be so beastly? I've heard of such things in Moulmein but I have never been assaulted before in this beastly way."

Blair was encouraged by the betel spitting; it proved him right, it might keep them at home. He said, "So you see what I mean by being careful. You were rash this morning, going out alone."

"I was rather hoping to have a look at that depot upriver," Frank said. "The one your friend Thackeray mentioned."

"Moedar," Blair said. "We'd need a proper boat. The police launch is spoken for. I suppose I can put in a request on Monday."

"I take that to mean we cool our heels," Frank said, with a trace of exasperation. "I reckon we could look in at the club."

Not that, Blair thought. *Never that.* He said, "There's a *nat pwe* tuning up at the pagoda, so I hear."

"Maybe tomorrow," Frank said. "Think I'll have a lie-down."

With a look of suffering, Kathleen rose slowly and went to her room, shutting the door. Frank yawned and stretched himself on a deck chair on the veranda and was soon snoring.

Blair was relieved that they were content to stay inside. He had the abiding fear that he associated with a parent looking after two small children that, out of his sight, they'd do themselves an injury.

Another day, he murmured, when he woke up on Saturday morning, listening for the movements of Frank and Kathleen. He'd warned Kathleen against going out for a stroll—it seemed she'd heeded his warning, because she'd finished breakfast and was engrossed in her needlepoint on the veranda by the time Blair sat down to his kedgeree.

"A creditable kedgeree," Frank said, pushing his empty plate aside. "I do hope you can arrange a little tour of the teak depot."

Blair said, "I'll make inquiries," and knew he would do no such thing; but he was unable to say, *It's impossible, I will never get a boat, it won't be authorized, you're wasting your time, you're on a fool's errand—don't you see you're unwelcome?* It seemed proof of Frank's failure, and a clear example of his desperation, that he was depending so heavily upon his disgraced nephew for help.

And Frank's sighs and Kathleen's silences seemed to suggest that they knew Blair was stalling, that they were inconvenient, their request at an impasse. They were good, kind people, they didn't judge him, but they were also simple provincials, baffled, up-country, in a small station. They were small, in the vast mechanism of the empire, and didn't see it was a despotism. They were prisoners of the Raj, habituated to its deceits, who couldn't live anywhere else. But they were utterly lost here, and he had failed them.

Yet they also annoyed him in their colonial manners, accustomed to servants. He wanted to say, *You don't stir yourselves to do a hand's turn to help!*

Frank had begun to regard Gugu as his personal khidmatgar, calling out to the old man, "Gugu, fetch me a cup of tea, there's a good lad."

Late that afternoon, to keep them busy—Frank kept inquiring about the Katha Club—Blair sent Gugu to find a tonga and the three set off for the pagoda.

Boys were lighting lanterns at the bamboo enclosure, musicians were setting out their instruments, rows of gongs and drums, an assortment of flutes, and a narrow table resembling an altar, a gilded Buddha as the centerpiece, garlanded with marigolds.

"What have we here?" Frank asked.

"This is a *nat pwe*," Blair said. "Or will be when they get underway."

"Nats are pagan ghosts," Kathleen said.

"Spirits, rather," Blair said.

A crowd had gathered and now seemed interested in the three visitors—the fat old Englishman in a topee, the immensely tall young Englishman, the young half-blood woman—more interested in that than in the preparations for the pwe. Self-conscious, feeling once again conspicuous, Blair called to one of the musicians and palmed him some rupees, saying, "Please start."

The man called out to the others, and a drum was thumped, gongs struck, flutes warbled. That same man began singing in a screech that resembled someone in pain and after a while, the screech becoming more urgent, a woman entered, shuffling from the back of the bamboo enclosure. She moved in jerky dance steps as though controlled by strings, like a life-size marionette. And swaying, she raised her arms, displaying a glittering sword in each hand, slashing them as she spun in her halting motion to the rhythm of the drums and gongs. She rolled her head, her eyes whitened, and within a few minutes she seemed to enter a trance state, but still flashed her swords.

"Absolutely fascinating," Frank said in a flat voice, sounding unconvinced, and covering his mouth to yawn.

"You have this in Moulmein?"

"No idea."

"Kathleen?"

The dancing puppetlike woman, swiping with her sword blades, might have noticed the look of disapproval on Kathleen's face, because she came near, stamping her feet—her face was clownish, green eye shadow, floury cheeks, a painted mouth—and she manipulated the swords, swishing them before Kathleen's terrified eyes. It occurred to Blair that the dancer might be drunk or drugged, she was without inhibition, she staggered, she was loose jointed, becoming more entranced as the music built in tempo.

"It is heathen," Kathleen breathed as the woman danced away.

"There's something sinister in it," Blair said, inclining his head so that he could speak into Kathleen's ear. He remembered what Robinson had said in Mandalay at the pwe he'd shown him. "There's a hint of the diabolical in all Mongols. But look at her—what she's doing. There's centuries of culture behind every movement. That dance has been handed down through generations."

"What's that, Eric?" Frank asked. "Can't quite hear you."

Raising his voice, Blair said, "Whenever I see something of this kind I think how it represents a civilization stretching back for centuries. Look at the way she's flicking those swords—her hands, her hips, the way she jerks her head, those minute gestures. The whole life and spirit of Burma is summed up in those movements."

But the music had grown louder, the clanging of the gongs drowned out his words; the woman had become frenzied, as the onlookers shouted encouragement, pushing forward, soaked in sweat, their faces shining, their teeth reddened with betel giving them death's heads with ghoulish grins.

Blair's hip was bumped by Kathleen, who was speaking rapidly, but incoherent because of the music and the shouting. He leaned near her again.

"I want to go home!" she howled. She wasn't angry, she looked tearful.

Blair signaled to Frank and they made their way through the crowd to the waiting tonga.

They sat in silence in the carriage, the only sound the clopping of the horse's hooves, the ring of its iron shoes on stones, the rumble of the wheels.

"Crikey," Frank said.

Blair wondered if he should apologize when they arrived at the house, but before he could speak, Kathleen sighed with satisfaction and relief, saying, "I know what I'm going to do tomorrow."

"Jolly good," Blair said and braced himself for what was to come.

"Church," she said.

Blair said, "I wasn't planning—"

"It's Easter. You can't call yourself a good Christian if you don't go to church on Easter Sunday."

40

GET ME OUT OF HERE

B lair could not think of church without thinking of chapel at Eton, the boredom, the nonsense, the smelly hymnals, soiled and smudged—and all the bibles had a peculiar odor from being handled, their gray pages thickened by licked fingertips, bindings cracked with age; they stank abominably. As for the preposterous beliefs, the scolding, the damning, the pomposity of the Anglicans, the rottenness of Catholicism—*Get me out of here,* was his constant thought. After Eton he had vowed never to return to the cant and the sanctimony, the oppression of Christian authority.

He'd vowed to keep his promise, to refuse to kneel, yet, as in so much else—Burma was a test of his beliefs—he'd failed, one of many self-betrayals. The empire was conscientiously Christian and uncompromising in religious matters. Law and life found their justification in the Bible, the king on all coinage was IND IMP—Emperor of India—and also FID DEF, Defender of the Faith. A simple silver one-rupee coin announced all the militancy of the Raj.

He'd weakened, of course, given in, sung hymns in Mandalay in training, showed up for the sake of appearances at various churches in Rangoon, attended a service in Insein with Mrs. Jellicoe and Muriel, and there was the lugubrious funeral of Grandma Limouzin in Moulmein. Months before, around the time he'd first come to Katha—when Selkirk's niece Elizabeth arrived and Slattery tried to woo her—there had been a church service, and Blair had agreed to it, the first time he'd attended St. George's. Slattery had begged the other club members to attend, to buck him up, to prove him respectable, to make it seem that Sunday service was part of the week's routine. He needed to convince the young woman that he was not a lout but a proper gentleman and a good prospect. Slattery who disparaged churchgoing—"Knee drill! The snivel parade!"

Blair had finally agreed because Slattery's attending was a charade, like the service itself, a moth-eaten ritual he'd loathed since St. Cyprian's and

All Souls Church in Eastbourne. He'd boasted of being an atheist at Eton ("I rather enjoy the sight of bare ruined choirs"), but morning chapel was compulsory—he'd been caned for missing prayers—and he remembered the fanfare at Easter, the procession, the gowned chaplain, the absurd solemnity of the choir—well, give them credit, the choir was full-throated and harmonious, those sweet-voiced boys. But the service itself was mockery and mimicry, a pantomime. Here, the Scots embraced it in their dismal Jock theology of Calvinism, but even at its best churchgoing meant joining a cult of killjoys. Blair would have laughed to think that Kathleen had press-ganged him into prayers, returning him to childhood and his schoolboy agony of enduring an entire Sunday service—would have laughed hard, except that in this case it meant he would be sitting in full view of the sahibs in Katha; no laughing matter.

Seeing Kathleen on the veranda on Easter morning he said, "I'm feeling a bit ropy."

"You'll feel better after you pray."

Frank said, "Cup of tea, Eric, might put you right."

"No tea—we're taking Communion," Kathleen said. She was slipping her cloth of needlepoint from her hoop. "There, finished just in time. I'm presenting this to the vicar."

Blair saw that picked out below the rose-entwined cross were the words *No Cross No Crown.*

"Communion?" Frank said. "But I'm feeling peckish, love."

"You'll have to wait, Daddy. Communion is more godly on an empty stomach."

Swallowing high church wafers! Candles and robes! No cross, no crown! How unlike the mean little service and bare altar of the Reverend Grover Albee in Twante. But Blair was not surprised to hear her speak this way. It often seemed to him that Eurasians took refuge in the Anglican church. It was their way of identifying with the British, defying the Buddhists and Hindus, grasping at Englishness, believing that a show of faith would offer protection, not acknowledging that all religions were alike, the Christians and their cruelty just as much a sham as the elephant worshippers and the animistic Buddhists, with their ghost-hunting and their nat obsessions and magic tricks.

"Might as well get cracking," Uncle Frank said. "The sooner this hoo-ha finishes, the sooner we eat." He hobbled toward the stairs, and seeing Gugu with a tray of breakfast cups, called out, "Gugu, fetch me my stick—there's a good lad."

In the driveway, Blair said, "I'm sure we can find a tonga," but Frank called out, "I've got me stick—let's walk. I can see the church from here." And to Kathleen, "Mind how you go, love. This waste ground's a caution."

"Maidan," Blair said.

Frank hooted. "Maidan! Pull the other one, Eric!" and he slashed at a clump of grass on a tussock.

Churchgoers had already emerged from the other bungalows, and the upper compound of government houses, Selkirk and Eastwood with their memsahibs, Slattery and Wraggett conferring, Mavis Wraggett walking in front of them in a disapproving hurry. They'd gone ahead and were walking in a file, nearing the church, where a group of Chinese, and the half-castes, Cecil and Samuel, were waiting, all of them deferential, natives delaying their own entrance until the sahibs had gone inside.

Blair had slowed his pace when he'd seen the others. He was determined to be the last to arrive at the church, so as not to be spotted, to sit unseen near the back. But Cecil and Samuel were still at the church door, and when Blair passed with Uncle Frank and Kathleen, the two men peered, pursing their lips in puzzlement.

Holding her folded cloth of needlepoint before her in both hands like an offering, Kathleen brushed past Blair and walked down the main aisle. She was headed toward the front pews, where the club members and the wives were seated. But Blair took two long strides and cupped her elbow, drawing her back, steering her to a pew halfway down the aisle. He then made way for Uncle Frank, and just before he sat down he looked around and saw how the congregants had sorted themselves out, the sahib log at the front, the Karen and Chinese Christians at the back, but sitting apart; the half-castes midway up the aisle on the far side about level with Blair—not many in the church, perhaps twenty altogether, and near the altar Mrs. Selkirk seated at the big boxy harmonium.

When the harmonium began to wheeze, Mrs. Selkirk stamping on the pedals, pumping air into it, Blair was reminded of his own breathing, the catch in his throat, the bronchial rattle that often woke him in the night— lying in bed seem to bring it on.

The vicar had been sitting to the side of the altar in a high-back chair, wearing a white smock over his black gown, and now, as the music grew louder, losing its wheeze, he stood. His hair was pure white, swept back, combed close to his head, its whiteness matching the tuft of his mustache. He had a discolored face, yet an air of refinement, excellent posture, and full sleeves that hung like limp wings when he lifted his arms. He held what appeared to be a hymnal.

The music ceased, leaving wisps of its echo in the air, and the vicar in-

toned what Blair first took to be a verse. But it was the title of a hymn—
Kathleen had heard, she had begun to stand before the vicar finished. She
had snatched up a hymnal and was flicking pages. Blair leaned to look past
Uncle Frank to see what page she was on, as the others in the church stood
and prepared for the cue from the harmonium.

Kathleen sang with gusto, and so did Frank—it was "Christ the Lord Is
Risen Today"—and behind them the Karen Christians were moaning the
words, the half-castes across the aisle sang loudly, and up front the sahib
log were shouting the words, with lusty "Alleluias."

The rest of the service was rigmarole and pack drill, the vicar chanting
over the fat Bible that lay open on a lectern, and more hymns, then more
readings, kneeling for prayers—and Blair was a restless schoolboy again,
sighing, sniffing the dusty air, and wishing for a cigarette. And he began
plotting how, at the end of the service, he would step smartly into the aisle,
beckon Frank and Kathleen to precede him and, hovering so as to hide
them, hurry them away and up the hill, unseen.

"Welcome to St. George's, Katha, and happy Easter," the vicar said. He
had climbed to the pulpit while Blair had been planning their escape. "I
greet you on this holy and hopeful day—and why hopeful? Because Easter
means renewal, the resurrection of Christ. It means 'He is risen.'"

Blair became agitated—It did not mean that. The word *Easter* meant
spring; it was a pagan vernal festival, barefoot maidens with flowers in their
hair, wearing diaphanous gowns, skipping through meadows, shaggy-
haired druids in greasy robes and long beards clumping heavy staffs, their
eyes upturned to the equinox. It had nothing at all to do with Christ, it was
a ritual in praise of the Dawn Goddess that somehow coincided with the
Christian mumbo jumbo.

But when Blair looked over at Kathleen, he saw her face illuminated, a
soft smile on her lips, and she gently nodded as the vicar spoke, her hands
clasped to her breast. Blair was touched by her piety that seemed to make
her beautiful in a way he had not seen before. It was her confidence in the
vicar's words, a belief that was valuable, that would help her, because as a
half-caste she was an outsider, on her own, and this belief would always
make her welcome in a church.

"A time for renewal," the vicar was saying, "to gather the strength to
seek new endeavors. When I was a boy in the West Country, the parish of
Plympton in Devon, we made a point of wearing a new shirt, a new jacket,
an article of clothing we'd not worn before—to remind ourselves that this
day marked a beginning, a fresh start."

Exactly what I need, Blair thought, and he saw the use of the service.

He was here to contemplate the future—and calmed to think that, as far as Frank and Kathleen's visit was concerned, today was taken care of. All he needed to do was to spirit them out of the church before any of the sahibs saw them. Tomorrow he would think of an excuse for not conveying Frank to the teak depot of Moedar. The days would slip by, and soon Frank and Kathleen would be back in Moulmein, and he would be free of them.

"The maypole, Morris dancing," the vicar was saying, still speaking of his youth in Devon. "Hot cross buns—"

All pretty pagan, Blair was thinking, but his thoughts were jarred by a sudden crash—had someone fallen?—but it was the bang of the church door flung open, its handle smashing the wall, and what followed was a screech that silenced the vicar in his reminiscences.

Everyone in the pews at the front turned as the screech grew louder, their faces looking stricken. To his horror, Blair saw Mee Hla was advancing up the aisle, shuffling in torn slippers, her hair wild, her blouse rumpled, her gray face seemed ghoulish—it was smeared with patches of yellow thanaka, adhering to her cheeks and chin.

"*Pite-san pay-like!*" she howled. "*Pite-san pay-like!*"

Give me the money! Give me the money!

Blair's face was burning, his first thought: Did the sahibs understand her words? Probably not. But the Karens and the other Burmese and the Chinese certainly did, and from their expressions—gaping mouths, widened eyes—Cecil and Samuel also did. But no one moved, the howls keeping them frozen where they sat.

Mee Hla advanced toward the pew where Blair was rigid, clutching his knees, alarmed at the sight of her, a disheveled version of the frantic wild-eyed woman who'd danced with swords at the *nat pwe,* except that instead of swords Mee Hla used her hands, her long painted nails, twisting her fingers and talons to threaten. But she was no less intimidating than the pwe dancer. Her shrieks echoed in the church and, because it was a wooden church, the sounds rang against the walls and rattled the paneling and pricked the splintery timbers.

"*Pite-san pay-like!*"

"Please," the vicar called out from the pulpit. "Don't be alarmed. But we must endeavor to calm this unfortunate woman."

Fear had transfixed the congregation. Had it been a crazed man or boy they would have pounced—Wraggett and Slattery certainly—snatching his arms and frog-marching the interrupter away. But this was a small howling woman, like a wicked imp, and she stood at the level of Blair's crimson face and was screaming into it.

"Who is this *ka-pyar*? What are you doing with her?"—she slashed at him with her fingers as she shrieked. "I am your *bo-kadaw*! She cannot take my place. She must go! You have betrayed me, your own *bo-kadaw*. You called me your kitten. Send her away and give me money!"

Blair was hot, he was trembling, his face was on fire. *Get me out of here.*

The Europeans cannot have understood her shrieking in Burmese, but they had no need to. Mee Hla was so demonstrative they must have had an inkling of her accusations. A *ka-pyar* was known to be a half blood, and *bo-kadaw* was an expression used with a nudge, by Europeans who knew few other Burmese words.

And even if they knew nothing of the language, those sahibs in the church would have known everything by the look of pure horror on Blair's tortured face.

"Stop this," he said, hissing in Burmese. "Stop this at once."

But Mee Hla was facing the sahibs now, screaming, "Look at me, you white men and you white women, too—look at me! Look at how he has ruined me. Look at these rags I am wearing! And the *thakin* is sitting with his *ka-pyar,* pretending not to see me. He would let me starve at his gate like a pariah dog." She tore at her blouse. "Look at this body you have kissed a thousand times—look, look!"

Her blouse had come adrift and it was this glimpse of her nakedness now that roused the men to act. Wraggett climbed past his wife and out of the pew, but Cecil and Samuel were quicker, dashing toward Mee Hla, gathering her loose clothes about her.

"I beg you to sort that woman out," the vicar said, recovering. "Take her outside."

As Mee Hla was dragged away, whimpering in exhaustion, Blair saw that the sahibs and the memsahibs in the front rows had stopped looking at her. They were gaping at Kathleen who was clinging to Blair, like a terrified child cowering and blubbing. The sight of the young half-caste holding him in desperation seemed to fascinate them as much as the complaints of the demented woman.

The heavy door slammed on Mee Hla's shrieks. At the back of the church Blair saw a family of Karens, shocked by the outburst, their faces set in suffering. Shattered by the spectacle, Blair gripped the side of the pew, dizzy, faltering from standing so abruptly. Kathleen stumbled past him and ran ducklike down the aisle, snatching open the door. Just outside, Cecil and Samuel were trying to pull Mee Hla away, but she fought them when she saw Kathleen and screamed, "*Hpa-the-ma!*"

Taking Kathleen's arm, Blair was about to say, *She's not a whore—she's my cousin.* But what was the point? Cecil and Samuel held Mee Hla back, as the others in the congregation began to leave—confusedly, as though escaping. Kathleen broke away, and Blair fled into the road, saying nothing, hearing the scolding mutters of the sahibs. He could scarcely keep up with Kathleen, who seemed propelled by an outside force, Uncle Frank lumbering after them, pushing himself along by his stick.

Once in the house, Frank and Kathleen disappeared to their rooms but with a clatter of tramping feet and slammed doors that provoked Flo to bark. Gugu crept from the back, concerned by the noise and by the agonized expression on Blair's face.

"*Thakin?*"

Blair waved him away. He lit a cigarette but was too winded to smoke it. He stood stunned, breathing hard for a moment, then walked slowly toward his bedroom. He didn't enter, he lingered by the door, his shoulder against the jamb, and he was on a sudden seized with fatigue, weakened, all his vitality drained from him. He tottered, he could not stand, he slipped toward his bed and collapsed into it, feeling leaden, sinking into the mattress, his humiliation like a sickness.

Between daylight and dark, sleeping and waking, Blair became dimly aware of urgent movement in the house, footsteps pounding the floor planks—the sound of a sahib was so much louder than a Burmese, you knew the race of a person from their footsteps. Foot thumps and the smack of dropped objects, boxes being dragged, the snap of orders ("See here, Gugu"), and finally the shadow of Frank bending over him, Frank's face lowering, the peaty tang of Frank's tobacco breath.

"Eric, lad."

"What time is it?" Blair was clawing at the counterpane, still groggy, gathering it in his hands.

Frank was talking, but too rapidly to be interrupted or easily understood, but Blair heard "motorcar," and "Naba," and "Night Mail." Frank then straightened and paused and spoke a final sentence.

Blair said, "Pardon?"

He had tugged himself upright with the counterpane, and he now saw behind Frank the squat shape of Kathleen, her blue dress, her hat that was like an upside-down bucket. She was slowly raising and lowering her arm, pawing the air, saying goodbye.

"I said, we mean to spare you your blushes"—the words suffused with stale tobacco.

Frank backed away, shutting the bedroom door, and at last the house was silent.

Blair lay back and slept, waking much later—noon, probably, he could tell from the heat and the sunlight. Gugu brought him a cup of tea, but Blair groaned. He couldn't speak, he could barely move, he was weary. He kept seeing Frank, hovering over him, the odor of tobacco, the sight of Kathleen looking diminished in the pale dawn light, and *Spare you your blushes.*

Blair had always thought of embarrassment as a psychic wound inflicted on him by someone stronger, a sharp-tongued boy or a moneyed beast in an upper form, a confident girl in her rebuff. It was a condition one had to overcome, brazening it out with a clever reply, snapping back. He remembered his exasperation with Jones long ago in Rangoon, calling him "Lofty," and the satisfaction he'd felt on the train to Mandalay when he'd taken Jones by the throat and screamed into his face. From that moment Jones was respectful.

But this embarrassment was something physical, a sickening humiliation. A cup of tea was no help. He was nauseated, his head hurt, his arms were heavy, his pajamas were clammy with sweat. It was worse than Mee Hla howling in the church, worse than her tearing at her clothes, looking frightful, interrupting the Easter service like a demon from the underworld. It was the look on the faces of the club members, the vicar, Mrs. Selkirk rigid, horror-struck at her harmonium, their shock at seeing Kathleen clinging to him, a frightened Eurasian in a ludicrous hat, the fat affronted man in the pew next to Blair, these strangers intruding. And because there was no way that Blair could explain, it was another failure, like the elephant, and Thackeray, and—he now remembered—those schoolboys at Pagoda Road Station, whom he'd thumped, the shame he'd felt when they'd followed him into the carriage, hectoring him before the other passengers.

Unable to rise above the pain, he suffered it and sweated. He sent Gugu with a chit to Eastwood saying, *Below par, rather subfusc, I hope to rally in a few days.*

But after those few days Blair still felt unwell, and weak, with a sick headache, the sense of having been punched in the gut, his face slapped. And when he finally rose from his bed and shaved and dressed, he did not go to the station at once, but waited until late afternoon—it was Thursday—seeking out Eastwood in his office, still somehow shamefaced and fragile.

Eastwood canted himself back in his chair and smacked the blotter on his desk, jarring a cheroot in an ashtray, half laughing in his shout.

"You're a dark one, Blair!"

"Rather unfortunate, I'm afraid. I reckon I'm the talk of the club now."

"You've always been the talk of the club, my boy. That elephant. That Indian."

Blair had sat, he put his face in his hands. He whispered, "Christ."

"The chaps will be dining out on this for months," Eastwood said.

"I can explain," Blair began.

Eastwood thumped his desk. "No explanations!"

He picked up the cheroot and puffed it. That seemed to soothe him a little. Blair lit a cigarette, to calm himself, to listen.

"I was young like you once, Blair," Eastwood said. "Tangle yourself up with these yellowbellies—see what happens! It ends in tears." He laughed again, then became serious. "But what about this tart you were running around with?"

"She was nothing of the kind, sir. I don't think it's fair to use such terms—"

"You see, Blair," Eastwood said, twirling a finger to disperse the smoke he'd just exhaled, "we white men have to think of something besides ourselves. We are, so to say, in a garrison here. We've got to keep the flag flying. As soon as you go mixing yourself up with these natives and Eurasians it's a loss of prestige. Lower your prestige and it's all up with you. Where are you then? Ruined!"

Blair sat, wondering how to reply. There was too much to tell, and was it even worth the telling? Every time Eastwood used words such as esprit de corps or prestige, Blair felt even more a failure. He'd stopped believing. Had he ever believed?

Eastwood drew a file folder from his in tray. He opened it and tapped a document.

"Says here you're due for home leave in six weeks. Good show. Nothing like a spot of leave to set your mind to rights."

Yes, leave. Get me out of here. Blair said, "Thank you, sir."

Before he could return to work, while he was still recovering, still prostrate with humiliation, he was stricken again, this time with a severity that knocked him sideways. A blazing headache, slack muscles, searing pain in his bones and his joints, his skin so sensitive to the slightest touch even the weight of his bedsheet caused discomfort. Unexpectedly, he was tearful. When had he ever wept? He couldn't stir from his bed. Gugu brought him brown sticky beads of opium, which he swallowed to ease his mind, to stop the pain. He thought of Robinson's addiction, and he thought of his father, Subdeputy Opium Agent Blair, but he was too ill to smile.

"It's dengue—break-bone fever," Eastwood said, on a hurried visit. "I'd send a quack if I could find one, but he'd just hand you pills. I have laudanum, which is more efficacious. Dengue's going round—you'll pull out of it. I may say, Blair, you've got all the luck!"

He'd had fever in the Delta, and had been laid up in Syriam with serious headache and squitters, but this was worse than anything he'd known. It was ten days of misery. In his delirium, and tears, and in the fevered loneliness of his bed, Blair wrote and rewrote a letter to Mrs. Jellicoe in his mind, murmuring it to himself.

> *You asked me not to forget you. Do you think I ever will? My heart was shriveled—that heart, which, when I was a young boy, I used to think was capable of such passion—and I used to think that passion awaited me somewhere, somehow, some time. The years went by and I was reconciling myself to a life without passion. And then, miraculously, this encounter, the unexpected flowering.*

He knew it would be another sad unsent letter. His fever was alleviated by Gugu's opium, bits of it, the size of sultanas. He lay immobilized, spared from having to go to work, and it excused him from seeing anyone at the club.

His fever and this immobility helped him in another way: He was so rarely ill that he was surprised to find something important in his misery, the way sickness concentrated his mind and made him decisive. The fever forced upon him the reality of where he was, and he lay like a castaway, staring upward, dreaming of rescue. He could no longer endure his life as a sahib in Burma. He needed to leave immediately to survive, no matter the consequences—to divest himself of his uniform and all thoughts of prestige, become smaller and anonymous, simplify his life. He had not known how a fever could fuel him in his yearning, burning away his pretensions, giving him a direction. His fever showed him how lost he was, how little time he had, how mortal he was, and what mattered.

How to do it? *Vanish into the crowd,* he thought, *become one with it, lower myself, lose myself—no more whips, no more pomp, no belts, no badges.*

Eastwood visited again. "Buck up, lad. We can move your leave forward. Medical leave, as soon as you're fit to travel."

To Blair's great surprise, Thackeray showed up. He said he'd ordered a new suit from a tailor in Katha and stopping by the police station had been told that Blair Sahib was poorly. He was wearing the new suit, whitish and ribbed, with faint blue stripes, the texture of the cloth reminded Blair of a tea towel, with broad lapels and the trousers so flared at the cuffs they covered Thackeray's shoes. His waistcoat was white, his foppish tie yellow and loosely knotted. The suit looked crushed and wanted pressing and made Thackeray seem untidy.

"New suit," Blair said. "Good business, Thackeray."

Thackeray pinched the lapel of his suit jacket and smiled. "Thanks to you, sahib."

"What is that cloth—looks like nightshirt stuff."

"Seersucker, sahib. Best fashion."

"You wrote to my uncle."

"Limoojeen Sahib, yes."

He explained that he'd hoped to benefit Blair's family, by telling Uncle Frank of the timber opportunities in Moedar. He wondered why Frank hadn't made the trip. The shroff Pramod had also been prepared to help.

"Ample of red tape, sahib," Thackeray said. "But uncle is welcome."

Blair said, "I'm leaving soon for England, my friend."

Tears welled in Thackeray's eyes. He clasped his hands before him. He had, as always, a look of suffering.

Finally he said, "Tell me there is hope for us."

Blair started to speak, but his throat burned—from the residue of dengue fever, from his scorched lungs, from disgust and shame and disillusionment.

"I beg you, sahib," Thackeray said softly with a gummy tongue. "Tell me." And breathed again, "Lie to me, sahib, tell me there is hope for Burma."

Blair shook his head, and cleared his throat with a fruity cough, and smiled, but hadn't the heart to reply.

41

THE *SHROPSHIRE*

Homeward Bound

Gugu got the chickens and ducks, Eastwood took on whimpering Flo. Without saying goodbye to anyone at the club (he knew what they'd say afterward: *Bloody Blair, not so much as a by-your-leave*), he caught the fastest train via Mandalay to Rangoon, offered no farewells, and boarded the *MV Shropshire*, bound for Liverpool. He kept to his cabin, or the smoking room, or idled unseen in the breeze at a corner of the bow. He dined alone, and when the mood took him, he wrote about his alter ego, John Flory. He was glad to be gone. *Medical leave*, he thought—*Yes, I have caught an everlasting cold.*

Through the green wastes of the Indian Ocean, glittering shoals of flying fish skimmed past. He did not go ashore at Colombo or Aden, and after the Canal the sea was blue enamel, pods of sleek porpoises streaming alongside the ship, at night the phosphorescent wash at the bow an arrowhead of green fire.

He spoke to no one, he told himself he was still ailing and needed a change of air and, impatient on the ship, hearing Hindustani spoken by surly sahibs to Indian stewards ("Chotapeg!" "*Jildy!*"), found himself again murmuring, *Get me out of here.*

As the ship approached Marseilles, the fragrance of hot sunlit Provence fluttered to him in wisps in the breeze from shore, the aromas of pale green shrubs and trees on the baked, summer-dry hills, the scent of pine and juniper, the perfume of roses and lavender, herbal notes—thyme and rosemary and marjoram. He inhaled the sweet odors in a great dizzying haust that cleared his head like a tonic, and he made a decision to disembark.

He sent his luggage on to Birkenhead and descended the gangway with one small bag, waving away a pleading porter, unthinkingly and absurdly addressing the Frenchman in Burmese. He had no direction on the quay until he saw a great crowd of men—thousands—gathered in the Old Port, many of them carrying signs, "Nous voulons la justice pour Sacco et Vanzetti" and "Ils sont innocents," a man standing on a crate among them, speaking in measured tones.

They were decent working people, simply dressed for the summer afternoon, unsmiling, defying authority. They had bunked off from their jobs and forfeited a day's pay to demand justice for the innocent anarchists falsely convicted of robbery and murder. Blair quickened his pace, heading toward the indignant men, indistinguishable from them in his old linen jacket—no tie, no badges, no puttees or boots, no sahib's topee—and vanished into the crowd.

Postscript

From Marseilles, Blair took the train to Paris, where he stayed with his aunt Nellie Limouzin and her Esperanto-speaking lover. Soon afterward he left for England, showing up at his parents' house in Southwold in that same month, August 1927, saying he'd been granted medical leave. Toward the end of September, on a holiday in Cornwall, he told them that he was resigning from the Indian Imperial Police.

He descended into the netherworld. He swapped his decent clothes for shabby ones, as Jack London had done in *People of the Abyss,* and became a tramp, lodging uncomfortably in squalid doss-houses and living among homeless wanderers, beggars, gypsies, and hop pickers. Wishing to sink further and to know more, he went back to Paris and found work washing dishes in a restaurant. By 1932 he had completed a manuscript for a book he planned to title *Confessions of a Dishwasher.* But the publisher preferred *Down and Out in Paris and London.* Blair asked for it to appear under a pseudonym, suggesting some names, adding, "I rather favor George Orwell."

In his last year as a policeman in Katha, he'd started working fitfully on a novel set in Burma, about his alter ego, John Flory, living in a small town on the Irrawaddy called Kyauktada, which much resembled Katha and its club and its torments. He finished it toward the end of 1933 and it was published the following year, as *Burmese Days,* to mixed reviews and poor sales. Nevertheless, he kept writing.

Ten years after returning from Burma, Blair wrote in *The Road to Wigan Pier,* "When I came home on leave in 1927 I was already half determined to throw up my job, and one sniff of English air decided me. I was not going back to be a part of that evil despotism. But I wanted much more than merely to escape from my job. For five years I had been part of an oppressive system, and it had left me with a bad conscience. Innumerable remembered faces—faces of prisoners in the dock, of men waiting in the condemned cells, of subordinates I had bullied and aged peasants I had snubbed, of servants and coolies I had hit with my fist in moments of rage (nearly everyone does these things in the East, at any rate occasionally: Orientals can be very provoking)—haunted me intolerably. I was conscious of an immense weight of guilt that I had got to expiate. I suppose that sounds exaggerated; but if you do for five years a job that you thoroughly disapprove of, you will probably feel the same. I had reduced everything to the simple theory that the oppressed are always right and the oppressors are always wrong: a mistaken theory, but the natural result of being one of the oppressors yourself. I felt that I had got to escape not merely from imperialism but from every form of man's dominion over man. I wanted to submerge myself, to get right down among the oppressed, to be one of them and on their side against their tyrants. And, chiefly because I had had to think everything out in solitude, I had carried my hatred of oppression to extraordinary lengths. At that time failure seemed to me to be the only virtue."

Acknowledgments

For their kind assistance and advice, I wish to acknowledge Jin Auh, Millicent Bennett, Bob Bookman, Pancho Huddle, Doug Kelly, Madam Khine, Laurie McGee, Ferdinand Mount, Bill Monahan, Jeffrey Meyers, Tristram Powell, Simon Prosser, Jonathan Raban, Alexander Theroux, Jonathan Tucker, and Andrew Wylie.

Kyay zuu tin par tal to my Burmese friends for their wisdom and guidance, though because they live in an unforgiving military dictatorship, I dare not name them.

For his securing me a University of Hawaii library card I offer my special thanks to Dr. Clem Guthro, university librarian.

For her love and support, my wife, Sheila.

ABOUT

MARINER BOOKS

MARINER BOOKS traces its beginnings to 1832 when William Ticknor cofounded the Old Corner Bookstore in Boston, from which he would run the legendary firm Ticknor and Fields, publisher of Ralph Waldo Emerson, Harriet Beecher Stowe, Nathaniel Hawthorne, and Henry David Thoreau. Following Ticknor's death, Henry Oscar Houghton acquired Ticknor and Fields and, in 1880, formed Houghton Mifflin, which later merged with venerable Harcourt Publishing to form Houghton Mifflin Harcourt. HarperCollins purchased HMH's trade publishing business in 2021 and re-established their storied lists and editorial team under the name Mariner Books.

Uniting the legacies of Houghton Mifflin, Harcourt Brace, and Ticknor and Fields, Mariner Books continues one of the great traditions in American bookselling. Our imprints have introduced an incomparable roster of enduring classics, including Hawthorne's *The Scarlet Letter*, Thoreau's *Walden*, Willa Cather's *O Pioneers!*, Virginia Woolf's *To the Lighthouse*, W.E.B. Du Bois's *Black Reconstruction*, J.R.R. Tolkien's *The Lord of the Rings*, Carson McCullers's *The Heart Is a Lonely Hunter*, Ann Petry's *The Narrows*, George Orwell's *Animal Farm* and *Nineteen Eighty-Four*, Rachel Carson's *Silent Spring*, Margaret Walker's *Jubilee*, Italo Calvino's *Invisible Cities*, Alice Walker's *The Color Purple*, Margaret Atwood's *The Handmaid's Tale*, Tim O'Brien's *The Things They Carried*, Philip Roth's *The Plot Against America*, Jhumpa Lahiri's *Interpreter of Maladies*, and many others. Today Mariner Books remains proudly committed to the craft of fine publishing established nearly two centuries ago at the Old Corner Bookstore.